MW01076073

WICKED SEXY

WICKED GAMES BOOK 2

J.T. GEISSINGER

This is a work of fiction. Names, characters, organizations, places, events, and incidents are either products of the author's imagination or are used fictitiously.

Text copyright © 2016 J.T. Geissinger, Inc.

All rights reserved.

No part of this book may be reproduced, or stored in a retrieval system, or transmitted in any form or by any means, electronic, mechanical, photocopying, recording, or otherwise, without express written permission of the publisher.

Published by J.T. Geissinger, Inc.

ISBN 978-1733824309

Cover design by Letitia Hasser RBA Designs

Editing by Linda Ingmanson

www.jtgeissinger.com

For my rock and my best friend, Jay.

TABBY

$\mathcal{T}$he key to infiltrating a highly secure, access-controlled building that houses multimillions of dollars of technology and proprietary trade secrets lies in one word.

Confidence.

"Good morning!" I say brightly to the receptionist seated behind the large mahogany desk in the posh lobby of GenCeuticals, the top biotech firm in Washington, DC.

She looks up and smiles. "Good morning. May I help you?"

Making sure to maintain strong but nonthreatening eye contact, I say, "Yes. I'm Dena Johnson from corporate. Bob McKenna said I could stop by and take a tour of the facility."

I hand her my card, which I made yesterday on my home printer. It identifies me as a Senior Vice President of Information Technology.

Of course I'd researched the company and knew what names to use. Dena Johnson and Bob McKenna are actual employees of GenCeuticals. The devil's in the details, as they say, and successful espionage requires total command of details.

The receptionist—twenty-something, friendly—doesn't even

glance at the card in her hand. "Certainly, Ms. Johnson. Let me call the general manager for you. Pease have a seat."

"Thank you." While the receptionist makes a phone call, I make myself comfortable on a leather sofa in the seating area nearby.

After a brief conversation, she hangs up the phone, beaming as if she's just won a prize. "Mr. Hoffmeier will be right out to see you!"

Smiling blandly, I tick off a mental list of failures so far. No inspection of my business card. No request to view my company security badge. No request for a second form of identification. No call to the corporate office to confirm my visit.

Stupid people make my job so much easier.

Never let a sheep guard the chicken coop. The wolves will always find a way in.

After a short wait, the glass doors to the left of the reception desk slide open with a gentle *siss* of air. Through them bustles a man. He's fiftyish, balding, wearing a navy blue suit and a tight smile. He looks at the receptionist. She gestures to me.

"Ah!" The man scurries over, hand extended. "Ms. Johnson! Welcome! I'm Donald Hoffmeier, General Manager here at GenCeuticals, DC. We don't often have visitors from corporate —what a wonderful surprise!"

I stand and shake his hand. It's clammy. His brow is speckled with shining drops.

It's all I can do not to smirk. I know I'm a bitch, but making people nervous sort of gets me off.

"Thank you, Mr. Hoffmeier," I purr, batting my lashes. "It's *so* nice to meet you. I'm sorry I didn't call ahead to arrange a visit, but I was on business in the area, and I've heard such wonderful things about your operation here that I couldn't resist taking a look for myself."

Hoffmeier looks positively dazzled. He stammers, "W-well

that's great to hear! You never know what the higher-ups think of all the hard work you're putting in."

He leans closer. His voice gains a conspiratorial tone. "I'd heard rumors of restructuring. Getting rid of some of the middle management, things like that."

I give his sweaty paw a final shake and then wave my hand dismissively in the air. "Oh well! You know how the rumor mill works. But I can assure you, everyone at headquarters *loves* what you're doing here." I drop my voice. "You didn't hear that from me, though. Gotta keep the troops on their toes, right?"

Hoffmeier nods so enthusiastically, I think his head might fly clear off his shoulders.

"Okay! Great, great!" He claps like he's calling a class to order. "So—the tour. Shall we?"

When he motions to the sliding glass doors—accessible only through an electronic badge reader, which mine won't open because it's fake—it's all I can do not to break into a big, shit-eating grin.

"Yes," I say. "Let's." I follow behind him as he leads the way.

Chickens, meet the wolf who's about to devour you.

Half an hour later, I've toured the executive offices, the acres of employee cubicles, and the enormous manufacturing facility, where I had to don booties and a cloth hair cap and pass through two sets of air locks that whisked away any stray dust, airborne microbes, and aerosol particles from my person, all the while exclaiming my delight at how well managed and efficient everything seems.

Now it's time to thrust home the sword.

"Mr. Hoffmeier, this is incredible." I pull off my cloth cap and hand it to a pimply tech in a white lab coat who looks about fifteen years old. He deposits the cap in a wastebasket and helps me wrangle the booties from my heels. I had to leave my briefcase outside the clean room—the briefcase the security guard stationed at the entry didn't bother to look inside because I was with Hoffmeier, mistake number five—but retrieve it as we exit. "I can only imagine how impressive the IT department is."

"Oh yes, you'll want to see that." Hoffmeier hands his booties and cap to the tech. "The boys in there are top-notch, I tell you. First-rate. Smartest guys in the industry. Though what they do is a little beyond me, it's all a little hush-hush." He looks with alarm at my briefcase as if just realizing it's there. "Oh dear."

My brows climb my forehead. "Is there a problem?"

"No, no, of course not." There's a pregnant pause. "Only, to be completely honest, I think you'll have to let them search your briefcase before you go in. You know, protecting the trade secrets and whatnot."

Here we go. So far this has been pathetically easy.

"Of course! No worries at all. I wouldn't want to get you in any kind of trouble."

Hoffmeier looks ridiculously grateful that I didn't try to bluster or pull rank, which makes me wonder how many other people have tried to bully their way into IT. Judging by the way he fawns all over me as we make our way from one building to the next, still happy I didn't bust his balls, probably more than a few.

We pass through a set of pneumatic metal doors, accessed by Hoffmeier's security badge and a ten-digit code punched into the keypad on the wall. Inside the doors is a desk with a uniformed guard sitting behind a bank of monitors. The guard slowly rises.

Even in four-inch heels, I'm looking *up*. The dude is psychotically tall.

"Morning, Mr. Hoffmeier." The guard nods at my companion. Without waiting for a response, he turns his gaze back to me. "Your name and company name, ma'am?"

I hold his gaze and keep my expression impassive. "Dena Johnson. I'm a Senior VP visiting from corporate."

The guard nods, punches a few keys on his keyboard, scans the monitor for what I assume must be a list of employee names, and then nods again, apparently satisfied that I am who I say I am.

Mistake number six: No picture to accompany the executive personnel name in the computer file.

"Do you have your security badge with you, ma'am?"

I have the fake badge in my pocket that would pass a visual inspection—I googled what they looked like, laughing that the information was accessible online because some dummy posted a shot of himself on Facebook at the company picnic with the security badge clipped to his shirt pocket for all the world to see—but if the guard runs it through the scanning unit on his desk, I'm dead in the water. So I wing it.

"Sure. It's here in my case." I set my case on the edge of his desk, open it, make a big show of rifling through it, and then frown. "I thought it was in here. Oh, shoot—did I leave it in the car?"

Hoffmeier says impatiently, "Surely you can let her in—you see her name there on the roster. And," he adds, sounding pompous and smug, "she's with me."

When the security guard's expression sours, I know Hoffmeier has said the wrong thing. Obviously there's no love lost between the two.

Wide-eyed and blinking, I protest, "Oh no, no. Please. I don't want to be any trouble." I turn to the guard. "You have a very important job to do, sir, I *completely* understand. I'll just go get my badge from the car." Patting my pockets, I mutter to myself, "Gosh, I hope I didn't leave it at the hotel."

Then I hesitate as if something has occurred to me. "Or

maybe you could just give a quick call to Cathy Suzinski in corporate HR? She could verify my identity."

Cathy Suzinski does indeed work in corporate HR, but today any calls to her from *this* facility are being rerouted to my home in Manhattan, where a skinny, scary-smart high school kid named Juanita "One Eye" Perez who has a voice like a forty-year old woman with a two-pack-a-day habit is lounging in front of my TV, feet up on my coffee table, stuffing her face with Cheetos and Red Bull.

I pay Juanita well for the work she does for me, but she'd probably do it for free just to get out of her house. She's the youngest of seven kids—who all still live at home.

But the guard, after a moment's thought, shakes his head. "That's all right. Cathy's got her hands full this week with new-hire orientations. I probably won't be able to reach her for hours."

Another reason I picked a Friday afternoon for this sting is that people aren't nearly as diligent at their jobs when they're counting down the minutes to the weekend.

The guard notes my arrival time on a clipboard, prints out a sticker bearing my name that I affix to my blazer's lapel—avoiding the dragonfly brooch that's really a tiny camera I've been using to photograph everything—and then takes a cursory look inside my briefcase. Then Hoffmeier and I walk through another set of locked doors.

We enter a large room inhabited by quietly humming towers of computer mainframes arranged in long rows. Everything is white and gleaming. Combined with the chill in the air and the faint scent of ozone, it puts me in mind of virgin snowfall in a winter woods.

I grin. *This virgin's about to get her cherry popped.*

"As you can see, we have state-of-the-art equipment in this facility," Hoffmeier says, chest puffed. He adds, "It has to be kept air-conditioned for the computers, you see."

I bite my lip to resist unleashing a scathing tongue-lashing on him. Because apparently the Senior VP of Corporate Information Technology would be ignorant of the fact that large banks of computers have to be temperature controlled on account of her vagina. Which makes her stupid.

Obviously.

Mistake number...oh, hell I've lost count: Don't put the sexist dipshit in charge of VIP tours. Or anything else for that matter.

"Hmm," I respond, acting impressed and clueless, a nearly impossible combination for me. "And where does the IT team work?"

"They're just over here." He holds an arm out, allowing me to move in front of him as we walk the length of one wall, our heels clicking on the tile.

Now comes the risky part.

There's a chance any one of the guys in the information technology department has actually met Dena Johnson in person during the interview process. If that's the case, I'm screwed. She's a sixty-year-old stick-thin blonde with a fondness for pearls and pastel sweater sets, and I'm a twenty-seven-year-old curvy redhead who wouldn't be caught dead in a cardigan, much less a lavender one, much less a set of pearls.

My heartbeat picks up as we approach a mirrored door. We stop in front of it. Hoffmeier swipes his badge through the reader mounted on the wall, enters his pin number into the keypad, and presses his thumb to a square black biometric scanner.

Nothing happens.

He gives the scanner a quizzical tap, waits, and then tries the whole process again. When there's still no result, he glances at me with an embarrassed smile. "Must be on the fritz."

Then—in a breach of security protocol so fantastic I nearly squeal in glee—he simply raps on the door with his knuckles. It opens from the inside.

"Ruben," he says curtly to the bearded hipster in the skinny jeans and untucked T-shirt who stands inside the door.

Ruben replies drily, "Hoff."

Hoffmeier stiffens. Brushing past Ruben—who is now openly staring at my chest—Hoffmeier mutters, "Don't *call* me that," and disappears into the dim interior of the room.

I hold out my hand to Mr. Ruben. "Hi. I'm Dena Johnson." I smile. "But you can call me John."

All the risks pay off when my new best friend Ruben, who clearly has never set eyes on the real Dena Johnson in his life and hates Mr. Hoffmeier with a passion, raises his gaze from my boobs to my face and drawls, "Don't mind if I do, John."

With a lazy grin, he takes my hand in his and leads me inside.

Twenty minutes later, I've met the three other guys on the team, gotten a detailed description of all their security measures, secretly taken dozens of pictures of the equipment, and installed a bot into their mainframe via a USB drive I had stashed in my bra that will allow me access to their network via my own servers.

To say I hit the mother lode would really be understating the situation.

"Well!" I say brightly, smiling at Hoffmeier. "This has been wonderful! But I don't want to keep you any longer on a Friday." I turn to the four IT guys standing in a cluster to my right. Ruben is still staring at my boobs. *This guy must not get out a lot.* "Thank you so much for showing me around, guys. I really appreciate it. Corporate will hear *exactly* what kind of a job you're all doing here."

Hoffmeier beams. The three other guys—whose names I've forgotten—smile sheepishly and shift their weight from foot to foot. Ruben, coming out of his breast-induced stupor, says, "Sure, great, I'll walk you out," and takes me by the arm. He steers me out the door before Hoffmeier can get a word in.

"Nice meeting you!" I call over my shoulder, listening to Hoff exclaim behind me.

Ruben takes a shortcut through the facility. We're in the lobby in no time. We stop beside a stand of potted palms in one corner, near the front door.

Ruben shoves his hands into his front pockets and stares at the floor. "So, uh, if you have any other questions, uh, I could, you know, take some time to answer them. Over drinks. Tonight."

Aww. He's asking me out.

It's too bad I've sworn off men, because he's actually really cute with his messy man-bun and scruffy beard.

It's also too bad I'll be costing him his job.

"Thanks, but I've got an early flight in the morning."

He nods, looking like he knew a *no* would be forthcoming. Feeling bad for him, I lower my voice and lie, "Actually, I live with my boyfriend, or I totally would."

Surprised, he looks up. I blink like a baby bird, which is what I do when I'm trying to look coy. I'm crap at flirting, but it seems to work, because Ruben breaks into a bashful smile.

"Okay. Well…if you guys ever break up…and you're in the area again…"

I smile back, nodding, wondering how long it will take him to try to connect with Dena Johnson on Facebook or Instagram and get the surprise of his life.

I'm giving it an hour.

I murmur a goodbye, head out to my rental car, and tear out of the parking lot, tires squealing. In twenty minutes, I'm back in my suite at the Four Seasons Hotel. There's a bottle of Dom Perignon on ice waiting in my room. The note accompanying the bottle reads:

A little gift to take the sting out of failure. Yours, Roger Hamilton.

I laugh for longer than I probably should, but honestly,

showing a man his weaknesses after he's insisted he doesn't have any is a perversely satisfying part of this job. I can't wait to demonstrate to the vastly overconfident CEO of GenCeuticals— Roger Hamilton, my client—exactly how much of a non-failure today was.

The bigger they are, the harder they fall. And nothing is ever completely secure, no matter what fail-safe systems you think you've put in place.

I kick off my heels, strip out of the loathsome tailored suit I wear only on jobs, ignore the champagne, and pour a sparkling water into one of the crystal flutes beside the ice bucket. I get into the bathtub, where I luxuriate in victory and soak until I'm almost a prune. Then I climb out, dry off, wrap the fluffy white towel around my body, and head to the bedroom.

Where I find a man—a huge, tanned, dark-haired beast of a man, clad all in black—sprawled in the middle of my bed with his arms propped behind his head and his giant booted feet crossed at the ankle.

I scream and drop the glass. It shatters against the marble floor.

The beast grins, revealing a set of perfect, gleaming white teeth.

"Howdy, sweet cheeks. It's nice to see you again too."

2

CONNOR

"Son of a *bitch*!" Tabby shouts, red-faced, and I just can't help myself.

I burst out laughing.

It becomes immediately apparent that's the wrong thing to do when she picks up a glass paperweight from the coffee table and hurls it at me. It smashes into the wall inches above my head, dislodging a shower of plaster, and then lands on the spot where my face was half a second ago.

"Temper," I chide, now standing beside the bed with my arms folded over my chest. "Tsk, tsk."

"I'll give you a fucking *tsk*," she growls, grabbing a cut-crystal ashtray.

"Whoa!" I throw my hands up. "Jesus, sweet cheeks, who shit in your cornflakes?"

She does this puckering thing with her whole face—like a scowl only times ten—that's supposed to look menacing but instead is cute as fuck.

"That would be *you*, jarhead! I hoped I'd never see you again!" She cocks her arm, readying her aim. "And what the hell are you doing *in my hotel room*?"

The last part is shouted so loud, people in the lobby can probably hear it.

"To talk business." My gaze drops to the towel she's clutching against her chest. Her grip is so tight, her knuckles have turned white. I let my eyes drift farther down, taking in dangerous curves and lean legs and bare toes—painted black, naturally—and drawl, "Though if you had any other ideas, I'd be open to hearing 'em." I meet her gaze to find her glaring at me. I crack a cocksure grin. "That bed's *mighty* comfy."

The ashtray sails through the air. It misses my left ear by a breath and smashes into the wall. I turn and inspect the damage, and then turn back to her with my cocksure grin still firmly in place.

"You're a shitty aim, sweet cheeks."

Her nostrils flare. Her chest heaves. She says in a low voice with an edge like a blade, "Call me sweet cheeks. One. More. *Time.*"

I laugh again. I'd almost forgotten how much fun it is to piss this woman off.

Red hair and long legs flying, Tabby darts over to the dresser next to the bed, grabs a lamp with an inconveniently heavy-looking ceramic base, whirls around, and brandishes it at me like a weapon. She yells, "Get out!"

I rest my hands on my hips and look down my nose at her. "You would bash me with a lamp after I got you the GenCeuticals job?"

She freezes. Her expression registers horrified disbelief. "What?"

"Seriously, Tabby. You think a guy like Roger Hamilton would pay a *woman* eighty thousand dollars to conduct a penetration test if someone he trusted implicitly hadn't suggested it?"

"*You're* the Special Ops guy he mentioned he had on retainer?"

I nod.

Tabby closes her eyes. "Mother*fucker*." Defeated, she lowers the lamp to the dresser.

I feel kinda bad for how hard she's taking the news, so I add a bit of truth to lessen the sting. "If it makes you feel any better, I thought walking right through the front door and pretending to be an executive was a ballsy move. Brilliant. And unexpected. Hamilton will shit his pants."

"Why didn't he just have *you* do the job? I'm sure you could've rappelled onto the roof from a black helicopter or something macho and melodramatic like that."

I shrug. "I'm outta the pen testing game. Not enough money in it. Metrix has moved on to higher-level stuff."

She narrows her eyes at me. Another thing I'd forgotten in the three years since I'd last seen Tabitha West is how brilliantly, lucidly green her irises are. Like an emerald held up to the sun. Like a big cat stalking its dinner in a jungle, its eyes illuminated in a slanting shaft of light.

Fuck. Now is *so* not the time to get a boner.

"Such as?"

"Extractions."

She processes that for a moment, her thumb working the knot between her breasts where the towel edges are joined.

Never thought I'd be jealous of a knot.

"People," she guesses correctly. "Politicians, royalty, wealthy businessmen, like that?"

I nod.

"Makes sense," she muses, turning her attention to the view of the city outside the windows. "Kidnappings, natural disasters, hostage situations... There are a million different scenarios where rich people might need their asses saved."

"Most people think I'm talking about teeth when I say extractions."

She snaps her head around and stares at me. "I'm not most people."

"No," I agree, holding her fierce gaze. "You're not."

We stand in silence for just longer than is comfortable, while I wrestle with a surprisingly strong urge to stride over to her, whip off the towel, throw her over my shoulder, and then throw her down on the bed.

My thoughts might show in my expression, because she turns abruptly away.

"I'm going to get dressed. Meet me downstairs in the bar in ten minutes. And don't touch anything on your way out, jarhead."

She heads into the bathroom. I call out after her, "Don't put clothes on for my sake. Make yourself comfortable, sweet—"

The bathroom door slams shut with a window-rattling *bang*.

Half an hour later, I'm about to go back upstairs and pound on Tabby's door when she walks into the bar like she owns the fucking place. She stands in the entrance, looking around with her nose in the air. The old guy on the stool next to me spots her and does a double take that might cause him whiplash.

I have to put a hand over my mouth to hide my smile.

I'll start from the feet up.

Black stilettos that don't say "fuck me" as much as "fuck *you*." Bare legs, tattoo of a green fairy decorating the inside of her left ankle. Black leather miniskirt with *suspenders* attached. A midriff-baring sleeveless T-shirt the color of Barbie puke that has, stretched out of shape over the fullness of her breasts, the words "Deal With It." Belly-button piercing with some dangly stuff, like a piece of jewelry. Colorful left arm tattoo sleeve that ends at her wrist. Studded necklace that looks exactly like a dog collar. Hair the color of a fire engine, drawn into a sleek ponytail that shows off aristocratic cheekbones and a long, elegant neck.

Over her right arm is slung a white purse with a giant logo of a cartoon cat on the flap. Because nothing shouts *I'm an adult with serious emotional baggage* better than Hello motherfucking Kitty.

Tabby spots me. Her lips twist into something that's probably disgust. I chuckle, watching as she makes her way across the bar toward me while a dozen heads turn in her wake.

Damn. Knows how to use those hips.

She stops next to me and drops her bag on the bar with a hostile *thunk.*

"You could've used this newfangled invention called a *phone* to contact me instead of wasting your time coming all the way to DC, jarhead."

"But then I wouldn't have gotten to see you in all your glory, sweet—"

She gives me a look that could wilt crops.

I amend it to, "Tabby."

The bartender, a dude with one of those pansy-ass over-groomed mustaches that are all the rage and I fucking hate, walks up smiling.

"What can I get you?" he asks Tabby's tits.

I growl, "Johnny Walker Blue Label and a strong length of rope."

The bartender frowns at me. "Rope?"

I lean closer to him. "For a noose."

His Adam's apple bobs as he swallows. He laughs—sounds like he's coughing—and scurries off.

Beside me, Tabby sighs. "Charming as ever, I see."

"Asshole was being disrespectful," I mutter, glaring at his retreating back.

There's a shrug in her voice. "Men can't help themselves, Connor. Boobs are your gender's Kryptonite. I don't take it personally."

Still bristling, I look at her. "Well, I do. You could be mine, for all that asshole knows."

She arches one elegant eyebrow. "Sure. In an alternate universe where I don't have an IQ approaching two hundred points and you're not a knuckle-dragging Neanderthal with a god complex and one too many pairs of cargo pants, I suppose that could be a possibility."

It's my turn to raise a brow. "You're in no position to diss my wardrobe, sweetheart. The fuck is that thing dangling from your belly button, a fishing lure? You trolling for largemouth bass?"

I suspect she wants to laugh. Her lips press together as if to keep a rogue grin at bay. Instead, she says coolly, "Hey, I'm not the one who always dresses like he's going to a military funeral. You realize they make clothes in colors other than black, right?"

"I'll wear something other than black when they make something darker."

The bartender returns with my scotch. His gaze firmly affixed to the bar, he politely asks Tabby, "And what may I get for you, miss?"

She shoots me a sour look. I grin.

"Ice water with lemon, please."

"Ice water?" I ask once the bartender has left.

Something odd crosses her face, there but quickly gone. "I don't drink alcohol."

"Lemme guess. Vegan?"

She curls her lip. "Please. I eat so much meat, I'm practically a meatatarian. And what does drinking ice water have to do with being vegan?"

"The fuck should I know?"

She inspects my face for a moment, and then says, "One of these days, I'll ask what you have against the words 'what' and 'how.' Until then, why don't you tell why you're here."

She slides onto the stool next to me, crosses her long legs, props her chin on her hand, and waits.

I can almost feel the old guy behind me having a heart attack.

Must be staring at her legs. They're pretty fucking spectacular, if I do say so myself.

"Got a client," I say. "High level. With a delicate situation. Knew you'd gone freelance after Victoria, heard through the grapevine you were killin' it. Today proves I heard right."

She tries not to look smug about that last part but fails. "What's the situation?"

I shake my head. "That's classified unless you've signed on the dotted line."

"What's the job?"

"See my previous answer."

She looks at the ceiling as if for divine intervention. After a moment during which I imagine her counting to ten to control the urge to stab me in the eye with the shiny lure attached to her navel, she says, "Can you at least tell me who the client is?"

"Miranda Lawson."

Tabby's eyes widen. "*The* Miranda Lawson?"

I knew that would get her. There's nothing Tabitha West likes better than another ball-busting woman who had to claw her way to the top over a pile of male corpses. "Yep."

The bartender sets a glass of water in front of her and leaves without a word. She takes a sip from the glass, thoughtfully crunches on an ice cube. "So the job's in LA."

"Maybe. Maybe not."

"Will I be working at her movie studio?"

"Can't tell you that."

"What else can you tell me?"

"That's it."

She stares at me like I'm a complete idiot. "You expect me to commit to a job based on no information other than a name."

"Pays half a million."

That stops her cold. She freezes with her glass halfway to her mouth, and then slowly sets it down and looks at me. "Nobody pays half a million for a pen test."

"Never said it was a pen test."

She studies my face, but she won't find anything I don't want her to see.

"You have to give me something else, Connor. I don't go into situations blind. It's not how I work."

She's serious. I can see that much. Stalling, I take a swig of my scotch. I relish the burn for a moment, considering my answer. "You have a particular skill set that's necessary for this job. None of my guys can do what you can do."

"*You* can't do what I can do," she shoots back, challenging me.

I know a lot of men who'd never admit a woman was better than them at anything. But I'm man enough to admit the truth. "Nobody can do what you can do, Tabby."

She blinks.

I sense a chink in her armor and press my advantage. "I'm flying out in the morning. Got a meeting with Lawson tomorrow. If all goes well, we're looking at maybe a week before the job's done. Then you can go back to your life and you'll never see me again. Only you'll be half a million bucks richer."

She sniffs. "I don't need the money. I never have to work again if I don't want to."

It's another challenge. So I challenge her right back. "Okay. But I'm betting you'd go out of your fuckin' mind if you didn't have a puzzle to solve. Right?"

She doesn't answer for a second. Then she turns away and mutters, "Bullshit doesn't suit you, jarhead."

I lightly grasp her chin, turn her face, and look her right in the eyes. "You're the smartest person I've ever met. I'm including myself in that statement, and I'm one smart motherfucker. I want you on this job. I wouldn't ask if I didn't know you were perfect for it."

She stares back at me silently. A furrow forms between her

brows. When she pulls her full lower lip between her teeth, I realize how close my face is to hers.

She has a beauty mark near her right eyebrow, a tiny, perfect spot of velvet brown. Otherwise, her skin is flawless. Creamy, I think you'd call it. And those eyes, sweet Jesus, those eyes that can turn a man to stone can also light his imagination on fire.

Smelling her skin, sitting so close, looking into those jungle cat eyes, my imagination is definitely ablaze.

Tabby abruptly withdraws. She licks her lips, swallows, turns her attention back to her glass of water. In a flat voice, she says, "Well. Thanks for that, but I work alone. Also I just remembered I hate you." She downs the water all in one gulp like it's whiskey, stands, and, without looking at me, says, "See you in another life, jarhead."

She turns and walks away.

Fuck.

I call out after her, "Think about it, Tabby. I'm at the Carlisle until six tomorrow morning if you change your mind."

She keeps walking, making no indication she's heard me. Feeling a little desperate, I add, "You got something better to do, sweet cheeks? Go back to New York and work on your Hello Kitty handbag collection? Get a few more tattoos?"

Over her shoulder, she flips me the bird. The old guy on the stool next to me cackles.

I turn around and give him my signature death glare, the one that always shuts dumb motherfuckers up.

But he's a scrappy old goat, not easily scared. He just cackles again, shaking his head. He says, "Don't worry, son. I'm sure someday you'll figure out how to talk to a woman."

I growl, "Mind your business, Grandpa."

Another cackle. Must be his signature thing, like my death glare. He says, "A little finesse wouldn't kill you, boy."

The fucking balls on this geezer! "*Excuse* me?"

"Convincing a woman to do something you want her to do

isn't like Operation Desert Storm. You can't go in all shock and awe, balls to the wall. Trust me, I been married four times. You gotta make her think it was *her* idea. You know." He wiggles his fingers in the air. "Finesse."

I look back to the entrance of the bar just in time to see Tabby disappear around the corner, her shoulders stiff, her head held high.

Finesse, he says. Not exactly my strong suit.

Fuck.

TABBY

*W*hen I get back to my room, I lie on the sofa and do deep-breathing exercises for ten minutes before the urge to break something passes.

What. The hell. Was *that*?

Just seeing him was strange enough. Out of the blue after three years, Connor Hughes materializes from thin air in my hotel room like fucking Cowboy Dracula, all *Hiya! Howdy, pardner! Have I got an offer for you!*

As if we don't have history.

As if he doesn't *know* I hate him.

And then the mysterious, cloak-and-dagger, I'd-tell-you-but-then-I'd-have-to-kill-you job offer.

I admit I was tempted by the thought of meeting Miranda Lawson. I've always admired her. She's a true genius, and those are rarer than unicorns. Graduated MIT—my alma mater—at seventeen, then attended USC film school and received an MFA in film and television production. Became the youngest female studio head in any movie studio's history at twenty-five. Founded her own studio at thirty. In the decade since, she's churned out blockbuster after blockbuster, attributed to a proprietary statistical analysis software she developed which can apparently predict what the movie-viewing public will enjoy with frightening accuracy.

She's fiercely intelligent, utterly unapologetic, and more competent than any man.

What's not to like?

Sure, she's got haters. A lot of them, from what I've read in the press. But the number of fucks she gives about what people think of her is equal to the number of times Connor Hughes has said, "I don't know."

Arrogant prick.

Although I grudgingly admit he shocked the hell out of me with that "you're the smartest person I've ever met" shtick. Not sure if it was even in the neighborhood of genuine, but he definitely managed to *look* sincere.

He looked a few other things too. Like…intense. Intimate.

Aroused.

And we're breathing.

I'm sure there are women who'd consider his kind of rugged, mountain-man type attractive, but I'm definitely not one of them. Two-day growth of beard, thighs like tree trunks, shoulders like a linebacker…ugh. He's fucking uncivilized is what he is. A big, barbarian ape. He probably chews with his mouth open.

Why would he even think I'd *consider* working with him?

The last time I saw him, I was in crisis mode. My best friend and employer, Victoria, had disappeared, the police had just interrogated me about my relationship with her, and in walks Victoria's ex, Parker, with his hired gun jarhead, demanding answers. It all turned out fine in the end, but I'll never forget how insensitive Connor was. How he *laughed* at me.

How small he made me feel.

Yeah, he's a prick. A self-involved bulldozer of a man who I want absolutely nothing to do with. And, more importantly, any job I take has to be within driving distance. I've never been on a plane in my life. I'm not about to start now.

Not even for Miranda Lawson.

Right, I think, sitting up on the sofa. *Moving on.*

I'm driving back to New York first thing in the morning, so I put together the report for Roger Hamilton, order room service, and pack. Then I eat my dinner on the couch while watching TV.

Just as I'm about to get into bed a few hours later, someone slips an envelope under my door.

I stare at it like it's full of anthrax. Who would be slipping me notes? At this hour? *Here?*

Only one way to find out.

I walk with trepidation to the door, open it, and peek out. The hallway is empty and silent. I close the door, pick up the envelope, and pull out a single sheet of paper. It's handwritten in blocky, blunt print. The first line alone has me gasping.

I owe you an apology.

It wasn't my intention to insult you, but I think that's what I've done. I'm not very good at treading lightly. Truth be told, I have one setting, and that's full steam ahead. Sometimes I forget my manners.

Sometimes I'm a dick.

You were right to flip me off, and I can't honestly say I blame you for walking out. What I can say is that I wasn't bullshitting you when I said I wanted you on this job. Not to sound like a stalker, but I've kept any eye on what you've been up to the past three years, and I'm damn impressed. I think you could rule the world if you wanted to, Tabby.

Anyway. Since I won't ever see you again, I'll take this opportunity to say I'm sorry. Sincerely. Best of luck to you. I'm sure whatever you're working on next will be much more interesting than meeting Miranda Lawson.

Yours,
Connor

I stand there with the letter in my hands for what feels like a long time. Then I crumple the letter in my fist. "Nice try, jarhead."

I throw the letter in the trash.

～

The drive from DC to Manhattan is just under five hours with no traffic. Since it's a Saturday and I left with the sunrise, I expected to be home by noon. Unfortunately, there was a pileup on the New Jersey Turnpike, so it took an additional few hours. By the time I get home, I'm crabby and ravenous.

"Honey, I'm home!" I call out as I walk inside.

"We're in here!" answers a faint voice from the direction of the living room.

My townhouse is in the swanky part of Greenwich Village. I bought it two years ago and promptly tore out all the hideous purple carpeting the previous owner favored, along with the blood-red Victorian floral wallpaper that made my skin crawl. It was like living inside a rotten plum. Now the walls are painted delicate eggshell, the floors are glossy ebony hardwood, and the furniture... I'm still working on the furniture. In five stories with six bedrooms, the only places to sit are behind the desk in my office, on the sofa in the living room, on the floor, or on my bed.

I drop my bags near the stairs to the second level and make my way down the hall. When I get to the living room, I prop my hands on my hips and smile, amused by the scene.

Juanita, my fifteen-year-old neighbor, is sitting cross-legged on the floor in front of the sofa with an open bag of Cheetos in her lap and a can of Red Bull in one hand. She's in her school uniform of white shirt and plaid skirt, but her skinny legs are bare, as are her feet. Her wild mop of curly dark hair is pulled back in a sloppy ponytail. The floor around her is littered with candy wrappers, empty soda cans, discarded bags of chips, and schoolbooks. She has her laptop open on the coffee table in front of her and is watching MMA wrestling, her favorite thing in the world.

Trying to sound stern, I say, "When someone tells you 'make yourself at home' while they're gone, Nita, it's a euphemism for be comfortable. Not move in and turn the place into *Animal House*."

She doesn't bother to acknowledge that or look over in my direction. "When are you gonna get a TV, man? What kind of weirdo doesn't have a TV?"

"I'm not weird. I'm limited edition."

"Tch."

"I'd also like to point out that I'm the only person in this room not wearing a rat."

Juanita's pet rat, Elvis, is perched on her head. He's white with big black patches, like a dairy cow. Juanita rescued him from a storm drain when he was a baby, and they've been inseparable ever since. He travels with her on her shoulder or in her backpack, to the dismay of her mother and teachers at school. When the principal said he'd suspend her if she didn't stop bringing Elvis to class, Juanita threatened to call the civil rights division of the US Department of Justice and report that her rights were being violated under the Americans with Disabilities Act, because Elvis was a service animal like a seeing-eye dog. When asked what service he provided, Juanita replied with a straight face, "Emotional support."

I love this kid.

She comes over every day after school to escape her six siblings, who all still live at home. She tells her mother I'm helping her with her calculus homework, but the reality is that Juanita could teach her AP calculus class herself.

"You say that like it's a good thing," says Juanita, reaching up to scratch Elvis on his belly. He shivers in delight, white whiskers trembling. "How'd the job go?"

"How do you think it went?"

Juanita snorts. "I think you shriveled another rich old white dude's balls to the size of peas."

"That I did. Another pea-sized pair of balls to add to my collection." I sigh in satisfaction. I really do love my job. "I'm going to make a sandwich. You want one?"

Her attention still glued to the computer screen where two shirtless, barefoot guys are beating each other to within an inch of their lives, Juanita says, "Nah. I'm good."

I eye all the junk food wrappers scattered around her. "It wouldn't kill you to eat some real food once in a while, kiddo."

Juanita makes a face. "Sure thing, Lourdes."

Lourdes is her mother's name. It's what she calls me when I'm meddling.

She calls me Lourdes a lot.

"Suit yourself," I say breezily, and leave Juanita and Elvis to enjoy their show.

In the kitchen, I kick off my shoes and open the fridge. Unlike the rest of my home, it's packed. An empty refrigerator is one of the few things that frightens me.

"Roast beef, provolone, tomatoes, lettuce," I say, gathering everything. "Hello, my beauties!"

I get the bread from the pantry, make myself a sandwich, and eat it standing up over the kitchen sink. Then I make another sandwich, tuck it inside a Ziploc bag, and slip it inside the backpack Juanita left on the console by the front door.

Then I go upstairs and unpack. When my things are put away, I pad down the hallway to my office, fire up my computer, and check my email.

Zip. Nada. Crickets.

And the old, familiar loneliness pops its head around my shoulder and gives me a kiss on the cheek.

This is the worst time, when I come home from a job and don't have anything else lined up. When I'm working, my mind is occupied, and when my mind is occupied, I can go days or weeks without once wondering what the point of everything is. But when I'm not working...

"I'm betting you'd go out of your fuckin' mind if you didn't have a puzzle to solve. Right?"

Jarhead and his annoyingly astute observations.

The thought of him is equivalent to a migraine. How can anyone stand to be around that cocky, irritating jerk? I know he runs a successful business, so he's got employees, clients, vendors, people he has to interact with on a daily basis. He's probably even got friends...girlfriends?

No, I think, wrinkling my nose. *He wouldn't call them "girlfriends." He'd call them...gashes. Or something equally repulsive.*

I really hate that chauvinistic prick.

"And we're breathing," I remind myself as my stomach tightens. "*Again.*"

Connor Hughes is bad for my blood pressure.

From downstairs Juanita yells, "We're outta here! See you after school Monday!"

I yell back, "Good luck on your calculus test!"

"Suck a bag of dicks, hooker!"

A laugh, and then the front door slams.

"Love you too, kiddo," I say, smiling.

I change into my running clothes and head over to Washington Square, the big park a few blocks away. I run my regular circuit on the paths that wind through the park, nodding at the old guys playing chess, dodging the street performers and families and couples walking their dogs. It's a bright, beautiful spring afternoon, and the park is crowded with people picnicking around the main fountain, enjoying the weather.

This is why I run in the mornings. All these people make me twitchy.

An hour later, sweaty, my thighs aching, I head back to my

house. I finish a book on the Chernobyl disaster, recategorize my CD collection by genre, and then decide to shower before I head out to find a place for dinner. Saturdays I usually head over to a little French wine bar in my neighborhood. I like to watch all the date-night couples gazing adoringly at each other over their overpriced glasses of Bordeaux and speculate about who's cheating on who.

I almost always decide it's everyone.

I take a long, hot shower, condition my hair, and shave all my lady parts that need shaving. Not that anyone's going to touch said lady parts, but I like to keep my garden free of weeds, so to speak. In case I'm ever in an accident and I have to be examined at the hospital by some insanely hot doctor. Why he'd be examining me nude I don't know, but in my fantasies, these kinds of odd scenarios regularly occur.

In reality, it's been years since a man saw me naked.

It's easier this way. Sex leads to feelings, and feelings lead to disappointment, so it logically follows that celibacy leads to no disappointments. Especially since I can get myself off in under sixty seconds. So it's easy *and* efficient.

I dry off, wind my hair in the towel, and wrap it around my head, and head naked into my bedroom.

Where I let out an earsplitting scream.

Connor Hughes, reclining on my bed with his arms behind his head and his feet crossed at the ankle, grins at me. "That's twice now I've made you scream, sweet cheeks, without even laying a finger on you."

His gaze, searing hot, travels down the length of my naked body. His voice grows husky.

"Imagine what I could do with all ten."

4

TABBY

I leap backward into the bathroom and slam the door. "You fucking *asshole*!" I shout.

In response, I hear a deep, satisfied chuckle.

So furious I'm shaking, I tear the towel off my head and wrap it around my body. "This is breaking and entering! I'm calling the police, you goddamn maniac!"

There's a short pause, and then Connor's voice, low and rich, comes through the door. It sounds like he's standing right outside. "You're not gonna call the police."

Red-faced, I stalk back and forth in front of the vanity, deeply mortified that animal saw me naked. "Oh yes I am!"

"Tabby. Be reasonable. Do you really think it's the best idea to invite law enforcement over to the home of the woman who once hacked into NASA's mainframe and intercepted the source code of the International Space Station? NYPD might not be the sharpest tools in the shed, but they'll take one look inside your office and know they're not dealing with the average computer hobbyist."

The bastard is right. My office is packed floor to ceiling with hard drives, servers, monitors, modems, wireless networking equipment, soldering equipment, lock picks, ham radios, crypto-phones, and all the other tools of my trade. I'm careful to always flush data from every device after a job is done, but you never know if some rookie officer who wants to make a name for himself decides to invoke probable cause in the name of post-9/11 public safety.

I imagine Connor smirking on the other side of the door and feel a profound desire to bury a hatchet in his skull.

"You're right. I won't call the cops. But you just made yourself an enemy. Consider it open season on Metrix."

Silence.

Now it's my turn to smirk. Connor knows I can make good on my promise. If I wanted to, I could have his entire company's network fucked six ways to Sunday before he could even figure out how I snuck in.

"How 'bout a compromise?"

"Compromises require two parties to make concessions in order to get what they want. *You*, asswipe douche bag megaprick, have nothing I want."

Connor chuckles. "I ever tell you I love that dirty mouth of yours?"

Oh my God. I'm seriously going to open the door and punch him in the face.

He taps on the door. "C'mon, Tabby. I promise I won't surprise you again, okay? No more showing up unannounced when you're coming out of the shower." Pause. "Though I have to admit, seeing you naked has been like the highlight of my entire fuckin' life. Nipple piercings? Jesus *Christ*, that's hot. And was that a tiger tattoo on your stomach?" He chuckles again and then growls, "Rawr."

I stare at the door, blood pulsing in my cheeks. "I will kill you with my bare hands."

A gently teasing *tsk*. "You love me. Just admit it, sweetheart.

The only time you feel alive is when you're screaming insults in my face."

I close my eyes, pulling in deep breaths through my nose, and count to ten. "How did you even get here so fast?" I ask through clenched teeth. "I thought you had a meeting in LA?"

"TSA global security pass, private jet, yada yada. Plus, manipulating time is my superpower." His voice drops. "Wanna know what my other superpower is?"

"*No.*"

"I'll give you a hint. It's between my legs."

I look around the bathroom for something sharp to stab him with.

I freeze when the door swings open. Connor leans against the frame, dwarfing it. He drawls, "Forget to lock something, girl genius?"

I stare at him with what I hope are death rays emanating from my eyes. "I hate you. With a heat like a thousand suns, I hate you. With the force of a million tons of TNT, I hate you. With every fiber of my being, I—"

"Hate me, I get the picture," says Connor drily. "But you also think I'm kinda cute, right?" He winks.

The nerve. The *nerve* of this man. My voice shakes with rage. "Get out. Get out of my house. Now."

Connor looks at me for a long, measured moment. "Sure thing, Pop-Tart. But there's something you need to see first." He turns around and disappears.

I find him in the kitchen, leaning against the counter, calmly eating an apple as if it's the only thing he's got on his schedule for the rest of the week.

"Liked you better in what you were wearing upstairs," he

remarks, eying my baggy jeans and even baggier Nine Inch Nails sweatshirt.

I say coldly, "If I had one, I'd also be wearing a hazmat suit. The thought that you've seen me naked is traumatizing."

He crunches into another bite. I wonder if he's got his arms folded across his chest like that on purpose, to show off his ridiculous, oversized biceps. They're so big, he could be one of those strongmen in an old-fashioned circus, the guys in the stretchy leopard-print unitards, hoisting barbells over their heads.

I'd like to hoist a barbell over his head.

"What's so important you just doomed your network to an early death over it?"

He motions with his chin to a laptop on the opposite counter.

"You brought me a gift? How sweet. But I don't accept candy from home-invading strangers. Now get out before I remove your spleen. With a rusty knife. *Through your nose.*"

Connor takes a final bite of his apple—*my* apple!—swallows, and licks his lips. He manages to make the entire thing look both sensual and provocative. A dare.

A growl builds in the back of my throat.

He says, "Open it. You can kill me after." A dent forms in one of his cheeks.

I'm not sure which infuriates me more, him seeing me naked or finding my anger about it a source of entertainment.

"I'll leave you alive just long enough to appreciate my skill at creating the metamorphic virus that's going to devour every line of code in every piece of software your company owns. How's that?" I smile sweetly and head to the laptop.

I open it, expecting to see anything but what I find, which is Miranda Lawson staring back at me from a live camera feed.

In a clipped voice, she says, "Tabitha West. I'm Miranda Lawson."

So much for the preliminaries. I look at Connor, who nods at the screen as if to say, *Pay attention.*

I turn back to Miranda, an elegant, icy-blonde ringer for the actress Sharon Stone. Straight-backed and pale, she's sitting at a desk in what appears to be a spacious home office. Bookcases and photographs line the wall behind her right shoulder. To her left is the view of a spectacular sunset over the ocean through a wall of glass.

If she's cutting right to the chase, I am too. "I understand you have a situation."

She offers me a pinched, unhappy smile. "Yes. My situation is that Mr. Hughes requires you to assist him in a job I've hired him to do, and he informs me you've refused."

With a clenched jaw, I look over my shoulder at Connor. He blows me a kiss.

I turn back to Miranda. "Correct."

"What is your reason for refusal?" she demands.

This entire situation is really starting to chap my ass. "Well, if you must know, I despise him."

She makes an elegant little movement of her hand as if she's swatting away a fly. "Your personal feelings about Mr. Hughes are immaterial."

I can see why this woman has such a bad reputation. I understand that highly intelligent people are more often than not absolute disasters with interpersonal skills. All I have to do is take a look in a mirror to get that. But that isn't what I take offense to. It's the arrogance that gets me. The presumption that what she wants is more important than what I want.

Before I can speak, she says coolly, "No, I don't care about your feelings. And you don't care about mine, nor should you. We're strangers, after all. What I do care about is that you are regarded highly by a person I regard highly, and therefore I'm willing to negotiate on price. I authorized Connor to offer you five hundred thousand. Now I'm offering a million. Will that be sufficient?"

I'm surprised she actually stooped to ask my opinion. I take great pleasure in saying, "I'm not interested in the job, Ms. Lawson. At any price."

Her icy-blue eyes don't blink. Her elegant features don't move. But I *feel* her disapproval, like a glass of cold water poured down my spine. "You," she says, barely moving her lips, "are being unreasonable."

If she's an iceberg, I'm a forest fire. I feel heat sweep up my neck from my chest, feel my ears go hot, feel the pressure build behind my eyeballs. "And *you*, Ms. Lawson, along with that high horse you rode in on, can go fuck yourself."

I slap the laptop closed.

Behind me, Connor sighs.

I glare at him. "That was *beyond*, jarhead, even for you."

"Well, my finesse didn't work, so I thought I'd bring in the big guns."

"Your finesse?" I repeat, astonished. "I didn't realize you were familiar with the word."

"The letter," he replies patiently, as if it should be obvious.

"Ah yes. The letter. I wonder, how many tries did it take before you could actually bring yourself to write the dreaded words 'I owe you an apology'?"

At the sarcasm in my tone, his brows lift. "You think I lied?"

"I think you'd rather stab yourself in the eye than admit you were wrong."

"Well, yeah." He shrugs. "But that doesn't mean it wasn't the truth."

I narrow my eyes and inspect his expression, which remains suspiciously bland. I can't tell if he's lying.

I *hate* it that I can't tell if he's lying.

He says mildly, "You have trust issues, you know that?"

"Ha! *Me?* With *you*? No!"

His smile is wry, that amusement again. He inclines his head, as if to say *Fair enough.*

"Are we done here? Because I'd really like to get back to my life now."

"There's really nothing I can do to persuade you? Nothing you want from me in exchange for doing this job?"

The way he said that last part, the hint of innuendo along with a sparkle in his eyes, makes me grimace. "Please tell me you didn't just offer to service me sexually. Tell me I'm wrong, jarhead. Restore my faith in humanity and tell me you're not that much of a pig."

He makes big, innocent doe eyes at me. "What? Geez, Tabby. Sex on the brain much? How long has it been since you've gotten some?"

Then he smiles.

And he does it with his whole goddamn body.

I shudder. "You're a real piece of work. How do you ever get a date? No wait, don't tell me—with cash!"

His lashes lower. He looks at me with so much smugness oozing from his pores, I'm afraid I'll need to get out the mop. "Never had to pay for it in my life, sweetheart. Though I've been on the receiving end of that offer more times than I can count."

I stare at him, amazed by the sheer size of his ego. "You're so full of shit."

His full lips curve into a wicked grin. "You'd like to think I am."

I cross my arms over my chest, shaking my head in disbelief. "Okay. I give. Uncle! Now *vamanos, por favor*, and don't ever darken my doorstep again."

"She's bilingual," he murmurs, as if that's some kind of giant shock.

Is he fucking with me? Making fun of me? Baiting me? I can't tell! Fuck!

In spite of myself, I can't resist correcting him. "Not bilingual. Septalingual."

He slow blinks, the very definition of droll.

Impatiently, I explain, "Spanish, French, Italian, Latin, Portuguese, Romanian, and Catalan. I speak seven languages, not two."

"The Romance languages," he says, drawing it out as if he's expecting me to give an explanation as to the origins of my knowledge. Which, obviously, I'm not.

But I am the tiniest bit impressed he knows what the Romance languages are. I doubt they teach that in jarhead school.

When I don't reply, Connor prompts, "You forgot English."

I'm momentarily thrown off balance. "Oh. Right. English. Well, that goes without saying."

In a tone so banal he could be examining his cuticles, he corrects me. "Actually it doesn't. Including English, you're octolingual, not septalingual." That roguish dent in his cheek makes another appearance. "Technically speaking, that is."

With a shock like sticking my wet finger into an electrical outlet, I realize several things at once.

First, he's right. He was right about the police thing earlier too.

Cue brain cells fainting.

Second, he's much smarter than he lets on. He plays the blunt, sexed-up, muscle-bound military man to absolute perfection so no one will think to look closer. But it's an act. A brilliantly executed, nuanced disguise.

Third, the preceding realizations rearrange something in my head, and I feel the first stirrings of something other than anger or contempt for Connor Hughes.

The world tilts on its axis. I pull my lips between my teeth and stare at him, for once at a total loss for words.

"Wow," says Connor. "There's smoke comin' outta your ears, sweet cheeks. What gives?"

"I-I...I'm..."

The dent in his cheek becomes an apostrophe.

"Nothing. We're done here. Get out." My voice is empty of all emotion. My eyes unflinchingly meet his.

For a moment, his mask slips. I see disappointment. I see frustration. I see something that might be defeat. But he quickly gathers himself, pushes off the counter, runs a hand through his dark hair. He shakes his head like a dog shaking off water and huffs a short breath through his nose. To himself, he mutters, "Roger that. We'll get Maelstr0m some other way."

He looks up at me, gives me a tight smile along with a curt salute. "See you in another life, maybe. Sorry to have wasted your time."

He moves past me, graceful even at his size, his step improbably silent against the floor, but I can't focus on the elegance of his movement because I'm too busy rewinding and replaying what he just said.

"Wait!"

In the doorway, Connor pauses. He looks at me over his shoulder.

With my heart in my throat I whisper, "Did you say...Maelstr0m?"

Connor frowns. "Yeah. Some hacker who goes by the alias Maelstr0m, with a zero for the 'o.' He's Miranda's situation." A heartbeat, and then, sharper, "Why?"

I inhale. It's like trying to breathe underwater. The room seems too warm, too bright, too close.

"I hope you're prepared to go to war, Connor. *I'm in.*"

CONNOR

_T_he trendy French restaurant Tabby insists I take her to before she'll talk is way too froufrou for my taste, but I have to admit the food is incredible. And the pair of young, hot chicks at the bar who've been staring at me since we got here are incredible too.

Not because I'm interested. Because Tabby's noticed the way they've been looking at me and is making a valiant effort to pretend not only that she hasn't, but that she doesn't care.

It's fucking beautiful is what it is. This is my new favorite place.

I say, "Enough with the suspense. Tell me what you know about this Maelstr0m."

Tabby delicately licks her fingers clean of truffle salt from the _pommes frites_ she's been scarfing down. I shouldn't be surprised that she could make such a simple act look sexy as fuck, but she does. And she's not even trying.

I shove aside the picture that pops into my mind of my hard cock in place of her fingers. Unfortunately, the big guy downstairs has already started to react to the brief but incredible illusion and twitches against my thigh.

I don't know what it is about this woman—bad-tempered, foul-mouthed Hello Kitty fiend with a constellation of tattoos on her body and a mind like a maze—but she really does it for me.

"I was living in Boston, in my third year of college—"

"MIT," I clarify, just because it's incredible to me that any person would be smart *and* self-confident enough to graduate high school at fifteen and go right into the most intellectually rigorous college in the nation.

She glances at me with a wry smile. "I take it you've been reading about me in a file."

"It's my business to know things about people I work with. Information is power. You know that. Although I have to admit I was surprised there was any information to be found at all after how perfectly you scraped Victoria's past clean."

Tabby's smile falters. When she looks away, I know I've hit a nerve.

Victoria Price was Tabby's best friend and a Bitch with a capital B. She had more skeletons in her closet than shoes. Until a few years ago when Victoria's past finally caught up with her and she fled to Mexico, Tabby's existence revolved around erasing information about Victoria, hiding her past, making sure no one discovered her entire identity had been manufactured. Tabby did her job so well, even *I* couldn't find anything on Victoria, and that was unprecedented.

Tabby says in a hollow voice, "I don't have anything interesting enough to hide."

"This from the woman who single-handedly shut down the government's space program for three weeks."

She dismissively waves her hand. "I meant personally. My hacks are another story, but Polaroid can't be traced back to me."

Polaroid is her hacker alias, so named for her photographic memory. She's infamous in hacker circles, revered not only for the brilliance of the jobs she pulls off, but also for never getting caught. She went legit after her time with Victoria, started doing white hat corporate jobs for guys like Roger Hamilton, and Polaroid went dark.

Curiosity prompts me to ask, "You still talk to Victoria?"

Toying with her fork, Tabby shrugs. "Yeah. I saw her a while back too. Darcy and Kai honeymooned in Mexico, and we all got together. It was fun."

I sense the sadness behind her words. "But?"

Looking uncomfortable, Tabby hesitates before she answers. "But she's busy living her happily-ever-after, and I'm busy... doing my thing."

It's obvious that she's happy for Victoria, but the undercurrent is loneliness. I want to reach out and squeeze her hand but know I risk losing it, so instead I try to lighten the mood.

"Don't worry, sweet cheeks, I'm sure you'll get your happily ever after too."

Unsmiling, she looks up. "There are no happily ever afters for people like me."

People like me? I tilt my head, studying her, fascinated. When she flushes and looks away, I decide to leave that subject for another time.

"Back to you attending MIT barely out of diapers."

She rolls her eyes. "Getting in at fifteen isn't that impressive, Connor. My first year there, a twelve-year-old graduated with a PhD in molecular biology. Geniuses are a dime a dozen at that school."

"Just because you're used to being surrounded by other stars doesn't make your star shine any less bright to the rest of us down here on earth."

Taken aback, she blinks and self-consciously laughs.

I wonder how often she's been on the receiving end of a compliment. Judging by her surprise, not often.

Why that should irritate me, I don't know.

She says, "Anyway, as part of a project in my quantum

computing class, we were assigned to work on a cryptology software program for businesses that could theoretically be hack proof. Protection for data at banks, universities, hospitals, that kind of thing. Totally hypothetical, of course, but we were supposed to come up with a new way of protecting data, and then test it in a real-world environment."

"Like with an actual business?"

"Bank of America of all things." Her lips twist. "I think someone at the bank must've been in on it because whoever thought it was a good idea to give a bunch of geeky teenagers with gigantic intellects and no impulse control access to billions of dollars' worth of financial information was definitely guilty of something. Criminal short-sightedness, at the very least."

I lean back in my chair and take a swig of my beer. From the corner of my eye, I see one of the girls at the bar who's been watching me lean over and whisper something behind her hand to her companion. They both look at me and then giggle.

Tabby didn't miss it either. A muscle in her jaw flexes. That small reaction makes me want to jump from my chair and do a touchdown victory dance, complete with chest pounding and Tarzan roars.

I say mildly, "Go on."

She takes a breath. "There were four teams of six students. Maelstr0m and I were on the same team. His real name is Søren Killgaard, by the way. But don't bother looking for him. You won't find any data about anyone, living or dead, with that name."

I keep my face and body perfectly neutral. Not even a muscle twitches. I hardly even breathe. But the odds that Tabby went to school with the very man I'm searching for are staggering.

I don't believe in fate, but there's something really creepy about this.

I motion for her to continue.

Fingering her fork, Tabby looks down at her plate. "He was different, even in a roomful of kids who were definitions of the word 'different.' He was..." She searches for the word. "Wrong, somehow. I don't know how else to put it. He was wrong."

"I know exactly what you mean. Some people look right, they say all the right things, on the surface they appear to be normal, adjusted members of society, but you can sense on an animal level that they're off."

Tabby's nodding. "I was the only person who felt that way about Søren. Everyone else was dazzled by him. In complete awe. I think in part it was because he was so beautiful—"

"*Beautiful?*" I drawl. "Did someone have a crush?"

She looks at me for a long, silent moment. She's not wearing any makeup, and in the candlelight, her bare skin gleams like a polished stone.

"No. I didn't have a crush. Even at eighteen I knew that beautiful things can be toxic. I'm simply speaking the truth. Søren Killgaard looked like a Renaissance painting of an angel. Golden hair and fair skin and eyes the color of ice in an alpine lake that never thaws. A body so proportionate and perfect, it was made to be sculpted. I always thought he looked like a fairy-tale prince, he had that sort of untouchable, otherworldly beauty."

Slowly, my brows lift. This Søren Killgaard must be some looker to get the rabid Tabitha West waxing poetic.

I decide I hate him.

"So what happened?"

Tabby's expression hardens. "He skimmed millions of dollars before they caught on to what was happening. He used a loop-hole in the bank's code to divert money into an account he controlled. Fractions of pennies at a time, so no single transaction would be detected—"

"Salami slicing. Classic hacker technique."

"Yes," she agrees. "Classic. Except the account he controlled was in my name."

In the silence that follows, the muted noises of the restaurant seem overly loud. Voices, music, the clatter of silverware against plates, the sounds clang around in my head.

"He set you up."

Tabby nods.

"Why?"

"Because he could. He could do anything he wanted."

"No. Why *you*?"

She looks over my shoulder. I sense she's deliberately avoiding my eyes.

"You'd have to ask him."

I stare at her long and hard. "Tabby."

She glances at me.

"Don't bullshit me. If we're gonna work together, there won't be any lies between us. Why did Søren Killgaard set you up?"

Her expression is unreadable. "Why do some boys like to pull the wings off flies?"

I say bluntly, "You were fucking him."

Something flickers in her gaze, a deep distaste or disappointment. "Not everything is about sex, Connor."

"Yes, it is. Except, like Oscar Wilde said, sex itself. That's about power."

Her head tilts. She appraises me with those beautiful feline eyes, a long, searching look that's strangely intimate. The distaste in her gaze changes to something else, something warmer. In a husky voice, she murmurs, "*Finally*, something on which we agree."

Heat surges through my body.

Desire is a strange animal. Elemental like hunger or thirst, but unlike hunger or thirst, it has the power to rob you of reason with the speed of two fingers snapping, so that you'll do things so out of character you don't recognize yourself, the creature you become in service of the primal, irresistible urge to mate.

The tone in her voice, the look in her eyes, the memory of her wet, naked body—all of it conspires to wipe my mind clean of all logic, and suddenly I'm just...*gone.*

I reach across the table, take her face in my hands, pull her toward me—knocking over glasses and rattling plates—and kiss her.

For a moment, there's nothing. Resistance, her mouth firmly closed, her lips hard. But then a softening, a quick intake of breath through her nose, and she gives in.

Her lips part. She takes my tongue into her mouth. She makes a sound deep in her throat, a low, feminine noise of pleasure, and my cock instantly stiffens to steel.

She tastes sweet, so fucking sweet, warm and soft and yielding, like a ripe piece of fruit. A peach, melting in my mouth. Our tongues sweep against each other, delicious sliding and pressure, suction, gliding, easy and perfect, like they were meant for exactly this. Then it's more urgent, a rising demand, a jolt of pleasure when she nips my lower lip, my hands tightening around her jaw, her hands fisted in my hair, urgently pulling me closer, deeper, my mind fried as my body throbs and pulses, every beat of my heart a roar in my ears, my blood pounding like drums, wanting wanting wanting—*Sweet Jesus this woman is heaven*—

She yanks away and slaps me.

Hard.

We stare at each other. She's standing up, I'm sitting down, we're both panting. Her face is bright red. My cock is so hard, it hurts.

The two girls at the bar are openly gaping at us. So is the waitress, who just arrived to clear our plates.

Tabby staggers back a step. She drags the back of her hand across her mouth. She rips her gaze from mine and looks at the girls at the bar.

"He's all yours," she says hoarsely. She spins around and strides away.

"*Goddammit*, Connor," I mutter. I throw some money down on the table. Ignoring the titters of the girls, I follow Tabby.

~

When she walks in the front door of her house, I'm already there, leaning against the counter in the dark kitchen in the same spot I was standing before we left.

She flicks on the light and stares at me. I've seen her angry before, but this…

This is something else altogether.

Eyes glittering, she says with dangerous softness, "Don't ever do that again."

Not chancing what might come out of my mouth if I open it, I simply nod.

She slowly exhales. "And no more appearing out of nowhere. Respect my privacy or fuck off. Permanently."

Again I calmly nod, but my heart leaps with hope. She's laying down terms, which means she's still in.

"I don't travel by plane. Ever. Anywhere. So if the job is in another country—"

"It's in LA. We can drive. If we leave tonight, we can be there in—"

"Three or four days, give or take," she says flatly. "I know. I've made the trip before. Only not with someone I detested, so I imagine it'll seem like much longer."

If a man could be murdered by a look alone, I'd already be dead. I decide to take a gamble and go out on a limb. "It won't happen again. I'm sorry."

"Yes," she replies. "You really are."

Ouch.

"Give me the contract."

Earlier I'd left the job contract, along with my standard, iron-clad nondisclosure agreement, beneath the laptop on the counter. I retrieve the paperwork and hand it to Tabby. She flips through it, quickly scanning the pages, her mouth tight, her face pale. When she gets to the end, she finds a pen in a drawer, scratches her name on the signature line, and thrusts the contract back into my hands.

"I'll tell Miranda to wire payment into your—"

"I already told you," Tabby grinds out through clenched teeth, "I don't need the money. In this case, I don't *want* it." Her eyes meet mine, and in them I see entire cities burning to the ground. "And no more questions about Søren."

I keep my voice carefully measured to hide the unease I feel hearing her say that. "I need to know whatever you know about him. It's critical information that could have a major impact on the success or failure of the job."

"There's a ninety-nine percent probability the job will fail, no matter what you know."

Her lack of confidence is surprisingly painful. "You don't even know what it is yet."

Tabby stares at me, her chest rising and falling in irregular bursts. I feel the tension in her, the weight of it in her body, how much effort it takes to stand motionless when everything inside her is pure violence. I recognize it because it's something I've felt myself countless times, on countless missions. Gun in hand, crouched low against a wall in the dark, counting my breaths as I lie in wait for an enemy.

Whatever happened between the two of them, she carries it with her like the lone survivor of a battle, standing in the middle of a field gory with bodies and blood.

She says, "The only thing you need to know about Søren Killgaard is that he's more clever than the devil, and not nearly as nice. If you show any weakness, he'll exploit it. Whatever you think his endgame is, you'll be wrong. He'll always be five moves ahead of you, no matter how well you plan, and there's only one way you'll ever catch him."

"Which is?"

Tabby smiles. The cold pragmatism in it sends a chill down my spine.

"By using me as bait."

6

CONNOR

*W*e leave for LA at midnight. And for the next
nineteen hours, Tabby doesn't speak to me.

I'm comfortable with silence, but her silence is so loud, it
screams. She's furious about that kiss, but it goes deeper than
that. I took something from her when I didn't give her a choice.
Worse, I suspect, is the way she feels about her own reaction to
having my mouth on hers.

She liked it, which makes her hate me even more.

Women.

"Are we driving straight through to LA?"

Startled, I glance over at her. She's staring out the window of
the car, refusing to meet my eyes, the question asked in a tone
that suggests she doesn't care one way or another.

Her choice of travel wear raised my brows when I returned to
her place after making a quick trip home to pack my bags, and I
let my gaze rake over it once again, if only to satisfy my growing
need to look at her. Tight black leather everything, including
gloves, motorcycle jacket zipped up to her chin, and combat
boots. The only thing she's missing is a helmet. Except for her
face, not an inch of skin is showing.

I recognize this outfit for what it is. Armor.

It's a good thing it's only March and the weather is cool, because August in that getup would be murder.

"No. Wanted to get into Tulsa before we stopped for the night."

We've had three short stops so far at gas stations along the interstate, just long enough to hit the head and refill the tank. If I were alone, I'd push straight through, but then again, if I were alone, I wouldn't be driving.

I know from my research that her parents were killed in an airplane crash when she was eight and wonder how much of her avoidance of flying is based on that.

I also wonder how much of who she's become is based on those deaths, and the death of the uncle she went to live with after the loss of her parents. By eighteen, she was all alone in the world.

Except for Søren Killgaard, whose relationship to her remains a mystery.

For now.

Suddenly she mutters, "I'm so fucking pissed off at you!"

I stare straight ahead at the twin beams of the headlights illuminating the highway and wait.

After a moment, she says, "I can't think when I'm mad. When I can't think, I feel out of control. When I feel out of control, I panic. Are you seeing the pattern here?"

I keep my voice low and calm, nonthreatening. "It won't happen again."

"You said that before," she says crossly, "but the problem is that I think I want it to."

I nearly drive off the road. This kind of straightforward admission is the last thing I expected, and I'm totally unprepared for it. I quickly decide the only way to handle it is in kind.

"I'm not sure how to respond to that."

She sighs, pulls the elastic out of her ponytail, and drags her hands through her hair. "Forget it. Tell me a story."

Hello, fly ball out of left field.

"Sure." I think for a moment, and then my brain presents me with a sly idea I have to admit I find totally genius, even if I did think of it myself. Well, probably especially since I thought of it myself.

"Once upon a time, there was a boy and a girl."

She looks over at me sharply.

"Don't get your panties in a twist, sweetheart. Am I telling this story or not?"

She leans her head against the headrest and closes her eyes. "Yes. Make it good."

"I will if you'd shut up long enough to let me talk."

I have to pretend I don't see the stabby look she sends me. "As I was saying: boy, girl. The boy was strong and smart, self-less and courageous, a natural leader, and, of course, very hand-some. And incredibly popular. Your real hero type."

Tabby's groan is pained. "For fuck's sake, Connor."

I push on, ignoring for the moment how much I like hearing her say my name. "The girl was strong and smart too, but in a way that most people couldn't understand. And because most people didn't understand her, it was hard for her to make friends. So because it was hard for her to make friends, she learned to rely on herself instead of anyone else."

Beside me, there's silence.

My voice grows quieter. "The girl lived alone in a castle high on a hill. She was a princess, you see. But her parents were dead, and she was an only child. An orphan. She had no one to play with and no one to talk to and no one to tell her how amazing she was." I glance at her. "How beautiful."

She's sitting very still, staring straight ahead, her posture stiff and guarded. It's all I can do not to reach out and stroke my fingers down her satin cheek.

"One day an evil wizard came to town. He'd heard of the beautiful princess, lonely and vulnerable in her castle—"

"Vulnerable!" Tabby scoffs.

"—and hatched a plan to steal her heart and then take over her kingdom by making all her subjects think she'd done something terrible. He began to woo the princess with jewels and gold and promises of forever—"

"Tread carefully, jarhead," says Tabby, her eyes on the road and her jaw set.

"You already know I'm no good at that," I reply softly.

She swallows and looks down at her hands clenched in her lap. "I don't like this story."

"Should I jump to the ending? Spoiler alert: the hero saves her."

Tabby looks over at me, her eyes shining like gems in the dark. "A real hero would teach the princess how to save herself."

Our eyes hold. A flutter works its way through my chest. I murmur, "Noted."

She breaks eye contact first. We drive in silence for miles, until finally she says almost inaudibly, "He never promised me forever."

Søren. His presence between us is palpable, a heavy weight in the air. A darkness.

"What did he promise you?"

Tabby looks out into the night, to the dark landscape passing by the windows in a blur, and says nothing.

We find a Best Western hotel in Tulsa and take adjoining rooms on the fourth floor. I'm impressed that Tabby has brought only one small suitcase for her clothes, but judging by the size of her normal wardrobe—skirts that make the word "mini" seem overgenerous and child-size tops—I can't say I'm really surprised.

Her computer gear, on the other hand, could have its own zip code.

"Good thing I drove the truck," I mutter, hauling a fifty-pound black case from the back of my Hummer.

"Truck?" says Tabby, standing next to me in the parking lot as we unload our bags. "Is that what you call this monstrosity?"

I drag another of her bags out, this one even heavier than the first, and drop it at her feet. "Spare me the tree-hugging psychobabble about gas consumption and emissions, will you, sweetheart? This vehicle is built for a specific purpose—"

"Overcompensation for feelings of penis size inadequacy?" She smiles.

"Safety," I correct and smile back. "As if you haven't already noticed, I'm not exactly lacking in the size department."

Involuntarily, her gaze drops to my crotch. Then she catches herself, blinks up at me, and flushes. Her voice comes out of her mouth with the cutting power of a sword.

"As a class three truck, this vehicle is exempt from many DOT safety regulations and lacks standard safety features, including side air bags and stability control. In addition, its large blind spots make—"

"Don't change the subject."

"Don't make me murder you in the parking lot of a one-star hotel."

"Yeah? You think you could get the drop on me?" Amused, I look her up and down. "You're lookin' at two-hundred-forty pounds of grade-A Marine Corps male, sweetheart. You're what, a buck ten, tops?"

She says, "First of all, you're shit at judging a woman's weight. I haven't been one hundred and ten pounds since junior high school. More to the point, I'm an expert in Krav Maga. Not that I'd need it to lay you out."

I prop my hands on my hips and grin at her. "Really. You got something more effective to take me down than the lethal hand-to-hand combat system developed by the Israeli Defense Forces? I can hardly wait to hear it."

Looking right into my eyes, she calmly answers, "Two things, actually."

"C'mon. The suspense is killing me."

Her smile could melt steel. "My tits. If I unzipped my jacket right now and showed you the girls, you'd definitely be distracted long enough for me to bury a knife in your chest."

She slings her laptop bag over her shoulder, grabs the handle of her suitcase, and jerks her chin at the rest of her bags that I've already unloaded. "By the way, all that gear can stay in the car. I won't need it until we set up a COM center at Miranda's."

Still reeling from the mention of her breasts and the image it conjured—the accurate image, because I've seen her in all her bare-assed glory coming out of her shower—I ask, "You're not worried about leaving your precious computer equipment in the back of my truck in a public parking lot all night long?"

"Give me a break, jarhead. I know an armored car when I see one. Someone would have to use a fifty-caliber machine gun to get through the amount of ballistic composites you've got on this thing."

Should've known she'd notice the mods on the Hummer. She notices everything. "Thought you said it wasn't safe."

"Oh, it's safe when it's parked. It's only a death trap when you're behind the wheel. Has anyone ever told you that you drive like a twelve-year-old with ADD who forgot to take his Ritalin?"

Then she sashays away, hips swinging. I throw my head back and laugh, because *goddamn* she can give as good as she gets.

I stop laughing when I realize how much I like it.

A little flirtation is one thing. But I know how fucked a man's judgment can get when he's distracted by a woman. I've seen it before. When the friendly jabs become serious attraction and your concentration is shot because all you can think of is getting her beneath you in bed, that's when mistakes happen. And in my line of business, any mistake could be deadly.

I've already seen how easily this particular woman can snap my self-control. The kiss in the restaurant was proof of that. I've never done anything remotely like that before, suffered an instantaneous, lust-fueled brain blackout, and I should be worried about it.

I should be, but I'm not.

Which is a problem.

Watching her walk through the sliding doors of the hotel, I resolve that there will be no more flirting. Until this job is over, I'll be strictly professional. I can't afford to be otherwise.

Now I just have to convince my dick to get with the program.

7

TABBY

*a*t five a.m., I finally give up the battle with insomnia and rise from bed.

I go for a run, trying to wipe all thoughts of the past from my mind and focus on the task at hand. Finding Søren Killgaard. Or, more precisely, getting him to find me. It won't be hard. But Connor isn't going to like what I have in mind.

Not that I'm going to tell him what it is.

There's only one thing in this world I value more than my privacy, and that's my sanity. It took me years to regain my mental footing after what happened between Søren and me, years of therapy that forced me to take a hard look at myself and the way I'm wired, but it only took Connor Hughes a single evening to unravel all those years of work.

It only took him a single kiss and I was undone.

In front of everyone in that restaurant, in front of those two ridiculous, simpering girls staring at him from the bar, undone.

And I don't even *like* him.

I don't understand it. It makes no sense. There's no logic to what happened to my body when he put his mouth on mine, the sheer electric jolt of pleasure I felt, right down to my toes. It was only a moment of utter madness, but I was shaken to my foundations, and still am.

"Stupid," I mutter. I pump my arms and legs faster, driving myself hard until I'm drenched in sweat.

By the time I return to the hotel, the sun is rising, the birds are chirping, and I'm slightly less inclined to take off someone's head. I go around the back, skirting the main lobby because the rear stairs are a more direct route to my room, and pass the pool. Someone else is up early, swimming laps with powerful, efficient strokes that make hardly a ripple in the surface.

When the swimmer ascends the pool steps and rises from the water, I stop dead in my tracks.

It's like porn. There's no other way to properly describe it. It would only be more perfect if I were watching it in slow-mo and there were a cheesy soundtrack playing in the background.

The swimmer is very muscular, broad through the shoulders and back, but with narrow hips that highlight the bulk of his upper body and thighs. On anyone less well-proportioned, his substantial muscle mass would make him look thick and ungainly, but with his height and that tapered waist, the overall effect is one of balance. Power, perfectly aligned with grace.

Water runs in rivulets over acres of tanned skin, streaming down his back and legs. His wet black swim trunks cling to his spectacularly perfect ass. Even his bare feet are perfect, masculine and brown as a nut against the pale concrete coping.

He reaches for a towel tossed casually on one of the chaise longues that line the pool and proceeds to dry himself, supple as a cat. I watch in fascination. He has no tattoos, no scars, no visible body hair. His virgin skin is completely unblemished, gleaming like rubbed wood in the morning light.

My brain and my ovaries are in total agreement: This man is *stunning*.

Then he turns around, catches me staring through the

wrought iron fence that surrounds the pool, and calls out, "Morning, sweet cheeks. You're up early."

Of course. Of *course* it's Connor. The universe has decided it would be amusing to watch me grapple with a sexual attraction to a man I want to slap most of the time. When I'm not wanting to roll my eyes in disgust or douse myself in antibacterial spray so I don't catch one of the virulent strains of STD he's probably carrying.

The way the blood rushes to flood my face is actually a relief, because it's diverting some of the blood that was throbbing between my legs.

"Good morning, Marine," I say coolly. "Just getting in from the strip clubs? Needed some chlorine to get rid of all that rainbow glitter and dime store perfume?"

He grins, slings the towel over his shoulders, and ambles closer to the fence. The light catches the silver chain around his neck, glinting off his dog tags. I try not to look at his abdomen, because I'm pretty sure he's got an eight-pack—not that it's even physically possible—and I don't want to stare.

Any more than I already have.

Don't notice his hard nipples, don't look at how perfect and brown they are or how there isn't a single stray hair on his entire gorgeous chest.

There's a border of low shrubs planted on the inside of the fence. Connor stops just in front of it. He runs a hand through his wet hair, pushing the dark mass of it off his forehead. I stifle the urge to laugh because I find the simple motion completely erotic and I'm the biggest idiot to ever walk the face of the earth.

His gaze flicks over the length of my body, my sweat-drenched T-shirt and little nylon jogging shorts. His grin dies. A muscle in his jaw flexes. In a different tone than moments before, he says, "We should be on the road within the hour. I've spoken to Miranda. She's expecting us by—"

"I'll be ready," I say indifferently. "Meet you at the car in thirty." I turn and walk away, trying to convince myself I really can't feel the weight of his stare on my back as I go.

～

I wake up with a start sometime in the late afternoon with a crick in my neck and my heart pounding. I'd been having a dream that I was falling from a great height, freezing wind tearing at my clothes and snapping through my hair, the air so thin it swallowed my screams the moment they left my lips.

From the driver's seat, Connor says, "You twitch in your sleep like a dog."

I mutter, "I was having a nightmare. I dreamt I was you."

He chuckles. "Aw. Am I annoying you already? You just opened your eyes."

"You only annoy me when you're breathing. Where are we?"

"Close to Albuquerque."

I'm surprised. "New Mexico already? We're making good time."

I regret that instantly when Connor smiles. He says, "Of course we are. I'm driving."

"God. It's too bad arrogance isn't painful."

Another mistake, because it causes Connor to laugh. Loudly.

I sit up straighter, scrub my hands over my face, and take a swig of water from the plastic bottle in the holder between the seats. Right after swallowing, I realize this bottle wasn't there when I fell asleep however long ago. Connor must have put it there.

For me?

He says, "Sorry there's no ice or lemon in it."

He remembered I ordered ice and lemon with my water at the bar in DC. Unsure what to make of that, or that he anticipated I might be thirsty when I awoke, I return the bottle to the cup holder with no comment.

After another few miles of driving in silence, I ask, "So what's the plan?"

Connor's dark brows lift. He glances over at me. "Oh, *now* the Abominable Snow Queen wants to talk plans?"

I exhale a long, pained sigh. "Did your parents ever ask you to run away from home?"

He laughs again. It's a big, unselfconscious laugh, deep and natural. In spite of myself, I smile.

"No," he says, "although I gave them plenty of reason to."

I'm intrigued. "Really? The strong, smart, courageous, popular hero who's the star of his own fairy tale wasn't a perfect little boy?"

"You forgot handsome," he says with a straight face.

I shoot back, "Handsome? You look like a before picture."

He pretends outrage. "Are you getting smart with me?"

"How would you know? If you had another brain, it would be lonely."

"Ha! Just remember Jesus loves you, sweet cheeks, but everyone else thinks you're a pain in the ass."

Trying not to laugh, I snort instead. "Oh, I forgot to tell you. The village called. They said they were missing their idiot."

Connor looks over at me. A brilliant grin spreads over his face. Behind him, the setting sun flares into a golden nimbus around his head, and he looks so heart-stoppingly handsome, it takes my breath away.

He teases, "Earth is full. Go home."

Our eyes lock, we stare at each other, and I can't look away. Slowly, his smile fades. With the sensation that we've just driven off a literal and figurative cliff, my stomach drops.

I finally break eye contact and stare out the windshield, blinking hard into the distance.

I don't like him. I don't. I *refuse* to. He's everything I detest in a man.

And yet...

"Let's talk about Miranda," I say abruptly, gazing at the range of blue-purple mountains we're headed toward. Their tips are lit fiery red by the setting sun as if they've been dipped in blood.

"Fine." His voice is low, slightly rough, all the teasing gone.

"When did she first contact you about her situation?"

He clears his throat. "I've been on retainer with her for years—"

"For security?"

"As a technical advisor," he says, gripping the steering wheel so hard, I think it's in danger of breaking. "Stunts, fight scene coordination, training actors in weapons handling, anything military related that needs an expert to add realism to a movie."

"Oh." I'm impressed. "That sounds cool."

"It is."

He says it flatly. I resist the urge to glance at his face to see what it's doing.

"So what happened?"

He's quiet for a moment, tapping a thumb against the steering wheel in a restless, staccato rhythm. "She received an email a few weeks ago. It said she was to deposit ten million dollars into an account in the Cayman Islands or there would be a serious data breach on her company's network. One that would make the Sony hack in 2014 look like child's play."

"Blackmail."

Connor nods. "What was unusual is that serious blackmailers already have the information they want to extort money for. In this case, it was simply a threat of a breach. One hadn't actually occurred."

"That fucking colossal ego," I murmur, watching the craggy mountain tops fade from red to purple.

"Pardon?"

Feeling the beginnings of a headache, I close my eyes and

pinch the bridge of my nose. "Søren. He wanted to give Miranda a heads-up that her system was going to be attacked so she'd close any holes there might have been in the network."

"Why would he do that? It makes no sense to forewarn your enemy that you're on the march."

I smile, but it's humorless. "Because he doesn't want it to be easy. He wants it to be as difficult as possible, so that when he beats you after giving you fair warning, it will hurt twice as much."

Silence as Connor digests that. I open my eyes and glance at him.

I say, "So let me guess how this went. You couldn't trace the source of the email because an anonymous proxy server was used to hide the IP address. You didn't think it was a credible threat because not only did he forewarn his intentions, his alias isn't identifiable with any known hacker collective or has been associated with any prior hacks, high level or otherwise. How am I doing so far?"

"Pretty fuckin' spot-on." He sounds lethally mad.

"Right. Then, after you checked to confirm there were no network breaches and made the system tighter than a virgin's asshole, you told Miranda she was probably dealing with an amateur and not to worry about it. And then he raped her network. And then the price doubled."

Connor's murderous expression tells me I'm right again.

"How long ago was that?"

"Four days."

"How are you stalling him?"

"She's saying she has to put together the money, she isn't that liquid."

"Has he given her another deadline?"

"Not yet."

"Has any of the data he stole been leaked?"

61

"No."

Good. So we still have some time. I pause, reflecting. "What did he get?"

"Emails. Everyone's, right down to the interns'. Executive salary information. Copies of unreleased films. Copies of scripts on future projects. And the source code for Miranda's proprietary algorithm software, InSight. We think that was the main target."

I snort.

Frowning, Connor looks at me. "What?"

"He's not interested in her software. If anything, he probably looked at it and had a good laugh."

"Why would he take it, then?"

I shrug. "To piss her off. To make it even more personal. She didn't do as he asked, so she got her hand slapped. Big-time. So what happened next? Did you bring in the feds?"

"Yes—"

"And did you confirm that the people who arrived at the studio with FBI badges were, in fact, FBI agents?"

"Yes."

He looks uncomfortable with my question. I suspect I'm echoing some of his worst fears about who he's dealing with. "How?"

"I've got contacts inside the agency."

"Let's hope those contacts are who they say they are."

He growls, "I've known them for over twenty years, Tabby!"

"Oh, please. You're not that naïve."

Connor's face flushes. He turns to me with a glint of steel in his dark eyes. "I was in the corps with those men. I'd trust them with my life. They *are* who they *say* they are."

After a quick mental calculation, I switch gears because my curiosity is getting the better of me. "Exactly how old are you?"

He turns his glower back to the road. "Older than you."

"By how many years, precisely?"

"More than ten. Now back to the subject."

Obviously he's not going to divulge his precise age, but "more than ten" puts him at *least* at thirty-seven or thirty-eight, depending on the month he was born. I look closely at the skin around his eyes, his jaw, the backs of his hands. It's all unwrinkled and tight, just as perfect as it looked in the pool. I wonder if he uses special cream, or if he's just genetically blessed, because to have skin that gorgeous at his advanced age—

"Jesus Christ, princess, cut a guy a break, will you?" he snaps, bristling under my microscopic inspection.

Perversely pleased I've been upgraded from "sweet cheeks" to "princess," I smile. In a teasing tone, I say, "Look at you, Mr. Senior Badass Hot Guy, still gettin' out there with the young whippersnappers to fight cybercrime! Impressive! But I'll understand if you need to be in bed by seven tonight. Gotta rest those creaky old bones. We don't want you breaking a hip."

Slowly, Connor turns and looks at me, only now the aggravation is gone, replaced by a sly *gotcha!* smugness.

He drawls, "Hot?"

Oh shit.

I attempt an attitude of nonchalance. "It's good manners to be polite to your elders." When his look of smugness only deepens, I hastily add, "Actually, I think your hearing aid is malfunctioning. I didn't say 'hot,' I said…um…something else."

Nonchalance = epic fail.

"Oh, I must have misheard!" says Connor, all wide-eyed, blinking innocence. "This pesky hearing aid is always malfunctioning on me. Let's see, what rhymes with 'hot'? 'Trot'? No, that doesn't work. 'Cot'? Hmm. 'Badass Cot Guy.' Unlikely. What could it be, what could it be?"

He pretends to think hard, while I slide lower in the seat, trying to make myself invisible.

He keeps guessing all the way into Albuquerque, gleefully

torturing me with words that rhyme with "hot" while I keep trying to steer the conversation back to Miranda, until finally I give up and sit with my arms crossed over my chest and my eyes closed he as proceeds to shove a giant fistful of crow down my throat, and all I can do is swallow.

Bastard.

8

CONNOR

*S*o getting my dick on board with my "strictly professional" plan with Tabby is a spectacular failure, evidenced by the way it reacted when I saw her at the pool in her running outfit, and in the car on the way to Albuquerque when her voice was breathless with stifled laughter and she looked at me as if she actually *liked* me.

In the second case, not only did my cock get hard, my chest went tight and my throat felt like I'd swallowed a rock. All from a look.

Imagine what might happen if she looked at me like that while she was naked. I could spontaneously combust.

And then she said I was hot, and my dick got so excited, I was worried I'd make a mess in my pants if I drove over a stray bump in the road. It's like I'm a teenager again, all boner and no brains.

I can't stop thinking about it. I can't stop thinking about her. I've already jacked off twice since we checked into the hotel, and if I don't figure out a way to manage this soon, I'm in big trouble.

Unfortunately, I know of only one way to satisfy an itch.
Scratch it.

9

TABBY

*T*he Hotel Andaluz is a vast improvement over the Best Western in Tulsa. I appreciate the Spanish-inspired décor, the russet pavers underfoot, the dark wood ceilings and bisque stucco walls. My room is lovely, spacious and quiet with a claw-foot bathtub big enough for two that keeps leering at me. I wonder if it's coincidence the room is called the Romance Suite.

Connor was the one who arranged the rooms with the front desk, and hell if I'm about to ask him.

I take a shower, change into a pair of black leggings and my favorite travel top—a body-skimming, tie-dyed, one-shouldered number in brilliant blues made of some kind of space-age knit that folds to the size of a hankie and never wrinkles—and slip on my casual shoes, the ones with only a four-inch heel.

Then I get a text from Juanita: *Hey. Can I use ur shower? Water is out at my house.*

"Oh God," I mutter. "Did your mother forget to pay the water bill again?"

I answer: *Yes, of course. I'm on a job for a few days. Clean up after yourself, plz.*

She responds: *Suck a bag of dicks.* With a minion emoji flipping me the bird at the end.

I reply: *Charming. I'm sure Sister Mary Claire is so proud of you.*

Two seconds later: *Sister Mary Claire can suck a bag of dicks.*

I chuckle. We really need to get Juanita a new catchphrase.

I'm starving, so I decide to go up to the rooftop bar, order some tapas, and enjoy the view of the mountains.

Unfortunately, my travel companion has had the same idea.

Connor spots me the second I walk out onto the patio. He's sitting across the bar at a long, raised stone table with a fire glowing in a low trough down its center. He lifts a hand as if he's been expecting me.

Which he shouldn't be, because we left each other in the lobby with a "See you at six a.m."

Feeling self-conscious, I make my way slowly across the patio toward him, weaving through tables. He watches me, his gaze contemplative and intense. The firelight lends his face a soft, pleasing glow. I wonder cynically if that's why he chose that particular seat.

Yes, I've noticed the knot of girls at a table on the other side of the patio who are gaping at him over their margaritas. This fool has groupies everywhere.

"Great minds think alike," he says as I stop beside him. He gestures to the next seat.

"Let's not get carried away." I lower myself to the stool.

He smiles. Catching the eye of the waiter who's making the rounds, Connor calls him over with a crooked finger.

"Yes, sir?" asks the waiter.

"Johnny Walker Blue and an ice water with lemon."

The waiter gives a short bow and retreats.

Now my self-consciousness turns to irritation, because if those girls don't stop staring and whispering, I'm going to go over there and smack the giggles right out of their stupid little mouths.

Noticing where my attention is, Connor drawls, "Guess they like hot senior guys," and chuckles.

"God, you're like a dog with a bone. Can we be done with that, please?"

Looking at me from the corner of his eye, he only offers a noncommittal "Hmm."

How are his biceps bulging when he's not even using them? How is his jaw so sharp, it could cut glass? How are his lashes that impossibly thick and long?

How the hell did all of that suddenly go from irritating to interesting?

"I like this outfit," he says, eyeing me. "You almost look like a normal human being."

I make a disgusted noise. "I'll be sure to never wear it again."

I'm aware that I'm being a bitch to manage my discomfort over my inconceivable attraction to him, but hopefully he won't catch on, because I've pretty much been a bitch to him from the get-go, so I think this is a safe course of action. It's the logical course of action, at any rate. Just stay on the bitch train, get through this job, and we can both go our separate ways without him ever guessing I might have once had a wee lady boner for him.

Because honestly, I can't think of anything more mortifying than Connor discovering that. The "hot" slipup was one I cannot, under any circumstances, repeat.

Connor says, "You've got that look again."

Startled, I glance at him. "What look?"

"The one you get when your brain is tripping all over its own feet."

I toss my hair over my shoulder and gaze off into the middle distance like a disinterested cat. "I have no idea what you're talking about."

He gives me another mysterious "Hmm."

For a moment, he just examines my face in silence. There's a strange tension in him, a stillness, like a held breath but in his entire body. Then he abruptly swings around in his seat so he's facing me, his massive thighs on either side of my barstool, his booted feet planted on the floor.

Trapping me.

"What do you think you're doing?" I ask, my voice high with panic.

"Got something to say to you. It's important, so don't talk until the end."

He looks dangerously intense. His dark eyes are heated, drilling into mine. His cheeks are flushed from the fire, or from something else, but I don't have time to think about what that something else might be, because he opens his mouth and starts to speak, and my brain faints dead away, leaving me to fend for myself.

"I want you. Bad. Don't know exactly why, you're a complete pain in my ass and pretty much the most contrary, foul-tempered woman I've ever met, and you've made it really clear what you think about me, but every time I look at you, I have an almost overpowering urge to touch you, kiss you, do a lot of bad things to you, and I don't know how to manage it. Yeah, it might be more prudent for me to keep this shit to myself, but I know that when you don't talk about shit, it festers, gets worse, and if the way I feel about you gets any worse, I won't be able to put my goddamn shoes on in the morning. So I'm puttin' it out there."

He takes a breath. Deeply shocked, I stare at him with my mouth open, my heart up in my throat.

"We're both professionals. We have a job to do. And I don't mix business with pleasure. Ever. But the way I figure it, we've got one more night until the work actually starts, and if I don't do something to get you straight in my head, I won't be able to do the job at all."

He stops abruptly. Then he waits, watching me with unwavering intensity as I attempt to digest what just happened.

I whisper in disbelief, "You're propositioning me?"

His gaze drops to my lips. When he looks back into my eyes, his own are burning. "You liked that kiss."

He gives me time to deny it, but I don't. How could I? We both know I'd be lying.

He adds, "And you called me hot, so I know you don't think I'm a complete troll, even though you act like you do."

"That was an accident."

"Yep." He nods. "And you fuckin' hated yourself for it. Which is why I know it was true."

Things are happening in my body. My nipples harden, my breath quickens, there is a distinctive throb and ache between my legs. All because this jarhead I hate just told me he wants to do bad things to me.

Bad things. Dear God, were any two sexier words ever spoken?

Connor says tersely, "It's your turn to talk."

Staring at him, I bite my lower lip. Seeing that, his eyes flare. He leans closer, and then closer still, until I can smell the fresh, soap-scrubbed scent of his skin, count every piece of stubble glinting copper along his hard jaw.

In a voice like sandpaper, he says, "Tabitha."

I hesitate for a moment, fighting the simultaneous urges to slap him and surrender to him, hating myself for being intrigued, hating this excruciating disconnect between what my mind insists is logical and what my body is loudly demanding. Ultimately, my curiosity wins out by a hair.

I say, "About those bad things you mentioned..."

He reaches out and takes my wrist in his big, warm hand.

He gently pulls me off my chair and toward him, so I'm standing between his open thighs, our chests almost touching. Our gazes locked together, he murmurs, "I want to make you come."

I exhale, a small, astonished noise, my eyes flared wide and my heart pounding.

At my reaction, he presses closer, his mouth at my ear, his voice gruff with desire.

"I want to put my face between your legs and eat your beautiful sweet pussy until you come so hard, you forget your own name. Then I want to slide my hard cock inside you and fuck you, slow and deep. And when you're about to come again, I'll put a finger in here—" He reaches around, palms my ass, slips a finger between my cheeks until he hits the tender spot that makes me gasp—"and kiss you, so that when you go off, you're full of me everywhere, your whole body is full of me, and all you can think of is me, all you can do is feel me fucking you, how much you love it, how incredible it feels, and how you never, ever want it to stop."

A noise involuntarily escapes my lips, a low, breathy moan that sounds as if he's already inside me.

A loud throat clearing. "Excuse me, folks."

The waiter has arrived with our drinks. Connor and I ignore him completely. He sets the drinks down and quickly leaves.

Into my ear, Connor breathes, "Talk to me, sweetheart."

I close my eyes, losing myself inch by inch to the most powerful desire I've ever felt. "We can't."

"Yes, we can. One night. Just to get it out of our system." His other hand finds my hip, curls possessively around it. He drags me closer to his body, so we're flush against each other, crotch to chest.

He's hard everywhere.

Nearby, someone snickers, enjoying the scene we're making, but I could care less.

My trembling hands climb iron pecs and flatten over them. "We shouldn't."

Connor's soft lips hover over the wildly fluttering pulse in my throat. He whispers, "We definitely should," and touches his tongue to my skin.

Electricity crackles through me. I arch instinctively, sucking in a breath, my fingers digging into Connor's chest. He makes a sound like an animal and takes a hot mouthful of my flesh.

The instant my eyes roll back in my head, an ear-piercing alarm sounds, shattering the moment. People start to shout. Chairs scrape back from tables. Connor and I break apart, panting.

He says, "It's a fire alarm." Then, angrier, "A fuckin' *fire alarm*," like he can't believe the timing.

Saved by the bell. A semihysterical laugh bursts out of me.

Connor grabs my hand. We move in the opposite direction of the rest of the crowd and run to the door with the red Exit sign illuminated above it on the opposite side of the patio from the main entrance. Inside, a stairwell leads to the ground floor.

We take the stairs two at a time, Connor ahead of me, still gripping my hand. The stairwell echoes with the sound of our footsteps pounding against metal, the blare of the alarm. We burst through the door on the first floor and out into the night. We're on the side of the hotel, on a lit pathway that leads to the parking lot.

Before I can get my bearings, Connor pulls me off the path into the shadows of the building, presses me back against the wall, and takes my face in his hands.

"One night," he says roughly, staring at me like he's starving. "Say yes."

We're both out of breath. I know it's not from the sprint down the stairs.

"Connor, the building could be about to burn down—"

"Let it burn. Say yes."

I laugh. A wild, dangerous feeling is growing inside me, a chafing at the seams, like an animal that has grown too large for its cage. "You said you wouldn't kiss me again."

"Only because you were about to cut off my balls. *Say yes.*"

The way he's staring at me, the heat in his eyes, the hardness of his jaw, the raw, unmistakable *need*—I've never been looked at like this by a man. I feel as if I'm standing in the sun for the first time. I feel like I've been living underground my entire life, and I've just crawled out of a hole into glorious, burning sunlight.

Burning being the operative word.

Things destroyed by fire: the earth in 2 Peter 3:10 in the Bible; Rome in 64 A.D.; London in 1666; Chicago in 1871; Boston in 1872; San Francisco in 1906; the Hindenburg in 1937; much of Europe in WWII.

Tabitha West in 2016?

When I freeze, Connor says, "Stop thinking."

"That's like asking me to stop breathing."

One of his hands drifts down and very lightly grips my throat. His thumb rests over the pulse throbbing hard in my neck, betraying me more than any words ever could.

He murmurs, "Give your brain a night off. Your body wants this. And so does mine." Slowly, he presses his pelvis to mine, his chest to mine, his thighs to mine, until our bodies are flush together and I have irrefutable evidence of how much his body wants me.

I squeeze shut my eyes so I can't see that incredibly enticing look on his face turn into something a little less enthusiastic. "It's called nonconcordance."

A pause, and then, "What?"

"My body and my brain sometimes don't work together. Especially in things like…this. I can't help it. I get stuck in my head. I'll start reciting lists, narrating what's happening, anything to distance myself. It's like being a spectator in my own body."

He gently thumbs over my cheekbone. He doesn't speak, but his silence has a quality of thoughtfulness to it, as if he's working through what I've said.

"Once it happens, I can't...that's it. So." I give Connor's chest a gentle push, but he doesn't budge.

After another moment, he says quietly, "Permission to engage the enemy, ma'am."

Furrowing my brows, I open my eyes. "Um...I don't know what that means."

"I want to kiss you," he breathes, staring at my mouth.

When I don't respond because my mind is in a death match with my hormones, Connor simply lowers his head and brushes his lips along the length of my jaw.

I shudder. He nuzzles his nose beneath my ear, inhaling against my skin, which makes me shudder again. He releases my throat and slides his hand into my hair. He takes a fistful of it and gently tugs, tilting my head back to expose my throat. He murmurs, "Just feel this. I'll stop in ten seconds. And I want you to count the time. Out loud."

He opens his mouth over the pulse in my neck. The unexpected heat of his lips and tongue feels so amazing, a low moan breaks from my chest.

I can't remember the last time I was kissed on the throat. Before Connor, I can't remember the last time I was kissed anywhere, by anyone.

It's fucking *amazing*.

"One," he prompts, his voice muffled against my skin.

"One."

The word is so soft, it doesn't qualify as a whisper. Connor sucks on my throat again, this time using a hint of teeth. My eyes slide shut with pleasure.

"Two."

His mouth drifts closer to my collarbone, his tongue gliding like silk, raising goose bumps on the back of my neck. I inhale, arching toward him. In the distance, the whine of sirens competes with the intermittent squawk of the hotel's alarm. I barely notice either.

"Three."

He bites me softly on the long muscle above my clavicle. Heat pulses between my thighs, and I restlessly squeeze them together.

I breathe, "Four."

His fingers find the hem of my shirt and slip beneath. When his fingertips brush my bare skin, I jerk, gasping. He kisses a soft trail from my shoulder back to my throat, his lips leaving sparks in their wake. I can hardly concentrate on counting, and have to think for a moment to remember what number I'm on.

"Five."

His fingers drift up my waist and over my rib cage, tracing their shape, the hollows and ridges. His gentle kiss turns more insistent. His tongue laps at the dip in the base of my throat. My nipples harden and begin to ache.

I want his mouth on them. I want his hands on them. I want to feel the pull and tug of his teeth—

"Six," he reminds me gently. When I breathlessly repeat it, I feel his lips curve against my skin. He whispers, "Good."

He flattens his hand over my rib cage, just under my breast. His palm feels as if it's scorching my skin. I wonder if he can feel my heartbeat, the wild hummingbird thrum of it, rising to a crescendo beneath his hand.

The sirens grow closer. Voices murmur nearby. People. People are close.

People can go fuck themselves.

The slow, upward drifting glide of his hand. The heat of it. The strength of it. The way he's in no hurry, the way his lips feel, fire and satin, oh God this is good this is so, *so* good.

He stills for a moment, waiting.

Number. What number? I mumble, "Seven."

Connor moves to the other side of my neck, repeating the process of slow kisses, nibbles, gentle bites, but leaving his hand just below my breast, unmoving. Everything inside me is aching, clenching, surging. All my nerve endings are firing at once. My arms tangle around his neck. My head drops back against the wall.

"Eight," I whisper, and adjust my body so the weight of my breast rests in his hand.

Because I hate them, I'm not wearing a bra.

Connor exhales softly. From somewhere very far off, I think it sounds like my name.

His mouth glides up my neck. His fingers slide together. He pinches my hard nipple between two calloused fingers, and I softly cry out. Into my ear, he says gruffly, "I want this in my mouth," and flicks his thumb over the small silver stud pierced through it.

I like how verbal he is, how explicit. I wonder if he'd be this explicit during sex, talking in that low, rough voice about how I feel, how I taste, what he's going to do next.

Between my legs, I'm drenched. The ache has turned into an insistent throb. I can't concentrate on anything else. There's only his mouth, his hand, and my body, reacting to both.

Connor says, "Nine, beautiful girl."

In response I simply moan.

His thumb circles my taut nipple, over and over, sending shockwaves through my body. His erection presses insistently against my lower belly.

"Say it and you'll get a reward." His voice is a husky, wicked whisper. His breath is hot at my ear.

"N-nine."

He dips his head, slides my shirt up, exposing my bare breast, and takes my rigid nipple into his hot mouth.

The noise that comes out of me doesn't sound human.

Then a fire engine comes to a screeching, rubber-burning

stop not thirty feet away, driving right up over the parking lot curb and onto the grass. When my body goes stiff, Connor pulls away, throws a glance over his shoulder at the fire truck and the men in yellow gear and hats hopping out of it, and mutters a curse.

Flushed and trembling, I scramble to pull my shirt down. By the time Connor turns back to me, my arms are crossed over my chest and I'm shaking my head in disbelief at what I just allowed to happen.

Looking at my expression, he says flatly, "Ten."

When I wordlessly turn and run away, Connor doesn't follow.

10

CONNOR

*I*gnoring the fire alarm and the fact that the hotel might soon be engulfed in flames, I trudge back up the stairs to the bar, willing my feet to climb instead of running after Tabby like they want to.

She needs space, not pressure. Though I'm almost positive I could convince her body to push past the constraints of her mind, it's obvious that would only serve me in the short run.

I'd probably wake up tomorrow morning with a hatchet buried in my skull.

If I woke up at all. Can a man die from too much pleasure? Because if the little taste of Tabitha West I just got is any indication, climaxing inside her might send me straight into cardiac arrest.

Sweet. Everything about her is sweet. Beyond that thorny wall she hides behind is the fucking Garden of Eden.

I want her so much, it's like holding your breath for too long under water and needing a big gulp of air. That desperate ache. That painful demand. I want to apologize to my cock for what he's going through, but it seems my heart is first in line for any mea culpas, because you could drive the Hummer through the hole in my chest.

The horror on Tabby's face when she broke away from me was like…a grenade. Right in the heart.

So my plan now is to finish my scotch, take a shower—if my room isn't on fire—and get some shut-eye. Tomorrow we can both pretend nothing ever happened. And after the job is finished and we return to New York, I'll try again. Only maybe with a little less waving my hard dick in the poor girl's face like it's a trophy for best in show.

Finesse, right?

The bar is deserted except for an old Native American janitor sweeping the floor. He has a gray braid that reaches his waist, tied at the end with a thin piece of leather. I make my way to the table where Tabby and I were sitting and down the glass of scotch I'd left behind.

"Kid at the pool pulled the alarm," says the janitor, his eyes on his broom. His voice is smooth and smoky, like good whiskey. "Third time it's happened this year. There's no fire, in case you were wondering."

Except for the one in my pants.

The intermittently ringing bell abruptly stops, punctuating the old man's words with welcome silence. He squints up at the dark sky. "Electrical storm comin' tonight."

I follow his gaze. I see sapphire sky pricked with the glimmer of stars, but the mountains in the distance are blanketed with thunderclouds. As if on cue, a streak of lightning cuts a jagged white path through a cloud bank.

"Gonna be a big one," he says, and chuckles. When I glance over at him, he isn't looking at the sky or the mountains. He's looking at me. "Just remember to keep yourself grounded so you don't get electrocuted, son."

I frown at his back as he turns and disappears, still chuckling, through the patio doors.

~

Back in my room, I strip and take a long, hot shower. My thoughts are too scattered to focus on any one subject for long, and the attempted distraction is useless anyway. All I can think of is her.

My sweet, vicious, passionate, distant, marvelous, maddening riddle. If she'd let me, I'd spend a lifetime trying to figure her out.

Catching my own thoughts, I groan.

Ridiculous romantic notions like *that* tell me exactly how much trouble I'm in. If I ever repeat anything remotely similar to Tabby out loud, I'll have to send out a search-and-rescue team for my manhood.

It's tempting to relieve the ache in my groin, but my heart is too heavy to bother. So I ignore my erection—the fucking thing is becoming a cliché—and just let the water pound me.

After ten minutes with my head bent under the spray, some of the tension in my shoulders is gone, but none of the ache in my chest. I figure it's about as good as it's going to get, so I turn off the water, dry off and brush my teeth. Sleep is the only thing that's going to help me now.

If it even comes.

Towel in hand, I push open the bathroom door—

And freeze.

"Well," says Tabby, reclining on my bed with her arms behind her head and her booted ankles crossed, "I must say my timing is excellent."

Her voice is tranquil, bordering on disinterested. Her expression reveals nothing. The lines of her body are completely relaxed. Only her eyes show anything other than perfect composure. They glitter in the low lamp light, edgy and steely as knives.

After the moment it takes me to overcome my surprise, my voice comes out roughened. "You're angry."

She ignores that. Her gaze drifts down my chest, over my abdomen, lingers on my groin. Still with that disinterested tone, she says, "Perhaps you should seek treatment for that. It seems to be a chronic condition."

I move to cover my erection with the towel, but Tabby says sharply, "Don't."

My fingers curl around the towel, bunching it in my fist. I hold still as she inspects me minutely from head to foot.

I deserve this. For her hotel room in DC, for her house in New York, for everything I saw without permission, I deserve this. So I hold still and allow it, watching her face as she looks with cool composure at my naked body. I feel equal parts unsteady, uncomfortable, and fantastically alive.

After a moment she inquires, "Aren't you going to ask why I'm here?"

A dozen responses come to mind before I finally settle on "I suspect you're about to tell me."

Those glittering eyes flash to mine. Her hair falls loose around her shoulders, but no other sign of softness remains. She's changed back into the black leather armor she wore yesterday in the car. I wonder if she's hiding a cache of weapons beneath it.

"One night, you said." She pauses, staring at me with something like rage. "I'll take it."

I feel the painful beat of my heart, and say quietly, "No."

Her brows shoot up. "No?" she repeats, drawing it out.

"Not like this. Not with this..." I struggle to find the word. "Resentment."

The fierce look in her eyes softens. She drops her gaze again to my cock, standing at full attention. Her lips curve. "I'm not sure your opinion is the one that really matters."

A gust of pent-up breath leaves my chest. "Tabby—"

"Come here," she says, and holds out her hand.

My mouth goes dry. I feel like a teenager again, trembling with nerves on a first date.

"Connor," she says, softer, still beckoning me with those eyes, that outstretched hand. When I don't move, she adds, "Please."

I close my eyes, swallow, take a breath to try to slow my pounding heart. What she's offering is everything I want, yet a part of me is holding back, still listening to the old man's warning: *Keep yourself grounded.*

I'm not grounded. I'm fucking unmoored. I'm so full of crackling, unstable energy, I feel like I might break the bonds of gravity altogether and rocket off into space.

Ultimately, my feet move me forward. Tabby on my bed is too great a compelling force for them, for any part of me, and so I walk.

When I get to the edge of the bed, Tabby stretches her leg out and stops me with her boot planted flat on my stomach. I halt, taken aback at her sudden change of mind, but as she lies there staring at me and patiently waiting, it dawns on me that this isn't a reversal.

It's a command.

Without looking away from her face, I take her boot in my hands, untie the laces, and slide it off. I drop it to the floor, where it lands with a flat thud that momentarily blocks out the roar of my blood in my ears.

Her knee bent, she sets her bare foot on the bed, and then lifts her other foot to my stomach.

I moisten my lips. She watches the motion of my tongue with a flush creeping over her cheeks, but no other sign of emotion.

I drop her other boot to the floor and then stand motionless, holding myself in check with sheer force of will.

She says, "Well, if you don't want to fuck me, maybe you

could just kiss me. Since I went to the trouble to break into your room."

Hearing her say the words "fuck me" makes my cock twitch. Slowly, she smiles. It's ruthless, satisfied, and now I recognize the game.

Payback. For everything I've done, and made her feel, so far.

But I'm not having it. I'm not playing. With anyone else, at any other time, this would be fun. A lark. But not with this woman. Not tonight.

Tonight, she's mine.

For *real*, or not at all.

I slowly lower myself to my knees on the bed, between her spread legs. Unmoving, she watches me. Her breathing is coming faster and her pupils have dilated, but she makes no effort to do anything other than lie still as I crawl up her body until I'm hovering over her, our noses inches apart.

Looking into her eyes I say, "All right. I'll kiss you. I'll give you the kiss I should've given you the first time. And depending on how well you kiss me back, we'll see what happens next."

I watch her face change, feel the tension invade her body, watch as she struggles to keep control of her breathing, and am so satisfied with all of that, I almost smile. Instead, I lower my head and gently, ever so softly, press my mouth to hers.

Her lips yield, opening.

Outside, a distant rumble of thunder echoes over the mountains.

I'm careful, oh so careful not to rush. I want to remember this moment, every second of it, every slight restless shift in her body, every telling flush on her skin. She takes my tongue into her mouth with a hesitancy that's so sweet it's heady, because I know that beneath her veneer of calm, she's exactly as affected as I am by what it feels like when we touch.

I take my time, exploring her mouth, letting my tongue learn the shape of her lips, how much pressure and suction will elicit that soft, feminine sound in her throat that I crave. When she finally makes it, inhaling and arching but then almost instantly suppressing her reaction, I feel like I've won a victory.

I take her wrist, press it above her head to the pillow, hold it there, captive. She flexes against my hold, but doesn't break away. Her other hand lightly rests against my shoulder. Her fingertips are five points of fire on my skin. I'm aware of her leg drawn up against my hip, of the heat of her body beneath mine, the feel of leather against my bare skin, and purposefully restrain myself from giving in to the drumbeat of *yes more deeper* that has begun to pound inside my head.

When I draw back, it takes a moment before Tabby opens her eyes. She's breathing erratically, gentle, ragged breaths that match my own. Her fingers on my shoulder slide to my neck, slip into my hair. She pulls me down to kiss her again.

This time it isn't quite as gentle. Need—both hers and mine —is growing, and it's much more difficult to hold myself back. My cock is trapped between us, stiff against her thigh, and when she subtly shifts her hips, it twitches in reaction, an unmistakable pulse that makes Tabby smile.

"Is he always this eager?" she murmurs against my mouth.

"No," I say, letting her hear the raw honesty in my voice. "No, only with you."

We gaze at each other in silence as another boom of thunder rolls over the valley outside. Then her lashes lower. She whispers, "I'm wondering whether it would be possible...to ask you to...kiss me anywhere else?"

Her cheeks turn scarlet.

An invisible hand takes hold of my heart and squeezes to a fist. I'm shaken with a sudden certainty that there isn't anything this woman could ask me, sexual or otherwise, that I could or would refuse. It surprises me and scares me in equal measure, because it's new. And extremely dangerous.

I turn her face to mine. Flushed and faintly trembling, she opens her eyes.

"Give yourself to me, Tabby. All of you. I want everything. If we're gonna do this and I only get one night, I want it to count. No holding back. No games."

She swallows. "I...I'm..." Her eyes close again. Her voice comes out small. "I don't want to disappoint you."

My heart threatens to burst inside my chest. "My God," I breathe, "how could you possibly disappoint me? You're the most beautiful thing I've ever seen."

Sounding miserable, she says, "I don't think I'm very good in bed."

I resist the urge to laugh in disbelief, because I know it would be mistaken for mocking, and I know how excruciating that admission must have been for her. I can't imagine where she could have gotten the idea that she's not desirable or perfect just the way she is, but it's obvious the nonconcordance she mentioned earlier has been a major problem in the past with other men.

But now isn't the time for psychoanalysis. Or for making her tell me who those idiots might be so I can break their skulls.

Now is the time to make her feel as beautiful as she is.

I lower my mouth to her ear and very deliberately say, "I think you're the sexiest fucking woman alive. You've been driving me wild since the moment I set eyes on you three years ago, and even if you just laid here snoring while I made love to you it would be the best sex of my entire life because it's with *you*. Now I'm going to get you naked and eat your pussy like it's the last supper and you don't have to do anything but enjoy it, do you understand me?"

Her shy smile is worth more to me than all the gold in Fort Knox.

"Good." I kiss her softly on the lips. "Oh, and one more thing."

She drowsily blinks up at me.

"You're not allowed to come."

Her eyes snap open. "What? Are you joking? Connor—"

Before she can say more, I sit back on my heels, yank down her zipper, and drag the leather pants down her legs.

CONNOR

"*F*ucking hell," I mutter, staring down at Tabby's spread legs.

"What's wrong?" she says, panicked. She rears up on her elbows.

Wrong? Nothing's wrong. Everything in the universe is perfectly *right*.

First, she isn't wearing panties. It's an unexpected, thrilling shock to find her laid bare to me like that, open and vulnerable and deliciously pink where only seconds before there was an impenetrable wall of black leather. The sheer decadence of it takes my breath away.

Second, she's a natural blonde. That's almost as much of a surprise as the first thing. I reach out and softly brush my fingers over pale gold curls, and hear a choked exhalation pass my lips. Why it should please me so much that she isn't shaved I have no idea, maybe it's the animal in me, but I know exactly why I like it that she dyes the hair on her head red, but down here she's au naturel.

Because it's a secret. No one else gets to see it but me. It's a secret I now know, and feel privileged to know, and will always remember.

Third, and perhaps most astonishing of all, her clit is pierced. I've never seen that in real life. I stare with my mouth open, drinking her in, loving everything I'm looking at.

Unfortunately, I'm so busy enjoying the visual feast that I've momentarily forgotten who I'm dealing with.

Cursing and red-faced, Tabby tries to roll out from under me, but I catch her and press her back down against the bed before she can escape.

"You're incredible," I blurt, holding her wrists above her head and gazing into her eyes. "I didn't mean to scare you or be disrespectful. It's just…you're even better than I dreamed."

She stares up at me, breathing hard, her gaze darting all over my face. "You've seen me before, coming out of my shower. You've already seen me naked."

I make my voice as gentle as possible. "I didn't see all of you. Just, well, your breasts, yes, and the tattoo on your stomach, but lower only—impressions—you covered yourself with your hands before I could see that you were"—my voice turns husky—"blonde. And *pierced*."

She asks cautiously, "And you…like that?"

I grind out, "I fuckin' *love* it, princess. When I'm eighty years old, I'll be jerking off to the memory of what I just saw."

She stares at me a moment, and then turns her head to the side, but not before I see the pleasure flash in her eyes, quickly veiled. "You're a perv," she says primly, which makes me grin, because I know we're past the danger.

"You bring out the beast in me."

I lower my head and indulge myself by nuzzling her jaw. She lies very still, allowing it, and stays still when I slide my hand down her arm to the collar of her jacket. I tug down the zipper a few inches, exposing pale skin and the pulse beating hard and fast at the base of her throat.

That stops me cold.

A swell of unidentifiable pressure rises from my stomach, spreading through my chest, tightening my lungs. I marvel that the simple sight of the blood rushing through her veins—blood made to rush by *me*—could have the power to strip me of all other thought, even as I lie on top of her, our naked legs tangled together, my straining erection so close to the place I want to bury it.

I stroke the fluttering vein with my finger. Tabby closes her eyes.

Adjusting my weight so I don't crush her, I carefully rise to one elbow and inch down the zipper again, stopping just below her navel. It's missing its ornament. I slide my hand inside her jacket, feeling the warmth and silken softness of her skin, and she inhales, her lips flattening. When I gently stroke my fingertips around the outer curve of her breast, her lips part, but she remains silent and perfectly still.

I feel the tension rising in her body like a wave.

This is why I told her she couldn't come. She'll repress her own pleasure, think herself out of it, unless I can short-circuit the system by giving her something to distract the problem-solving, frantic part of her brain. Against the wall before the firetruck arrived to spoil the mood, I made her count out loud. But for this, to get her where I want her to go, we have to up the ante.

I nuzzle her ear, lightly take her earlobe between my teeth. "I'm gonna touch you everywhere, Tabitha. Anywhere I want, anywhere it pleases me. And my mouth is gonna go anywhere it wants too. If you want that, say yes."

Her eyes stay closed. Her breathing is shallow and fast. "Yes."

The tone is faint but unequivocal. Desire surges through me. "Good. But I want you to remember, you can't come. The goal tonight is only pleasure, not orgasm. If you feel like you might be getting close to coming, I want you to recite the names of every flower you know." I pause. "In Portuguese."

"Wha—"

"Shh!"

She bites her lip, acquiescing. I say a silent word of thanks that her eyes are closed, because if she saw the grin on my face, she'd probably kill me.

I slide the zipper down with exquisite slowness, tooth by tooth, watching arousal and apprehension play over her face. When the zipper reaches the end, her jacket falls open, exposing both her breasts. This woman seriously dislikes underwear. I might be the luckiest man on earth.

Her nipples are already hard, peaked and rosy, fucking gorgeous.

"I love these." I thumb over them, back and forth from one breast to the other. "I love how responsive they are to my touch." I lean over and blow on one, and watch it harden even more. I whisper, "And to my tongue," and suck it into my mouth.

Her gasp is quiet and utterly satisfying.

I take my time with her breasts, gently fondling them, pinching and stroking the nipple that isn't being attended to by my tongue, holding her lower body in place with the weight of my pelvis, one leg flung over hers. Her hands are still above her head, clenched in the pillow. Her head is turned to the side.

Her cheeks are still stained that appealing, embarrassed red, almost as red as her hair.

I love all her contradictions. I love that she wears sexy, revealing outfits, has tattoos and piercings, swears like a sailor, and knows Krav Maga, but a single kiss can undo her. I love that she's brilliant and bold and mercilessly independent, but manages to make me feel like a king when she blushes. I love all her sharp edges and all her soft, hidden spots and *if you don't watch yourself, idiot, you'll find yourself with a much worse problem than a perma-boner!*

Inhaling a sharp breath, I pull away.

Tabby turns her head and searches my face with big, dark eyes. She whispers, "No holding back, remember?"

Jesus Christ. She knows what I'm feeling. I can't decide which is worse, having the feelings, or having only one night with a woman intuitive enough to guess at them.

Breathing raggedly, I lower my forehead, rest it between her breasts, and close my eyes.

I feel her fingers stroke my hair, and it's wonderful. Soothing. I turn my cheek to her chest and listen to the wild clamor of her heart. She takes my face in her hands and forces me to look at her.

"Tell me."

My voice is raw and unsteady when I answer. "I don't know if I can have only one night."

She says tenderly, "Don't wuss out on me now, jarhead, a deal's a deal," and kisses me.

I slide my open hand up her thigh, over the crest of her hip, up her rib cage, and over her breast until her jaw is cupped in my hand. My other hand tangles in her hair. We kiss deeply but with no hurry, luxuriating in it, our breathing falling into rhythm, our bodies fitted together. She makes a slight movement with her hips, and I groan, lust flaring hot inside me.

"Maybe I should be the one telling you not to come," she teases, drawing away with a soft, pleased laugh.

"You could tell me to do anything and I would."

It's out before I can stop it, a bald admission made even more plain by the tone of quiet vehemence with which it's spoken. Tabby's gentle smile slowly fades. We stare at each other, the moment stretching out past retraction, past any chance of reclamation with forced laugher we can hide behind and tell ourselves it means nothing, it's only a stolen moment, soon to be forgotten with the morning light.

"Then, do anything," she whispers, holding my gaze. "Do it all."

I feel like a flock of birds has taken flight inside my chest. To distract myself from the imminent possibility that I'll open my mouth and deliver this true but entirely emasculating line, I slide my hand down her body and slip my fingers into the tight heat between her legs.

"Wet," I growl as she arches, gasping, her eyes gone wide. When I slide my fingers up and stroke them over her swollen clit, she moans.

It breaks the spell I'm under. Her moan takes me from swooning Romeo to snarling caveman in two seconds flat.

"*You will not come,*" I command, slide down the length of her body, spread her pussy open with my thumbs so that glistening pink nub at the top is exposed, and apply my mouth to it.

I suck. Greedily.

Her back bows from the bed. I push her down by her hips and hold her still like that, stroking my tongue over and around, sucking, making a meal of it and not caring at all how carnal it sounds, how loud it is in the stillness of the room. Tabby's hands fist in the bedspread. Her entire body trembles beneath my hands.

When I feel her pleasure plateau, that inevitable flattening that reveals her brain is in a snarl, I lift my head and direct, "Flowers, Tabitha," then go back to sucking.

She exhales a long, shaky breath. "*Girassol,*" she whispers.

I have no idea what that means, nor do I care. Here, at the core of her, she isn't sweet. She's salty and tangy and a little like the ocean, or grass. Grass drizzled in crack cocaine. It's fucking intoxicating. I hear myself making animal sounds deep in my throat, like a bear neck-deep in honeycomb.

A delicate shudder works its way through her. "*Tulipa.*"

A sudden dazzling bolt of lightning illuminates the room, and the lights flicker. The sound of thunder rolls through the walls. I slide a finger inside her, feel her muscles contract, add a second finger.

"*Orquídea.*"

With my teeth, I tug gently on the small silver stud in her clit, pressing my fingers deeper inside her, and get the immediate and gratifying feedback of the roll of her hips paired with a long, low moan.

"*Íris, jacinto, ervilha doce,*" Tabby pants, writhing.

"Don't. Come."

She makes a small, pleading sound, her lips pressed flat together, her chest rising and falling, her pelvis flexing, riding the strokes of my tongue.

It takes every ounce of self-control I have not to sit up and sink my throbbing cock as far as it will go into her delicious cunt and start pounding. I'm out on the ragged edge of my own restraint, watching her fall apart, stunned by how beautiful she is, how brave, and by the force of how much I want from her.

How much more I want from her than this.

You're mine, I want to say, but can't, because she isn't.

With deliberation, I suckle her, reach up with both hands, and firmly pinch her nipples.

"Connor," she says, stiffening.

"Yes, sweetheart," I whisper, watching her face. I return to my sucking.

She says my name again, a fractured sound, cut off at the end when she cries out, her body taut as a piano wire, her arms outflung, still entangled in her jacket.

With convulsions that shake the bed, she orgasms in my mouth.

Thunder booms. Lightning flashes. The first of the rain begins a soft, drumming song against the roof.

And for the first time in my adult life, I discover the true meaning of the word *yearning*.

This—this moment, this feeling—is everything I didn't know I wanted or was missing, made all the more agonizing by the freezing realization that it's precisely this that Tabby *doesn't* want.

At least not with me, for longer than one night.

She's crying a soft repetition of *oh God oh God oh God*, still straining against my mouth, her heels digging into the mattress, hands bunching the covers in her fists, and I can no longer wait.

"I need to be inside you," I say, my voice rough with desire. When she whispers, "Hurry," her hips still undulating, I don't hesitate.

My wallet is on the nightstand beside the bed. I reach for it, fumble out a condom, fling the wallet aside. With lightning speed, I roll it down my engorged, aching cock. Then I take my erection in my fist, pull her toward me with my other hand wrapped around her hip, and slide the head between her soaked folds.

I drop my weight to a hand, planted on the mattress beside her. Moaning, she cants her hips higher, using her thighs to lift her bottom off the bed, grabs my ass with both hands, and pulls me inside her body. Deep.

Slick, tight heat, still rhythmically spasming—I can't help myself. From my throat comes a loud, broken moan.

We stay locked like that for what feels like forever, suspended, unmoving, until finally the pulsing inside her pussy slows to a stop, and she collapses back against the bed, taking me with her.

I adjust my weight so I'm fitted more comfortably against and inside her, push her hair off her damp forehead, and give her a deep, heartfelt kiss. When I break away, she looks up at me through her lashes.

"Oops," she murmurs, smiling bashfully.

I'm so fucking helplessly charmed I might as well attach some strings and a pair of handles to my back, give them to her, and let her make me dance.

"Good?" I ask.

Her bashful smile takes on a hint of playfulness. "Mmm. I don't normally kiss and tell. Sorry—*come* and tell."

"But for me you'll make an exception."

Gorgeous, mussed, flush with afterglow, Tabby says, "All right. For you I'll make an exception." She looks deep into my eyes. Then, softly, "It was very adequate. Thank you for your services, soldier."

I chuckle. "Adequate, was it?" Flexing my pelvis, I make a slow circle, feeling that small stud of metal pressed right above where our bodies are joined.

Her eyelids flutter. Her fingers, still dug into the flesh of my ass, twitch. "So very, very adequate," she breathes, arching.

Watching her reaction, I want more. I slide my hand down her thigh, feeling her muscles flex under my hand, and pull her leg up so its wrapped around my waist. It changes the angle between us, opening her slightly, allowing me to press deeper inside. I slide in and out, then back in again, amazed she's allowing this, wishing it would never end.

Tabby, so beautifully responsive to me, wraps her other leg around my waist and rocks her hips. "Almost...mediocre," she says between breaths.

The feel of her rocking against my cock, using her hands and hips to manipulate my body to her own pleasure, is so hot and amazing, I shudder. Tabby looks up at me with dark, half-lidded eyes.

And then I'm fucking her. Slowly, deeply, the entire time staring down into her eyes. She stares back at me in a hazy sort of amazement, like she can't believe it's happening either.

It's intense. Intimate and personal. Quiet, unlike the beat of my heart, which is deafening.

Her brows pull together. She whispers, "*Lírio*," and I'm almost out of my mind with masculine pride.

"Already?"

She nods, biting her lip.

"You're so goddamn perfect." My voice is hoarse, the words torn out of me against my will. "Sweetheart. I want...I—"

Tabby kisses me, swallowing my words and the emotion that's threatening to drown me.

It's never been like this for me before, the pleasure of the physical act of sex overwhelmed by a sheer enormity of feelings. Part of me hopes it will never happen again. I'm a soldier. A mercenary. A Marine with twenty-three confirmed kills. And yet, with her, I'm as weak as a newborn baby.

She makes an inarticulate sound of pleasure, slides her hands up my back, and suddenly I need something more.

Taking her with me, I roll to my back. She settles on top of me, blinking in surprise for a moment before gazing down at me with a smile. "Getting lazy, are we? Or just running out of gas? I know at your advanced age—"

"I want to see your face. I want to see everything. I want you to ride me and come again that way, and I want to watch as you do it."

I push the jacket off her shoulders, let it fall to the floor. She's fully bared to me now, straddling my body, her long hair brushing her breasts and the flare of her hips warm in my hands. She watches me with those piercing eyes, and I know she sees more than I want her to, because her smile slowly fades.

The sound of the storm outside grows louder. Wind whistles through trees.

She encircles my wrists with her hands, slides them up her body to her breasts. The silver studs in her nipples wink, catching the light. I cup both her breasts in my hands, softly squeeze them so they spill out, more than a handful, and she sighs.

I would kill a man to hear that exact sigh even one more time.

"Tabitha," I growl, and she moves.

A stroke and a slide and an easy, graceful flex, her body

begins to move over mine. The pleasure is intense. I look at her bitten lips and pink cheeks and the rosy flush on her chest, and fight against my instinct to drive hard up into her, force those wanton cries from her throat. I want her to set her own pace, find her own rhythm, using me as a tuning fork to find the perfect pitch at which her body will sing.

The rhythm she finds is agonizingly slow, minute sliding and grinding movements that have me panting and sweating within seconds. I stroke her rigid nipples with my thumbs, and she rewards me with a moan of such voluptuous sensuality, I almost come.

When I apply one of my thumbs to her clit, she moans louder.

A moment later, rocking faster on my cock, she whispers something in Portuguese.

My smile is savage. *Adequate, my ass.*

"Feel my cock deep inside you, sweetheart. Feel how hard I am for you. Now tell me you like it."

Her breasts bounce. Her lips part. She says breathlessly, "You know I do."

"Say it."

She groans, her head falling back. I stroke her clit between two fingers, tugging at the stud. She gasps, her entire body jerking.

I pant, "Talk to me, sweetheart. Tell me...tell me how it feels."

A short silence, faster rocking, the tension in her body rising until her back is stiff with it, and then words burst out of her in an almost incoherent rush.

"God you're so hard and big and good it's so fucking good I love it oh God Conner I love it please don't ever stop!"

Yes. The sensation that sweeps through my body is one big, epic *yes.*

I roll her to her back, take her face in my hands, kiss her deeply, and thrust into her.

Hard.

Moaning into my mouth, she throws her arms around my neck, wraps her legs around my back, and moves her body in perfect counterpoint to my every thrust.

And I'm gone. Destroyed. The restraint I'd been so carefully maintaining snaps. I become a slave to sensation, to instinct. With some vague part of my brain I hear the sounds I'm making, the animal grunts and groans, but I don't care. In part because she's making the same sounds, but from her they're deeply sexy, viscerally beautiful.

She sounds, tastes and feels like art, she smells like heaven, she fucks like she's possessed, and she is the single most perfect woman I've ever met in my entire existence on this planet.

My final coherent thought is *I'm so fucked.*

Her pussy clenches around my cock once, and then again. Her body stiffens. She sucks in a sharp breath through her nose. I slide my hand over her ass, find the tight, puckered bud between her cheeks. When I stroke it, she shudders and makes a sound like a plea.

I gently push. Her body opens to me. I push deeper, sinking my finger to the knuckle, and Tabby convulses around my cock.

I try to hold on, desperate to experience everything just a moment longer because I know tomorrow it will all be gone, but my body is relentlessly pushing me toward the end that aches inside me, and all I can do is helplessly ride the wave of pleasure as it crests over me, breaks, and sends me crashing into oblivion with the boom of thunder in my ears and her name a strangled cry on my lips.

CONNOR

*N*ear dawn, the rain tapered off. I was awake to hear the wind die too, and the sounds of a new day beginning: birds chirping, the hushed murmur of voices down the hall, the low drone of a garbage truck lumbering down the street.

Outside the world is stirring, but here, in this shadowed room, in this warm, rumpled bed, I'll make time stand still for as long as I can.

Tabby is a soft weight beside me. Her head tucked into my shoulder, she slept deeply all night. Now with the first of the day's light, her breathing changes. With a quiet sigh, she shifts against me. Her eyes drift open. Sleepily blinking, she looks up at me, and I experience a tightness in my chest at the simple pleasure of watching her come awake in my arms.

Her shy smile unwinds the knot of worry in my stomach. I didn't know how it would be, if she would bolt in horror or be filled with regret, but she's smiling at me so sweetly, I let the anxiousness go and gently press my lips to hers.

"Good morning."

"Good morning." Her voice is drowsy and warm. "I suppose I have you to thank for my incredible night's sleep."

The tightness in my chest turns into an ache that I'm astonished to realize is happiness. I can't think of anything to say but a husky "You're welcome."

She gazes at me in silence for a long moment, and then curls a finger around the chain on my neck and uses my dog tags as a leash to pull me down.

Then we're kissing. Slow, amazing kisses that ignore the clock, the rising sun, everything we have ahead of us. Her arms slide around my neck. Our legs tangle together. I grow hard.

With a soft laugh she says, "You're insatiable."

"Yes." The word is raw in my throat. "For you."

She traces the outline of my lips with her fingertip. Her touch is tender, thoughtful, and sends a rush of hope through me. Hope that's smashed when she says, "So our one night is over."

I swallow. There isn't a word for what I'm feeling or a way to deny the obvious truth of her statement, so I say nothing at all.

Softer, with such innocent hesitance it nearly breaks my heart, Tabby asks, "And...what did you think?"

Groaning, I drop my head and hide my face in her neck.

Mistaking my longing for something else, she tenses. "I'm sorry. That was stupid of me—"

"I loved it. Every minute." I say it roughly, against her neck so she can't see the wild hunger in my eyes. I'm afraid of what she might do if she sees how much I want to keep her. How much I want her to be mine.

A shade of the tension fades from her body. After a while she says quietly, "It's still early."

I lift my head and stare at her. Color suffuses her cheeks. Her lashes sweep downward.

She clarifies her meaning by wordlessly pressing her pelvis to mine.

"And I'm the insatiable one? You're downright greedy!" I tease, enormously pleased. I'm even more pleased when she echoes my words from moments before, with a smile made all the more beautiful because it's genuine.

"Yes. For you. Now make love to me before you say something stupid and ruin the moment."

With a glad heart, a hard cock, and a head full of possibilities, I oblige.

~

Afterward, I drowse. When I awake several hours later, I'm dehydrated, disoriented—

And alone.

"Fuck," I mutter, leaping out of bed. I grab my watch from the dresser and check the time. It's late, much later than I thought. I jump into my pants, drag a clean T-shirt over my head, strap my watch to my wrist and shove my feet into my boots. I'm about to call Tabby's room when I notice a note on the floor near the door.

Heart pounding, I snatch it up. When I read its contents, I groan.

Jarhead,

In order to avoid what is sure to be an even more awkward drive together to LA, I left first. You're welcome. And thank you. Even writing this is ridiculously awkward, which convinces me I've done the right thing by going. My cell phone number is below. You probably already have it, having done your "research" on me, but just in case. It won't be turned on until I arrive in LA. Text me the address of the job.

As you said, we're both professionals, so I know I can trust you not to mention this again.

For the record, I won't either.

T.

. . .

It could only be worse if she'd signed it "Friendly regards."

I curse again, passing a hand over my face, and then crumple the note and throw it on the floor. Fuming, I stare at it for several seconds, but then expel a hard breath and pick it up. Smoothing out the creases, I carefully fold it and tuck it into my wallet.

I pack up the rest of my things in my duffel bag and head out.

I arrive in Los Angeles eleven hours later, overcaffeinated and jumpy as hell. True to her word, Tabby has had her phone turned off all day. I've dialed her number no less than ten times, my frustration growing each time I hear the toneless electronic voice on the recording directing me to leave a message. I never do.

Finally, on the eleventh try, she picks up. Her voice is mild, businesslike, impossibly impersonal.

"You were supposed to text me an address."

I don't bother to ask how she knew it was me. "Are you all right?"

That might have come out more brusquely than I intended, judging by the surprised pause on the other end of the line.

"Of course. Are you?"

No. Standing in my dark hotel room overlooking the bright lights of Century City, I bite back the word and rake a hand through my hair. "How did you get to LA?"

"I rented a car. Did you think I sprouted wings and flew?" She's amused.

"Where are you now?"

Another pause. "Venice."

I release a breath. From my investigation of her background, I know she grew up in Venice Beach, blocks from the ocean. Her parents were well-educated, a political science teacher and an artist, bohemian and antiestablishment, basically hippies.

And then they were dead.

"Visiting the old neighborhood?"

The pauses in this conversation are growing longer and longer.

"Connor." Her voice is soft around my name, a caress. I close my eyes and listen to it, let it steady my jagged nerves. "I'm fine. Thank you for asking. And I'm ready to go to work. Whatever I need to know, text me—"

"I'll email—"

"*No email.*"

Something cold snakes through my gut. "I use the highest encryption protocols commercially available, Tabby, and tweak them to my needs. You know I take precautions. It's my business."

"I'm sure Miranda took precautions too. You know as well as I do that email can never be one hundred percent secure."

"The encryption I use is the closest thing to bulletproof. It's based on what they use at the National Security Administration, customized for me."

Her tone goes flat. "I see. And I suppose you think a universal encryption key is a myth."

The cold unfurls, spreading to my chest. "Of course it is. Not even the NSA or Homeland Security has that kind of technology."

"No," she says after a moment. "They don't."

"Are you telling me—"

"By the way, if you've ever used this phone to contact Miranda, assume all your voice communications are compromised as well. My advice is to get a few burners for this job, use a new one every day. It won't matter in the long run, but it might slow him down a little."

Him. Søren. Like a bad rash, he's suddenly back.

I say slowly, "If someone is intercepting my calls, watching my electronic activity, that means you've been exposed too."

That charming sound on the other end of the phone is Tabby softly laughing. "Just text me the information about where we're setting up shop, Connor. Leave the heavy lifting to me."

She disconnects the call.

I stand there in the dark, staring at the phone in my hand, wondering why it never before occurred to me to ask her the reason she took the job in the first place, and understanding with sudden, awful clarity that it was the most important question of them all.

I'm in, she'd said. *I hope you're prepared for war.*

With new foreboding about what that might mean, I take the elevator to the lobby of the hotel, in search of a payphone.

13

TABBY

*T*he first thing that happens when I meet the venerated
Miranda Lawson, CEO of Outlier Pictures and a long-
time girl crush of mine, is that I hate her.

With a capital H.

Glaring at me, she snaps, "You're late."

Her words crack like a whip across the space between us,
spookily echoing off cement floors and columns before fading
into silence. We're at her movie studio, in one of those creepy,
subterranean parking lots featured in slasher films, where the
female victim is hurrying to her car, looking over her shoulder in
fear of the boogeyman she senses is waiting for her with a
chainsaw somewhere in the dark.

"That's on me," says Connor calmly, standing beside me.
"Got a late start this morning out of Albuquerque." A short
pause. "Caught in one mother of a storm."

Because I now have intimate knowledge of all the gradient
inflections of his voice, I know what the slight drop in his tone
over the last few words means, and who they're meant for. I'm
thankful for the cover of shadows, because I feel heat creep into
my cheeks.

It blazes hotter as Miranda turns her icy-blue gaze on Connor and then breaks into a dazzling smile.

"Connor. *So* good to see you again." She crosses the space between us with a few graceful strides of her long legs, her heels smartly clicking against the floor, and presses her cheek to his. She's slim and immaculate, dressed in a perfectly tailored ivory Chanel suit, nude heels, and pearls. She smells like mint Lifesavers and money.

After a murmured hello, Connor introduces me. "Miranda, this is Tabitha. She's—"

"The woman who works for free, apparently," says Miranda, still with that dazzling smile. It's toothy and predatory, and would look at home on a wolverine. "Not that I'm complaining, of course. Lucky me! I suppose we all have our quirks."

Her gaze travels over my outfit as she says "quirks."

I'm in my usual hacker chic outfit I wear on jobs, lots of tight black everything, punk meets goth, short on class and full of sass.

Because fuck you, that's why.

I smile sweetly at Miranda. "You have lipstick on your teeth."

She replies coolly, "If I did—which I don't—it would be easily remedied. Unlike your unfortunate fashion sense. Or perhaps you got dressed in the dark this morning?"

Beside me, Connor bristles. "Enough."

I think he's chastising both of us, but when I glance at his face I'm surprised to see his ire is directed straight at Miranda.

He's angry with her for dissing my outfit. Which he himself has done on more than one occasion.

Before last night.

This is new. What is this feeling? Pride? Satisfaction?

I don't know what it is because it's completely unfamiliar, but I decide I like it.

Miranda's gaze snaps to Connor. She studies his face for a

moment in silence and then looks at me. "I apologize. As you can imagine I've been under a great deal of stress. I'm grateful to have your help." She turns her attention back to Connor. "Both of you. The FBI so far has gotten nowhere, and we're running out of time."

"You've had more contact from Maelstr0m?"

Miranda nods. "He's begun erasing data from the servers. It started an hour ago. He says he'll erase a terabyte every hour that he doesn't get the money."

"So he's installed malware," I say, unsurprised. "Good."

Connor and Miranda stare at me. "*Good?*" she repeats, astonished.

"The malware will have a specific digital fingerprint. If I can capture some of the code, I can link him to other malicious cyber activity through it. Which means he'll be on the hook for a helluva lot more than just this job."

"*If* you can capture the code," says Miranda. "None of my in-house computer experts or the FBI have found anything so far to trace the source of the breach."

There's something unpleasant in her tone, but I merely smile. "That's because the malware is written so it destroys itself after it delivers its payload. But I know where to look."

Miranda inspects my face in the same way she did Connor's moments before. I can almost see the wheels turning behind her eyes. She says quietly, "You admire him. This hacker, whoever he is—you admire him."

My smile fades. "In the way one admires a shark for being a perfect killing machine, yes. But that doesn't mean I like him."

A new look comes into her eyes. Her voice drops in shock. "You *know* him."

Connor says roughly, "She was victimized by him once too."

Looking straight into Miranda's wide eyes, I emphasize, "*Once.*"

I feel Connor's attention shift to me, feel his need to question me about Søren like a razor slicing over my skin, but I know he won't ask in front of Miranda.

The funny feeling from before intensifies when I realize that I know it's respect that will keep his mouth closed. He might try to pummel me with questions in private, but he won't bring it up in front of other people because he knows I wouldn't want anyone else seeing how weak and stupid Søren made me feel.

I never would have imagined myself describing Connor Hughes as a gentleman, but I'm starting to believe that underneath the swaggering G.I. Joe sex-machine routine, that's exactly what he is.

Miranda lets out a relieved breath. "Well, this is fantastic news! We need to inform the FBI immediately—"

"Oh, we will," I say, waving my hand dismissively in the air. "But it won't matter. They'll never find him. He's a digital Jedi. A ghost."

Connor mutters, "A *digital Jedi*?" When I glance at him, his jaw is as hard as a rock.

Not understanding what caused the look on his face, I frown. *Why is he angry?*

"Whatever he is, let's get on with trying to stop him," says Miranda, turning brisk. "The FBI has set up a command center upstairs and has cyber forensic agents working twenty-four-seven on this. Shall we?"

We turn and follow her through the shadowed parking lot to the elevator bank, where she hits the button for the seventh floor.

The FBI's COM center is something straight out of a spy movie. They've set it up in the empty office adjacent to Miranda's executive suite, and even at this late hour, it's buzzing with activity.

It's got "waste of taxpayer money" written all over it.

By my count, there are fifteen fully equipped computer

stations set up, arranged in a semicircle in the middle of the room. Each bristles with wires and is covered in monitors and hard drives, staffed by a young man in a suit, tapping diligently at a keyboard. A large desk has been set up to one side, where I suppose a more senior man sits, although it's currently unoccupied. On the wall has been hung a large dry-erase board, with a mishmash of case facts, website URLs, and hypotheses scrawled over it in red pen. In the center of the board is a large circle, drawn by hand, with a big question mark at its center.

"Why are there so many government employees in this room?" I ask Miranda. "They usually sent out two or three guys for this kind of thing."

"Because the Sony hack was traced to North Korea and the feds are concerned that this is the North Korean government upping their game. Apparently there have been some recent threats of nuclear strikes from the regime that are credible. These gentlemen are from the Cyber Action Team, the FBI's rapid deployment group."

I sigh, because this is going to be a real pain in my ass.

I stride across the room and pick up the red Erasermate pen from the thin metal lip at the bottom of the board. In the big circle, I write, "Søren Killgaard."

When I turn around, everyone in the room has stopped to stare at me.

"Hello, humans," I say, looking at each one in turn. "Take me to your leader."

"That would be me."

I look in the direction of the gravelly voice. A man stands in the doorway I just passed through. He's built like one of Juanita's MMA fighters, barrel-chested and short-necked, with a big red face that betrays his fondness for alcohol. His head is shaved. His tie is askew. His eyes are bloodshot and squinty. He looks as if he was woken up by gunfire halfway through a bad dream.

"Mr. O'Doul," I say, recognizing him. Everyone in the

hacking community knows who all the top government cyber dogs are. "I'm a big fan."

He takes me in with a single, sweeping glance, his expression unchanging. "Executive Assistant Director O'Doul. And you are?"

Standing beside a tense-looking Connor near the doorway, Miranda says, "This is Tabitha West. She'll be assisting in the investigation. I expect your team to give her its full cooperation. She's a computer specialist, subcontracting with Metrix Security."

Connor and O'Doul nod a greeting at each other. I take it this is one of the FBI guys Connor mentioned he knew.

O'Doul's steady gaze comes back to rest on me. "What's your specialty?"

I flippantly reply, "Destabilizing governments."

His expression sours. "You're a hacker," he says flatly. The young men sitting at the computers shift in their seats, glancing at one another in surprise.

I give him my most winning smile. "I prefer the term social engineer. By the way, congratulations on being promoted to the head of the National Cyber Investigative Joint Task Force. Your predecessor was a total moron."

His squinty eyes narrow. He says slowly, "Tabitha West, is it?"

Connor says tersely, "You won't find anything."

"We're the FBI. We always find something."

"Really?" My brows lift. "How's that working out for you with Maelstr0m?"

The mood in the room is growing decidedly tense. I'm used to aggravating people, so it's no skin off my back, but Miranda looks as if she's already regretting the decision to bring me on board, while Connor is glaring a warning at me from beneath lowered brows. The guys at the desks have their hands poised over their keyboards, as if waiting for a command from O'Doul to enter my name into one of a dozen databases.

O'Doul asks, "You an associate of Maelstr0m's?"

"Nope."

Connor says, "She's clean, Harry."

A pause as O'Doul examines my face. "You vetted her?"

"Yes. You know no one gets on my team without a squeaky-clean file."

That's a stretch, considering Connor has witnessed in the past one or two of my less "squeaky-clean" activities, but he's technically correct. My file is clean.

My hands are another subject altogether.

I wait for O'Doul to decide whether or not he's going to allow me into the boys' club before a full government background check can be completed and he's convinced I'm not collaborating with the enemy, a worm sabotaging the investigation from the inside. When he takes too long, I say with exasperation, "Okay, I'm not being conceited when I say this, but I'm your only hope here. You'll never catch him without me. Dicking around is only going to make the situation worse."

A few snickers and rolled eyes from the guys at the computers. Someone chuckles and says under his breath, "Is that a Hello Kitty watch she's wearing?"

I turn to glare at him, my hands curled to fists. "Yeah, motherfucker, it is. And in two seconds it's going to be telling the time inside your colon."

Connor coughs to cover his laugh. Appalled, Miranda lifts her hand to her throat. O'Doul says wearily, "Shut the fuck up, Rodriguez, my daughter loves Hello Kitty."

Abandoning my attitude of nonchalance, I turn back to O'Doul. "The name of the man you're looking for is Søren Killgaard. I went to school with him." I glance at the jerk who made the watch comment. "MIT, in case you're wondering." Back to O'Doul: "I know how he thinks, I know how he codes, and I know it's him using that hacker alias, because he's eliminated anyone else who ever tried to use the name."

At the same time, O'Doul and Connor say, "Eliminated?"

"Use your imagination," I respond, looking back and forth between them. "The part where all the monsters live."

Connor does this thing where he seems to inflate, like a cat when it bristles all its fur upon sensing danger. I can't decide if it's interesting or ridiculous, but all the other men in the room except O'Doul definitely seem to think it's intimidating as hell. I've never seen a group of men shrink as a collective.

Before Connor turns into the Incredible Hulk, I say, "I can make contact with Søren in five minutes. In under an hour, I can have a program installed on Miranda's server to counteract the damage his malware is doing. And if you don't get in my way, by tomorrow at this time I can—most likely—find out exactly where he is. If I fail, you've lost nothing."

The room is silent. When I look at Connor, I feel everything he's feeling as if an invisible wire is connected to our chests.

In a low, controlled voice, he asks, "You know how to contact him?"

I know he's not asking for a yes or a no. He's asking for an explanation.

"He left me a channel. A way to reach him in case I ever changed my mind."

O'Doul steps farther into the room, his eyes sharpening. "Changed your mind? About what?"

All at once, the room feels too hot. My skin feels too tight. My hands are cold and clammy. I say simply, "About joining him."

And because of that invisible connection between us, I feel the exact moment Connor begins to doubt me.

TABBY

*J*t takes several hours to unload all my equipment from Connor's Hummer and set it up. During that time, Miranda retires to her office to get some sleep on the couch—it's past midnight—O'Doul and I have arrived at a tenuous truce brought about by my successful effort to thwart Søren's malware attack with an antimalware program of my own, and Connor has become increasingly agitated.

I'm not sure anyone else would notice it, but I'm attuned to him now. To his facial tics and the timbre of his voice, to the way he holds himself when under strain yet trying to look as if he's not. He's exceptionally good at maintaining his composure... except when he looks at me.

When he looks at me, his eyes blaze so hot, I think I might ignite.

This time, however, it's unclear if the fire in his eyes is lust.

"Can I have a word?" he says under his breath, leaning over my shoulder.

My hands freeze on the keyboard. I glance up to find him staring down at me, his face like a slab of granite. "Now isn't really a good time," I say, stalling. "I'm searching the root directory for—"

"I'll meet you in the ladies' room." He turns and strides away, his back stiff.

I glance around. In spite of my warnings to the contrary, all the agents are at their computers, avidly searching for the name Søren Killgaard in every directory and database they have access to, including O'Doul, who is pecking away relentlessly with his stubby index fingers at a laptop.

They won't find anything—as I told them they wouldn't—but the real problem is that now Søren will know they have his name.

And he'll start wondering who gave it to them.

I rise as casually as I can and wander out of the room as if I just need to stretch my legs.

The ladies' room is down the hall. I enter with trepidation, dreading what's on the other side of the door:

Connor, arms crossed over his chest, legs spread apart, scowling.

"Funny meeting you here." I let the door swing shut behind me.

"What was your relationship with Søren Killgaard."

It isn't a question, it's a demand, delivered with dangerous softness. I decide to sidestep. "In the words of your client, my feelings about the subject are immaterial."

"I didn't ask about your feelings. I asked about your relationship."

We stare at each other. The color is high in his cheeks. His breathing is slightly irregular.

"Why?" I ask softly. "Are you jealous?"

"Fuck yes," comes the instant, husky response. "But that's not why I'm asking."

A little thrill burns through me at his admission. "Then why are you asking?"

"Because there's a hell of a lot you're not telling me, and that lack of knowledge could compromise this job."

"We've already been over this."

"Let's go over it again."

After a long, tense interval, I say, "No."

His arms unfold. He takes a step toward me. I take a step back.

"Why not?" he asks, and his voice is velvet darkness.

My heart begins to beat faster. I'm not afraid of him; it's his intensity that's getting to me. His proximity. The way I can recall with perfect clarity how he sounds when he comes.

I moisten my lips. "Because it's none of your business."

It's the wrong thing to say. It stops him dead in his tracks with a look of incredulity on his face. Slowly, he shakes his head. "Don't do that. Don't pretend it didn't happen."

My ears go scalding hot. "We had a deal. One night, remember? One night to get it out of our systems, and then we'd never mention it again."

He softly corrects me, "One night and one morning."

The way he's looking at me makes my nipples hard and sends a rush of heat between my legs. I can't help it, my body responds to this man like nothing else I've ever experienced. I'm an addict, he's a needle full of heroin, and even though I know I'm not supposed to want it, I do.

He must see something in my expression, because his dark, dark eyes turn an even deeper shade of black. He takes another step toward me.

"Connor," I warn, backing up.

"Yes, Tabitha?"

"I'm going to touch you everywhere, Tabitha. Anywhere I want, anywhere it pleases me."

The way he says my full name, the deeply sexual tone of it, sends my heart racing. I retreat another step until my back comes in contact with the door.

Connor advances. Lifting his arms, he sets his palms flat against the door on either side of my head. He leans in close to my face. "You were about to say something."

"You said we were both professionals." I try to keep my voice stern, but fail. The words are a breathy whisper, more *come closer* than *stay away*.

"We are. And I'm asking—from one professional to another —what your relationship to Søren Killgaard was so I can then determine how much satisfaction I'm going to get from putting the bastard in prison."

He's betraying himself. A moment ago, he said it was about compromising the job. I'm amazed to find myself reaching up to touch his face. He stills when my fingers come in contact with his skin. His breathing goes ragged. I see the pulse pounding in his throat.

In a shaking voice, I tell him the truth. "I was the only person who ever told him no, and he punished me for it."

His hand covers mine. If I'm not imagining it, his tone is hopeful. "You weren't in love with him?"

I want to laugh. Or maybe vomit. "Love? There are things much stronger than love, Connor."

His eyes glow with emotion. "I thought nothing was stronger than love."

Unthinking, I blurt, "Fear. Hate. Self-loathing. The way your own mind can betray you if it's left alone in the dark for too long."

Connor takes my face in his hands and gazes down at me, his brows pulled together, a look of something like fury darkening his face. "What the hell did he do to you?"

Flooded with shame, I close my eyes. I whisper, "He held up a mirror to my soul and showed me what it looked like."

After a while, Connor says, "Open your eyes."

I obey him and stand there helplessly shaking, feeling as if my heart is exposed, dangling out of my chest.

"Let's put aside the question of Søren for the moment. I want to make a new deal."

I can't speak. I can hardly even breathe. I wait, my nerves standing on end like a million screaming exclamation points.

"Let's extend the one night to one week."

My breath leaves my chest in an expulsive rush. He makes it sound so rational. So businesslike. So simple, when it's anything but.

"You said you didn't mix business with pleasure. Ever." I take no joy in turning his words back at him, but it has to be said.

"I did say that," he admits, nodding. "Because I never have before. But in this case, I'm willing to bend my rules."

His thumbs gently stroke over my burning cheeks. Why does he have to do that, be so distractingly tender when I'm trying to concentrate on all the reasons why what he's asking for is insane?

"It's a terrible idea," I say. "It will be too much of a distraction."

"I'm aware."

He's aware but obviously doesn't care. His face is getting closer to mine. I'm beginning to feel a little desperate.

"I'm not sure I like you."

His lips curve. Faint amusement is reflected in his eyes. "I'm not sure I trust you."

Touché.

I put my hand flat on his chest and push. "I'll think about it."

"You'll think about it," he repeats slowly.

"Connor. We're in a women's bathroom—"

"You'd prefer the men's?"

"I'm exhausted, hungry, and wrestling with some very dark personal demons. All while standing ten feet away from a row of toilets. It's hardly conducive to romance."

"Is it romance you want?" he asks softly, reaching for my hand. "Or is it this?"

He presses my hand to his crotch. Beneath my fingers, he's rock-hard.

My patience snaps.

All my initial irritation with him, my original assessment of his character that concluded that most of his brain power is contained in his underwear, comes flooding back. I jerk away from him, spinning out of his reach. "Jesus! You're nothing but a...giant...*animal*!"

His jaw hardens. He folds his arms across his chest, draws himself to his full, considerable height, and looks at me down his nose. "Volatile little thing, aren't you, sweet cheeks?"

Sweet cheeks. Not "sweetheart" or "princess" or even Tabby—the mocking, derisive "sweet cheeks," which he knows I detest.

I feel as if the wind has been knocked out of me. Like he just punched me right in the chest.

Watching my face, Connor curves his mouth into a grim smile. When I realize he was counting on this reaction from me, that he was *baiting* me, I want to scream.

He says, "If you're telling yourself last night meant nothing, you're not half as smart as I thought you were."

He opens the door and walks out.

A moment later, all the lights go out, plunging me into darkness.

When I stumble into the COM center, I hear O'Doul shouting, "And why isn't *her* station out?"

"Because I'm not on the grid," I answer from the doorway. "I have my own power source."

My computer station is the only one with monitors that are lit up. All three of them glow cheerfully, lending my corner an ethereal electronic light in contrast to the rest of the room, which is in blackness. Agents mill around with their hands on their hips, muttering to each other, unsure what to do.

It's ridiculous how unprepared people are to be cut off from electricity.

"What are you talking about?" snaps O'Doul, coming closer. The others turn to look at me. Connor is nowhere to be seen.

"I'm using a portable generator." I cross to my station and point at a black piece of equipment the size of a printer, gently humming on the floor beneath the desk.

The guy who had a problem with my Hello Kitty watch also evidently has a problem with my energy source, because he pipes up with a snotty "Generator power fluctuates too much—there are too many variable voltage issues for it to be a reliable source to power your computers. Your hard drive is probably already fried."

I clap, slowly, three times. "Very good, Einstein. But I'm using a UPS that employs double conversion topology to provide continuous pure sine wave output."

Even in the low light, I can see how ruddy his face gets. "Well...that...that probably voided your warranty!"

"Yes," I reply with a straight face. "That is a *very* serious concern."

O'Doul interrupts our little love fest by standing between us and barking, "Shut your piehole, Rodriguez! And why the hell would you be using a *generator*, Miss West?"

Exasperated, I cross my arms over my chest and tap my toe against the carpet. "Because I needed my equipment to stay online when Søren found out what all you busy little bees were up to."

The room falls quiet. It's O'Doul who finally speaks.

"You're saying the hacker cut the power to the building? How? And how would he know we're searching for his name? We're on the FBI's secure virtual private network—"

I laugh. "Spare me your 'secure' crap, O'Doul. The FBI's VPN is about as solid as Swiss cheese."

My new arch nemesis, Rodriguez, drawls, "Riiight. Let me guess—you think *you* could hack it."

The energy in the room changes. I've got fifteen guys—sixteen including O'Doul— looking at me as if I'm either full of shit or off my rocker. They're shaking their heads and rolling their eyes, like I couldn't possibly be legit because *no one* can hack the FBI's site, and probably also because I don't have a dick.

I grin. *Oh, this is going to be so much fun.*

"O'Doul, I need you to guarantee me immunity from prosecution by the FBI or any other law enforcement agency for what I'm going to do in the next five minutes."

Rodriguez snorts. "Five minutes? Are you high? You can't hack into the FBI's VPN in five—"

"I'm not in a position to grant anyone immunity," lies O'Doul, making me laugh again.

"C'mon, buddy. You're the head of the NCIJTF! I wasn't born yesterday." When his expression sharpens, I add, "You've got fifteen witnesses who can attest to what happens in case anything goes sideways, which it won't." I glance at Rodriguez. "This is just a little pissing contest." I turn my attention back to O'Doul. "If it makes you feel better, you can consider it a bit of free security consulting for Uncle Sam. And after I win, you and I will have a nice long talk about the man you're dealing with at the other end of cyberspace."

O'Doul says drily, "Yes, about that. No one by the name Søren Killgaard exists. We've been checking for the last two hours."

"And don't you find that interesting, that on this planet with a population over *seven billion* people, not a single one of them has the given name Søren with the surname Killgaard? Not one social media profile? Not one utility bill? Not one birth—or death—certificate, driver's license or credit card? What do you think the odds are of that?"

"About one in seven hundred trillion."

It's Connor, from the doorway, holding a flashlight in his hand. The yellow beam sweeps across the room, landing on O'Doul's scowling face. He adds, "The guards at the security desk downstairs confirmed the power outage isn't anywhere else on the local grid or the rest of the studio campus. It's only in this building. And it's not the circuit breakers either."

Someone says, "I'm sure the backup generators will come on any second—"

"Those will be disabled too," I say. "He's hacked into the servers of the local power station, along with the studio servers. Consider the power out in this building for good." Smiling broadly, I add, "Except for over here, of course," and make spokesmodel hands at my computers.

I can tell O'Doul is trying to decide if he should arrest me on the spot and ask questions later, so I throw him a bone.

"How about this? While I get busy winning my hundred bucks from Rodriguez—"

"I never said we were betting a hundred bucks!" protests Rodriguez.

"*Two* hundred bucks from Rodriguez, why don't you get Professor Alfredo Durand in the Computer Science department at MIT on the horn and ask him about the Bank of America incident in 2007. He and other professors at the school can confirm the existence of Søren Killgaard, even if all the records of his attendance have been erased."

I look at my watch. It's glow-in-the-dark, and therefore easy to read. "It's after three a.m. in Massachusetts, but I'm sure Professor Durand won't mind assisting the FBI, no matter the time. He's a good sport like that."

O'Doul cocks his head, his sharp eyes studying me. He says to one of the agents standing nearby, "Special Agent Chan."

A young Asian man with glasses and unruly black hair, says, "I'm on it, sir," takes a cell phone from his shirt pocket, and walks several feet away to make a call.

I point to my computer. "May I?"

O'Doul growls, "You've got five minutes, Miss West, and not a second longer. Don't make me regret this." He throws a shady look at Rodriguez, who I can tell he doesn't particularly like.

I sit down in front of the computers. Everyone gathers around me, including Connor, who asks, "What are you doing?"

His voice is suspicious, but even more than that, it's worried. I don't look at him when I answer. "Oh, just this little thing called a bitch slap. It'll only take a sec."

Behind me, there are snickers. Ignoring them, I log onto my computer and begin.

For a full minute, there's silence. The only sound is my fingers rapidly tapping the keyboard. Over my shoulders, everyone raptly stares.

At two minutes, a hushed voice says, "There's a vulnerability in the web server."

Still typing, I chuckle. "There always is."

After another interval of silence: "Holy shit. Is that the remote login for the...*crime database*?"

"Yep," I say cheerfully.

The agents behind me are getting restless, starting to mutter to each other.

"There's no way she can get into the mainframe. They fixed all the holes after the Trilogy software disaster."

"She'd need an administrator password—"

"Forget about passwords, she's already at the Unix shell!"

I say, "Oh look, the mainframe directory listing. Tsk. Your system architect should be tried for treason."

Shocked silence. After typing for another few moments, I ask no one in particular, "Should we add Darth Vader to the Most Wanted list?"

Nobody answers.

Finally, Connor says, "Four minutes, twenty-six seconds."

"Hold on, I'm looking for the president's cell phone number. Let's text him a dick pic—"

O'Doul slaps the laptop closed, cutting the connection.

I swivel slowly around in my chair, look at the stunned faces staring down at me, and smile. "Any questions, ladies?"

Connor's flashlight provides enough light that I can see how pale Rodriguez's face is. He says, "That was pure luck."

Connor is the one who responds, in a voice like silk. "No. That was pure talent."

Our eyes meet. He gives a slight, annoyed shake of his head, chastising me for showing off, but I see the admiration in his eyes.

O'Doul snaps, "Posell, coordinate with studio security to find us another space to set up. Rodriguez, get all this shit ready to be transported. And you," he says, jabbing a finger in the air in my direction, "come with me."

He spins on his heel and heads for the door.

I stand and follow, Connor right behind me. Over my shoulder, I call, "When I get back, you better have my money, Rodriguez!"

I'm gratified to hear a low, aggravated, "Fuck."

CONNOR

*T*he elevators are out, so we take the stairs to the ground floor. The yellow beam of my flashlight leads the way. Harry doesn't ask why I'm following along, but he doesn't tell me not to, which is good because I don't want to have to knock him on his ass.

From now on, wherever Tabby goes, I go. Hearing her tell Harry that Søren had "eliminated" people activated every protective cell in the caveman part of my brain. Which would account for my decision to corner her in the women's restroom and start demanding answers and trying to renegotiate our agreement.

Damn, this woman gets to me.

We pass through the darkened lobby. An armed security guard unlocks the doors for us, letting us out into the night. It's cold. The air is a bracing snap in my lungs, a welcome broom to sweep the cobwebs of jealousy, desire, and frustration from my head.

Whatever Søren did to Tabby, I'm going to make him pay for it.

In spades.

"Where are we going?" Tabby pipes up as we pass between two buildings along a red brick path.

"Coffee," growls Harry, and keeps going.

In a few moments, we round a corner and enter a courtyard lined with palm trees. A patio is filled with tables with umbrellas, and through a wall of glass behind them I see a brightly lit cafeteria. I'm surprised it's open all night, because the lot is deserted. We must have the FBI to thank for that.

Tabby groans. "Food! Thank you, baby Jesus!"

Once inside, we get coffee and sandwiches from a sleepy-looking young girl behind the counter and find a nearby table to sit down. The place is empty except for us. Tabby starts wolfing down her sandwich as if she hasn't eaten in weeks, while Harry just drinks his coffee and watches her, his gaze contemplative and deeply unsettled.

A look I'm sure I've worn many times myself.

Deciding to keep my trap shut to see how this plays out, I take a bite of my sandwich.

Harry says quietly, "Tabitha Anne West, age twenty-seven, five-foot-six, one hundred thirty-five pounds, verified IQ of one hundred ninety-eight."

Ah. So while his boys were searching for Søren Killgaard's name in databases, Harry searched for Tabby's. It doesn't surprise me. He's one sharp son of a bitch and damn good at his job. He wasn't really cut out for the corps—lotta guys aren't—but he's a perfect match for the FBI. He's a no-nonsense straight shooter with just enough balls to make him dangerous.

He continues, "No known religious or political affiliations, no history of substance abuse, no outstanding traffic tickets, property and income taxes never paid late. Mother Laurel, father Christopher, no siblings, grandparents on both sides deceased. Went to live with her uncle Scott in Boston after her parents' deaths in a plane crash when she was eight. Graduated high school at fifteen, accepted to MIT on full scholarship. At seventeen, she discovered Uncle Scott with his face in a bowl of cereal at the breakfast table, dead from acute arsenic poisoning."

I freeze. *Poisoning?*

The file I read listed her uncle's cause of death as heart attack, and that it happened a year later, when she was eighteen. Stunned, I glance over at Tabby. She's pale and unmoving, her eyes downcast, her gaze on her plate.

"Due to the presence of a note and her uncle's history of depression, the death was ruled a suicide. Department of Children and Families was brought in to choose a guardian, and the minor was placed in foster care...for a period of one month, until she disappeared. School records show she continued attending classes, but officials were never able to locate her—"

"They never looked," she says quietly.

"Wait," I say, an odd tightness growing in my chest.

"—and when she became legally an adult at eighteen, the case was closed. Address records show residences for every year except 2007." Harry gazes at her, long and hard. "So my first question is this. Where were you for that missing year?"

She raises her head and stares at Harry. When she speaks, the floor drops out from under my feet.

"Living with Søren Killgaard, of course." Her laugh is low and bitter. "Actually, that's a gross misuse of the word 'living.'"

Shocked past words, I stare at Tabby. An interval of four heartbeats passes before Harry turns his hard gaze to me. "You said you vetted her."

"I...I did...there was no missing year, there was nothing to indicate—"

"It's not his fault," says Tabby. "The FBI are the only ones who have the accurate data."

My head is swimming. My heart is hammering. She *lived* with Søren. She told me she wasn't in love with him. She led me to believe she hated him, but she spent a year of her life under the same roof with the man.

She fucking lied to me.

Anger turns my vision red. I'm trying to get my thoughts straight to ask a coherent question, but Harry beats me to it.

"You've made it obvious you can bypass our firewalls without even breaking a sweat, Miss West. Which means you can just as easily access any other database. So my next question is, why would you change those few details in public records but leave the truth for the FBI?"

She looks at him first, and then turns her eyes to me. "Because I knew someday I'd be having this conversation."

Through gritted teeth, I ask, "What does that mean?"

She holds my gaze for a moment, her expression unreadable. She's searching my face for something, but the only things I'm feeling are fury and betrayal, neither of which seem to satisfy her. She finally abandons her search and looks to Harry. "You're familiar with Stockholm Syndrome, I assume."

"Capture-bonding," comes the immediate reply. "Where hostages express empathy for their captors, to the point of defending or sympathizing with them."

"*Or falling in love,*" I hiss, hackles raised.

Tabby ignores me. "It's a form of traumatic bonding—"

"You're saying he held you hostage?" I interrupt angrily. "For a year? While you attended school during the day?"

She ignores me again and keeps speaking to Harry in a cool monotone as if discussing the weather. "An adaptive psychological defense built into our DNA. Identifying with an abuser is one way the psyche defends itself, especially in women."

Harry's calmly nodding. I want to tear out every strand of hair on my head.

"When my uncle died, I had no one left. No one. The government put me into foster care. The first week I was there, my foster father came into my bedroom in the middle of the night and tried to rape me. He didn't succeed—he was a fat fuck, and I've always been strong—but my foster mother didn't believe me when I told her. Neither did anyone at the DCF. I was denied transfer. The family had been fostering for years with no problems, they said. It must be me, they said."

Her pause is fraught with anger. "He tried to rape me again a few weeks later."

Listening to her speak, my rage turns to horror which then turns to a violent urge to take her into my arms. I don't know if I've ever felt as helpless in my life as I do right now.

"But that time was different, because someone was there to help me. Someone had been watching me carefully, and when my stepfather pulled the covers off my bed and I screamed, he got a very unpleasant surprise in the form of a baseball bat to his balls."

Into the silence I say, "Søren."

Tabby swallows, and then nods. "He came through the window and beat my foster father to within an inch of his life, and I crouched on my bed and watched him do it. And did nothing to intervene. There was..." She clears her throat. "A lot of blood. Afterward, Søren told me that he saw me in class, that he knew something bad had happened to me just by looking at my face, and that he wasn't going to let anything bad happen to me ever again. Then he left."

Her voice grows quiet. "It didn't occur to me until much later that I might not have been placed in that foster home by chance...or that my uncle's death might not have been a suicide."

Horrified, I lean forward. Harry murmurs, "Go on."

As if gathering her strength, Tabby inhales and then lets the breath out slowly through her nose. "From my first memories, I was used to being different, which meant that I was used to being looked at oddly. That was a disadvantage. For all my precociousness, I never learned to recognize when a strange stare in my direction was dangerous. I was naïve."

Lost in some dark memory, she closes her eyes. "When I

later investigated my foster parents, I found that they had multiple complaints against them which had somehow been erased from the DCF's files. When I further investigated my uncle's death, I found it troubling that there was no arsenic found in the house, and the level in his blood indicated he'd been ingesting relatively small quantities for a long time. Which—if you're going to kill yourself, why do it slowly? He owned several handguns, could have shot himself, jumped from the roof, any number of options seemed more logical than poisoning himself over a period of months."

"But there was a note," Harry points out. "In his handwriting."

Tabby looks at him. "And some people can forge a painting so perfectly not even an expert can tell it isn't an original."

I say in disbelief, "You're saying Søren met you at school, became obsessed with you, murdered your uncle so you'd be put in foster care, manipulated the system so a rapist would get you, and then waited for his chance to rescue you so you would then feel…grateful to him?"

"Pretty sophisticated for a teenager," says Harry doubtfully.

"He was twenty-one," replies Tabby. "And already a multi-millionaire from stock market speculation. And yes, I think that's exactly what he did, though I have no proof. All I know is that Søren is a master manipulator. He can make people do things and convince them it was their own idea."

There's something strange in Harry's face that I can't put my finger on, something darker than doubt. Studying her, he tilts his head in thought. "Or maybe the master manipulator is someone else."

Suddenly, I'm out of breath.

I look at Tabby with wide eyes. When she sees my expression, she looks as if she's been slapped.

We stare at each other. My brain says *No, no, no*.

And then, more faintly, something not so unequivocal.

Into our silence, Harry says, "I have no proof this person Søren exists, except for your insistence that he does. I *do* have proof that you're perfectly capable of breaching extremely sophisticated network systems, because you've given me a lovely demonstration. I also know you recognized me the minute you saw my ugly mug, which strikes me as incredibly coinciden-tal. Too coincidental. And judging by the way our boy here keeps staring at you, I'm guessing there's a lot more going on between you than could be considered strictly professional."

When he pauses, I look at him. He says, "Which may or may not also be coincidental."

I cut my gaze back to Tabby.

She whispers, "Connor. You can't believe that."

I stare at her, remembering how upset she was when I kissed her against the wall at the hotel, only to show up in my room half an hour later, demanding sex. My brain is recoiling in horror from the idea that…she…

"*You* came to *me* for this job!" she cries.

You knew I would, I think, but can't bring myself to say it.

Harry muses, "I also find it interesting that Victoria Price, your employer from the time you left MIT until she disappeared under mysterious circumstances three years ago, left you every-thing in her will. Including a twenty-five-million-dollar pent-house in Manhattan." As an afterthought, he adds, "Her body has never been recovered, correct?"

A crackling pause follows.

In the moment before Tabby jumps to her feet, time is suspended. I see her lips flatten, see outrage flare in her eyes, see the exact moment her opinion of me goes from "not sure if I like you" to "wouldn't spit on you if you were on fire." Then, with a lightning-fast unfolding of limbs, she's up, and then I'm up too, and my hand is wrapped firmly around her bicep.

Stiffening, she bites out, "Lay another uninvited finger on me and you'll lose the whole goddamn hand."

Looking back and forth between us, Harry says, "Well. At least I know one of you isn't in over your head."

I growl, "Tabitha—"

Before I can finish the sentence, someone calls Harry's name from the other side of the room.

He rises. I turn and see one of his agents, the one named Chan, at the entrance to the cafeteria. He's holding out a cell phone.

"It's Professor Durand from MIT." His gaze skips to Tabby. "He'd like to talk to you, sir."

Harry waves him over.

As Chan walks closer, Harry says calmly to me, "You got your cuffs on you, Connor?"

Staring at Tabby, I nod once, a curt affirmative.

"Excellent," he says, taking the phone. He smiles at Tabby. "Because depending on what the good professor says, you might need 'em."

CONNOR

*W*hile Harry has a muted conversation a few yards away, Tabby and I stand in frosty silence, staring at each other. I've still got her arm in my grip.

Fighting the adrenaline coursing through my veins, I keep my voice controlled when I say, "Tabby—"

"Fuck you," she snaps, eyes blazing. Her cheeks are bright red, she's breathing hard, and there's a good chance I'm gonna get a knee in the balls any second.

I try again. "Tabitha. Listen—"

"Off is where you should fuck," she hisses. With a swift, practiced move, she manages to twist away.

All my muscles tense. I'm braced to chase after her if she tries to break and run, but she doesn't do anything except angrily brush her hair out of her eyes. Then she glares at me with what looks to be hatred.

I open my mouth, but she cuts me off.

"Go. Fuck. Yourself. *Asshole*."

Heat radiates up my neck. I curl my hands to fists and count to ten.

Then I count to twenty.

"You lied to me." It's fast and cutting, spoken before she can curse. Her response is just as quick, just as angry.

"Never."

I have to breathe deeply for a few seconds before I can control the scream crawling its way up my throat. When I speak, my voice is raw. "You said he was 'wrong.' That you were the only one who thought so. That you weren't"—my voice grows louder—"*fucking him.*"

Special Agent Chan, standing off to one side, throws us a curious glance, and then looks away.

"All true! And then you shoved your tongue down my throat before I could say anything else!" she spits back at me, so furious, she's trembling.

The anger gives me some hope that she's telling me the truth. I've met plenty of people who can convincingly lie, but I've never met anyone who can force the physical signs of anger. The red face, the shaking hands, the ragged breathing, the dilated pupils, they all tell a tale. Rage is distinct, and honest.

The only other option, I force myself to admit, is that she's angry she got *caught* lying.

I lower my voice so Chan can't hear me. "You're not gonna want to hear this—"

"Then don't say it."

"—But you worked for a *huge* liar for years. You helped Victoria create an entire identity that was a lie. You helped her lie to my friend Parker—"

"Because he screwed her and her entire family over! He ruined her life!" She throws her hands in the air. "Or so we *thought*! You know exactly what happened. Don't turn it around on me!"

When I don't respond, Tabby says bitterly, "Why don't you just say it, Connor. Just say that you think I made up Søren. That

I made up *everything*. That I'm the one who pulled the studio job, and being here to watch the chaos is just a big ego stroke. That the blackmailer is really *me*."

I say nothing. She turns her back on me and stands with her arms crossed over her chest, shaking.

Then Harry walks over and casually says, "Nice guy, your Professor Durand."

Tabby turns her head, listening.

"Spoke very highly of you. Fondly, in fact. Says you were the most brilliant student he ever had." Pause. "Aside from one Søren Killgaard, that is."

The breath I didn't know I was holding leaves my chest in a gust.

Over her shoulder, Tabby says quietly, "You should send an agent to Durand's house to verify it was him you spoke with. At some point, it will occur to someone on your team that phone numbers can be spoofed and rerouted, and we'll be right back to square one. Go to his house and talk to him face-to-face, and then you can be sure."

Harry looks at Chan, who says, "On it," and leaves.

Then Harry says to Tabby's back, "You ever think about joining the FBI?"

By the time the sun comes up, the COM center has been moved to another building on the studio campus, two agents from the Boston field office have interviewed Professor Durand at his home, and Harry has given me the rundown on the infamous Bank of America incident.

"Took Tabby weeks to convince the cops she was innocent," he'd said. "Mainly by proving it wasn't her who opened the bank account where the stolen money was deposited. Security footage showed an older woman, taller, different coloring. They weren't able to identify her other than to rule Tabby out. The bank employee who opened the account couldn't recall anything unusual about the woman that could've helped the investigation. That, added to the lack of any other evidence linking Tabby to the crime, made the DA decide not to pursue charges. And that was that. Subsequently, she dropped out of school, and Durand never heard from her again."

"If there was no evidence," I'd said, "that means the police searched her computers. Which means they searched her home. But you said there was no address on record for her that year."

"She rented an apartment near the campus a few days before she got nabbed—"

"And before that?"

"She said she'd been living in her car."

Harry and I had looked at each other then. I knew we were both thinking the same thing. Either Tabby lied to us about living with Søren, or she was protecting him by not giving the police his home address.

Neither option worked for me.

"Did the police interview Søren? And why was it handled by the cops, anyway? A case like that, the FBI should've been involved."

Harry had shrugged. "They went to the address the school had on file for him, but it was one of those UPS mail centers. And by that time, he'd stopped attending classes too. Because it had been a woman who opened the account, they assumed Tabby's insistence it was Søren who did the job was just a case of sour grapes."

"What do you mean?"

His steady gaze had stayed on mine. "A lover's quarrel."

"Lovers," I'd repeated, feeling sick.

"Apparently Professor Durand often observed Søren

sketching pictures of Tabby during class and saw them together around campus. He assumed they were an item."

"Did he ever see them…"

He picked up on what I'm not able to speak aloud.

"He didn't say. As for why the FBI wasn't involved, a decision was made by someone high up at the bank to keep the incident as quiet as possible. Hacks are bad for business. The public gets skittish when they know their money is vulnerable. And for a seventeen-year-old to be accused of making off with millions right under their noses… I guess they decided the public relations shit storm wouldn't be worth it. Besides, they recovered all the money very quickly. No harm, no foul."

Something wasn't making sense. "You said you couldn't find Søren's name in any database."

"Right."

"What about his school records?"

"Disappeared, like he never existed."

"But the police knew about him back then?"

"I know a guy in the local PD, asked him to copy the reporting officer's handwritten case notes. That was the only place Søren was mentioned. After the woman on the video, they decided Søren was a dead end."

I'd passed a weary hand over my face and asked Harry what he thought. About Tabby, about all of it.

"I think there are a lot of unanswered questions," he'd said, watching me closely. "But mainly I think this girl is a wild card and dangerous to the clarity of your thinking. Mainly I think you're balls-deep in trouble, my friend."

It's really inconvenient when motherfuckers are so observant.

I'd avoided his all-seeing eyes and stared morosely out a window instead. "I don't know what it is between us."

"It's something, though, isn't it?"

Respect for him had made me nod instead of offer a denial, which would've been a lie anyway.

He'd sighed and downed the dregs of his cold coffee. "You've never been one to think with your dick, buddy, so I won't give you a lecture. Just watch yourself. I have a feeling this thing is much bigger than it looks."

I wasn't sure if he'd meant the situation with Miranda and Søren, or the situation with Tabby and me, but for the moment, I'd dropped the conversation with Harry due to sheer exhaustion. I'd been up for twenty-four hours and needed to sleep.

I needed to get my head screwed on straight before I talked to Tabby.

Whether she'd let that happen was up in the air. She'd curled up in a chair in the new COM center and gone to sleep without once looking in my direction. Or accepting my suggestion that she sleep on the sofa I'd had brought in for her.

Harry had asked that we both stay on premises until further notice...though I knew it really wasn't a request.

So I'd found a quiet spot for a nap in someone's office and gone to sleep.

And now someone is shaking me awake.

I open my eyes to find a man—goateed, tatted, grinning—standing over me.

"Gettin' your beauty rest, pumpkin?"

"Ryan." I'm on my feet and slapping him on the back in greeting before the word is all the way out of my mouth. I'm surprised how relieved I am to see him. Impulsively, I pull him into a hug.

"Gee, boss," he says, my arms still around him, "one day in LA and you're already battin' for the other team? What're they puttin' in the water out here?"

"Fuck you," I say with gruff affection and push him away. "And if I *was* going to bat for the other team, your ugly ass is the last place I'd start."

Still smiling, he crosses his arms over his chest. At just over six feet tall, Ryan McLean is a few inches shorter than I am, but bigger than pretty much everyone else. We served together in the corps, and as soon as he aged out of Special Ops, I recruited him to Metrix. He's an expert in close-quarter battle tactics, weapons, and recon.

And despite my teasing, he's not ugly. His nickname is Thor, because the resemblance to the Norse comic book superhero is uncanny. All he needs is a flowing cape and an oversized hammer and he could star in the movie. Add a sleepy Georgia accent and a pair of baby blue eyes to the mix, and he's the kind of "not ugly" that melts panties.

Those blue eyes now squint at me. "You all right?"

I drag a hand through my hair, shake my head to clear it. "Been a strange coupla days."

"So you said. Wasn't sure what to make of your phone call last night, brother. You sounded...not like yourself. Got on a plane fast as I could."

I don't want to get into exactly how much I'm not myself at the moment, so I deflect with a question. "You see Harry yet?"

Ryan nods. "He brought me up to date. And they just got another email from the target. Apparently this Maelstr0m is none too fuckin' happy someone on our team cock-blocked his malware. Says he wants the name of who did it. Threatenin' all kind of mayhem if we don't give it up."

"Fuck. All right. Let's hit it."

I leave the room, Ryan by my side. When we reach the COM center, Miranda is already there, pacing back and forth in front of the windows. Harry and his boys are gathered around a desk set up with computer equipment, staring at a single monitor. Tabby is noticeably absent.

"Heard you had contact," I say, stopping next to Harry.

With a subtle smile, he jerks his chin at the screen. "Looks like this Killgaard character doesn't like sharing his toys." He sends me a sidelong glance, which I don't take the time to interpret because I'm too busy staring in fascination at the screen.

Appearing in rapid succession on the monitor is a series of pictures of battle: atomic mushroom clouds, planes dropping bombs over targets, buildings exploding under heavy mortar fire. At the bottom left of the screen is a white skull and crossbones—the skull has flaming eyes—with a bar of text. Ryan reads it aloud.

"'Give me a name, or there is no avoiding war.'" He snorts. "Melodramatic much?"

"That's Machiavelli, not melodrama."

Everyone turns to the sound of the voice.

It's Tabby, standing in a doorway on the opposite side of the room. She's obviously dead tired, but still sexy as fuck in spite of it. Her eyes are heavy lidded, her hair tumbles over her shoulders in an appealing mess. She's wearing the clothes she had on earlier, but pared down: unlaced combat boots, skintight black jeans, a black T-shirt that's about three sizes too small and does an incredible job of showcasing her slender waist and the fullness of her breasts.

She yawns and stretches, arms overhead, arching her back. The T-shirt rides up her flat stomach to display the glittering jewel tucked into her navel and part of the tiger tattoo lower down. I know it's not my imagination that the temperature in the room seems to jump by several degrees.

Standing next to me, Ryan mutters, "Mercy."

I don't like the way he's looking at her. The way everyone is looking at her.

The way she's now looking at *me*, with complete disgust.

Harry says, "Pardon?"

Tabby moves into the room. Nineteen pairs of eyes follow her every move. She stops on the other side of the desk from me and stares down at the screen.

"Niccolo Machiavelli, the Renaissance philosopher. It's part of a quote of his. 'There is no avoiding war, it can only be postponed to the advantage of others.'"

When no one responds, she looks up and around. "None of you has read Machiavelli?"

"No, ma'am," says Ryan. "But he sure sounds fascinatin'. I'd love to hear all about him real soon."

While I feel the hair on the back of my neck stand on end the way it does just before I pull the trigger on a kill, Tabby blinks at Ryan and looks him up and down.

"Who are you?"

"Ryan T. McLean, ma'am. At your service." His gaze rakes over her. "And you are?"

Before I can snarl *Off limits!* Tabby says, "Tabitha West. But you can call me Tabby."

Ryan grins. "I once saw a thoroughbred named Tabby win at Belmont Park. Most beautiful thing I've ever seen in my life."

Obviously charmed, Tabby grins back at him. "What's the 'T' stand for?"

"Tiberius."

Her brows shoot up. "Like Captain Kirk or the Roman emperor?"

Impressed, Ryan blinks. "Like Captain Kirk. My parents are huge Trekkies."

"Well," Tabby says, looking him over, "it suits you. You have the look of a man who could captain a starship."

"Why thank you, ma'am," he drawls, crossing his arms over his chest so his big, tattooed biceps are on full display. "And may I say I really like that T-shirt. Does it, uh…have any special meanin'?"

Tabby's T-shirt reads: "Pussy Riot." She glances down at herself. "It's a Russian feminist punk rock protest group."

Ryan thoughtfully strokes his goatee. "Oh. And here I thought it might be somethin' straight outta one of my wet dreams."

Heat sweeps up my neck and into my face. Tabby looks at me...and smiles.

I think if I look anywhere but right at her, I might accidentally murder someone.

Harry clears his throat. "Miss West, your friend Søren is a little pissy about that antimalware program you ran that disabled his intrusion attacks. Having a bit of a meltdown. I'm worried what his next move might be."

Tabby looks at the screen again. Her smile dies. "Well. Let's give him what he wants then, shall we?" Then under her breath, "God forbid the son of a bitch is kept waiting." She pulls the chair out from under the desk and sits down.

I blurt, "Don't—"

Harry stops me short with a hand flat on my chest.

Looking into my eyes, he says quietly, "Rein it in, or I'll throw you out. Decide now."

Everyone's looking at me, including Ryan, whose brows are arched in surprise. I take a deep breath, nod, and step back.

To Tabby, Harry says, "This isn't your show, understood? I'm in charge here. I make the decisions about how to proceed. So before you put a finger on that keyboard, we're gonna have a talk."

Tabby slowly swivels around in the chair. She crosses her legs. She folds her hands in her lap, gazes up at Harry with a chastened look, and bats her long eyelashes. "Yes, *sir*," she says demurely, and waits.

Harry scowls at her, but I sense it's more to maintain the status quo than from actual irritation. In spite of any doubts and questions he still might have about her, I can tell he's just as impressed by Tabby as everyone else is.

Except Rodriguez, who's glaring at her with all the intimidation he can muster. Which isn't much.

Harry says, "Tell me what you're thinking. Are you just going to flat-out tell him who you are?"

142

"What fun would that be?"

"We're not here to have *fun*."

It's Miranda, coming to stand near, her pacing abandoned. Though she's still perfectly coiffed and there's not a wrinkle on her expensive clothing, her face is pale and strained. It looks like her rest break didn't take.

Tabby says, "*You're* not. But he definitely is. And the only thing that can distract Søren from his game is another game. So I'm going to give him one." She looks at Harry, and her voice loses some of its edge. "With your permission."

In silence, he assesses her face. After an uncomfortably long pause, he says, "Go on."

Tabby nods. "Okay. So in addition to having a malware blocker, the program I've uploaded to the network backbone automatically responds to any new attempted breaches with a counterstrike—"

"It *automatically* returns fire against a threat, without human direction?" interrupts Rodriguez incredulously. "Like the NSA's MonsterMind program, which isn't even supposed to be in existence yet?"

"Yes. Exactly like that."

Under the weight of her simple admission, the room falls into stunned silence. Harry shoots me a stony glance, and I know with chilling certainty what he's thinking.

Tabby hacked the National Security Administration and stole their software.

If that's true, she'll spend the next few decades in prison.

All the blood drains from my face.

Tabby rolls her eyes and sighs. "You guys, relax. It's *my* program, okay? I can prove I developed it. And I'd never go near the NSA servers, anyway—even I'm not that crazy."

After a moment, Harry asks, "And what does this program of yours do in terms of counterstrike? Specifically."

A smile works its way over Tabby's face. "Well, without

getting overly technical, once the program detects an attempted breach, it follows it back to the source and launches malicious code in the originating system."

Harry looks dubious. "Which then does what?"

She shrugs. "Anything from wiping out data, to gathering data, to making a little white cat dance on every network monitor that can never be bypassed, thereby rendering the system useless. That's why Søren's so mad right now. He's getting a taste of his own medicine, and it tastes like shit."

Rodriguez frowns. "A dancing white cat..." His gaze falls on Tabby's Hello Kitty watch. His eyes widen. He sucks in a breath.

Harry asks irritably, "What now, Rodriguez?"

Rodriguez breathes, "She's...*Polaroid*! She broke into NASA's mainframe, Citibank's, the Church of Scientology's, the Department of Defense...you name it, Polaroid's done it, and always left behind a dancing white cat, just like that one!" He points accusingly at her watch.

The sound of fifteen FBI agents gasping in unison is one I'll never forget.

Undaunted, Tabby says calmly, "Oh keep your panties on, Rodriguez. I've never heard of this Polaroid, but I'm sure only a *guy* would be smart enough to do all that, right? Besides, lots of girls like Hello Kitty." She smiles sweetly at Harry. "Including your daughter, as I recall."

When Harry cuts his gaze to me, my blood freezes inside my veins.

This is highly dangerous. I have a millisecond to decide which side of the law I'm on, because if the FBI thinks Tabby is a threat to national security and I defend her, then I'm a threat too.

But as fast as I have the thought, I just as fast realize I don't care. Somehow over the course of the past few days, protecting her has become my number one priority.

I'll think about what that means later.

I'm standing in front of Tabby in full-on bristling battle mode before anyone can even blink an eye, my legs spread apart, my nostrils flared, every muscle in my body tensed to steel.

I snarl, "Anybody wants to try to get to her, they have to go through me!"

CONNOR

*N*o one moves.

After a long, silent moment, Ryan says drily, "Brother, you've got a *lot* to catch me up on."

Harry sighs and looks at the ceiling. He mutters, "Lord, give me patience." Then he looks at me. "No one's trying to get to anyone, all right? Now stand down, we've got a job to do."

Rodriguez protests, "But sir! She—"

"Shut the fuck up, Rodriguez!" thunders Harry, red-faced. "If I wanted your opinion I'd give it to you! Make yourself useful and go get me a cup of coffee!"

A livid Rodriguez glares at Tabby, and then spins on his heel and stalks out.

Harry irritably instructs the rest of the gathered agents, "Everyone else take a meal or rest break. Have your asses back here in an hour. Chan, you stay."

Slowly the agents disperse, whispering among themselves, shooting Tabby curious glances over their shoulders as they leave the room. When the last of them are gone, Harry turns to Tabby.

"I think we need to have another talk, Miss West. But for

right now, let's get on with it. What were you saying about a game?"

With a hand on my shoulder, Ryan gently pulls me a few feet away so I'm no longer blocking Tabby.

"Hide and go seek," she says, looking at me with even more curiosity than the agents looked at her.

My heart is throbbing wildly from all the adrenaline coursing through my body, and I'm having a hard time controlling my breathing. I have the vague thought that it might be useful for me to go find something elsewhere to break to relieve some of my tension. I haven't felt this fucked up and pretzel brained in...

Ever.

"What does that mean?" asks Miranda. She's been watching us all so quietly, I'd almost forgotten she was here.

Tabby replies mysteriously, "It was Søren's favorite. He won't be able to resist."

Something about the way she says it makes my skin crawl. Ryan's grip on my shoulder grows a little tighter. He murmurs, "Easy, brother. Take a breath."

"And?" prompts Harry.

"And if I can distract him long enough, we might have a chance to gather some clue as to his whereabouts. I've started a traceback. The longer my program spends in his system, the better chance it has to gather data before he discovers it and shuts it down. But if I engage with him, it might stall him a bit."

Harry narrows his eyes at her. "You said earlier you knew how to contact him."

"I do, but it won't give us his location."

"How do you know? Have you tried to contact him before?"

"No. But I know it's only an origination point, not direct access. He'll have built in layer after layer of obfuscation. I can reach out, but that's all. It's like firing a flare into the night sky. He'll see the flare, and then respond when he's ready. But even then his location will be cloaked. He'd never be stupid enough to give me a direct line."

"Hold on," I say, understanding dawning. "You're saying you have his *phone number*?"

Tabby stares at me for a while before she answers. I can feel how carefully she's choosing her words.

"I'm saying I have *a* phone number. I don't know whose it is, I've never called it. But if I reach out to him that way now, as all his systems are under attack, he'll not only know it's me, he'll know it's a trap."

In a tight voice, I ask, "You don't want him to know it's you?"

Miranda says, "No enterprise is more likely to succeed than one concealed from the enemy until it is ripe for execution."

Tabby looks at her in surprise. "I see someone other than me *has* read Machiavelli."

Miranda's smile is pinched. "Yes. I've studied his writings extensively."

I don't know what to make of the expression on Tabby's face. She says, "'It's double pleasure to deceive the deceiver.' That was always my favorite of his lines. You?"

Miranda locks eyes with Tabby. "'Nothing great was ever achieved without danger.'"

Some unspoken understanding passes between them. Tabby murmurs, "Indeed."

Harry is irritated with the interruption. "If we're done quoting a dead guy to each other, ladies, can we get back to the situation at hand?"

Tabby turns her attention back to Harry. She leans forward in her chair. "Give me a chance to engage him, distract him, play with him a little. He won't let it last long, but once he's shut down his servers, we can analyze whatever data my program has scoured from his system."

"And if your program comes up with nothing useful?"

Tabby leans back in her chair and lifts a shoulder. "Then we can make a phone call. But once we do that…once he knows I'm involved in this…" Her voice darkens. "The game will change."

"How?" I ask, my voice hard.

Tabby looks at her hands when she answers. "We'll no longer have any control whatsoever."

My throat is tight, crowded with every question I want to ask her about Søren, but won't. Not here. Not now.

Harry, however, has no problem getting straight to the point. "Why not? What will he do?"

Tabby looks at me. She says softly, "He'll end it."

Harry crosses his arms over his chest. "Miss West. Please. I don't have the patience for puzzles. *What will he do?*"

It's Miranda who answers, her voice strained. "It's obvious, isn't it? He'll release all the data he stole from me to the press and my competition—including my proprietary software—cut the power to the entire studio, and destroy my business. Every production will be shut down. Every office and soundstage will go dark, possibly permanently, depending on how much control he has over the Department of Water and Power's computers."

"We've got agents working on that," says Harry. "The DWP has been notified there's been an intrusion into their network—they're executing breach protocols as we speak."

"If they block one hole, he'll find another," says Tabby. "There's always a way in. Also, there's the possibility he has people inside the DWP assisting him."

Harry nods. "We're working on that theory too."

"The bottom line," says Miranda in a shaking voice, "is that everything I've worked for and created over the last twenty years will be *gone*. So please—let her go to work!"

It's so unusual for Miranda to show strong emotion that I'm momentarily distracted from Tabby. Next to me, Ryan watches everything with hawk-like focus, taking it all in. It's one of the reasons I wanted him here. He can see whatever I might be missing because I'm too close.

Because I'm too emotionally involved, and can't trust myself.

Harry says, "Chan, sit down at the desk. Miss West, you can tell him what to type."

Tabby sends Harry a grim smile. "Don't trust me, O'Doul?"

"Of course not. I don't trust anybody, it's bad for business. Now move."

Agent Chan makes a *sorry* face at Tabby. When she rises from the chair, he takes her place. Fingers poised over the keyboard, he says, "Ready."

Standing behind him, Tabby instructs, "Get rid of that shit on the screen. Take us down to the C prompt."

Chan starts typing. The pictures of war flashing on the monitor vanish, replaced by a normal Windows desktop. A few more keystrokes and the screen goes black. A green cursor flashes at the top left.

Tabby says, "You know your stuff."

"That's why I'm the only *Special* Agent in this group, Miss West."

As Tabby softly chuckles, Chan waits, eyes fixed on the screen.

"All right, then. Here we go. Type 'What is divisible by zero?'"

Chan answers automatically, "No number is divisible by zero."

"I didn't say what *number*, did I? Now type."

After a quick glance at Harry, who nods, Chan begins to type. He presses Enter, and waits.

And keeps waiting. The cursor flashes, but nothing comes back.

A minute passes. Then two. Harry says, "He's not answering."

Her gaze fixed on the screen, Tabby murmurs, "Wait for it."

Then a message blinks up: *To whom am I speaking, please?*

Ryan snorts. "Pretty polite for a bad guy."

"Manners make the man," says Tabby thoughtfully.

Is her tone *admiring*? I want to reach through the computer and strangle whoever is on the other end.

Tabby instructs Chan, "Now type 'What is the meaning of life?'"

The instant the question is entered, an answer flashes back: *42.*

On the next line: *I didn't realize the FBI had a sense of whimsy. How refreshing. With whom do I have the pleasure of communicating, please?*

"Jesus Christ," I mutter. "Does he always talk like this?"

"Not everyone has a dirty mouth," says Tabby. When she slides me a smoldering look, my heartbeat goes arrhythmic.

Our gazes hold. Still looking at me, she says to Chan, "Type, 'If you can answer my first question, I'll give you my name.'"

After Chan complies, on the screen flashes an animated gif of a cartoon dog with its paws clasped, eyes closed, heart pumping wildly outside of its chest. Beneath the dog are the words *Be still my heart! A challenge!*

Then a T-Rex bursts onto the screen and devours the dog in one giant bite. Blood spurts from its grinning jaws. The dinosaur runs off, trailing intestines.

"What the fuck is wrong with this guy?" I bark, making Miranda jump.

Tabby says softly, "Everything." She's still looking at me.

When she looks away, it feels as if something tears inside my chest.

She instructs Chan, "Type 'Your paleontology is as weak as your hacks.'"

Harry says drily, "I don't think poking the bear is the best strategy here, Miss West."

"We need the bear distracted, and so we poke it with as big a stick as we can. Type, Chan."

Special Agent Chan looks at Harry. "Sir?"

After a moment of thought, Harry nods and waves his hand, resigned.

Chan's fingers fly over the keys. The response arrives at light speed.

Explain yourself.

Tabby's smile is savage. "Canids didn't exist concurrently with tyrannosaurus in the Late Cretaceous period, dumbass."

"Leave out the 'dumbass,'" says Harry.

Chan types.

There follows an interval of screen silence. Then: *You are reckless. I enjoy that in an enemy. Toying with overconfident fools makes for excellent sport.*

Tabby smiles. "You should know, having toyed with yourself so much. Tell me, how calloused are your palms?"

Before Harry can protest, Chan has typed it out and hit Enter.

If you are too much a coward to reveal your name, let me see your face, comes the immediate reply, *so I may know what it looks like while still alive.*

"Ooh," says Tabby with bitter cheer. "Is someone miffed?"

I step forward. "That's a threat on your life. Disconnect."

"Back off, jarhead," answers Tabby offhandedly. "The adults are handling this."

Harry shoots me a warning look. Ryan clears his throat. Chan looks up at me sheepishly. And I turn away with my hands clenched in my hair so I don't do anything stupid, like throw Tabby over my shoulder, bolt from the room, and find the nearest bed to tie her down to so I can fuck some sense into us both.

I hear Tabby's voice from behind me. "Chan, type, 'I'll show you mine if you show me yours.'"

As Chan starts tapping away, Harry says wearily, "You don't

really think that will work. No criminal mastermind who's gone to the trouble to erase every trace of his existence would ever…"

When Harry trails off into astonished silence, I turn around to find the computer monitor flooded with image after image. Windows pop up on top of each other, piling so fast the screen is a blur.

Tabby says softly, "Everyone has an Achilles' heel. Søren's is his ego. He could never let a challenge go unanswered." She folds her arms over her chest and turns away. Her posture changes, becomes smaller somehow, as if she's drawing into herself. Protecting herself from what's on the screen.

Like a fairy-tale prince, Tabby had described him with the face of an angel. I'd thought it over the top at the time. A silly exaggeration. But now I see it was something far worse.

Accurate.

I don't find men attractive. I've never considered another man beautiful in the physical sense, would never have thought it possible that I could. But now I'm forced to admit that the face splashed all over the monitor isn't only beautiful. It's *perfect*.

Miranda's soft gasp indicates she concurs.

His features are fine and sculpted, like those of a Greek god. His hair is rich golden blonde. He's got a pair of lips any woman would covet, full and berry red, offset by a cleft chin and strong, angular jaw.

But it's his eyes that are most arresting. Pale, icy blue, heavily fringed with dark lashes, his eyes have an arrogance and cruelty that the rest of his elegant features can't soften.

Taken from various angles, the pictures of his face are accompanied by dozens of pictures of the rest of him. Striding through an airport, crossing a busy intersection, waiting on a subway platform, always standing a head taller than anyone else. Always looking at the people around him like a king surveys his subjects. Always alone, regal, dressed in beautifully tailored suits.

I can't help but glance down at myself, clothed in a black T-shirt and cargo pants.

Harry leans closer to the monitor, squinting at it. "These are all taken from surveillance cameras. Look at the angles. They're all from above."

"If that's true," says Chan slowly, "he's hacked into the entire infrastructure. Transportation grids, law enforcement grids, traffic cams…you name it."

"He's already proven he's in the power grid," points out Miranda.

"If he had that much access, he'd have caused a lot more problems than what we're dealing with here," I counter.

Tabby asks quietly, "How do you know he hasn't?" She glances at me over her shoulder. Her normally bright green eyes are troubled and dark.

"What do you mean?"

She looks at Harry. "How many terrorist acts go unclaimed?"

"Almost all of them," he replies, watching her closely. "Only fourteen percent of the more than forty-five thousand terrorist acts that have occurred since 'ninety-eight have credible claims of responsibility."

"What are you saying?" As my heart starts to beat faster, I move closer to her. "That Søren's not only an extortionist, he's a terrorist? You have proof of that? What do you know?"

Her prolonged silence infuriates me. My patience, worn to a shred, finally snaps.

I growl, "Tabby, whatever problem you have with me, you better spill your fucking guts before Harry decides you're withholding evidence, because I *will not* stand here with my dick in my hand while you get hauled away to prison and interrogated by the FBI! Am I making myself clear?"

Faint color rises to her cheeks.

Ryan says, "Lady, start talking, because if he squares off

against the feds, so do I, and that is one shit storm you definitely don't wanna get in the middle of."

"I'm going to pretend both of you idiots didn't just threaten me," says Harry between gritted teeth. "But if it happens again, you're *all* going to prison. Miss West, you're walking a very fine line here. *Talk*."

She looks at the three of us, then at Chan, then at Miranda. Finally, she heaves a breath that sounds exhausted and flops into a nearby chair. She rests her elbows on her knees and puts her head in her hands. When she speaks, her voice is hollow.

"I don't have proof of anything. All I know is…Søren. I know Søren. Whatever his interest is in this studio, it isn't money. He doesn't care about money. He's an anarchist, not a capitalist. What he cares about is *chaos*. Instigating it, creating it, and then sitting back with a bowl of popcorn and enjoying the show. He likes to set things in motion. He likes to destroy things." She pauses, and when she speaks again, her voice is shaking. "He just wants to watch the world burn."

Her pain is so obvious, it seems like another person has suddenly appeared in the room, an invisible, heavy presence, indelibly dark. With a shock, I realize this is the thing she hides at her core. Beneath her smart mouth and rebel attitude and odd costumes, all the walls she's built around herself, lies a lost soul, alone and in pain.

My sweet Tabby is in so much pain.

"Shut it down," I instruct Chan, my voice thick.

Tabby raises her head. Our eyes lock. Her lashes are wet. It sends a flood of emotion coursing through me, fury and possessiveness and a need to protect her, stronger than everything else.

"Shut it down right now," I repeat, turning to Harry. "Get that asshole off the screen."

While looking at me, Harry says to Tabby, "Has it been long enough for your pro—"

"I don't care about the *program*," I snap, squaring off to face him. "Shut the fucking thing down!"

"You're being *paid* to care about the program," says Miranda stiffly, sending me an arctic stare.

Special Agent Chan says, "Too late. He's out. He must've spotted the trace."

When we all look at the screen, the monitor has gone dark. All the pictures of Søren have vanished. Only a blinking green cursor remains.

With quiet resignation, Tabby says, "It will take hours for the traceback to compile a report. Then more hours to comb through it to see if there's anything useful. In the meantime, to appease him a little, we should give him some money. Make it look like we're trying to comply with his demands."

Miranda points out, "You said he doesn't care about money."

"He doesn't. But it's our only play if we want to stay in the game. It'll buy us time to try to figure out what he's really after, and maybe unruffle a few feathers so he doesn't blow the whole thing to shit." Her voice drops. "Obedience is always rewarded."

That last part sends a rash of chills down my spine. I share a look with Ryan. I know our thoughts are aligned: *This freak Søren Killgaard needs to be put down.*

Tabby glances at Miranda. "His demand is now at twenty million, correct?"

Miranda nods. "But my assets are primarily real estate, stocks, equity in the studio. I don't have that kind of cash just lying around."

Tabby stands, pulls her shoulders back, takes a breath. She lets it out in a noisy rush.

"I do."

18

TABBY

The first thing out of O'Doul's mouth is a flat, "No."

His tone suggests there's no room for argument. Naturally, I do anyway.

"Miranda can pay me back—"

"*No*. As soon as he has the money, he'll make good on all his threats. We never negotiate—"

"This isn't negotiating," I interrupt wearily. I'm so tired, my eyes are crossed. "This is stalling. It's strategic—"

"Tabitha."

Connor says my name so gently, it startles me. I look at him, standing next to the blond, tattooed bulk of Ryan T. McLean, who, though large and intimidating in his own right, is dwarfed by his boss. Between the two of them, there's so much free-floating testosterone in the room that a girl could get pregnant through osmosis.

But the look in Connor's eyes…oh God. My poor heart can't take much more of this.

He murmurs, "Please. Listen to Harry."

When I open my mouth, Connor holds up a hand. Even more gently than before, he says, "Please."

You son of a bitch. Please? After you practically accuse me of setting this whole thing up, you have the nerve to say please? Nicely?

But I don't say anything out loud, because his eyes are wrecking me. His voice is wrecking me. The memory of his face is wrecking me, how he looked when his body was moving inside mine, his expression of adoration, of reverence, as if what he felt wasn't just physical pleasure, but something a little more...

Sacred.

Connor didn't just fuck me. He made love to me. And no matter how much I might want to deny it, what happened between us was far more profound than a casual screw.

One night, he'd promised.

I don't know which one of us is the bigger fool.

"So what are we supposed to do now?" Miranda starts up her pacing again, back and forth over a few feet of carpet, her arms crossed tightly over her chest. "Just wait and see what happens?"

"Go home," answers Harry. "Get some sleep. There's nothing more you can do here. If anything happens, we'll call you." He glances at me, and then at Connor. "The same goes for you—"

"I already slept," I say dully, dragging a hand through my hair.

Harry looks at me, his lips in a wry twist. "Forty-five minutes curled up in an armchair doesn't count as sleep, Miss West."

"I'm fine."

"You're not fine," says Connor, still with that soft voice. He must see my anger at his contradiction, because he adds, "I know you need to be clear-headed, and I also know you need *sleep* to be clearheaded. Let your program do its work. Harry's right. There's nothing more we can do for now."

Waiting. I'm no good at it. I'm even worse at taking directions. But judging by the expression on Harry's face, it looks like

I'm going to be doing both of those things whether I like it or not.

Slowly, I stand. Miranda stops pacing long enough to send me a cool glance. "You said you know him, this Maelstr0m."

I nod, feeling Ryan's eyes on me. For such sweet baby blues, they're downright scary.

"And that he likes to create chaos."

I nod again.

Miranda says, "What if—to unruffle his feathers, as you put it—what if we give him the *appearance* of chaos?"

Harry asks, "How?" but I'm already on the same page with Miranda.

"A press conference," I say, staring at her. "But you'd have to act really—"

"Devastated," she murmurs, warming to the idea. She moves closer, her eyes brightening. "Tears?"

"Gallons. If you can pull it off realistically, faint."

Her smile is savage. "I've spent the last twenty years around actors. I can pull it off."

With narrowed eyes, Connor looks back and forth between the two of us. "I thought you didn't want publicity, Miranda. If you give a press conference—and *cry*—it'll be a media circus. You'll be all over the news, here and abroad."

At the same time, Miranda and I say, "Exactly."

Harry says flatly, "No press conferences."

Miranda looks at him. "You'll speak too," she says in a tone reserved for royalty addressing peasants. "What should he say, Tabitha?"

My lips curve into a smile, just as savage as the one Miranda wore. "That the studio has experienced a major breach in its network and you're coming forward with it because Miranda thinks it's important to be transparent with the public and her shareholders. That the business and government communities can only catch these cyber criminals by working together. That the hacker responsible is the Hannibal Lecter of computer crime, the head of a highly sophisticated, vertically integrated global network of hackers, and his capture could have even more far-reaching effects than the capture of Bin Laden."

I pause. "Make sure you use both those names. He'll love that shit."

Harry erupts in anger. "Are you crazy?" he shouts. "I can't go on national television and compare a hacker to *Bin Laden*!"

"Leak it anonymously, then," responds Miranda calmly. "Or compare him to Hitler." Her eyes meet mine. "I know a thing or two about men with gargantuan egos. One thing they all have in common is they want to be recognized as the best. Even if being the best means being the worst."

"Absolutely not!" barks Harry, but Miranda isn't having any of his attitude.

"Would you like me to call your superior?" she asks, one blonde eyebrow arched.

Harry has to take several deep breaths before he managers to answer. Veins are popping out all over his neck. "My superior," he says between clenched teeth, "is the *President of the United States*."

Miranda's expression is serene. "I know. We've met on more than one occasion. He's a big movie buff. I gave him a personal tour of the lot." She smiles lazily. "He invited me to spend the night in the Lincoln bedroom at the White House."

The subtext is clear. The leader of the free world has the hots for Miranda.

You have to admire a woman who can render four grown men speechless. I cover my mouth with my hand to hide my smile.

Connor clears his throat. "Well. We'll leave you to figure out the details. Harry, you know how to reach me. Tabby..." He sears me with a look. "Let's go."

I snort. "You're funny, jarhead."

"I'm not joking. We're leaving. Together."

Now everyone is looking at us. Heat sweeps up my neck. I say quietly, "No."

Harry intervenes. "You can have two federal agents assigned to you, Miss West, or you can have Metrix. Your choice. But until this investigation is over, someone is keeping eyes on you twenty-four-seven."

Livid, I glare at him. "I know my rights—"

"Use that big brain of yours to think of all the perfectly legal scenarios where you end up a lot worse than simply followed, Miss West. I've got fifteen agents who'll swear under oath they saw you hack into the FBI's database like you'd been doing it for years."

It takes almost all my self-control not to execute a spinning axe kick on this turncoat and knock his head off his shoulders. "You gave me immunity for that!"

His brows lift. "Really? Because as I recall, those words never left my mouth. And we still haven't addressed the issue Agent Rodriguez brought up—Polaroid, in case you've forgotten —or the fact that you were once intimately acquainted with our new friend Mr. Søren Killgaard, hacker and extortionist, and, by your own admission, possible terrorist. I've got so much prob-able cause to lock you up, I could make a very convincing case for Guantanamo."

When I take a step forward, my hands curled to fists, Connor is there to stop me.

"Easy, tiger."

He stands in front of me, gazing down at me with that annoying look from before, like he thinks I'm made of glass and it's his job to make sure I don't get broken.

The only thing in danger of breaking here is someone's jaw.

"Fine." My voice is cold as I look up into his eyes. "Metrix it is. Ryan?"

"Yes, ma'am?" Ryan answers over Connor's shoulder.

Still looking into Connor's eyes, I say, "Will you please accompany me to my hotel?"

Ryan drawls, "Be happy to, Tabby."

Connor's face darkens. There's murder in his eyes.

Unintimidated, I stare up at him. "Move."

"If you think you're going anywhere without me," he says, deadly soft, "you're mistaken."

Ryan ambles over, slings an arm around my shoulders, and grins down at me. "Looks like it's a threesome, then." He winks. "Lucky girl."

I know Ryan notices the way Connor's nostrils flare, the way his lips flatten, the way his body, invaded with a sudden tension, falls perfectly still. I know because as Ryan leads me away toward the door, he leans down and murmurs into my ear, "He didn't tell me shit about what's goin' on between the two of you, Tabby, but I'll tell you one thing. I've never seen him like this. Not over a woman, not over anything. The rest of the boys at Metrix call him 'Teflon,' because nothin' ever sticks. So here's somethin' for you to think on. You fuck with my boy, you're fuckin' with me."

When he pulls back, his smile is gone. His baby blues drill straight down into my soul. "And I'm no sexist. I'll take you down even if you *are* a girl."

Strangely, this little speech endears him to me. My spirits somewhat lightened, I nudge him in the ribs. "You could try, but big guys like you are always super slow."

Unsure of what to make of my nonchalance, he cocks his head. "Is that a fact?"

I nod. "Glacially slow. On account of all that muscle mass. You're too bulky. Now, *me* on the other hand—I'm ninja fast. Like lightning fast. Like"—I snap my fingers—"*Shazam!*"

Ryan's trying hard to keep the stern look on his face, but I know that in spite of himself and the warning he just gave me, he's inclined to like me.

What surprises me is that I'm inclined to like him too. And not because I dig his tattoos or his dimples or his disarming combination of sweet Southern drawl and gun-toting badassery.

I like him because he's a good friend of Connor's. Because he obviously has Connor's back, and would do anything for him. Because somehow I'm living in an alternate universe where those things have become important benchmarks against which my opinion of people is measured.

Even if I despise him.

Which I do.

Which I keep telling myself as Ryan leads me out of the room while Connor follows behind us, burning holes in the back of my head with his eyes.

By the time we pull up in front of my hotel, I can barely keep my eyes open. I've slept less than one hour in the last day. Everything is getting fuzzy around the edges.

When Connor opens my door—I'm in the back of Ryan's rented Escalade because I refused to sit up front when Connor announced he was driving—I jump out and immediately stumble.

Connor catches me. His hands grip my arms for support.

"Do I need to carry you?"

I shake him off. "Try it and I'll introduce you to a thousand new forms of pain," I grumble.

Ryan rounds the front of the SUV. "You two lovebirds need a little privacy? I can make myself scarce—"

In unison, Connor and I snap, "We're not lovebirds!"

Then we stare at each other in silence while Ryan whoops with laughter. "Roger that! *Not* lovebirds!" Grinning, he comes to stand beside us. He slaps Connor on the back. "So, notlovebirds, you need a little privacy or what?"

"Is he always like this?" I ask Connor.

"He hasn't even gotten started," he sourly replies.

"Aw, c'mon now!" Ryan gives Connor's shoulder a friendly shake, which doesn't budge his big frame. "I'm just providin' a little relief from all the unresolved sexual tension, my friends! Thought I was gonna choke on it on the ride over!" Turning practical, he props his hands on his hips. "You two really should get it over with and bone so we can focus on work."

Connor's face turns red. Instead of being embarrassed, I'm amused. "What was it you said to me at the hotel, Connor? Oh yes—great minds think alike. I guess you two graduated from the same charm school?"

Ryan nods. "Oh yeah. We're a couple of real charmin' motherfuckers. Ask anyone." He spots a woman walking through the sliding glass doors to the lobby who's checking out him and Connor over her shoulder. His grin returns in full force. "You see? Proof's in the puddin'." He turns his grin on me and waggles his eyebrows. "Or should I say panties."

I roll my eyes. "It's like you're twelve."

Connor says drily, "That's giving him a lot of credit."

"Okay. Now that we've established my babysitters are the world's worst driver and a randy twelve-year-old, can I please go to my room and get some sleep?"

Ryan's brows pull together. "Randy? Is that one of them poo-poo British words for handsome?"

Connor's eyes briefly close. "Horny, brother. It means horny."

Ryan acts affronted. "Hey, don't get all uppity with me, boss, at least I'm not the world's worst driver." When he winks at me, I think he might be becoming one of my favorite people.

It's a short list.

"C'mon, then." Connor holds out an arm. "After you, Tabby."

When we enter the lobby, Ryan says to Connor, "I'll be down here if you need me." He ambles over to a sofa and makes himself comfortable with his feet up on the glass coffee table. The concierge looks at him with pinched lips, disapproving of him using their furniture like it's a frat house, but when Ryan notices his stare and raises his brows, the concierge sniffs and looks away.

I'm gifted with another of Ryan's winks. Shaking his head, Connor steers me toward the elevators.

"You're not coming anywhere near my room," I say stiffly, "so don't get any ideas."

Connor stabs his finger to the elevator call button. A muscle in his jaw is jumping like crazy. He doesn't say a word, just stands next to me in silence until the elevator arrives. We step inside.

"What floor?" he asks.

"Eight."

He presses the button. The doors slide shut. As soon as the car starts to rise, Connor presses the Stop button, and the elevator comes to a jerking halt.

"What the—"

"I'm sorry." He bites it out, moving in front of me. His body blocks the doors. I quickly back up, only to find myself up against the mirrored wall. To stop his advance, I brace my hand flat against his chest and lock my elbow.

"Don't you *dare*," I say through gritted teeth, staring him down.

He gazes back at me with fire in his eyes. Every inch of his body is filled with tension.

"I'm sorry," he says again, his voice husky. "But you're keeping so much to yourself and I have to find out secondhand about your uncle and that you *lived* with Søren—you won't just be honest with me. How was I supposed to react?"

"I *have been* honest with you," I counter, hearing how tight the words sound because my throat is closing with emotion. "I might be a lot of shitty things, but I'm *not* a liar!"

Connor blinks. His dark brows draw together. "You're not one single shitty thing."

I whisper, "You don't know me."

"Yes, I do."

"No you—"

"You live alone," he interrupts. "You don't trust anyone. Your only friend is a fifteen-year-old girl who reminds you of yourself, smart and odd and lonely. Before that, your only friend was a woman whose entire identity was made up...by you. Because she was like you too, completely alone in the world, mistreated and misunderstood, and by helping her, you did what no one had ever taken the time to do for you, namely—be on your team. You're a team of one. And I suspect that's because of Søren, because you've never gotten past whatever it was between you. Because he somehow taught you that trust is worse than anything else."

He pauses. "How am I doing so far?"

I swallow around the lump in my throat. The arm I have braced against his chest starts to tremble.

Connor's voice softens, and so do his eyes. "When the exact opposite is true. Trust is *better* than anything else. Ryan, that goofball downstairs? I trust him with my life. I'd take a bullet for him. There's nothing we wouldn't do for each other. Nothing."

He reaches out, gently brushes away a lock of hair from my cheek, cups my face in his hand. "I want that for us too."

I struggle to keep the waver from my voice. "You move pretty fast, soldier. First it was one night you wanted, then one week, and now it's bullet-taking trust?" My soft laugh sounds choked. "I think you've got the wrong girl."

"No, I don't." He takes my face in both his hands, forces me to meet his eyes. "You can trust me, Tabby. I'm not him. I'll never lie to you. I'll never let you down when you need me. I might irritate the shit out of you and say or do something stupid once in a while because I'm a guy and sometimes we're clueless, but if you want me to, I'll give you one thousand percent and have your back one thousand percent and be one thousand percent on your team."

His eyes shine so bright, they look unreal. "I want to be on your team."

I can't breathe. My throat has closed. There's water in my eyes—fucking *tears*! I want to slap myself.

"You're just trying to get laid."

He smiles. "Can you blame me? Look at yourself, baby."

"I'm not your baby!"

His smile deepens. "I stand corrected. Sugar? Sunshine? Angel?"

I shake my head to clear it and give his chest a push. He steps back, releasing me. He makes no move to come closer again, just keeps watching me with those warm, beautiful eyes.

Eyes that, if I'm not careful, I'll fall so far into, I'll never be able to crawl back out.

"Let's go." I cross my arms over my chest and stare at the sliding doors.

After a moment of silence, Connor says, "All right." He pushes the Stop button again, and the car lurches into motion. We stand unspeaking as my heart thunders. When the elevator stops on my floor and the doors open, Connor adds ominously, "But this conversation isn't over. And remember, I'm not *him*."

He steps out of the elevator and strides down the hall.

TABBY

hen I wake up, it's dark outside and I have no idea where I am.

I bolt upright in bed. It takes a moment for me to recognize the unfamiliar room and for my heart to slow from a gallop to a trot. I drag my hands through my hair, rub my eyes, get up, and use the toilet, brush my teeth. When my stomach starts to make angry growling noises I realize I'm ravenous. I think I had only one or two bites of the sandwich at the commissary at the studio before what Harry was saying made my stomach turn sour and my appetite flee.

I order room service and then take a shower, wondering where Connor is. He left me at my door with a promise that if I tried to run away, he'd find me, and then I slammed the door in his face. According to my watch, that was six hours ago.

Six hours of tossing and sweating and nightmares I thought I'd outgrown.

But no. Once horror sinks its claws into you, it never lets go. I should have known better.

The hotel's robe is one of those poufy white terry cloth

affairs that are totally impractical but highly comfortable. I put it on, turn on the TV, and wait for room service to arrive.

When I hear a noise outside my door, I cross the room and open it.

And find Connor asleep on the floor.

He's sitting upright, back against the wall, arms hanging over his bent knees, dark head bowed, breathing evenly. I don't know whether to knock him over or go back inside and call hotel security. It might be fun to see him try to explain himself.

Unmoving, he says, "If you kick me I'll take you over my knees, woman."

His voice is scratchy with sleep, low and impossibly sexy.

Irritatingly sexy.

"It's princess," I say impulsively.

Connor looks up at me. He blinks slowly several times.

"Not woman or baby or sugar or any of that other stuff. And especially not sweet cheeks." My face is red, I can feel it. "I like princess, because it's ironic. Okay?"

A smile tugs at the corners of his lips. He nods. He needs a shave and to run a comb through that dark mop on his head, but he still looks so goddamn handsome, I feel sorry for the rest of the men on earth.

Then I feel sorry for myself. I'm beginning to realize just how much it's going to hurt when all this is over.

At the end of the hall, the elevator opens. A uniformed waiter gets off, pushing a rolling cart. I lift my hand and wave.

"Down here!"

The guy—grinning and tanned, has the look of an aspiring actor—waves back. In the blink of an eye, Connor is on his feet. He stretches with his arms over his head. His black T-shirt is so tight, I can see every ridged outline of abdominal muscle through it.

I can see his nipples through it.

I find myself wondering if it's only the thought of food that's making my mouth suddenly water.

"Got a lot for you here, miss," says the waiter cheerfully. He glances at Connor and comes to an abrupt stop. "Should I set it up inside?"

I notice Connor staring hungrily at the cart. From beneath the domed silver plates, delicious scents waft up: cheeseburger and fries, chicken wings, mac and cheese, nachos with the works. I couldn't decide what I wanted so I ordered everything that looked good.

It's more than enough for two.

I wave the waiter in. "Yes, please. On the coffee table is fine." When he rolls past me into the room, I sigh and tighten the belt on my robe. "All right, soldier, you can come in for a minute. But just to eat, okay?"

Connor looks at me from under his lashes. "Roger that."

How he manages to make that sound so perilous, I have no idea. I decide to stay as far away from him as possible and get him out as quickly as possible because, judging by the tingling happening throughout my body from his look, I'm in serious danger of making a bad decision if he stays too long.

Another bad decision.

Shit.

The room service guy sets up the food, silverware, and a carafe of water on the coffee table, then has me sign the bill. He leaves, closing the door quietly behind him, and then Connor and I are alone.

"Where do you want me?" Connor asks.

I know it's only my imagination that makes it sound sexual, because he's not doing anything remotely suggestive, but damn if my vagina isn't shouting, *In here, big boy!*

"At the desk," I blurt, too loudly.

Connor gives me an odd look. Ignoring it, I make myself a plate, pour a glass of water, and go sit on the chair across the room, at a safe distance. After watching me for a moment, Connor gets himself a plate of food, sits down at the desk, and starts to eat.

I notice it again, how elegant he is for a man his size. He eats with perfect self-possession, almost regally. He walks the same way, easy, smooth, with an economy of motion that's unusually graceful. Normally, big men thump around noisily, eat noisily, take up too much space. Connor takes up a lot of space, but it's his presence—quiet and intense, dangerous and still—and not a loud, arrogant swagger that calls attention to itself.

I've seen it happen many times. When Connor is in a room, every eye instinctively turns his way, even if he's just sitting there not saying a word.

He notices me watching. "You're gonna give me a complex, princess."

I flush and look down at my plate. "Any news from O'Doul?"

He doesn't mention my awkward segue. "'Bout an hour ago. All quiet. Miranda scheduled the press conference for five tomorrow evening. Word is already all over the Internet. Speculation is tending toward two camps, her resignation or a major hack."

I'm relieved, both because Søren hasn't taken any action—yet—and about the rumors. I know they'll please him.

It was smart for her to do it later instead of the morning. If I know Søren, Miranda's just bought us another day. He won't want to do anything before he sees the show.

The television keeps us company as we finish our food. Having Connor here isn't as awkward as I thought it would be, and gradually I begin to relax.

Then, out of nowhere, he says, "When I was fourteen, my brother Mikey died."

Startled, I look up. Connor is staring at his plate.

"Fell out of a tree in our backyard. Wasn't even that tall of a tree, but it didn't matter. Mikey was five. The baby. I was the oldest. Of six, all boys, my poor mother. Anyway, after that I developed a fear of heights." He snaps his fingers. "Boom. Like that. Totally irrational, I wasn't even near Mikey when it happened, didn't see him fall, nothing. But from the day of Mikey's funeral on, I couldn't stand to be anywhere my feet weren't touching solid ground. I'd get dizzy going up ladders. Felt like my heart would explode if I had to climb a flight of stairs. Which was really fucking inconvenient considering my bedroom was on the second floor of our house. I even cried when my father made me go up into the attic to get the Christmas ornaments."

I'm astonished. "You? *Cry?*"

He lifts a shoulder. "Not my proudest moment, but yeah. My point is that I get it. Suffering over something you have no control over, that you picked up secondhand."

He looks up at me. His eyes are penetrating. "Your fear of flying, I'm talking about."

I don't know what to say. His confession and the direction this is taking are so unexpected, I'm literally speechless.

He wipes his mouth with a napkin, tosses it to his plate, and stands. When he looks at me his expression is empathetic. "What I'm trying so badly to say is that there's a way out."

This is dangerous territory. But after a moment, my curiosity overcomes my hesitation. "Which is?"

"Through."

When I blink at him, confused, he clarifies.

"The obstacle *is* the way. The thing that ails you is also the cure. There's no running away or going around or over. There's no avoidance. Avoidance is just a guarantee you'll never prevail. You have to push *through*, to the other side of your fear. The obstacle itself is the way through."

My heart is doing something strange inside my chest.

"You're saying I should suck it up, put on my big-girl panties, and get on a plane."

"I'm saying that the only way you're ever going to get this monkey off your back is if you give it the middle finger and tell it to go fuck itself. I *know* you're capable of that."

Give the monkey on my back the middle finger.

I study his face for a long time in tense silence before I speak again. "So that worked for you with your fear of heights?"

Connor slowly moves away from the desk. He looks at the bed, and then looks away quickly, almost guiltily, as if he caught himself doing something bad. Agitated now, he starts to pace back and forth across the room.

I can't help but think of a lion, pacing in his cage.

"My father—a Texas ranch man, raised longhorns, still does —said no son of his was gonna turn out to be a lily-livered sniveler, so he basically forced me to join the Marines. And thank fuck he did, because by the time I was seventeen, I was on the express train to the United States penal system. So I *had* to deal with my shit. The military doesn't care about your dainty little phobias. You *must* climb that rope, you *must* scale that wall, you *will* learn to be a team member and a leader and an example for others, in spite of yourself. Or you're out. Disgraced.

"And though I was a hardheaded little fucker, even at seventeen I knew I'd rather die than be disgraced. So it became about more than just me and my fear. It became about making my father proud. About making my brothers proud. About honoring Mikey's memory, instead of letting it cripple me."

After I overcome my shock, I say softly, "Connor. That's sort of...beautiful."

"Thanks," he says gruffly.

Then it seems neither of us knows what to say, because we just look at each other in awkward silence.

Finally, I draw enough courage to ask, "But you're not really talking about my fear of flying, are you?"

He looks at me for a long time, and then blows out a hard breath and looks away. "You said something to me in the car on the drive out here that stuck with me. After I told you the story about the hero and the princess, you remember?"

When he looks back at me, I nod.

"You said, 'A real hero would teach the princess how to save herself.' I thought that was so profound. I couldn't stop thinking about it." His voice gets gruff. "About you. What it might mean to you, if I could…help you save yourself."

There's no more air in the room. There's nothing left to breathe. When I look down at my hands, they're shaking.

Connor softly curses. "I'm sorry. I know you don't want to talk about him—"

"It's all right. You've been fair." I glance up and meet his eyes. "It's just that…some things shouldn't be said out loud. It's dangerous, summoning old ghosts. You never know what they might want from you in return for digging them out of their graves."

Connor looks disturbed by that but waits to see if I'll say more. There's so much I should tell him, so much I'd like to say but can't. But he deserves some explanation, at least, and so I try.

I rise from the chair, cross to the window, and stare out with my arms tightly wrapped around myself. I exhale a ragged breath.

"I have a little black box inside my head where I keep all the memories of that year I lived with Søren. It's this trick I learned. Compartmentalization, my therapist called it. The box is there to keep me safe. It has a big metal lock and sits in a dark corner with a layer of dust on top inches thick. Inside the box are monsters." As I speak, my voice is growing more and more constricted. "I can't open that box, Connor. Not even for you. But I will tell you this."

I swallow twice before I can continue. "I haven't lied to you about anything. I'm holding things back, yes, but it's only to protect myself, not to deceive you. And I don't…" My voice drops to a whisper. "I don't want you to hear all the ugliness. Especially now."

I hear him move behind me. I see his reflection in the glass. He's so close, I can feel the heat radiating from his body.

"Why especially now?"

My laugh is soft and ragged. "You know why."

When I feel his hands gently rest on my shoulders, I don't pull away. Then his mouth is next to my ear, and his voice is a low, sexy rasp.

"Because you're falling in love with me."

"Don't flatter yourself!" I scoff, but his words leave me breathless.

He threads his fingers through my hair, makes a fist, and softly tugs so my head falls back.

He whispers, "I'm not," and kisses me.

It's different, this kiss. So different from any we've shared before. It's not demanding but endlessly giving, tender and sweet, filled with unspoken promises.

"I want to be on your team."

Startled by the swell of emotion rising inside me, I break away, but he spins me around, pulls me back against him, and kisses me again. His strong arms wrap tightly around my body.

"I'll give you one thousand percent."

I want to pound against his chest but my arms are trapped between us, and they don't want to pound—they want to wind up around his shoulders and never let go.

"I'll never let you down when you need me."

When I make a sound of desperation, Connor breaks the kiss but keeps his tight hold on me, keeps me so close I can feel his heart hammering, like my own.

"That's why you were so mad at me in the cafeteria," he says roughly, breathing hard. "Why you're always so mad at me.

Because I keep hurting you. And I couldn't hurt you unless you *care*."

He kisses me again, but it's rougher this time, edged with raw emotion. I stumble backward, and we slam into the desk, rattling the lamp. It topples off the edge to the floor. Connor leans forward. I'm forced back. My leg instinctively comes up as I try to keep my balance. My robe slips open over my bare thigh.

His mouth is hot and delicious. His tongue knows exactly what to do. Though I hate myself for it, my body responds as it always does to his touch, and I allow the kiss to go on longer than I should just because it feels so good.

Connor groans softly into my mouth. With one hand under my butt, he lifts me and scoots me up onto the desk. Now my thighs are open around his waist and my robe has fallen away and his hands are buried in my hair and digging into the flesh of my bottom and I'm dizzy, so dizzy I think the room has started to spin.

My head drops back. I gasp for air. He moves his mouth to my neck, sucking and biting with just enough pressure to sting. I shudder with the pleasure of it, and my lips part on a moan.

He tears open my robe.

With a muttered oath, he takes my breast in his hand and sucks on my hard nipple.

Arching, I cry out. In one swift motion, he sweeps his arm across the desk behind me, shoving away the telephone, a stack of magazines, a cup filled with pens. In a clatter, they follow the lamp to the floor. Connor pushes me flat on my back on the desk. He ravishes my breasts, moving greedily back and forth between them, sucking, licking, biting, making hungry, masculine noises as if he's tearing into a steak.

From somewhere far away, I hear myself moan his name. My fingers twist in his hair. My hips rock helplessly.

Then he throws my legs over his shoulders, puts his face between my thighs and starts to feast.

And something happens that's never happened to me before.

My mind blinks offline.

It's not a slammed door, or a blackness like a curtain pulled across a window. It's a release, like when you let something heavy fall from your hands.

"Fuck me," I demand. "*Now*."

Connor looks up from between my trembling thighs. He licks his full lips. His black eyes are like an animal's. "I don't have a condom."

"I'm clean. Are you?"

"Yes." Then he straightens, rips down his zipper, frees his stiff cock, and pushes it inside me.

I cry out. My back bows from the desk. I grip the edge of the desk to keep myself in place as Connor starts to thrust into me, his hands on my ass and his eyes on my face, those black animal eyes staring down like they want to devour me.

"Take off your shirt."

He pauses for a fraction of a moment to comply, using one hand to grip his black T-shirt at the back of his neck and then drag it over his head. He tosses it away, and I'm treated to the sight of bronzed skin and hard abs and biceps that flex and bulge as he begins to thrust again. With every move, his dog tags glint in the light.

"You're beautiful, jarhead," I say brokenly.

He pants, "I'm yours, princess."

With a painful burst, my heart fragments into a million jagged pieces.

The world fades to nothing but sensation. The push and drag of his body inside mine, his heat, weight, and scent, the sound of our labored breaths, flesh against flesh, the complaining groan of the desk beneath me.

The taste of all I can never have bittersweet on my tongue.

With a helpless cry of surrender, I close my eyes and disappear.

20

CONNOR

*T*abby's orgasm is so abrupt, the force of it so violent, for a moment I'm stunned into motionless shock.

She's strong, with the thighs of a runner, a taut figure honed by what must be countless hours of the practice of Krav Maga, and so the flex of her legs around my waist is no small thing. But really it's her abandon that takes my breath away. The change that transforms her from one second to the next. The new way she gives herself to me, as if all her walls are crumbling, all the brakes have been stripped, everything she's been holding back has broken through and is flooding her at once.

As if she's finally *here*.

With this woman, you're always dealing first and foremost with her formidable mind. The force of it is evident in every look. She's beautiful, yes, blatantly, but the razor-sharp edge of her intellect gives her a prickly, untouchable quality. The rose is there in full bloom for you to admire, but watch out for those enormous thorns. They're full of venom and have a taste for blood.

But this new woman beneath me now, *this* woman is all emotion. All head-tossing, passionate abandon. She's writhing like a demon on my cock and begging me to fuck her, fuck her harder, and I'm three seconds away from losing control. So I do the only thing I can.

Slow it down.

I lift her, wrapping my arms around her back, and carry her over to the bed.

She moans as our bodies briefly disengage, then again, louder, as I lower her to the mattress, spread her legs, and gently push back inside her. She flings her arms and legs around me, turns her face to my neck, and shudders.

"Deeper," she pleads, sounding desperate. "Harder. More, Connor. *More!*"

"I don't want to come yet, sweetheart," I murmur. Sheathed deep inside her, my cock throbs.

"He does." She wriggles her hips.

I growl and then kiss her deeply, still not moving my pelvis.

She starts to rock underneath me, flexing her hips so my cock slides in and out as she moves. I hiss in a breath at the feeling, my balls tightening, sweat breaking out on my chest.

Tabby digs her fingers into my ass and bites me on the neck.

I can't help myself. I thrust into her, hard, a groan torn from my throat.

She makes an encouraging sound. Her bite gentles to a suck, her hands glide up my back. Her nipples skim my chest, twin points of pebbled flesh that need my mouth, and so I give it to them.

Tabby moans, bucking. "Yes," she breathes, eyes squeezed shut. "Oh God, Connor, yes."

Hot, concentrated pleasure coils at the base of my cock, an ache that pulses through my entire lower body. My thrusts become deeper, less controlled. My breathing turns to grunts and broken groans. She's so wet I feel it on my thighs, and something about that drives me insane with lust.

I release her nipple, grab her by the hair, and thrust my

tongue into her mouth. I hold her head in place as I fuck her pussy and her mouth, driving deep, feeling the last of my control begin to unwind, only vaguely aware of the hollow echo of the headboard slamming against the wall.

"No—you can't—in my mouth," she pants, breaking free.

Dazed as I am, I don't understand for a moment, but then with a push she rolls out from under me, flips around, shoves me to my back, straddles my face, and swallows my cock.

I lose myself. Thought ceases. My body strains up against her mouth. The sound of pleasure that breaks from my chest is loud and raw.

She draws up, sucking, and then furls her tongue around the head. Making a humming sound in her throat as if she's pleased with me, how I taste and feel in her mouth, she lowers her head again and opens her throat so my entire cock is bathed in wet heat, all the way down to the base.

When she gently squeezes my balls, I bury my face into her pussy and unleash my tongue.

She squeals and shudders. I hold her tight against me with my forearms locked at her waist, my hands spread over her ass, and suckle her swollen clit. She starts a breathtaking assault on my cock, up and down, sucking relentlessly, falling into rhythm with my desperate upward thrusts.

I hold on with sheer force of will. The impulse to release pounds through me, growing with every stroke of her clever tongue, but I won't let go until she does. I can tell by the trembling in her body, her noises and breathing, that she's close.

I slide a hand down the curve of her ass and slip a finger into her wetness. She moans around my cock, an incredible sensation I'll remember for the rest of my life. I let her ride my tongue and finger for a moment longer, feeling the tension in her cresting, almost ready to break, and then wet the thumb of my other hand.

I press it against the tight pink calyx between the cleft in her cheeks and push.

She comes almost instantly, shuddering and mewing, bucking against my mouth, completely abandoned to her pleasure. Her fist tightens around the base of my cock, stroking now in tandem with her tongue, and finally I can't hold on anymore.

My orgasm is an explosion, ripping through me, tearing me apart. Wave after wave after wave and I'm convulsing, moaning into her spread legs, fucking her mouth and eating her gorgeous pussy, knowing in some abandoned part of my soul there will never be anything as perfectly perfect as—

Her.

Us.

This.

❧

Afterward, we lie in each other's arms, stunned and silent, staring at the ceiling.

Finally, Tabby whispers, "Wow."

I turn my head on the pillow and look at her. A grin spreads over my face. "You're speechless, right?"

She sends me a sideways warning glance. "If you say 'I have that effect on all the ladies,' I'll be forced to do something violent." She pauses. "I can't think of what exactly because my brain is taking a nice oxytocin and dopamine bath at the moment. But it will be bad, believe me."

I roll to my side, gather her against me, and nuzzle my face into her hair, inhaling her sweet scent. "I'll die happy, though." My voice comes out thick, and for a second, I'm worried I've ruined this incredible moment by being a dumb, sappy fuck.

Her legs tangle between mine. When she settles into my embrace, sighing contentedly, my worry eases.

After another moment, her voice drowsy and sated, she asks, "You have kind of a butt thing, don't you?"

I burst out laughing. She raises her head and looks at me, a brow quirked.

I roll her to her back and throw my leg over her, relishing the simple fact that I can. "I have a thing for *your* butt, to be specific, yes," I answer, grinning down at her.

Her cheeks flush. She turns her head and lowers her eyes, but I can see she's pleased.

A thought occurs to me. "Would you want me to—"

"Fuck me in the ass?" she asks innocently.

I almost choke. "Jesus!" I say, racked with laughter. "Give a guy a second to make his point, would you?"

She rolls her eyes. "Oh please, don't tell me you're shocked Mr. 'I'm gonna get you naked and eat your pussy like it's the last supper.' That's practically sacrilegious."

It's my turn to pretend innocence. "I'd never say a thing like that to a delicate flower such as yourself."

Tabby smiles, curling her toes around the back of my calf. "Oh, but you would. And worse. And I love every second of it, by the way."

Love. It hangs in the air for a moment. We look at each other, breathless, and then Tabby looks away.

She stammers, "I-I…um, we should probably get going—"

"Look at me." When she doesn't, I take her face in my hand. "Tabby. Look at me."

The old tension in her has returned with a cold snap. I know she's hating herself for that slip, hating that we both noticed it, the elephant that's appeared like magic in the room.

She wants to push the elephant out the window. I want to invite it to stay for a drink.

Or forever.

I run my thumb over her lips. She closes her eyes. "Why do I get the feeling you're not going to let me pretend I didn't say that?"

I gently kiss her jaw, her cheek, the curve of her eyebrow. "Because I'm not."

"It was just a figure of speech. A random choice of words."

I whisper, "You'd like to think it was, wouldn't you?"

She's getting frustrated, fidgeting underneath me like she wants to bolt and run. "Let me up."

"No."

"Connor—"

Into her ear, I say very deliberately, "You can love how I talk to you without having to commit the rest of your life to me, princess."

She stills. The color is high in her cheeks. Her heart is pounding.

My heart is melting like a fucking ice cube in the sun.

"It doesn't have to be a four-letter word between us. Okay?"

Her lips twist. "Except it *is* a four-letter word."

"Hmm. You're right. Maybe we should add a letter to get us out of the danger zone if you feel the need to use the word again."

She glances at me warily, her cheeks still red.

"To describe how you feel about my sexual prowess, of course."

She groans. "God. I've created a monster."

Ignoring that, I muse, "How about…slove. 'I slove the way you talk to me.'" Then I make a face. "No. That's weird."

Tabby covers her face with a hand. "This is *all* weird!"

For whatever bizarre reason, this conversation is making me hard again. I guess my dick is as excited about Tabby's Freudian slip as I am. "What about this: 'glove.' That's an actual word so it's not as weird. 'Connor, I absolutely *glove* that enormous cock of yours! Will you please let me lick it again?'"

In spite of herself, Tabby laughs. She tries to smother it, keep her lips pressed together, but her body shakes with the effort.

"Too obvious? You're right. It should be something no one else would recognize. Our little code word, don't you think? Something that won't give it away if you accidentally slip and say it in front of anyone else." I think for a moment, and then pronounce, "Loathe!"

Tabby looks at me like I'm a nut job. "What?"

"Loathe. It's got three of the same letters as love but it's the *opposite*, so it'll make you feel really happy when you're saying it since you can't stand me and everything. For instance, 'Connor, I loathe your sense of humor as much as I loathe your face!' It's genius, right?"

Beaming, I look at her for confirmation. She's doing this adorable thing where she's laughing and groaning and shaking her head, all at once. "You're crazy!"

I give her a soft bite on her neck. "I was fine before I met you, princess. Now look at me. I need a straitjacket."

She freezes.

"What is it?"

She blinks rapidly, swallowing, the color draining from her face. "What? Nothing."

"Yeah," I say drily, "I'm calling bullshit on that, sweetheart. Spill."

With sudden vehemence, Tabby snaps, "We don't have to talk about *everything*!"

She shoves me in the chest, hard, and leaps from the bed, leaving me stunned by the sudden change in her mood.

I watch her stalk around the room, snatching up the clothes she'd left hanging over the arm of the sofa and the back of the chair, muttering something under her breath.

"You're giving me whiplash here, princess."

"Well, deal with it," she says, dragging her T-shirt over her head. She stops and looks down at herself, mutters, "Fuck," and tears the T-shirt off. She storms over to her suitcase lying open on a folding luggage rack against the wall. She rummages through it, tossing clothes aside, and then pulls out a pair of black leather pants I recognize.

I sit up in bed and drag a hand through my hair. "Not the armor again," I say wearily, watching her get dressed.

She barely glances at me. In less time than I've seen some bullets hit a target, she's dressed and pulling on her combat boots.

And I know our little oasis of happiness has vanished like the mirage it was.

I rise, and dress quickly and silently. Then I hear a small electronic alarm chirping somewhere in the room and cock an ear toward the sound. "What's that?"

Tabby pulls up short. "It's my phone." She bolts over to the dresser, snatches up her cell, and stares down at it. When she looks at me, there's something wild in her eyes. "The traceback program," she whispers. "It's compiled its report."

"Well then," I say, a brick inside my stomach. "I guess it's time to go."

We stare at each other silently across the room, until Tabby nods.

"Yeah. I guess so."

She turns to leave. I have no choice but to follow.

21

TABBY

*a*fter a tense elevator ride during which we both said nothing and tried to pretend nothing had happened, we come downstairs to find Ryan doing pushups in the middle of the lobby floor.

Connor stops several feet away and crosses his arms over his chest. "Working off some steam, brother?"

"Fifty," Ryan grunts. He's breathing a little harder than normal but doesn't look as if he's exerting himself all that much. I'd bet good money he could easily do another fifty more without breaking a sweat. With a pointed look at Connor, he says, "I could ask you the same question, brother."

He glances at me and then goes back to his pushups.

"Oh, for fuck's sake!" I say, aggravated because we're so obvious. I set my hands on my hips and huff out a breath.

Ryan stops at the top of a pushup and gives me some major side-eye. "Ex*act*ly," he drawls.

I throw my hands in the air. "That's it. He's your problem," I say to Connor, and storm off.

Yes, I'm acting nuts. You would be too, if you'd just had the best sex of your life and accidentally said the "L" word to your enemy/fuck buddy in the middle of an FBI investigation into the man who wrecked your trust in humanity and murdered your last living relative.

I really need to rethink this whole no-drinking thing.

I go outside to the valet stand and bark orders at the poor guy on duty to get our Escalade from the garage. When he asks me for my ticket, I snap at him just to bring whichever black Cadillac he finds first.

Then, from behind me, Ryan patiently says, "Here you go." He presents his parking ticket to the valet guy, who scurries off in search of saner people.

Connor isn't with Ryan. "Where is he?" I jerk my chin toward the sliding doors.

"Dunno." Ryan folds his arms over his chest and looks down his nose at me. "Probably in there breakin' a few heads to make himself feel better about whatever happened between you two upstairs over the last few hours."

"I slept!"

Ryan snorts. "Yeah? Was that before or after you gutted him like a fish?"

I stare at him, feeling the blood pounding in my cheeks, wishing I had it in me to poke his eyes out with my thumbs.

But I don't. I actually like the guy.

So damn inconvenient.

I cover my face with my hands and groan. Ryan slings his arm over my shoulders and gives me a little shake.

"Eh, buck up, kiddo. It's good you're both this fucked up. If I thought it was only him, I'd have to shave your head while you were sleeping." When I look up at him, he adds, "To *start*."

Somehow it isn't only his lack of a smile that indicates he isn't joking.

"Normally I don't like people who threaten me every time they see me, but for whatever reason, you're the exception, Ryan T. McLean. He's lucky to have you as a friend."

"I'd die for him," Ryan says bluntly, with zero self-consciousness. "He's saved my life more than once. Even if he hadn't, he also happens to be the best man I've ever known."

I look away, my eyes prickly. "He basically said the same thing about you." When my throat loosens enough for me to talk again, I murmur, "It must be something."

"What?"

I quickly swat at my eyes. "To have someone who'd die for you. How many people can say that?"

There's a long silence. I feel Ryan inspecting my face, but don't look over at him because I'm afraid what my expression might reveal. Finally, he leans in and says softly, "*You* can, you hardheaded woman."

My heart in my throat, I glance up at him. He looks both disappointed and angry, a combination that makes gazing into his baby-blue eyes almost unbearable.

"That's not...you're being—"

"Shut up," he sighs, and gives me another shake. He drops his arm from around my shoulders and stretches his head back. Under his breath, he mutters, "Fuckin' women."

At the same time the valet guy pulls the car around the corner and to a stop at the curb, Connor walks through the doors of the lobby and joins us. He nods at Ryan. He doesn't look at me.

It's all I can do not to reach for his hand, because what Ryan said keeps echoing over and over inside my mind, a record stuck on repeat.

You can.

I don't know whether that makes things better, or so much worse.

∼

When we get back to the COM center at the studio, I make a beeline for my computer. O'Doul's agents are taking a meal break, milling around a table someone has set up with platters of food. They fall into silence when we walk in. Everyone turns to look at us except Rodriguez, who sneers in my direction and turns away.

O'Doul quickly ends the phone call he was on. "Gentlemen." He nods at Ryan and Connor, and then looks at me. "Miss West."

I cut right to the chase. "I've got something." I sit down at my computer, enter the password, and hold my breath as I open the traceback program's compilation report.

Within seconds, I've got sixteen FBI agents and two ex-Special Ops badasses breathing down the back of my neck. Everyone watches in tense silence as numbers begin to stream across my screen.

"What're we lookin' at?" asks Ryan from behind me.

"Data points," answers Special Agent Chan. He's to the right of me, bent over my desk, staring in fascination at the display. "But this report is totally random—how can you tell what you're looking at?"

"I can't. Not yet, anyway. This is raw data from Søren's system. It has to be converted."

I sense the general disappointment from behind me. O'Doul asks, "I assume you have another program for that?"

"You assume correctly." With a few keystrokes, I've pulled up the remote access tool that allows me to log in to my home system. I upload the compilation report and hit Send.

"What now?" asks Chan.

I sit back in my chair and release a breath. "Now we wait."

"How long?"

I shrug. "Depending upon how much data we were able to extract, anywhere from a few hours to—"

I break off mid-sentence and jerk upright in my chair, gaping at the screen.

Instantly, Connor is behind me, his presence calming though I'm in complete shock. He says, "What?"

I point at the monitor. In the upper right-hand corner, the program displays a series of bar graphs, indicating how much time is left on various conversions.

Two of ten bars have already turned from red to green. Then, in rapid succession, all the remaining bars turn green.

O'Doul grunts, impressed. "Pretty fast converter you've got there."

"It never works this quickly," I say slowly, feeling a cold niggle of worry at the base of my spine. I open the file utility and look at the size. "According to this, there was a few terabytes of data to sort through—"

"Let's take a look and see what you've got!" interrupts Chan eagerly, crowding close.

Everyone is silent as I open the first report. I read through a few lines, stunned, and then read on all the way to the end to be sure I'm seeing what I think I'm seeing.

Finally, I'm convinced. I sag back against the chair and breathe, "Holy. *Shit.*"

Though he keeps his voice even, I can feel O'Doul's aggravation. "Please don't make us keep asking 'What?' Miss West."

I shake my head. "This is… I can't believe this."

In unison, O'Doul, Chan, Ryan, and several other agents bark, "*What!*"

I'm still staring in awe at the monitor, blinking because I can't believe my own eyes. "It's Søren's malware program. The entire thing. All the code he used to cripple Miranda's system. It's all just…here."

Electricity sparks through the agents. There are a few whoops, a few muttered oaths of surprise, one or two low whistles. Everyone knows what this means.

"Get it on disk," O'Doul says instantly to Chan. "See if we can get any hits in the database." To the other agents, O'Doul says, "Everybody get on it. I want to know if we've got something ASAP."

In a daze, I copy the report to a thumb drive and hand it over to Chan. He bolts over to his computer station and proceeds to run a virus scan on the thumb drive. When that comes up clear, he uploads the report to the FBI's system. The other agents head back to their computers as well, all thoughts of food abandoned.

This is big. Bigger than big. The footprint of Søren's malware can now be compared to a million different fragments of software gained from investigations into various computer crimes conducted by government agencies all over the world.

Whatever else Søren has been up to, the FBI will now be able to discover.

Finally!

"What are the other reports?" asks Connor, still behind me. I turn and look up at him.

"All kinds of digital artifacts from his system. RAM data. Cross-drive analysis—"

"His location?"

There's something scary in his eyes I've never seen before. Something deadly. It's like I'm looking at another person. He's wearing a flat, killer gaze.

"If we're lucky...yes."

"Thank you for your help, Miss West," says O'Doul.

I glance at him and notice he's sweating. His eyes are overly bright.

"Oh. You're welcome. But we still have a lot of work—"

"Step aside."

Caught off guard, I blink. "Excuse me?"

"The information on your system is crime scene evidence. Step aside, please."

It takes a second for me to comprehend him. When I do, I jump to my feet, spin around, and hold my arms out in a protective stance.

"You're not touching her!" I shout.

"Whoa, whoa," says Ryan, confused. "Her who?"

"My computer!"

Connor is still wearing his serial killer look. He says calmly, "You must've known this would happen, Tabby."

I look at him, my heart beating wildly in my chest. "Connor. No. Please. Tell him no."

"It's not his decision," answers O'Doul. "And anyway, he's right. Did you think we would just let you walk away with all this information? We're the Federal Bureau of Investigation, Miss West. You might play by your own rules, but so do we." His smile is a little apologetic. "And our rules say that your system and everything on it now belongs to us. We'll take it from here."

I say vehemently, "Touch my computer and I'll break your face!"

While O'Doul looks at the ceiling, Ryan tries to reason with me. "C'mon now, Tabby, it's just a computer."

"It's my life!"

"Well that's just *pathetic*," says Rodriguez, smiling broadly at me from his chair across the room.

I snatch up a stapler someone has left on my desk and hurl it at him. It hits him square in the forehead.

He squawks, covers his face with his hands, jerks out of his chair, and promptly trips over his own feet. He crashes to the floor, howling. "You crazy bitch! I'm pressing charges!"

I'm so furious, I can't even speak. I don't know where to look or what to do. They're going to confiscate my computer! I have half a mind to yank Connor's gun from that stupid holster at his waist and start randomly shooting.

"Not sure you want to press charges against the person who just handed us the biggest score I've seen in my time on this job," says Chan, staring in shock at his computer screen.

Everyone stops what they're doing and looks at him.

O'Doul strides over to Chan's workstation. "What've you got?"

Agent Chan says somberly, "Two dozen hits, sir. So far."

"Show me."

Agent Chan points at his monitor. "Shellshock, 2014. The huge slave botnet that took over the Department of Defense." He scrolls through several more screens and stops to point out something else. "GhostClick, 2013. Millions of computers infected with a surveillance virus." Another scroll, another point. "The attack on the Chinese central bank last year that put their economy into a tailspin and almost crashed their stock market."

"Jesus," mutters O'Doul. "We hit the mother lode." He flicks me an inscrutable look.

"The hack on Heathrow airport in September that shut down air traffic control for four days. The Ukraine power grid attack last month. The list goes on." Chan glances up at O'Doul and then over at me. "This guy's everywhere."

The room has gone silent. Even Rodriguez has stopped his bitching and is simply kneeling on the floor with his hand cradling his forehead, gaping at Agent Chan.

Into the stillness, Connor says, "Open the location file."

I make a move to sit down at my workstation, but Connor moves faster than I do. He's in front of me before I've taken two steps, holding out his hand to stop me. "Let Chan do it."

Blood rushes to my face. I glare at him, outraged. "It's *my* computer."

He shakes his head and doesn't budge.

"Oh, fuck this." I take two long strides, brushing past him, determined to sit down at my own damn computer in spite of what anyone says, when before I know it, I'm swept up off my feet and am staring openmouthed at the hideous gold carpet on the floor.

Connor has thrown me over his shoulder.

"Be right back, boys," he says calmly, turns around, and walks away.

I pound on the expanse of his broad back, sputtering, "You—you—*jerk*! Put me *down*! Right *now*! You giant—"

"Animal, I know," he says drily. In one smooth motion, he flips me over and sets me on my feet.

We're in the adjacent room. It's an average office with a desk and two chairs, a bookcase, a sofa along one wall. A poster of Arnold Schwarzenegger from *The Terminator* stares back at me from the opposite wall.

I wonder how it's going to look with Connor's blood splattered all over it.

With a kick of his boot, Connor shuts the door.

"You did *not*," I say, breathing hard with my hands balled to fists at my side, "just pick me up and throw me over your shoulder like a sack of potatoes. In front of everyone. In front of that epic asshole Rodriguez, you did *not* just do that. Right?"

Connor folds his arms over his chest. "Is that a trick question?"

"Because if you *did*," I continue, ignoring him, "I'm going to tell you that I loathe you." When his eyes flare, I add, "*And not in our secret code way!*"

He purses his lips. "Now you're just being mean."

I take a moment to try to calm myself. When I'm reasonably sure I'm not going to stab him with the scissors from the jar on the desk, I ask through gritted teeth, "Why would you do that to me?"

"Because I'm gonna look out for you," comes the instant reply, "even when you're not looking out for yourself."

I glare at him without speaking, forcing him to explain.

"Harry will arrest you if you interfere with the investigation."

"I just *handed him* the investigation!"

"It doesn't matter. He told you to step aside. If you don't listen to him, he'll have you removed from the premises with some shiny new metal bracelets decorating your wrists."

When I open my mouth to retort, Connor interrupts me.

"I know him, Tabby. This is as far as he'll be pushed." A muscle in his jaw jumps. "And I'm not taking a chance with your safety."

A noise is growing in my head. It sounds like a swarm of bees after someone has kicked their hive. "You don't get to tell me what to do," I say, holding his gaze. "Just because we've slept together doesn't give you *any* right to tell me—"

"I care about you." His voice is big and loud in the small room.

For so many reasons, that leaves me breathless. Unable to meet his eyes any longer, I turn away. When I can finally talk, it sounds like I've swallowed gravel.

"I know you have a hero complex, but I don't need you to save me. That includes saving me from myself."

He mutters an oath under his breath. "You can't do it, can you? You just can't let anyone in."

He's bitterly angry with me. It's obvious from his tone. That hurts so much, I find it hard to say what I know I have to say. But if I let this thing between us go any further, I'll hate myself.

I can't drag him down with me. I have to cut the cord before it's too late.

In a flat, emotionless voice, I set him loose.

"It's not your business what I can or can't do. Why do I have to keep explaining this to you? There's *nothing* between us, Connor. We have *nothing* in common. I thought we were both adults, on the same page about our agreement, but I have to admit I totally regret it, because it's given you some kind of bull-shit idea that you're entitled to an opinion about the choices I make."

I gather my courage, take a deep breath, and turn to look at him.

"Stop trying to convince yourself this thing between us is anything other than sex. It isn't. You said it yourself. I'm a team of one." I pause and then drive home the final nail in the coffin. "And that's how I want it to stay. Forever. So *back off.*"

His silence burns and lasts an agonizingly long time. A vein in his neck throbs. One of his fingers intermittently twitches.

Finally—so, so softly—he says, "I've always admired you. Respected you, for everything you are. But right now, I'm so disappointed in you, it's making me sick to my stomach."

I force myself to hold his gaze steadily, to keep my breathing slow and even, to stand upright when it feels like I might at any moment fall to the floor.

Without another word, Connor turns on his heel and walks out, leaving the door open behind him.

And what's left of my heart breaks a little bit more.

22

CONNOR

*A*s soon as I enter the room, I know something has happened in my brief absence. The mood has turned from excitement to frustration.

Almost as big as my own.

I walk over to Ryan. He's standing with his arms crossed over his chest, watching me with narrowed blue eyes.

"What's going on?" I jerk my chin in O'Doul's direction. He's huddled with Chan in a corner of the room, gesticulating and shaking his head, obviously annoyed.

"You tell me. Why do you look like your face was on fire and someone tried to put it out with a hammer?"

I sigh and run a hand through my hair. "Here's the part where I tell you to mind your own business, brother."

Ryan bristles. "I told that broad in no uncertain terms that if she fucks with you—"

I clap my hand on his shoulder and look him in the eye. "Number one, don't call her a broad. It's disrespectful. Number two, dial it down a few thousand notches. I don't like you threatening her." My voice softens. "Number three, I appreciate your concern, but this is one battle I've gotta face on my own."

His look sours. "Yeah, well, it looks to me like you're walkin' into this battle with a slingshot while the other side has a mile-wide fuckin' lineup of tanks pointed at your head."

I slowly nod. "Sounds about right."

"Listen, brother—"

"I'm a big boy, Ryan," I say, my voice nearly a growl in my throat. "Leave it alone."

He cocks his head, folds his tattooed arms across his chest, and thoughtfully strokes his goatee like he does whenever he's trying to suss something out. After a second, he says, "Huh. Never thought I'd see the day."

I drop my hand from his shoulder. "Don't even want to know what that means. And don't tell me either!" I snap when he opens his mouth to say more.

He shrugs. "Suit yourself, 'big boy.'" Then he smirks at me. "Just make sure I get an invitation to the wedding."

"Gimme a fuckin' break, will you?" I say, scowling.

Ryan has the balls to laugh.

Then O'Doul calls Tabby's name. Unsmiling, she appears in the doorway of the adjacent office, looking like she'd rather be anyplace else than here. She leans against the door frame and looks him up and down with her lip curled and her nose wrinkled, a hand on her hip.

Ryan says under his breath, "At least you're not the only one on her shit list."

I mutter, "Shut up."

O'Doul's tone is brusque. "The location file was corrupted. Whatever data your program extracted was useless in determining Søren's whereabouts. On that front, we're back at square one." A loaded pause follows. "So about that phone number you have."

Tabby says innocently, "Oh, so you need my help with your case again?"

I can already tell where this is going, but O'Doul doesn't

know her as well as I do, so he just nods as if he's not about to get his balls handed to him on a platter.

"Obviously we'll take every technical precaution so the call can't be traced from his end. On ours, you only need to keep him on the line for—"

"And what do I get out of it?"

After beat of silence, a flush of color crawls up O'Doul's neck. "You get to stay out of prison."

With perfect indifference, Tabby yawns and then inspects her manicure.

Ryan hides his chuckle by coughing into his fist. For my part, I don't think this is funny at all, but she's made it crystal clear how much help she wants from me, so I clench my teeth and keep my mouth shut.

O'Doul steps slowly forward. A flush rises from his neck to his face. Against the starched white of his shirt collar, his skin is the color of a boiled beet. He says, "There's this fun thing called 'obstruction of justice.' I'm sure you've heard of it?"

Tabby tosses her hair over her shoulder and looks at him down her nose. "There are also these *other* fun things called 'coercion,' 'undue influence,' 'duress,' 'illegal compulsion,' 'oppressive exaction,' 'extortion'—"

"What do you want?" he interrupts, exasperated.

"I want," she replies with the air of a duchess, "my computer, all my equipment, and a written statement from you that whatever happens from this point forward, I'll be immune from prosecution for any and all assistance I may give on this case." She bats her lashes. "Since I obviously can't trust you to keep your word."

I hope O'Doul doesn't have any undiagnosed heart problems, because he looks as if he's about to have some kind of major cardiac event.

"That's blackmail," he says, seething.

"No, that's negotiating. Blackmail is when you threaten to

send someone to jail unless they do what you want." She gives him a bland smile. "I forgot to mention that one in my 'fun things' list."

While everyone else in the room watches this interaction as if it's the best reality TV episode ever, Tabby and O'Doul stare at each other like pistoleros in a standoff.

Me? I'm wishing I had an Alka-Seltzer. This shit is hell on my stomach.

O'Doul takes a short, stiff walk around the office with his hands on his hips, shooting Tabby the occasional glare. Finally, he lets out an aggravated sigh and relents.

"Fine. Since we're 'negotiating,' how about this. *If* you successfully make contact with Killgaard, and *if* we successfully determine his location from that contact, and *if* we're able to apprehend him as a direct result of your assistance, then you can have all your equipment back—*after* we've extracted all relevant evidence to this case—and I'll write you a letter. But *if* your phone call produces nothing, I'm under no obligation to uphold my end of the deal."

Tabby considers his words for a moment. "That's a hell of a lot of *ifs*."

"Life is full of uncertainty. Take it or leave it."

Tabby purses her lips. She glances at me, and I incline my head. *Take it.*

"All right," she says breezily. "Deal." Like a boss, she struts over to him and sticks out her hand.

He shakes it.

Tabby adds, "But we should wait until after Miranda's press conference. That will give me a legitimate excuse that might not tip him off that I'm involved in the investigation."

"How so?"

"Because I saw it on TV, obviously." She shrugs. "Miranda can drop some obscure fact about the hacker's methods that I'd be familiar with, and I can say I decided to reach out to him."

"But why now?" My voice is a little too loud. Everyone except Tabby looks at me. I get the distinct feeling they're all thinking the same thing: *That dude is losing it.*

I clear my throat, try to act casual. Normal. Like I'm not out on a fucking ledge.

"You've known how to contact him for years. If I were him, I'd want to know why you waited so long to call."

Just to twist the knife a little deeper, she throws my words from our elevator ride back at me. "But you're *not* him, remember?"

She doesn't even bother to look at me when she says it.

O'Doul ignores our back and forth and accepts Tabby's suggestion. "Fine, we'll do it right after the press conference. Be back here at five p.m. sharp tomorrow. And in the meantime," he glances meaningfully at me, "*stay out of trouble.*"

Oh, great. Here's the part where I'm supposed to get Tabby to let me babysit her again. No problemo. I might as well just castrate myself first and get it over with.

"I'm staying right here," she says to O'Doul. To Special Agent Chan, she says, "No offense, but there's no way I'm not here to watch while you extract data from my baby."

Indifferent, Chan shrugs, but O'Doul is looking more and more like he's going to keel over from stress. He glares at me. "Will you deal with this, please?" he says gruffly, waving in Tabby's direction. Then he whips his cell from his pocket and stabs his fingers against the screen to make a call.

Tabby sends me a look that says if I take a step in her direction, I'll get a knife shoved through my thorax. Then she steps backward into the office and slams the door.

"Well," says Ryan beside me, "looks like we're hangin' out here for a while. I'll get us some chow."

～

By the time we're ready to make the call to Killgaard the next day, Chan has finished extracting the data from Tabby's computer, Miranda has given an epic performance as a damsel in distress at a mobbed press conference on the steps of the studio, and Tabby and I are apparently not on speaking terms because she's refused to acknowledge my existence every time we're in a room together.

I'm *persona non grata*, and it's really crossing my wires. I've got a head full of scrambled eggs.

As for the FBI, they're more hyper than a bunch of little kids on Christmas morning. I've never seen a bunch of grown men so giggly and excited. Apparently, Killgaard has been involved in so many previously uncredited high-level hacks, he's shot right to the top of the Cyber Most Wanted List.

Yes, they really have one of those. Which is where I suspect Tabby's name will appear if this all falls apart and I have to smuggle her to safety across some international border in the hidden compartment of the Hummer.

I'm pacing back and forth in front of the office windows when Ryan ambles in, fresh from a shower in the employee gym on the first floor.

"What's the 411?" he asks, dropping the duffel bag with his clothes and shaving kit on the floor beneath the window.

"Just waiting on these fucknuts to get their shit together."

Rodriguez and Chan are on the other side of the room at Chan's desk, arguing over who should sit where during the call. O'Doul and Miranda are deep in discussion outside the adjacent office, where Tabby's been for hours. She's emerged only once, to shower and grab a sandwich from the food platters delivered at regular intervals from the cafeteria.

She's not eating enough. She's not sleeping enough. I'm worried about her, but there's nothing I can do about it.

Which sucks so hard, I want to break something.

"Where's your girlfriend?" asks Ryan without a hint of sarcasm.

Knowing it will only wind him up if I deny Tabby's my girlfriend, I tip my chin toward the closed office door.

Ryan looks at me. I can tell he's trying not to smile. "You're still in the doghouse, huh?"

"Why is this so funny to you?"

He shrugs. "Because I've never seen you not get something you want." Smiling, he adds, "I think a little groveling will be good for your character."

"There's nothing wrong with my character. And I don't *grovel*."

"Not yet."

"Jesus," I mutter, aggravated. "Remind me why I thought it was a good idea to bring you here?"

Ryan's smile widens. "Because right now you've got a boner where your brain used to be, and I can see stuff that you can't. For instance, that little interaction between Tabby and Miranda, all that Machiavelli bullshit back and forth. What was that about?"

I think for a moment, recalling the scene. "The smart chick equivalent of a big dick contest?"

"Nope."

Realizing he's right, I slowly nod. Their exchange seemed weird to me at the time too. Loaded with unspoken layers of meaning. I glance at Miranda on the other side of the room. She must feel me watching, because she looks over and smiles.

It looks fake. As fake as the tears she manufactured for the press conference.

Ryan says quietly, "She's been a client for what? Three years?"

"Yeah. She signed on right around the same time..."

The same time I met Tabby.

When I stiffen, Ryan looks at me. "Get your game face on,

brother," he says under his breath, still smiling like he doesn't have a care in the world. "I have a feeling all the pawns are about to get moved around the board."

Ryan's mention of pawns jars my memory. It was something Tabby said to me right before we left for LA. We were standing in her kitchen, and she'd just told me the job had a ninety-nine percent failure rate no matter how well I was prepared to go up against Søren.

"Whatever you think his endgame is, you'll be wrong. He'll always be five moves ahead of you, no matter how well you plan, and there's only one way you'll ever catch him."

"Which is?"

"By using me as bait."

The hair on the back of my neck prickles. "Ryan. You ever play chess?"

"Yep."

"You any good at it?"

"Yeah, actually. My dad taught me. We played all the time when I was a kid. Why?"

Looking between O'Doul, Miranda, Rodriguez, Chan, and the rest of the FBI agents working at their various stations around the room, I ask, "What's the most valuable piece on the board?"

"Technically the king. The goal is to get him in checkmate. That wins the game. He's the most important piece, but he's not the most powerful."

"Who's the most powerful?"

The door on the opposite side of the room opens. Tabby stands there, outlined in light. Despite being pale and somber, despite the dark hollows under her eyes that betray her fatigue, her chin is up. Her back is straight. Her legs are braced shoulder-width apart.

She looks ready for battle.

Ryan says, "The queen."

23

CONNOR

"*A*re you ready, Miss West?"

In answer to O'Doul's question, Tabby nods. "But I'd like to request that the room be cleared when we do this. It could get a little...personal."

I wonder what the word is for when you feel jealousy, anger, hurt, betrayal, outrage, and the urge to scream, *Fuck!* at the top of your lungs, all at once.

"Fine." says O'Doul. "We'll need Special Agent Chan on this, though. He'll be recording the call."

"Okay."

O'Doul looks at his men and points at the door. "Everybody out." He glances at Ryan and me. "Sorry, boys."

"Connor can stay," says Tabby quietly. She doesn't look at me, instead walks over to the whiteboard, turns her back on the room, and folds her arms across her chest.

No one contradicts O'Doul's order. Even Rodriguez keeps his mouth shut as he rises from his desk and exits the room. They all seem to know how important this is, how much it would mean if they can locate Killgaard, and seem willing to set their egos aside if it means they get a little closer to their goal.

I, on the other hand, have just gotten a giant ego boost in the form of Tabby wanting me to stay. I feel like a cat that's just been stroked down its back. I'm so happy, I could purr.

Ryan leans a little closer. "Our client doesn't look too excited about the turn of events."

That's an understatement. In fact, Miranda looks as if she might curl her hands around Tabby's throat.

"Well, obviously, *I'm* not going anywhere," Miranda says, her fake smile replaced with a very real scowl.

O'Doul glances at Tabby. She's got her back to me so I can't see her expression, but whatever he sees on her face makes him shake his head.

"Sorry, Ms. Lawson. We really need to—"

"This is *my* studio. This person Killgaard threatened *me*, stole from *me*, is attempting extortion from *me*. I have a very personal investment in the outcome of this investigation. I've assisted in any way I can—"

"It's not about you," interrupts Tabby, still staring at the whiteboard. She turns her head and looks at Miranda. In profile, her face is lovely. But her expression…let's just say I'm really glad I'm not on the receiving end of *that*.

"It most certainly is!" protests Miranda, her voice shrill.

In contrast to Miranda's flustered heat, Tabby is cool as ice. In fact, it seems to me that the longer this investigation continues, the more Miranda's famous control unravels and the more Tabby's fire burns arctic cold.

With chilling calmness, Tabby says, "It's never been about you, Miranda. But if you don't get out of my face in two seconds, it will be."

Ryan chuckles. "Girl fight. Cool."

O'Doul intercedes before any punches can get thrown. "This might be your studio, Ms. Lawson, but this is my investigation." He jerks his thumb in the direction of the door.

Face flaming, Miranda looks to me for help. "Connor."

I spread my hands in a helpless gesture. "Sorry, Miranda. You heard the man. He's in charge."

Her exhalation sounds like a cobra hiss. Nostrils flaring, she turns on her heel and storms from the room.

Ryan says, "Maybe she needs a neck massage." He winks at me and then, with a swagger, follows her out.

O'Doul sighs heavily and scrubs a hand over his face. "Chan."

"Yes, sir, we're all ready. Miss West, all we need from you is the number we'll be calling, and then we can begin."

Tabby looks at him. "Walk me through it. Tell me about the software, the tracking, how you record it, everything."

Chan shakes his head. "I can't. Sorry." When her look sours, he hurries to add, "But trust me, the technology is state-of-the-art. Untraceable."

She looks dubious, most likely because he uttered the dreaded word "trust."

"Let's do a trial run. Why don't you call me on my cell first to see if I can detect anything unusual?"

O'Doul says flatly, "No. And don't bother asking again."

When I walk closer, it distracts her from the argument I can see coming. As if we're magnets repelling each other, she moves to the other side of Chan's desk. "Suit yourself."

I take up position directly across from her, the desk a buffer between us. O'Doul comes to stand beside me as Chan logs into his computer, navigates through a maze of prompts and pop-up windows, and then comes to a box with the words "Enter destination" beside it.

"Before we begin," says O'Doul, "a few words of warning."

Tabby cuts him a look.

"Obviously, you know that everything said will be recorded."

He doesn't have to explain the subtext: *Don't try anything funny, because we'll have it all on tape.* Also: *Prison.*

Tabby says drily, "Obviously."

"The object is simply to keep him on the line for sixty seconds. Keep him engaged, keep him talking. But if at any time I feel that the conversation is veering toward something that will compromise the investigation, I'll have Chan disconnect the call. Which will mean our agreement is null and void."

Again unsaid: *Prison.*

With her icy calm still intact, Tabby replies, "You don't have to paint the pictures on the walls for me, O'Doul. I get it."

"Good. One final thing." O'Doul turns his gaze to me. "No noise whatsoever from the peanut gallery. I want total silence in this room while they're speaking. If I get anything less than total silence, if you even clear your fucking throat, I'll consider it sabotage."

More prison.

I feel vaguely insulted and want to tell him so, but decide to bite my tongue so I don't get thrown out before we even start. I'd chew off my own arm to be in the room during this phone call. So I swallow my pride and nod.

He turns his attention back to Tabby. "The origin of the signal will be digitally cloaked, so if he asks why—"

"He won't ask why."

When O'Doul raises his brows, she explains. "I've been cloaking all my digital signals since forever. In fact, he's the one who taught me how. He'll expect not to be able to trace my location." Her voice darker, she adds, "Which is why he'll try to, so you better hope your shit is *tight*, or this whole thing will blow up in our faces."

Unthinking, Chan starts to give her an explanation of just how good the FBI software is, but O'Doul barks at him to shut up before he can get half a dozen words in. Chan turns red and mutters an apology.

O'Doul drags a chair next to Chan's desk and points to it. "Sit," he instructs Tabby. Uncharacteristically obedient, she sinks into it without a word.

She's pale. Her hands fidget on her thighs. She swallows, breathing shallowly. Beneath her veneer of calm, she's nervous.

Adrenaline snakes a jittery path through my veins.

Chan's hands hover over the keyboard. "Sir?"

"Proceed. Tabby, give him the number."

Tabby recites it robotically off the top of her head. I know she has a photographic memory, but it still irks me that she can recall so easily a number she claims never to have dialed in almost a decade.

Chan enters it, his fingers expertly flying over the keys. Then we wait.

A hiss, a faint click, and then the lonely electronic sound of a phone ringing somewhere out in the vast emptiness of cyberspace.

Three rings. Four. Five. The tension in the room ratchets higher.

When the line is finally picked up, the voice that barks through the speakers is so unexpectedly loud and jarring, I wince.

"*Bună ziua, cine este?*"

It's a male, his age indeterminate, the language—for the moment—unknown.

Without hesitating, Tabby answers in the same harsh tongue. "*Spune-master care iad are peste congelate.*"

I exchange sharp glances with O'Doul. His eyes tell me in no uncertain terms to keep my trap shut or get personally acquainted with a five-by-seven-foot cell. I look at Tabby, but she isn't looking back at me. She's staring straight ahead, unblinking. Her fidgeting hands have fallen still on her legs.

A pause follows. In the background, I hear street noise: traffic, a car horn, the squawk of a pigeon, people chattering nearby. I listen intently, trying to pick up any clues about who might be on the other end of that line, his location or even general whereabouts, when finally, in heavily accented English, the voice says, "He'll be pleased."

What the ever-loving fuck?

"How can the master contact you?" continues the voice.

My eyes bulge. *Master?*

Tabby looks to O'Doul for direction. He whips a yellow pad off Chan's desk, dashes off a number, and holds it out. Tabby reads it aloud.

The voice makes a noise of assent. "You will wait." Then abruptly, the call is cut off.

Bewildered, Chan says, "He hung up."

"He'll call back," Tabby says quietly. "It won't be long."

O'Doul is irritated. "Chan, did you get anything?"

Chan quickly navigates around the software interface and then shakes his head. "No. We need more time to dial down to the country and city."

"What's the country code at the beginning of the number?"

Chan types into his interface and then shakes his head. "No matches."

O'Doul curses and then turns to Tabby. "What language were you speaking?"

"Romanian."

Suspicion is etched into his blunt features. "So we just called Romania?"

"Maybe. Probably not. The man who answered the phone could know several languages. Today he could've been instructed to answer in Romanian...maybe last week his instructions were to answer in Italian. I don't know. We can't assume anything, except that that phone won't be anywhere near Søren's actual location. From the sounds of it, we called a pay phone on a busy street. He'd have picked a spot with bad cell phone reception, poor infrastructure, or an area where a sizeable part of the population doesn't own mobile phones. That pay phone probably gets used by dozens or even hundreds of people a day."

I hate to admit it, but that's a smart move. If that pay phone were located and put under surveillance, you'd have dozens of suspects to follow...and dozens more the day after that. And on and on. It would be a logistical nightmare.

O'Doul slowly lets out a breath. "So someone has been paid to answer that phone when it rings, and then relay any messages to Søren."

Tabby nods. "And there are probably several more someones in between who know nothing of the links in the chain beyond the one past themselves. And before the call even got to that pay phone, it was bounced through different telecommunications satellites in different countries and the encryption changed an infinite number of times before finally reaching its destination. I told you there would be layer after layer of obfuscation. His paranoia is almost as big as his ego."

"What did you say when he picked up the phone?" My voice is rough.

When Tabby turns her head and our eyes meet, I'm startled by how wide her pupils are dilated. It almost looks as if she's recently ingested drugs.

"I said to tell the master that hell has frozen over."

We stare at each other. The moment stretches out. I feel like I'm on the verge of understanding something important, something I've been missing that's the key to this entire mystery, when a distinct electronic ring comes through Chan's computer speakers.

Because we're looking right at each other, I see clearly how all the blood promptly drains from Tabby's face, turning it white as stone.

"It's him," she whispers.

She's terrified.

Operating on pure instinct, I stride over to her, kneel beside her chair, take her hand, and squeeze it.

She squeezes back, hard.

"Answer it," says O'Doul.

Chan taps a single key on the keyboard, and the ringing stops. There's dead silence.

No, not dead, I think, listening. This silence has a weight and a temperature, an actual presence, like it's alive. It takes a lot to rattle me—I've seen men trying to hold their bloody intestines in their mangled stomachs after being savaged by a grenade—but the texture of this silence makes my skin crawl.

Faintly, Tabby says hello.

The awful silence breaks with the sound of a low exhalation, and then a single word, murmured like a prayer.

"Tabitha."

Tabby's arms break out in gooseflesh. Her eyes close. She stops breathing.

I watch all that with impotent rage, not understanding what the hell is happening, only that I want it to stop. *Now.* I squeeze her hand again, but hers has turned limp and clammy in mine.

Perfectly still, Tabby sits. The air crackles with electricity.

"You've made me wait," says Søren, "a very long time."

His voice has the quality of a lullaby, soft and stroking, meant to soothe. It carries a faint and indefinable accent. Not British, but something equally refined. Aristocratic. Somehow it reminds me of winter snowfall, when the air is sharp and cold and everything is blanketed in powdery white.

Snow. Beautiful, frozen, and deadly if you stay out in it too long.

"But how do I know it's really you?" he muses. Soft tapping, like fingers drumming on a hard surface. "What could convince me?"

A change comes over Tabby's face. A flash of emotion disfigures it momentarily, as if a terrible memory has reared its head.

"I have a little black box inside my head. Inside the box are monsters."

She says, "I still have the dagger, if you'd like me to take a picture and send it to you. I'll focus up close on all the dried blood."

Her tone is flat and hard, edged with fury. Abruptly I understand that I was wrong before. Tabby wasn't terrified. It wasn't fear that made her face go white, her body stiffen.

It was hate.

She hates him. She hates him so much, she's shaking with it, breathless from it, frozen in place from the sheer enormity of the feeling.

And now we've got a bloody dagger to add to all the other weirdness. How fucking Shakespearean.

Whatever the meaning of the dagger, the mention of it makes Søren laugh. It's a ridiculously self-satisfied sound, low and infinitely pleased, and also pleas*ing*. This dickhead has a voice as pretty as his face.

God, I'm really going to enjoy mangling both.

"Oh pet," Søren says warmly, "I've missed you." A shade of melancholy sneaks into his cultured voice. "I've missed you so much."

A shudder runs through Tabby's body. She opens her eyes and stares at Chan's computer monitor as if she'd like to tear it to pieces with her teeth. "Really? No other gullible minions to mold in your despicable image?"

Søren's gentle sigh sounds perversely intimate, like he might be stroking himself, aroused by the sound of her anger. "Yes, of course, but none of them could ever compare to you. My fierce little *krijger*. My *liefde*."

Whatever those words mean, they really piss her off. Color burns over her pale cheeks. Veins standing out on her neck, she leans forward in her chair and says through clenched teeth, "I was never *yours*."

"On the contrary, *liefde*. You always were…and still are."

"You're wrong!"

"Am I? Well, that would be a first. Tell me, do you have a family? A husband? Children? Any connection to another human being that could be considered intimate?" He waits for a only a beat before answering his own question, smug as shit. "Of course you don't. And you never will. And—please be honest with me, you know I'll know if you're lying—why is that?"

Tabby vibrates fury. That and misery. She withdraws her hand from mine, sits back in her chair, and exhales hard, as if expelling a poisonous breath from her lungs.

"Because of you."

"Because of me," Søren slowly repeats. He lets it hang there, damning as a confession of murder.

Tabby says nothing. She doesn't move, with the exception of her lower lip, which starts to tremble.

I'm going to kill him.

The thought is bright and dangerously sharp in my mind, a knife blade catching the light.

Even if I never find out the details of what happened between them, it's clear as day that this motherfucker wrecked her in some profound, irreversible way. And so I'm going to kill him, and present his head to Tabby on a metal spike, and then feed his body to a pack of rabid dogs.

The thought makes me feel a lot better.

I rest my hand on her shoulder. Tabby blindly reaches up, grabs my pinky, and holds on tight.

"I saw what you did," she says, struggling to keep her voice even. "On the news, that movie studio in Los Angeles, the press conference. I knew it was you when they talked about *how* they'd been hacked. That's why I'm calling."

Søren says nothing.

His silence seems strategic, as if he's waiting for her to keep talking, to blunder, to give something away. Or maybe I'm just imagining it. Maybe he's just sitting there frantically jerking off to his reflection in a mirror and I've built up this whole vision of him as the great and powerful Oz because that's how Tabby thinks of him, when really he's just some insecure asshole pulling levers and operating machinery from behind a curtain.

Maybe he's all smoke and mirrors, and she's never been able to see beyond the screen.

Chan points to his watch, signs the numbers two and zero, and then gives a thumbs-up.

I squeeze Tabby's shoulder. *Twenty seconds. Keep him talking for twenty more seconds, sweetheart, and then we can nab his smug, psychotic ass.*

"Do you remember what I told you the last time I saw you?" asks Tabby.

She's beginning to look drained. Even this small amount of contact is taking it out of her. *How must it have been for her living with him for an entire year?*

I want to kick my own ass for doubting her.

"Yes," replies Søren. "Perfectly. You know I do."

"So you know what has to happen next."

"I know what you *think* has to happen next. But consider: Who would you be without me? *No one.* Just another squandered talent in a world littered with the corpses of the could-have-beens and the almost-hads and the settled-for-second-bests."

Chan taps his watch, signs, *Ten.*

"But you're none of those things," continues Søren, his voice growing softer with every word. "Are you, pet? You're not the frightened little lamb I saved all those years ago. What are you now?"

Tabby's voice cracks over her answer. "Frankenstein's monster."

"No, *liefde.* You're a survivor. You're a hunter. You're a lioness. And we both know what do lions do best."

Chan raises his right hand. All five fingers are splayed. He makes a fist, displays four fingers. Another fist, three. Then two. Then one.

Tabby whispers, "*They hunt.*"

Chan shakes his fist. He turns to O'Doul. Exultant, he mouths, *We got him!*

In a voice throbbing with intensity, Søren says, "So let the hunt begin."

And just like that, the line goes dead and he's gone.

24

TABBY

I'm shaking so hard, my teeth chatter. A trickle of cold sweat runs down the back of my neck. My heart is like a rat trying to claw its way out of a cage, and there's an invisible vise winching tighter and tighter around my lungs.

It's been nearly a decade since I've heard Søren's voice, yet it still has the power to shatter me like a hammer slammed against bone.

"Where is he, Chan?" barks O'Doul.

"Miami. South Beach."

Miami? Søren hates the beach.

I'm vaguely aware of Connor's hand on my shoulder, of O'Doul calling for the agents to return to the room, of a swarm of excited activity around me as everyone starts talking at once. Words tumble over me like water, a meaningless jumble of noise.

"I've missed you so much. My fierce little warrior. My love."

Air. I need air.

I lurch to my feet. Connor follows.

"Tabby?"

His voice is tight with worry, but I can't think about that now.

I can't think, I can't breathe, I can barely put one foot in front of the other *holy shit get me out of this room before I scream*—

I'm scooped up in a pair of strong arms.

"Wha—"

"I've got you," says Connor. I realize I'd been just about to fall. My legs are as wooden and useless as the rest of me.

As if he knows instinctively that I need to get as far away from this room as possible, Connor strides out of the office, carrying me in his arms. In the hallway, he pauses, looking left and right.

"Outside," I say, panting fast, shallow breaths.

Connor squeezes me. "You're hyperventilating. If you don't get your breathing under control, you'll pass out."

I drag in a huge breath, blow it out hard. It seems to help clear my head, so I do it again.

"Good. Keep doing that."

Connor starts to walk again. We move down the hall until we get to the elevators. He lifts a knee and presses it against the call button, and I'm distracted from my pending mental breakdown by how impressed I am that he can stand on one foot and knee a waist-high button on the wall while holding a grown woman in his arms, all without even a wiggle of imbalance.

Between breaths, I wheeze, "Do you do Pilates? Your balance is amazing."

"Yoga."

He answers with a straight face, so I know he's not making a joke. I picture Connor—macho man, hulking muscles Connor— on a yoga mat doing sun salutations and a downward-facing dog, and laugh. Unfortunately, it was badly timed as I was in the middle of gulping air, and so I start to cough, big, body-racking coughs that have Connor saying, "Whoa," and looking alarmed.

"Put me down," I croak, gasping.

He gently sets me on my feet and then puts his hands on my shoulders to steady me. I lean against the wall and cough and cough until finally I catch my breath and look at him, my eyes watering and my face red.

"Thought you were gonna cough up a lung, princess."

His voice is casual, but his expression is anything but. He's concerned. *Really* concerned.

A melty feeling expands inside my chest. It's definitely better than what was there a few moments ago.

I blurt, "Thank you."

His forehead wrinkles. "For saying you were gonna cough up a lung?"

"For getting me out of there. And for being..."

I flail around for the right word, but Connor supplies it before I can come up with anything.

"Supportive?"

"Yes," I say as the elevator dings and the doors slide open. "Supportive. Thank you."

He gazes at me for a moment. As if just realizing his hands are still on my shoulders, he withdraws, shoves them into his pockets, and clears his throat.

"Sure. That's what friends are for."

Friends. Why those seven letters arranged in that particular way and said in that particular tone should irritate me so much at this particular moment, I don't want to examine.

Yes, I'm going with denial, thank you very much. It's highly underrated.

We get in the elevator. The doors slide shut. Connor presses the button for the ground floor. We stand beside each other, subjected to a truly hideous Muzak rendition of the Rolling Stone's song "Under My Thumb" as the car descends.

I try not to read any significance into it.

When the doors open, Connor asks, "Where to?"

His assumption that wherever I'm going, he's going doesn't irk me as much as it should. In fact, I'm grateful for it.

I don't want to be alone with my brain right now. I can't trust it. I don't know what tricks it might play on me, what rabid-dog memories it might decide to unleash.

"A bar," I decide in a flash of inspiration. I look at Connor. "Take me to a bar."

He slow blinks, rubs his hand over the stubble darkening his jaw. "Thought you didn't drink alcohol, princess."

I shoulder past him on my way toward the lobby doors, and freedom. "Yeah, well, that was then and this is now."

"Sure thing," he calls from behind me, his voice wry. "Let me just put on my neck brace, and I'll catch up."

For the first time in hours—days?—a smile lights my face. It's faint, but it's there, and it's because of Connor.

My good "friend" Connor, who I might actually like, need, and want a hell of a lot more than I'll ever admit.

Because if anything goes wrong with O'Doul's plan to capture Søren, I'll have to intervene.

And then I'll never be seeing my "friend" again.

I stare in utter disgust at the shot glass in my hand. It's half full of a vile, black substance called Jäegermeister, the aftertaste of which is still searing my nostrils and throat with a bitter, cough-syrup flavor more suited to poison than a food product.

"That is *absolutely* the most revolting thing I've ever had in my mouth. How do people drink this shit? And why would you *pay* for it? *Yuck!*"

Sitting across from me in the booth at the trendy bar he chose, Connor chuckles. "You're not supposed to sip it. You're supposed to shoot it, like an oyster. Down the hatch in one swallow."

I shake my head and gulp water from the glass the waitress brought with the drinks. "Holy crispy pork belly Christ. It's beyond foul. It tastes like melted crayon and mint mouthwash. With some licorice and funky barnyard herbs mixed in just to make it even more disgusting. How can they sell this to the public? I bet it causes cancer!"

Connor leans back, swirls his whiskey around in the glass, sniffs it, and then takes a swig. "Guess it's an acquired taste," he drawls, sounding suspiciously like he's holding back laughter.

I glance sharply at him. He stares back at me with a bland expression but brightly twinkling eyes.

"You...oh my God. You dick."

He blinks innocently. "What?"

"You picked the worst drink for me, didn't you?"

A dent forms in his cheek.

I recognize that fucking dent. And now I want to slap him... although part of me also thinks it's funny. I can absolutely see myself doing the same thing to him if the situation were reversed.

"You could make a girl crazy, you know that?" I mutter, glaring at him.

"Me?" He snorts. "Uh, hello pot, meet kettle."

"Shut up."

"Make me."

"Don't tempt me. Seriously, I'll lay you flat on your back on the floor in front of all these pretty yuppies before you can say 'steroids are my soul mate.'"

He snorts again, louder. "I don't take steroids, Tabby. These muscles?" He makes a show of flexing his arms so his biceps pop out, big as boulders. "These babies are one hundred percent bonafide. I'm just genetically blessed."

Ignoring her boyfriend, who's studying a menu, the dishy blonde sitting in the booth across from us picks up her cell phone and discreetly takes a picture of Connor. When she notices me scowling at her, she blushes and looks away.

In a voice as sweet as syrup, Connor notes, "You're pretty territorial for a woman who only wants to be a team of one, sweetheart." He takes another swig of his whiskey, watching me over the rim of the glass.

"I just don't like the way people look at you like you're...meat."

He sets his glass down, runs a finger thoughtfully around the rim, glances at the blonde and then back at me. "And by people you mean women. You don't like the way women look at me."

I pick up the shot of Jäegermeister and drink the rest of it. It burns my throat, just like that nasty bit of truth I so stupidly blurted. Anyone who could develop an acquired taste for this putrescence deserves a gold medal.

Grimacing, I say, "Order me something better. Please. This can't be the first and last taste of alcohol I'll ever have. I'll be scarred for life. Well, *more* scarred."

Connor's eyes sharpen when I say that last part, but he lets me off the hook for the moment and motions for the waitress. She arrives quickly and asks him what he'd like.

"You have Krug Clos d'Ambonnay, 1995?"

She blinks in surprise but quickly recovers. "Oh, uh—no. We unfortunately don't carry that vintage, sir, but we have the 2007."

"Excellent. Thank you."

She realizes she's been dismissed and hurries away. She stops to confer with a gentleman in a suit at the end of the long wooden bar. They both turn to look in our direction, and the suit smiles. I get the feeling they're both happy with the order.

"I've read Krug is the champagne of true connoisseurs."

Connor shrugs. "Judge for yourself. And while we wait, you can tell me more about this little territorial problem of yours..." A loaded pause. "Or about the dagger."

Oh, goodie. Out of the frying pan and into the fire.

"How about a third option?"

Connor rests his elbows on the table, leans forward, and gazes intently into my eyes. "Sure. How 'bout this, Tabby. What's your plan here? Why did you really agree to help me find Søren?" When I open my mouth, he adds, "And don't say it's payback for the Bank of America thing, because that's bullshit. You could've done that years ago. There's something else."

My heart starts to pound. I look away, hating how easy it is for him to see me. He *sees* me, no matter how high or thick the wall I build, and I don't know what to do with that. I only know how to live behind walls. It's only with him that I've ever felt...

Safe.

I feel safe with Connor.

Suddenly, I want to scream.

Swallowing hard, I look down at my hands. He says my name, but I hold up a finger.

"Give me a minute. I'm getting my shit together."

I hear his impatient exhalation, hear all the other questions he wants to ask in it, but I'm concentrating hard on swallowing the swell of words rising fast on the back of my tongue, on tamping down the hot expansion inside my chest, the feeling of seismic shock, like the earth jumped ten feet sideways from one breath to the next.

You're in deep, Tabby. Denial will only take you so far. You might as well just fucking admit you have serious feelings for this irritating, overbearing, completely incompatible sexalicious stud of a man, and get on with your life.

And maybe take another amazing roll in the hay with him before the gig's up.

When I look up, Connor is staring with laser-like focus at me.

"I have something to say to you. When I'm done, I would appreciate it if you'd act like I didn't say anything and not ask me any questions, because I'm not sure exactly what shape I'll be in. Okay?"

Connor silently examines my face and then nods.

I draw in a breath, let it out, and let him have it.

"I like you. More than that. I don't know. I know a lot of words, but I don't know what the word is for this thing between us. It's confusing. And scary. And I don't scare. I don't know what to do about it, or if there *is* anything I can do, but I definitely don't want to feel this way. I don't like feeling confused. I like feeling in control, you know that, but with you, I'm not in control. I'm a passenger in a speeding car traveling down the side of a winding mountain road at top speed in the dark. I don't have my hands on the steering wheel or my foot on the brake, and it freaks me out, like, *hard.* And yes I know that hard is a ridiculous word to use to qualify an emotion but my brain is operating at about ten percent of its capacity right now because of all the stupid emotions running around in my body like kids left alone with a negligent babysitter who's fed them too much candy. I want to tell you everything, but I can't, okay? I just can't. I *won't.* I swore to myself a long time ago that no one would ever...that I wouldn't let anyone—"

I stop speaking abruptly when the waitress arrives with a bottle and a pair of champagne flutes. My face burns so hot, it might burst into flames.

The waitress sets the glasses down and presents the bottle to Connor. Without looking away from my face, he says gruffly, "Just pour it."

We stare at each other across the table as she removes the foil cap and the wire muselet, uncorks the bottle—the pop it makes is loud and cheerful—and pours a measure into each glass.

"Shall I put the bottle on ice?" she asks Connor.

He doesn't answer. He's staring so hard at me, it's like she doesn't even exist. He hasn't once shifted his gaze away from my face.

"Um, I'll just go ahead and do that, then." The waitress discreetly removes herself.

Connor extends his hand across the table, palm up. I hesitate but then reach out and rest my hand in his. His warm fingers curve around mine. He gently squeezes.

"Do you have any idea," he says softly, "what that means to me?"

With my free hand, I cover my face. "You promised you wouldn't say anything."

He squeezes a little harder. "I know the word you're looking for, in case you're interested."

"No. I'm not. Please stop talking now."

He strokes his thumb back and forth across my knuckles. "I'll stop talking on one condition."

I peek at him between my fingers.

He says in voice thick with emotion, "Come sit next to me, princess."

"Are you going to keep your hands to yourself?"

He says instantly, "No," and I can't help but laugh.

"Well, all right, then. Move over."

I stand. Mercifully, the ground feels solid under my feet. Connor slides over in the booth and reaches out. I take his hand, slide in next to him, and he immediately engulfs me in a giant bear hug. He buries his face in my neck.

"Goddamn you," he whispers.

"I know," I whisper back, my eyes squeezed shut. "I'm sorry."

We stay like that with our arms wrapped around each other, just breathing, for what seems like a long time. When the waitress returns with the champagne in an ice bucket, we reluctantly break apart. She makes an apologetic noise and quickly leaves.

I weakly laugh. "It's like we have a bet on how many poor waitstaff we can embarrass across the continental United States."

Connor slides a hand under my hair, wraps it around the back of my neck, and settles it there. He picks up one of the flutes of champagne and presents it to me. "Here. This will make you feel better."

I take it, hold it under my nose, and sniff. I get a fragrant whiff of fruit and flowers, along with a little zing of effervescence. "It smells good."

"Wait until you've got it on your tongue."

Our eyes meet. I know I'm not the only one who found that offhand comment enticingly sexual. Holding his gaze, I take a sip...

And groan in pleasure. "Seriously? That's like drinking happiness!"

Connor smiles. "You like?"

"Wait, let me be sure." I take another sip, and then an even bigger swallow. I nod enthusiastically. "Yep. It's official. This stuff is great."

"Well, at a thousand bucks a glass it should be."

I freeze, horrified, and stare at him with my mouth open.

He's unmoved by my shock. "It's been a strange day, princess. You deserve a treat. Drink up."

His cell rings. He fishes it from his pocket, answers it with a gruff, "Talk to me," listens for a while, and then grunts. "Roger that." He disconnects the call and looks at me. "That was Ryan. O'Doul and the agency have put together a local team in Miami to get Søren. Go time is zero six-hundred hours tomorrow."

I check Ms. Kitty on my wrist. It's eight minutes to seven p.m. on the west coast, which makes it almost ten p.m. in Miami.

In eight hours, the FBI will raid Søren's hideout. With any luck, in eight hours Søren will be in the custody of the United States government. In eight hours, I'll be able to breathe again.

Connor and I stare at each other. I feel every single throbbing beat of my heart.

"So what're we going to do for the next eight hours, jarhead?"

Connor downs his glass of champagne in one gulp. He looks at me, licks his lips, and growls, "Everything."

Then his mouth is against mine.

Even if I wanted to protest, I couldn't, because the man tastes better than a thousand-dollar glass of champagne.

25

TABBY

"*I* can't drive with you doing that, princess," Connor says, breathing raggedly, his hand fisted in my hair.

His hard cock is in my mouth.

I've just unzipped his pants and gorged myself on it, because I couldn't stand one more second of rubbing the pulsing length of it through the fabric as Connor tried to kiss me and concentrate on the road at the same time.

"Then pull over," I mutter, and take him all the way to the base. I fondle the heavy, velvet warmth of his balls, and he sucks in a breath.

The Hummer zigzags. A horn sounds. Someone yells a curse.

I slowly draw up, savoring him like a lollipop, my other hand curled around his girth, stroking my thumb up and down the thick vein on the underside of his erection. I slide my tongue over the slit in the head. Connor moans softly. His big hand spreads out to cradle my skull as he flexes his pelvis, wanting more.

"You like my mouth," I whisper, feeling powerful.

"Princess," he pants, driving so erratically, the car is swerving all over the place, "I *love* your mouth."

I falter for a second. *There's that word again.* But it only gives me a moment's pause before I go back to worshipping his cock.

When I fumble with my zipper and slide my hand into my pants so I can stroke myself while I suck on him, Connor almost drives off the road.

"Fuck," he says between gritted teeth, straightening the wheel. The car slows down and turns. My fingers are already slick with my own wetness. I rub my clit, making circles in tandem with the circles I'm making with my tongue. It feels so good, I moan and rock against my hand.

After a few more turns, the truck slows to a stop. Connor turns off the engine, pulls my head up with both hands, and kisses me so hard, it takes my breath away.

When he breaks the kiss, he demands, "You want my cock or my mouth first?

"Decisions, decisions." I slowly stroke my hand up and down. "Are we back at the hotel already?"

"Yes. Answer the damn question."

When I take too long to answer because I'm preoccupied with stroking him, Connor puts his mouth against my ear.

"You can't decide, I'll decide for you. You're getting my cock. From behind. I'm gonna get you on your hands and knees and fuck you until you come, and then I'm gonna fuck you some more, until we both come. And then I'm gonna fuck you again."

I thrill to his words, and to the look in his eyes, hungrier than a starving animal. I whisper, "Yes to all that. And Connor..."

"What?"

"Make it rough."

There's an electric pause. He licks his lips, and his voice gets all rumbly. "Rough leaves marks, sweetheart."

Without hesitation, I say, "I want your marks. I want my skin to show where your hands were, where your teeth were, how I make you lose control. I want to be able to look in the mirror tomorrow and see everywhere you touched me."

For a moment, Connor closes his eyes. He mutters, "Could you be any more perfect?"

One of his hands grips my head to hold it in place while he ravages my mouth. With his other hand, he pinches my hard nipple through my shirt. When I squirm in pleasure, he releases my nipple, slides his hand into my pants, and pinches my swollen clit.

My whole body jerks. I gasp into his mouth. He laughs against my lips, a low and satisfied sound, and then slides a finger deep inside me.

I say his name, my voice husky with need. My hips start a rhythm in tandem with the press and slide of Connor's big finger. His thumb goes to work on my clit, circling round and round. I groan. My eyes slide shut. I arch my back, opening my legs wider for him.

Connor bites my jaw. His hot breath fans down my neck. When he rubs his cheek against mine, his stubble is scratchy against my skin. "You like my fingers, Tabby? You like my tongue and my hard cock? You like it when I tell you how much I love your mouth and your pussy?"

I whimper.

"Yes, you do," he says roughly. "Because you're my beautiful, dirty, sweet, badass girl. Now let me watch you suck my cock while I make you come, sweetheart."

I obey without thinking, adjusting my position so I can take him down my throat while he works his magical fingers between my legs. The steering wheel is jammed into my shoulder, I'm getting a cramp in my arm, and I'm wound up like a pretzel between the seats, but I don't care.

He makes me forget everything else. He wipes my mind clear of all the garbage. Intellectually, I know it's only sex, but it's so much more because it's *him*, and he makes everything better just by being himself.

"Oh God, princess," he whispers, staring down at me as I suckle and stroke him. "Fuck yes."

He's rock-hard in my mouth, hard and throbbing, and I'm throbbing all over too. I feel like a lit stick of dynamite, ready to blow.

Connor's head drops back against the headrest. He starts to thrust up into my mouth, grunting in pleasure, his hand still working between my legs. I'm so soaked, I hear the sound it makes as Connor's fingers fuck me. I'm close to orgasm when I hear the electronic chirp of a car alarm.

Connor groans. "Got company."

I peek past the edge of the window and see a couple walking from the parking garage elevator. They're headed toward the BMW parked next to us.

I quickly sit up and adjust my clothing. Breathing hard, Connor stuffs himself back into his pants, zips up, and gives me a hard kiss on the lips. "Upstairs," he says gruffly, looking into my eyes. "Now."

My heart singing, I jump from the car. Connor follows just as fast. We get to the elevators, Connor pushes the button, and then we stand there staring at each other in burning silence as we wait for it to arrive.

The bell dings, the doors slide open, Connor pulls me inside. As soon as the doors slide shut, he pulls me into his arms. His mouth goes to my neck. He sucks, hard, and a moan escapes me.

"Do you know what you do to me? Do you have any idea?"

He whispers it into my ear, pressing me against the wall of the elevator, his big body hard and hot against mine. I feel his heart hammering against his breastbone, hear the need in his voice, smell the masculine scent of his skin, and wonder if anything else will ever be as good as this.

Our lips meet. It's anything but gentle.

I'm panting. Greedy for him. Wanting him inside me so bad, I'm trembling. He grabs my ass and grinds his pelvis against mine. His other hand gathers my hair. He wraps it around his wrist and uses it to hold my head in place while his tongue plunders my mouth.

The elevator slows to a stop, and the doors open. I open my eyes, and he's staring down at me with this ravenous, adoring look, like he can't get enough of me. I can't get enough of him either.

I say brokenly, "Connor."

"I know. Me too."

He kisses me one last time and then takes my hand and tugs me out of the elevator and down the hall. I follow him, almost tripping over my own feet in my rush. When we get to the door, he fumbles for the card key in his pocket, curses when I press my breasts against his back and reach around to stroke him, stiff and ready under his zipper.

He gets the door open, drags me inside, pushes me against the wall. The door slams shut. He pulls my shirt off over my head and tosses it aside. He bends down, takes my breast into his mouth, and bites.

It's soft at first, a nip just under the puckered bud of my nipple, but when I groan and arch into his mouth, Connor presses down harder until it stings. I cry out, loving the feel of his teeth against my tender flesh, loving it even more when he gentles and strokes his tongue over the place he just bit.

"More?" he whispers, his fingers digging into my hips.

"More," I beg. I'm instantly rewarded. He nips a stinging path all around my nipple, following each bite with a tender stroke of his tongue, so I'm overwhelmed with the cycle of pain/pleasure. I writhe against him, whispering *yes yes yes* as he moves to my other breast and repeats the process. When he finally raises his head, both my breasts are stinging and slick, and I'm wet between my legs like I've never been.

He demands, "Tell me what you want."

"You. Everything. Anything. Please."

My breathless pleading makes him growl softly in pleasure. "Get naked. And then get on the bed."

The intensity in his eyes and voice make my pulse fly. I quickly strip. When I go to the bed and sit on the edge, Connor shakes his head. "On your knees, princess," he says, his voice husky, and my pulse goes haywire.

I get on all fours and look at him over my shoulder. He walks closer, watching me. He pulls his shirt over his head and drops it to the floor. "Look at that beautiful pussy," he whispers, staring between my legs.

My face flushes. I've never been looked at like this. I've never *displayed* myself like this, and I'm shocked at how much I enjoy his devouring gaze roaming over my naked body. I feel both vulnerable and powerful, which is confusing, exciting, and the most addicting thing I've ever felt.

Connor stands at the edge of the bed. He reaches between my legs and lightly strokes me there, eliciting a soft whimper from me. Our eyes lock. He says, "Stay still and be quiet," and then slowly pushes a finger inside my slick heat.

I bite my lip to keep from moaning.

Gently he works his finger in and out, until I'm pushing back against his hand and gripping the blanket, my eyes closed. When he slides his finger over my throbbing clit, I moan.

He smacks me on the ass.

I jump, gasping.

"Quiet," he warns, and goes back to stroking me.

Now my ass is stinging along with both my breasts. If he smacks me again, I think I'll come instantly.

Connor goes to his knees. His big hands slide up the backs of my thighs. I feel the warm, soft wetness of his tongue tease the fold between my pussy and my thigh, and stop breathing.

His tongue caresses me, teasing all around the outside of my pussy, until finally he spreads me open with his thumbs and suckles my clit between his lips.

I cry out in pleasure, arching my back. One second later, Connor smacks my ass again.

But he doesn't pull away. He's got his face between my spread legs, eating my pussy while spanking my ass. I think I might die right now of sheer bliss.

I buck against his mouth. He slaps me again. It makes me moan again, and I get another sharp, stinging blow on my bottom. "Connor," I gasp. "Please."

"You can't come yet," he growls, and then sinks his teeth into my thigh.

I bury my face into the blanket and whimper.

He plays with me, taking his time, running his hands over my thighs and ass, up my spine, all the while murmuring words of adoration.

Beautiful.

So sweet, so wet.

Look at this—perfect.

God, you make me crazy.

I don't pay attention to the words themselves. It's the reverent tone they're spoken in that move me, the way he's so completely into this. Into *me*. It makes me feel safe and beautiful and reckless. At this moment he could tell me to do anything, and I would.

"Your cock," I beg. "I need your cock."

"And you'll get it, sweetheart. But I'm not done playing yet."

In one swift move, he flips me over so I'm on my back. My legs are spread open. My pussy is drenched. My nipples are hard and aching.

Holding my gaze, Connor slowly unbuckles his belt. He slides it through the belt loops, smiling this devilishly wicked smile, his full lips curved, his eyes heavy-lidded and hot.

A shiver racks my body. Dizzy with lust and anticipation, I wriggle my hips.

Connor chuckles. Still holding on to his belt, he unzips his pants. I see the big bulge beneath his boxer briefs and moisten my lips.

He walks slowly around the side of the bed. Leaning over, he gathers my hands in his and then presses them to the pillow over my head. He wraps his belt around my wrists, tightening the hold with a firm tug at the end.

Looking intently down at me, he whispers, "Okay?"

I nod.

"Say it, sweetheart."

"Yes. Okay."

He nods, satisfied, and then returns to the end of the bed. Slowly, never taking his gaze from mine, he strips out of the rest of his clothing. When he's fully naked, his erection jutting out proudly, a drop of moisture glistening on the slit in the head, he growls, "You look fucking *amazing.*"

He grips his cock in one hand. With the other, he reaches down and thumbs over my clit.

I close my eyes, lost in sensation. Beyond the excruciating pleasure, I hear his voice, praising me.

"Your tits are gorgeous. Your skin is perfect. And that ass." He softly groans.

"Fuck me," I whisper, "Please. I need you."

Instead of his cock, I get his mouth again, teasing my clit. My back bows from the bed. He pinches both my nipples. A shock wave of pleasure rolls through me. I moan his name.

"Fuck my face, angel," he pants. "Come in my mouth. Let me taste you."

My hips twitch involuntarily at his words. *God, that dirty mouth destroys me.*

His fingers dig into my ass as he lifts me, grinding his mouth against my core. I feel the rough scrape of his unshaven jaw against my thighs, the tug of his teeth against the most sensitive part of my body. The sounds he makes are loud and carnal, sucking and smacking, completely erotic. Moaning and rolling my hips, helplessly bound and abandoned, I ride the strokes of his tongue until I'm right at the razor's edge—

Then he presses a finger inside me, and I come.

It's violent, taking over my entire body. I can't tell where it starts or ends, it feels as if it originates from everywhere at once.

I scream.

It feels so good to let go, so good to give myself over to him. I never want it to end.

Connor moans into me, encouraging me as I explode, convulsing and writhing, oblivious to everything else but the pleasure he's giving me.

"Yes. Beautiful. You taste like fucking heaven," he whispers, licking me, kissing me, worshipping me with his mouth.

I'm full of him, coming for him, and still I want more. I groan. My thighs shake. Every part of me shakes. Every part of me is desperate for his touch, for his hot, filthy words and sweet, gentle possession. I want whatever he wants to give me, but most of all, I want it *now*.

Connor rises. He sets my ankles on his shoulders and pulls me down to the edge of the mattress so his cock is pressed against my pussy. I feel it twitch and pulse.

I rock my hips against his hard length, loving it when I hear him hiss out a sharp breath. He turns his face to my leg and bites me on the ankle.

"You good?"

His voice is gravelly with lust, but also soft with concern, and that shatters me. I open my eyes and look at him. He's flushed, breathing hard, the muscles in his chest and arms are corded and tense. Gorgeous.

When I nod, he bites me just a little harder. He watches me lick my lips. Trailing his hands down my calves to my thighs, he rocks his hips so that his cock slides through my wet folds, back and forth, slow and torturing.

My head tilts back. My eyes slide shut. I moan.

"Gonna fuck you now, princess."

"Thank God."

His laugh is soft and pleased. Then the engorged head of his erection presses into my heat.

He slides in agonizingly slow, so I feel every inch, until I'm so full, my moans are broken. When he stays like that, hot and throbbing inside me, unmoving, just running his hands up and down my legs and over my hips, I tilt my pelvis and whimper. "Now now now now *now!*"

His laugh is soft and dark. He slides halfway out and then grips my hips and plunges deep inside me.

I cry out his name. He starts to fuck me with short, hard strokes, his fingers digging into my flesh, grunts of pleasure torn out of him with every thrust. He's talking too, words of adoration whispered in his rich, husky voice, but I lose the shape of them beneath the crashing of my heartbeat in my ears, and just let myself fall deeper.

My legs slide off his shoulders. He falls on top of me, kissing me savagely on my belly and breasts, biting, licking, sucking, all the while grunting and panting, sounding wild. He rears up on his elbows and grips my head, pulling my hair, manhandling me, rough and tender at the same time. His chest is slick with sweat. My legs wrap around his waist.

My pussy clenches around him, and I arch, moaning, lost to the sensation. I'm close again.

He says hoarsely into my neck, "Not yet. Tabby—I can't —hold on—"

He shudders and groans, his words cut off, and I know he's about to come too.

I turn my face to his ear and plead, "I need you somewhere else."

He stills, lifts his head, looks at me. When I bite my lip, his dark eyes flash. He slides his hand down my ribs, over my hip to my ass. I feel a press and a stroke between my cheeks, a gentle push, and I gasp when he sinks his finger deep—

"Here?"

I mew, rocking against his cock and his finger, wordlessly begging.

He exhales a slow, ragged breath. His brows draw together. "Are you sure?"

I can see exactly how much he wants this, which makes his hesitation all the more sweet. I drop my bound arms around his shoulders and give him a long, passionate kiss.

"Yes," I whisper, nipping his full lower lip. Then I roll onto my stomach, spread my legs, arch my back and glance at him over my shoulder. "I'm sure."

He looks down at me, presenting myself for his eyes to feast on. His lips part. His nostrils flare. A sharp tremor runs through him. "I don't want to hurt you," he whispers, his voice throbbing with desire.

With simple honesty, I say, "I want you to come inside me. Like this." When he hesitates, his body radiating ambivalence, I add, "*Soon.*"

His eyes flash to mine. With my demand so clearly articulated, Connor can't find another reason to delay.

He runs his hand up my back, tangles his fingers into my hair. He presses himself against me for a moment, inhaling against my skin, letting me feel all his jumbled emotions through the wild pounding of his heart. Then he releases my hair, drags his hands down my ribs and over my waist, and with his hands flat on the small of my back, presses me against the mattress.

"Open your legs wider," he says, his tone full of command. My arms over my head and my face pressed to the blanket, I close my eyes and do as he asks.

He slaps my ass. Surprised, I yelp and jerk.

He smooths his hands over the sting, softly stroking, crooning words of praise. Then he slaps me again even harder on the other cheek, making me moan. After eight more sharp slaps alternating back and forth from left to right cheek, he whispers, "So fucking wet. Look at you. All down your thighs."

I can't help myself. I rock my hips wantonly, canting my ass in the air, desperate to have him inside me.

"God, Tabby. You're so—" His voice breaks.

"Hurry," I whisper, looking up at him. "Connor. Please, hurry."

His hand trembles when he curls it around my hip. His knees nudge my thighs farther apart. Then I feel his hardness, his insistent heat, sliding gently up and down over my tight, puckered bud. He licks his fingers, wets the head of his cock, gently moistens me, then positions himself.

With the head of his cock fisted in his hand, Connor slowly presses forward and enters me.

I shudder, groan, grip the blanket. When he freezes, I whisper, "Don't stop."

His hand tightens around my hip. He flexes his pelvis, sliding deeper inside me. With his other hand, he reaches around and softly strokes my pulsing clit.

I buck back sharply, taking him to the hilt.

The moan that breaks from his chest is loud, broken, totally undone.

I love that sound.

The thought rips through my mind as pleasure rips through my body. I'm bound, and he's enormous, but the control is all mine. And all I want is to force that helpless sound from him again. I tilt my hips and find a rhythm, fast and hard, because we're both so close and I can't hold on much longer.

With every flex of my hips, he whispers, "Fuck. Fuck. Fuck," an incoherent chant of bliss. His strokes on my clit get rougher, faster, pinching and sliding. I cry out, losing it.

He grabs both my hips and drives into me so hard, I feel bent in two. Then he bellows and comes, holding me against him as he empties himself in wild, jerking pulses that shake the whole bed.

So good. So good. So fucking good.

I listen to him roar in pleasure as my own pleasure crests over me, erasing all other thoughts. My cries are torn out of me, muffled by the blanket I'm biting down on.

Connor slows. His grip on my hips gentles. He lowers himself on top of me, taking us both down to the bed, covering me with his strength and heat, panting into my ear.

We're quiet for a while, just letting our breathing slow. I feel boneless and overwhelmed, the intensity of what just happened eclipsing anything I might say.

He kisses me on the shoulder, brushes my hair off my face, kisses me on the neck. "Tell me you're not hurting," he rasps.

I whisper, "I'm good. Better than good."

He reaches above me, unties the belt from my wrists, throws it away. He massages my wrists and arms, and then very carefully eases out of me.

We both softly moan.

He rolls to his side, curling me up against him, the length of our bodies pressed together. He wraps his big arms around me. They're shaking.

"That was…"

"Intense," I whisper. "I know. I wish we could do it every night for the rest of our lives." As soon as it's out of my mouth, I freeze in horror.

Dear God. The man just fucked the truth right out of me.

26

TABBY

nderstanding I'm utterly dismayed about what just left my lips, Connor clears his throat.

"I'm not saying anything."

"Good."

I'm surprised he's letting it go, and also relieved we're not going to have a conversation about the future, or commitments, or any of the other million off-limits topics about our relationship. Or whatever this thing between us is called.

Enemies with benefits?

After a moment, Connor adds, "But if I were to say something—"

"I knew it!"

"—it would be that you just made me really goddamn happy. That's it."

He peppers sweet, reverent kisses all over my neck and shoulder.

"You're a romantic, you know that?"

Connor chuckles. "And you're the only woman who'd accuse a man of that in a surly tone of voice."

I grunt. It sounds surly.

He turns me over so I'm forced to look at him. "C'mon. Admit it. There must've been a time when you weren't quite so..."

I narrow my eyes. He has the good sense to look wary.

"If I say 'cynical,' will that be the last time I'll ever see my dick?"

"Probably. Tread carefully."

He cracks a cocky grin. "We've already had the conversation about how good I am at that."

"Hmm. You're right. You admitted in your letter that you only had one speed. Full steam ahead."

Connor takes that as a license to bulldoze away. "Yep. And since we're on the topic, why have you never had a drink before today?"

"We weren't on the topic."

"I'm full steaming here. Go with it, woman."

"Just out of curiosity, how can people who aren't having sex with you stand to be around you for more than five minutes?"

"Because of my good looks and charm, obviously. Answer the question."

"Connor—"

"You've had my cock in every orifice in your body, Tabitha. Answer the question."

We stare at each other until finally I say, "Please, for the love of all that's holy, never, *ever* say the word 'orifice' to me again."

He smirks. "Start talking, princess, or it's 'orifice orifice orifice' until the cows come home."

I flop onto my back and stare at the ceiling. "God, why do you hate me? Seriously, what have I done to offend you so deeply that you'd burden me with this ridiculous—"

"Ahem. Heroic," Connor interrupts.

"—egomaniacal—"

"Brilliant."

"—*delusional*—"

"And yet somehow always right."

"—insufferable, asinine, jockstrap of a man?"

After a moment, Connor says, "Jockstraps are very useful, so I'm taking that as a compliment. And I happen to know that you don't believe in God, so cut the theatrics and answer the question."

"I don't believe in the traditional definition of God," I answer. "The Biblical God who throws tantrums and demands sacrifices and basically acts like a spoiled five-year-old who needs a time-out, but I do believe in...something. Some sexless, formless, benevolent energy that watches over us and lets us flail away in ignorance until we finally get old enough or lucky enough to figure out that all we basically should be doing is being kind to each other and to every other sentient being on the planet.

"That's all. Just be kind. Help old people. Help the weak. Don't be an asshole. And stand up to bullies, no matter the cost."

I count the cracks in the ceiling. There are seventeen. It seems prophetic, somehow, that number. Seventeen was the age I was when all my deepest cracks began to form.

More softly, I say, "That's the most important thing. Stand up to bullies. Even if you accomplish nothing else with your life, standing up to a bully is enough. Bravery is an end to itself. That's what God or the universe or the sacred sparkle pony or whatever you call it wants. For us to learn to be brave and to do the right thing. In my humble opinion, that's the real meaning of life."

After a moment when Connor doesn't say anything, I add sheepishly, "Sorry. I'm always tetchy right before I get my period."

I get a big, warm hand on the side of my face, gently pressuring me to turn. When I meet Connor's eyes, the look in his is breathtaking.

He says quietly, "You are the most interesting, thoughtful,

beautiful, weird, and perfect soul I've ever met, Tabitha West. It's an honor to know you."

My throat tightens. When I inhale, it's with a little, hitching breath that makes it sound like I might be about to cry.

I AM NOT ABOUT TO CRY.

"Don't try to butter me up so I'll answer you stupid questions." I sniffle, blinking hard.

"Just the one question," he corrects. "And you know you're going to answer it, so just get it over with already."

I look at the ceiling again. Connor moves his hand to my belly, where it spreads open, warm and strangely comforting.

"Like a flesh blanket," I say, sighing.

"Um. What?"

"Oh. Sorry. I was just thinking out loud. Disregard."

"Uh-huh. I did include 'weird' in that list a second ago, right?"

"You did. And I keep telling people I'm not weird, I'm limited edition."

Connor chuckles. "Sweetheart, they broke the mold with you."

That makes me smile. "I know."

He leans in and softly kisses my shoulder. He nuzzles my neck, tickling me with his beard.

"Okay. Here's the answer to your question. Are you listening?" I ask when he starts to nibble on my earlobe.

"Mmhmm." Nibble. Nibble.

Enjoying the feeling of his lips on my skin, I close my eyes. "My dad used to drink a lot."

Connor abruptly stops nibbling. I feel him looking at me but don't open my eyes.

"It wasn't tragic, he didn't beat us or break things in drunken rages, but he just…anesthetized himself. That's how he dealt with stress. He'd come home from teaching and pour himself a big glass of gin and sit in front of the TV until the gin was gone, and then he'd pour himself another. And another. It made my mother really sad that he was so distant. I don't know what the problems were in their marriage. They never fought in front of me. But I remember very clearly him drinking gin every night until he quietly passed out, and my mother being lonely and depressed. So I decided when I was six years old that I'd never drink because I'd rather feel everything, no matter how painful, than nothing at all."

The pause that follows when I stop talking is what you'd call pregnant. Third-trimester pregnant. It makes me edgy.

"Don't feel sorry for me!"

Connor props his head on his hand and stares down at my face. Heat begins to suffuse my cheeks.

"You've been alone your entire life, haven't you?" he murmurs. "Even when your parents were alive, you were alone."

Awash in some weird half-breed emotion that's part regret, part shame, part longing for something I've never had, I laugh. Even to my own ears, it's ugly.

"That's why it was so easy for Søren to manipulate me. I wanted so badly—"

I stop abruptly. When I make a move to rise, Connor throws his leg over me and pins me down.

"No way," he says softly. "You're not running away from me, Tabby. Not anymore."

I close my eyes and turn my head.

"Don't hide from me," he urges, squeezing me. "Tell me what you wanted."

I'm breathing fast and hard, choking on so many feelings, it's hard to decide which one is worst. And maybe because I know in a few hours it's possible that this chapter of my life will finally be closed, or because I've been slowly revealing myself to Connor, one crumb at a time, tiny truth-chunks that he's always gobbled up, but I don't want to hide from him anymore. At least, not right now.

Right now, I want there to be no walls between us.

For this one wild moment, I want to let him in.

I look at him. I let him see everything. All the pain and confusion, all the hope and tenderness and absolute terror of getting too close. In a raw, shaking voice, I say, "I just wanted to belong to someone."

Connor's face goes through a dozen expressions before it settles on adoration. He breathes, "And now you do."

He kisses me so passionately, I'm stunned.

I flatten my hands on his chest and push him away.

We break apart and stare at each other in throbbing silence, both of us breathing raggedly. Finally, I whisper, "What did you say?"

Connor's Adam's apple bobs as he swallows. "You heard me."

"Say it again."

Connor wraps his hands around my wrists. He carefully peels my hands from his chest, lowers them to the pillow above my head so he's on top of me, his chest pressed to mine, his nose inches from mine. Staring into my eyes, he says firmly, "You belong to me. You belong *with* me. You're mine, and I'm never letting you go."

There's a long, tense silence.

Then I burst into tears.

"Goddammit!" I sob. "You asshole! Look what you did!"

Connor kisses me all over my red, wet face, murmuring soothing words that I only catch snippets of because I'm bawling like a damn baby. He releases my wrists, and I fling my arms around his broad shoulders and bury my face in his neck.

"Love your tears, princess, 'cause I know you'd never give them to anyone but me," he murmurs into my ear. For once, I don't mind that he used that forbidden four-letter word.

I let him hold me and listen to his sweet, beautiful words, wondering through my tears and hiccupping breaths if this is what religion is like for some people, all this awe and mystery and the feeling of having found your way home.

Sometime shortly after my tears slow to sniffles, we fall asleep in each other's arms.

And sometime after that, I wake up sweating, with a pounding heart and an awful premonition that something is terribly wrong.

On the table beside the bed, Connor's cell phone rings. He's awake instantly, snatching it up.

"Talk to me," he commands.

He listens. After a moment, he wordlessly ends the call. When he looks at me, I know. I already know.

"Søren," I whisper, my heart in my throat.

Connor's body is completely still. In the shadows, his eyes shine with a strange, deadly light. "The team in Miami that went in to get him…" He hesitates. "It was an abandoned house. The place was rigged with explosives."

Horrified, I gasp. I bolt upright and clutch his arm. "Oh my God. How many were hurt?"

"Nine agents went in."

"How many came out?"

Connor says simply, "None."

CONNOR

On the ride to the studio, Tabby is silent. Unnervingly silent, like she might have lost the ability to speak. I keep her hand tightly wrapped in mine, but in spite of that physical connection, there's a chasm between us. She's beside me, but she's a million miles away.

I sense that somehow, with some twisted logic that only makes sense to her, she's blaming herself for what happened.

"It wasn't your fault," I say as gently as I can.

We're stopped at a red traffic signal only a few blocks from the studio. Her face is lit crimson, bathed in a devilish light. She doesn't answer me. She doesn't even blink. She just stares through the windshield into the gray dawn of early morning, her face as white as chalk beneath the traffic light's eerie glow.

"Tabby—"

"I should have known it was too easy. I should have known it was a trap."

Her voice is flat. Empty, like she's dead inside. I squeeze her hand, but she doesn't squeeze back.

When we drive into the parking structure at the studio, she's out of the car and striding across the dark lot before I've even turned the engine off, leaving the passenger door wide open behind her.

"Tabby! Wait!" I curse when she ignores me.

She enters the open parking garage elevator, punches the button, stands mute and stone-faced while I jog across the lot, my footsteps echoing. I run through the elevator doors just as they're sliding shut.

I grasp her shoulders, turning her to face me as the car begins to ascend. "We're in this together, all right? Don't shut me out. Whatever happens, I've got your back."

Tabby stares at me like she's never seen me before in her life. The bell dings. The elevator doors slide open. With a sharp twitch of her body, she shakes me off.

With frost on her breath, she says, "When I told you before that Søren would end it if he found out I was involved in the investigation, I didn't mean what Miranda thought I meant. I wasn't talking about what he'd do to the studio."

"What are you saying? I don't understand."

Her eyes are dark and endless, full of secrets only she knows. "I mean that all these years, we've both just been biding our time."

I'm so frustrated with this cryptic line of conversation, I want to shake her. "Tabby, what the fuck are you talking about?"

"I'm talking about fate, Connor. About physics. About how certain events have so much weight they create their own gravity, and you can waste your entire life in orbit around their memory, caught in their magnetic pull. And there's only one thing that can break that miserable, endless revolution."

I'm lost. I admit it. She's completely lost me. I stand with my hands spread open in a helpless gesture, waiting for an explanation.

It never comes.

Instead, she surprises me by reaching out and caressing my

cheek. Softly, with grave tenderness, she says, "You're a good man, Connor Hughes."

Something about her tone of voice makes all the hair on the back of my neck stand on end. "Why does that sound like a goodbye?"

She smiles. It's the saddest thing I've ever seen. Then she turns around and walks away without another word.

Into my mind a thought rises, unbidden.

I have a really bad feeling about this.

The COM center is buzzing with activity when we walk in, but as soon as we're spotted, it falls dead silent.

Miranda stands by the windows, her head bowed, her arms crossed over her chest, her complexion as pale and severe as the tailored suit she's wearing. The FBI agents are broken into several close-knit groups, standing together around their computers like satellites hovering around a mother ship. Special Agent Chan is standing beside O'Doul's desk, looking shell-shocked, his black hair standing at odd angles, his striped tie askew.

Off by himself near the whiteboard stands Rodriguez. He's staring straight at Tabby with an expression that can only be described as pure, unadulterated rage.

My nerves, which normally simmer somewhere around DEFCON 3, slam up to DEFCON 1. My ears prick. My muscles tense. Every sense screams into high alert.

Ryan makes a beeline for us from where he'd been standing at a respectful distance from Miranda near the windows. As soon as he's close, I ask in a low voice, "Where's O'Doul?"

Ryan glances at Tabby. His expression is neutral. "Went to Florida to head up the tactical op in coordination with SWAT, didn't he?"

Translation: O'Doul is scattered in a thousand bloody chunks over some neighborhood in Miami.

I look at Tabby, hunting for her eyes, but she keeps them averted. I feel her react to the realization that O'Doul is dead, and then force herself not to react. After a heartbeat of frozen silence, she gives off a dangerous, crackling energy, as cold as black ice and just as deadly.

Ryan feels it too. He looks at me with his brows quirked just so, in warning.

"You," hisses Rodriguez into the awkward quiet, "fucking *cunt!*"

Then somehow I'm across the room, standing over Rodriguez, who is writhing on the floor, clutching the bloodied pulp of his nose which I've just smashed with my fist.

The room erupts. Three guys are on me, then four, then five. It rapidly devolves to a free-for-all, a half dozen FBI suits vs. the dynamic duo of me and Ryan, shoving and shouting insults and really just letting off some steam. When it's over, we're no worse for the wear, but the suits are looking pretty goddamn rattled. No bones are broken. Other than Rodriguez, no blood has been spilled.

Across the room, past all of us as if we don't exist, Tabby and Miranda stare at each other. Tabby has this weird look, this thousand-yard stare that I've seen once or twice before on the best military snipers.

"Special Agent Chan. You're in charge here now, I assume?"

Tabby keeps her gaze on Miranda as she calmly speaks. Chan nods, rakes a hand through his disheveled hair, nods again. When he realizes Tabby's not looking at him, he says, "Yes."

"With your permission, I'd like to inspect the data you pulled from the phone call."

His look sharpens. "Why?"

Tabby is statue still, in full control of whatever she's feeling. Not even a muscle twitches on her face. But I know behind that mask of placid loveliness is a storm of biblical proportions.

"Because I think Søren fed false data points into your software. I think he led you where he wanted you to go. I think he knew he was being traced."

"That's impossible," says Chan.

Slowly Tabby turns to look at him. Pinning him in her icy stare, she asks softly, "Is it?"

For a long moment, Chan says nothing. Except for the sound of a fly buzzing against the windowpanes, the room is eerily silent. Then: "I can't trust you around a computer."

From the floor, still cradling his bleeding nose, Rodriguez says bitterly, "Amen."

When I glare at him, he blanches and looks away.

"I'm not asking for your trust," says Tabby, "or for anything else for that matter. I understand…"

She falters for the briefest of moments, her voice wavering before she reins it back under that tight, frozen control.

"I understand that what happened is because of me—"

"It's *not*," I say loudly, stepping forward. Without looking at me, she holds up a hand.

"But I'd like the opportunity to try to see if I can find anything that might be helpful."

"We've already looked."

"I haven't."

When Rodriguez realizes Chan is considering it, he explodes.

"She's a fucking *traitor*, Chan! She's a liar! She's the reason nine good men are dead! Did you know she lived with Mael-str0m? That's right," he says when Tabby recoils and several agents utter disbelieving gasps. "I looked through O'Doul's notes. This"—he stabs a finger in Tabby's direction—"is Mael-str0m's bitch!"

Ryan has to physically restrain me from tearing Rodriguez in two. He pushes me back several steps with his hands on my chest while I growl and seethe, straining forward, tasting blood. He murmurs calming, rational words, but to my furious ears, they all sound like *kill, kill, murder, kill.*

I wonder vaguely if I might need to spend some time on a psychotherapist's couch when this job is over. My entire body feels like an exposed nerve scraped raw by knives.

"As usual, you don't know your ass from your elbow, Rodriguez," says Chan. "And your reading comprehension skills are as shitty as ever. She was *victimized* by Maelstr0m, which is why she's assisting in the investigation. She has as good a reason as the rest of us to want to catch this bastard."

Rodriguez spits a mouthful of blood onto the carpet. He staggers to his feet. "You're a dope. You were only hired because of affirmative action, anyway."

Chan doesn't rise to the insult. He turns his gaze to Tabby. "Why don't you use this computer, Miss West?" He points to the desk where Rodriguez sits.

"Are you fucking kidding me?"

"No, Agent Rodriguez, I am not. Miss West—sit."

Rodriguez storms out. In his absence, the other agents seem at a loss for what to do. A few follow Rodriguez, a few sit at their desks, most of them just stay where they are, milling around, lame ducks in a swiftly draining pond. Tabby takes the opportunity to cross over to the empty desk, pull out the chair, and sit down.

Ryan gives me one final friendly shove, says so only I can hear, "Eyes open, brother. Pawns are moving."

"Don't I fucking know it," I say under my breath.

"What's the system password?" Tabby asks Chan.

When he looks at her sideways, she says patiently, "It'll be faster if you just give it to me."

He recites a list of words, numbers, and symbols that sound like some fucked-up form of haiku. Tabby rapidly types as he speaks. "I'm in. Where's the file?"

Chan points. Tabby clicks. Ryan and I move silently closer, watching everything with greedy, searching eyes.

We stand behind her as she opens a series of windows across three monitors and starts a scrolling view of all the code, stripped to its bare bones. It's like a scene out of *The Matrix*.

She's reading it. Jesus Christ. She's reading thousands of lines of raw code in real time.

Ryan and I share an astonished glance.

"Here," she says after a minute, pointing. With a click of her mouse, everything on the screen comes to a halt.

Chan gasps. "Well, I'll be a baloney sandwich. It's a patch."

Tabby grimly nods. "Undetectable by your software because there's no mathematical pattern. A computer sees it as completely random. It's technically not even a program. You have to scour the code manually line by line to find it. You have to look past all the noise and focus *through* the code to see the picture that emerges."

"Did he know you'd find this?" Chan asks.

"He knows everything," Tabby replies without a hint of irony.

That murdery feeling in my gut makes a reappearance. Ryan's hand clamps down on my shoulder. I close my eyes, breathe through my nose, and silently count to ten.

"Does this mean you can see his real location?" asks Ryan.

Something about Ryan's question makes her fall still. She stares in silence at the screen for a moment before saying, "No. Not yet. I need more time to go through the code."

Her tone is odd. Off, somehow. I want to ask her about it, but Chan interrupts.

"A group from Washington is due to arrive any minute."

Right. Nine dead federal agents gets you a shit storm of attention from Washington.

I say, "They'll relieve you of command, debrief the group, including us, and install another team to finish the op."

Agitated, Chan runs a hand through his hair and nods. "Working in conjunction with Homeland Security and the DOJ. And now that we know Killgaard's cybercrimes are international, the CIA and the NSA are involved."

Tabby repeats faintly, "The National Security Administration. Perfect." She laughs softly. It sends chills down my spine.

"There's nothing for you to worry about, Tabby. Your involvement in this job was at the specific request of Miranda Lawson. Everything you've done has been sanctioned by her and a federal agent. They can't blame anything on you."

She looks at me. In her eyes, I see that strange farewell again, the same expression she wore when she told me I was a good man, as if it would be the last time she'd ever see me alive.

She turns her faraway eyes to Chan. "Agent Chan, please. Let me try to find something before they get here. Just give me a few more minutes to look through the code."

"Tabby—"

She cuts me off. "Connor, I need to concentrate. Five minutes, okay? That's all I need, and then we can talk."

I look at Chan. He shrugs his shoulders, agreeing. I look at Ryan, at the remaining agents, at Miranda near the windows, her back still turned to us all. "Fine," I say, my voice low. "Five minutes. Do what you can to find this bastard, and then let it go and let the suits handle it."

Her eyes glimmer. She whispers, "I will."

She waits until the three of us have stepped away and then turns her attention to the computer screen in front of her. She bends her head over the keyboard and goes to work.

Five minutes later, as Ryan and I are talking quietly in a corner, the door to the room bursts open. Guys in matching beige trench coats and murderous scowls swarm inside.

Feds. Top brass, by the looks of 'em.

And supremely pissed off.

One of them, a tall, thin man with iron-gray hair and a voice like a bullhorn, holds up a cell phone and thunders, "The director of the NSA would like to know who in this room just hacked their fucking mainframe!"

Gleaming under the lights as they slip out from beneath trench coats, nickel-plated shotguns appear.

Time stops. All the air is sucked out of the room. I look over at Tabby, but she's not looking back at me. She's calmly looking at the man with the iron-gray hair, and she's standing. She's raising her hand. She's opening her mouth to speak.

"I'm your huckleberry."

It happens fast.

Handcuffs flash. Men shout. Trench coats flare around running legs.

I leap forward with a roar, adrenaline searing my veins, but they've slammed Tabby down onto the desk and twisted her arms behind her back before I can reach her. I shove through the crowd—

And get the business end of a Glock .40 caliber handgun jammed under my jaw.

"Hello there, Mr. Hughes," says the man with the iron-gray hair. His eyes, I note, are exactly the same color. "Now say good night."

The butt of a shotgun cracks hard against the back of my skull. Stars explode in my vision, flashing pinpricks of pain. The room slips sickeningly sideways.

The last thing I see is Tabby, handcuffed, being dragged away by a knot of armed men.

Why is she smiling?

Everything goes black.

TABBY

*a*fter a short flight on a C-130 military plane, I'm seated at a table in a small, cold room in a government complex in the middle of who knows where. I had a black hood over my head when they brought me in, but they took it off, and now I can observe my surroundings.

Cement floor. Cinderblock walls. Cement ceiling inlaid with a row of florescent lights. The black plastic eye of a closed-circuit camera high on the wall in one corner.

A glass of water sits on the table to my left. Beside it is a sleeve of Oreos, which I find amusing. Apparently, the government wants you to have a tasty snack before they start with the waterboarding.

At least they removed the handcuffs.

The door opens. A man walks in. Caucasian. Thirtyish. Built. He's tall with shaggy reddish-blonde hair, handsome with the exception of acne scars pitting his cheeks. His suit is black, as is his skinny tie. I've never seen eyes that color, pale amber, like honey. He looks like a friendly ginger tabby cat, which I know is intentionally misleading.

Beneath his suit, there's a bulge on his left ankle and one on his right hip. Tabby cats who wear guns strapped to various parts of their bodies are anything but friendly.

He sits on the edge of the table, casually tosses a manila file folder my way. It lands with a dull slap against the steel tabletop, slides a few inches, spilling pages from the sides.

"Is that me?" I ask, eyeing the file.

Shaggy nods.

"It's pretty thick."

"You've led an interesting life."

I cock my head and appraise him. "So have you, I bet. What's that accent? No, let me guess. Appalachia?"

He watches me with those unusual eyes. "Twenty years ago. You're the first person in fifteen to catch it."

We stare at each other. Without a hint of emotion, his gaze takes me in, moving over my face, my hair, my body, finally settling on my wrist. "Interesting timepiece."

"Thank you."

"Family heirloom?" His voice is faintly amused.

"Something like that. I'm surprised you didn't confiscate it."

"In my experience, plastic Hello Kitty watches usually aren't cause for alarm."

I smile, and the stare-off resumes. After a while I ask, "So are you going to tell me your name or should I just keep calling you Shaggy like I'm doing in my head?"

"You aren't scared," he notes.

"That's not really my thing."

"Right now it should be."

"My ride's on the way."

His expression doesn't change. "No one is coming to rescue you."

"I never said it was a rescue," I reply, holding his gaze. "But someone is definitely coming."

"Really? Who?"

I have to give it to him, this guy has an amazing poker face.

"Not into suspense, huh?"

He smiles for the first time. He has good teeth, straight and pearly white, like a movie star. "On the contrary. I'm all about suspense. Mysteries too. Like that cryptophone we took off you. *Über* mysterious. Never seen anything like it. Programmed in Sanskrit, encryption ciphers that blow all current known protocols away, even ours. Where'd you get a hold of technology like that? Bangalore? The Chinese?"

I blow a scornful breath through my lips. "I didn't 'get a hold' of it. I made it."

An infinitesimal pause follows. "I see."

"You don't believe me."

"Perhaps if you elaborated."

"Oh, you want schematics? Sorry, didn't bring them along."

Shaggy's smile grows wider. "That's all right. We'll get them from your home office. We're searching it now."

I can tell he expects me to gasp or go pale or lose my shit in some visible way, but as I already called Juanita from the bathroom at the hotel before Connor and I went back to the studio and told her to flip the red switch on the wall in my office that would melt down all the hard drives on my computers and fry every circuit board on every other piece of electronic equipment I own, I'm sitting pretty.

Hopefully the rest of the house didn't get melted down along with the computers, but I never finished decorating anyway.

I say, "You don't have to walk around like that, you know."

"Pardon?"

"With a face like a hundred miles of bad road. They have lasers that can fix acne scars now. There's no need to be mistaken for Tommy Lee Jones. I mean, you're a good-looking guy. The procedure probably isn't even that expensive. One, maybe two grand? You'd be Brad Pitt."

"He's a bit of a douche, though, no?"

Now I'm smiling. "Totally. Why you'd leave Jennifer Aniston for that psychotic witch Angelina Jolie I have no idea."

Shaggy shrugs. "Angelina is probably better in bed."

"Well, yeah, but you just *fuck* crazy. You don't marry it."

After a moment wherein we simply stare at each other, Shaggy decides to get down to business. "There are things we don't know. We'd like you to fill in the blanks."

I make a face. "Uh-oh. The royal 'we.' I'm in trouble now."

"For instance, when did you first discover Søren Killgaard was your brother?"

Slam! goes my heart against my breastbone. The friendly tabby cat just unsheathed his claws.

After I catch my breath, I say, "He's not my brother."

Shaggy opens the file with one finger, lazily lifts up a page to read something. "Half brother. I stand corrected." He lets the file drop closed, folds his hands in his lap, turns his golden gaze back to my face. "The unfortunate product of your father's brief affair with a Norwegian student of his."

I swallow. It feels like someone shoved a fistful of gravel down my throat. "Dutch," I whisper. "The student was Dutch."

We stare at each other. He doesn't look so friendly anymore.

"The plane crash that killed your parents."

Knowing what's about to come, I close my eyes.

"Forensics determined that interference with the airplane's onboard navigational system was the cause of the accident. Someone hacked into the in-flight entertainment interface, and from there…"

He snaps his fingers. *Poof!* "But you already knew that, didn't you?"

I open my eyes and glare at Shaggy. "News flash: I hate rhetorical questions. Fuck off."

"You had evidence that your half brother caused a plane crash that killed two hundred thirty-five people, including your own parents, and you did nothing with that information."

"Incorrect. I told the police about it. They thought I was nuts. At the time of the incident in question, he was *thirteen*."

"And by all accounts already a sociopath."

"All accounts? Like whose? The FBI didn't even know he existed until a few days ago."

"We aren't the FBI."

No, they aren't. The NSA is the agency that has the entire planet wire-tapped. Emails, Facebook posts, instant messages, phone calls—they record it all in cooperation with every major technology provider and sift through the data at a speed of seventy quadrillion bits per second. It would take the average home PC twenty-two-thousand years to do what their supercomputer at their headquarters in Maryland can do in the blink of an eye.

They're Big Brother's big brother.

I can't sit anymore. I jerk to my feet, start to pace, chew a hangnail on my thumb. Shaggy isn't concerned by my sudden need to rove around. He just watches me, tracking my every move with those cagey alley cat eyes.

"When I knew him—"

"At MIT."

"Yes! Shut up, will you, I'm getting things off my chest! Where was I? Oh yes. When I knew him, Søren was always taking credit for things. Anytime anything malfunctioned anywhere in the world—a roller coaster that went off its tracks at an amusement park in Paris, a broken water main that flooded a subway tunnel in Amsterdam, plane crashes, train derailments, terrorist bombings—you name it, he claimed it was his doing. If he could've figured out a way to take credit for going back in time and shooting JFK, he would have."

I swing around, enraged by all the memories, and look at Shaggy. "I thought he was full of shit!"

Shaggy replies calmly, "Until you found out he wasn't."

Yes. Until I found out he wasn't. Which is when everything fell apart.

I turn my back, fold my arms over my chest, and stare at the cement wall.

Shaggy keeps talking in this light, casual tone of voice, like we're two girlfriends having tea. "The FBI's theory is that you two met at MIT, and then lived together and hacked together until you had some kind of falling-out. After which Søren got payback for whatever you'd done to piss him off in the form of pinning the Bank of America job on you, and then he vanished. It's a solid theory, but the real question is, what caused the falling-out?"

When I don't respond, he asks, "Would you like to hear *my* theory?"

"Fuck no with a capital F-U-C-K."

"I think you tried to kill him."

Shaggy, you dick. This guy has X-ray vision. He sees through me even better than Connor does.

I exhale, hard. "In my defense, he really had it coming."

He ignores that. "I listened to the tape of the call between you two. Creepy stuff. 'Pet?' 'You've made me wait so long?' The way he said your name? I think your brother was in love with you, to the point of obsession. Still is, by the sound of it."

Between gritted teeth I say, "*Half* brother."

He ignores that too. "I think he constructed an elaborate web of mind fuckery with you, little fly, right in the middle. And by the time you realized that everything in your life had been manipulated by him, that he'd been pulling the strings all the way back from the deaths of your parents when you were eight years old to the death of your uncle when you were seventeen— which led to the foster home, which led to him rescuing you from the foster home—you were so far down the rabbit hole, you didn't know how to find your way out. And so, like every wild thing does when it's cornered, you lashed out."

"You got all that from reading a file, huh?"

Apparently his little speech is over, because he doesn't add anything else or answer my question. He just sits, waiting.

And because this game is coming to a close, I decide to tell him the truth.

I turn to look at him. "Are you familiar with *50 Shades of Grey*?"

Shaggy doesn't bat an eyelash. "The kinky sex book. My girlfriend loved it. Used to read it out loud to me in bed. Good stuff. And?"

"And," I say, looking him in the eye, "Søren Killgaard makes Christian Grey look like a Disney prince."

Another pause while he absorbs my words. "So in addition to being a sociopath, he's a sadist."

"If the Marquis de Sade and Steve Jobs had a love child, it would be Søren. He's brilliant, he's brutal, and he likes to break things."

"Again, and?"

"And he consumed me."

Shaggy waits, those amber eyes burning.

I turn back to the wall. Every beat of my heart is a little earthquake inside my chest.

"There's no other way to describe it. He fed on my loneliness like a snake feeds on a mouse. I was blinded by him. By his brilliance. By his mind, the way it worked. At the beginning—even though I knew something was wrong with him, that he was broken—I was so grateful that he took me in when I had no one else, that he *protected* me from something so terrible and stood up for me when no one else would, that I pushed aside my doubts. I went to live with him—"

"In a home owned by Professor Alfredo Durand."

My stomach tightening, I glance at him.

He says, "We had a little chat with your professor after the FBI did. He said you two were the brightest minds he'd ever encountered. Huge potential to change the world. So he took you under his wing and gave you the keys to the kingdom. Twenty-four-seven access to the best computer science and artificial intelligence lab on the planet."

"Which would have cost him his job if the university had found out."

"So you protected him during the investigation by saying you'd been living in your car."

I say forcefully, "Too many innocent people have paid for Søren's sins. I wasn't about to let Professor Durand be another one. He was a good man, trying to do a good thing. He had no way of knowing he'd made a deal with the devil."

Shaggy nods thoughtfully. "Okay. Back to the devil."

I blow out another hard breath, drag my hands through my hair. "He acted like my best friend in the world. That's what he said we were, best friends. Brother and sister. Two peas in a pod, so lucky to have found each other. And to his credit, he was a perfect gentleman." My voice gains an edge. "At first."

In the silence, I feel Shaggy searching for words. "How do I put this delicately... He forced you?"

"No. Or else I would have stabbed him much sooner. No, Søren would never take a woman against her will. He thought that was beneath him. Something only animals would do. And besides, he was beautiful. He had plenty of willing playmates."

I shudder at the memory of all those girls who'd arrive at the house smiling and coy in the evening, and leave in the morning walking gingerly, with bruises mottling their lovely necks.

"At first I thought it was all in my head, these little...attentions he would pay me. I mean, we were related, for fuck's sake! He showed me the DNA tests that proved it. It *couldn't* be happening. Only it was. And at seventeen, I had no frame of reference for how to deal with something like that. Something so...gross. It was just gross and twisted and unbelievable, and I kept pushing the thought away, and we kept working together, learning new hacks, creating new code, planning…"

Shaggy asks sharply, "Planning what?"

My exhalation sounds as if it comes from the body of a hundred-year-old woman. "The kind of Utopia only the truly naïve or insane believe can exist. Countries without borders. Societies without governments. Freedom and equality for everyone, of every race, color, and creed."

"And you thought you could do that through hacking," Shaggy says flatly.

I turn and look him in the eye. "If every electronic system on the planet went down, how many hours would it be before total chaos ensued? No lights, no refrigeration, no goods being transported because no fuel could be pumped from gas tanks. No hospitals. No medicine. No food. No Internet. No phones. No emergency response teams. No police. No *infrastructure.*

"Modern society is a sand castle, and all it would take to bring it crashing down is one good wave. That wave is the failure of technology. Knock out a single transformer manufacturer and just nine of our fifty-five thousand interconnected electrical substations, and all the power goes out in the US for eighteen months. *Eighteen months.* My best guess? At least half the population wouldn't survive it."

After a moment, Shaggy says, "Yes. Those equations have been run."

"So you see my point."

"All right. So you were an idealistic teenager, and he was your pervy older brother—"

"*Half brother!*"

"Excuse me. Pervy half brother with a penchant for sado-masochism and hobbies that included plotting the downfall of society and trying to get into his little sister's panties. Excuse me again," he says, seeing the violence in my eyes, "*Half sister's* panties."

"In a nutshell," I say stiffly, "yes."

"So what was the tipping point? What made you decide to take him out?"

I drop into the chair and slouch down. Looking at its scarred surface, I say dully, "When I discovered that he used some of my code, software that *I* had written, to hack into a military satellite and intercept a drone conducting surveillance over Kandahar. He changed the coordinates, gave it new orders." My voice drops. "The drone was armed with a Hellfire missile."

"What was the target?"

It's almost unbearable to do it, but I look up and meet his eyes. "A grade school. He bombed a fucking *grade school.* When I confronted him, he said he was doing a service to humanity by killing future terrorists. I could choke on the irony of that."

Shaggy doesn't even have the good grace to look disgusted. "When was this?"

"December 25, 2007." When I swallow it tastes like ashes. "He said it was his Christmas present to me."

I have to look away for a moment to compose myself before I can continue. "Before that, it was all talk. At least, I *thought* it was. He'd say casually, 'Tabitha, did you see the news today? Bomb went off in the British Prime Minister's office,' and he'd smile. I'd roll my eyes and tell him he was full of shit. It was a game he liked to play. A little deception. The boy who cried wolf. Only ultimately I realized it wasn't a game. I mean, for him it was. For everyone else, it was deadly real. But until the end, I had no idea that he was really...that he was capable of..."

I swallow, take another deep breath. "Once the cat was out of the bag about the drone, he told me the truth about the crash my parents died in. When we first met, he showed me letters between my father and his mother, detailing their secret affair. He said he'd found them along with the DNA tests after his mother died, and was overjoyed to discover he had a sister. What he left out was that his mother went into a deep depression after my father rejected her when he found out she was pregnant. A depression that years later led her to commit suicide.

"So Søren figured out a way to pay my father back for that betrayal. It didn't matter to him that all those other people, including my mother, died on the plane he took down. He called it 'collateral damage.' That's when I realized all the times I'd thought he'd been joking about the things he'd done, he hadn't been. And that's when I snapped."

Shaggy sees the despair on my face and moves in for the kill. "Where is he?"

I look up. "If I knew that, he'd already be dead."

His amber eyes narrow. He doesn't believe me.

"Okay. Let me tell you how this goes. If you don't cooperate and lead us to him, you'll spend the rest of your life here." He points at the floor. "Right here, in this room. No jury. No trial. You'll just disappear. You'll get a bucket to piss and shit in that will be changed once a week. You'll get a cot in that corner to sleep on. Maybe you'll get a pillow. Maybe not, but definitely no TV and no computer. You'll eat the same thing every day, for every meal. You like chicken soup?" He gifts me that celebrity smile. "Personally, I find it overrated."

He stands with a smooth unfolding of limbs. "So. Are you going to help us, or are you going to rot?"

I want to roll my eyes, but I'm too tired to expend the energy. "Honestly. Why do you think I'm here, Shaggy?"

"You're here because you hacked into our mainframe, which is the topic for another conversation." He pauses. "Incredible work, by the way. Off the record, that was the first time I've been truly surprised in years. How did you do it so fast?"

"Thank you. And *duh*, with a universal encryption key."

Shaggy's left eyebrow shoots up, like Spock when he's parsing some bit of human behavior that makes no sense to his Vulcan mind. "There's no such thing."

"Right. And there are no alien aircraft at Area 51."

His other brow shoots up.

"And no, hacking your database isn't why I'm here. Well, technically it is, but that's just what *got* me here. *Why* I'm here is to help you. By helping you, I help myself, and...well, pretty much the entire human race. It's time for me to put an end to this game, once and for all."

The man has the patience of a Buddha. He waits for me to explain myself as if he's got all the time in the world.

I rub a hand over my eyes. They feel gritty. Suddenly I'm more than tired. I'm completely spent.

The rows of fluorescents overhead flicker and snap. Shaggy looks up, frowning.

With a pop and a sizzle, they're extinguished, plunging us into blackness.

Into the dark, I sigh.

"It's been nice chatting with you, Shaggy, but my ride's here."

CONNOR

I don't know how long I was out, but when I come to, I'm on the floor in the office next to the COM center, flat on my back. They must've dragged me in while I was unconscious.

By "they," I mean the four FBI agents flanking either side of the closed door.

I sit up, wincing, and gingerly touch the back of my head. Sticky wetness, an open gash, a big-ass lump... Yeah, that's gonna leave a mark.

I've had worse. And right now, I've got something much more important to worry about.

One of the agents says into the mic at his wrist, "He's awake."

They're all miked, with small plastic receivers nested in their ears. Two of them have shotguns in hand. All of them are wearing their standard-issue Glocks on their belts. In appearance, they're almost identical. Average height, medium-brown hair, beige trench coat, utterly forgettable. One of them works a tooth-pick between his teeth, but aside from that, they could be quadruplets.

I know enough to keep my mouth shut until their boss arrives. I busy myself by wiping the blood from my fingers onto the leg of my pants.

When the door opens a few minutes later, it's the tall, iron-gray-hair dude who walks through it. He folds his arms over his chest and appraises me with an air of faint disappointment.

"Mr. Hughes—"

"Call me Connor. Where've you taken Tabitha West?"

Ignoring my interruption, he begins again. "Mr. Hughes, I'm Deputy Director Overton Downs."

I wait for a second to see if he's joking. When no one cracks a smile, I decide he's not. "That's a helluva name. Sounds more like a place. In England, maybe. 'Come visit the spectacular gardens at Overton Downs,' like that."

Downs finds my humor lacking. His gray eyes take on a distinctive chill. He gestures to a chair. "Have a seat, Mr. Hughes."

Guess we're not gonna be on a first-name basis, then. Somehow I didn't think we would be. Probably on account of that gun he shoved into my face.

I stand, cross to the chair he indicated, lower myself into it, and wait.

If he were going to arrest me, he'd have done it already, so this little meet and greet must be part of the debrief process. Most likely Ryan, Miranda, and everyone else have been separated and are getting raked over the coals as I'm about to be.

Deputy Director Downs—Overton? Really? What the fuck were his parents thinking?—pulls up a chair and straddles it backwards, very casual, very Mr. Government cool, very "we're all just friends here."

I'm not buying it for a second.

"I need to ask you a few questions, Mr. Hughes."

His voice is clipped, precise as a scalpel. I peg him as an

anal-retentive, by-the-book type, which won't leave me much wiggle room to negotiate.

I nod. "I understand. Where is Tabitha West?"

His look sours. He reaches into the pocket of his trench coat, removes a travel-sized bottle of Tums, flips the cap open, shakes a few pale pink tablets into his mouth, and grinds them between his molars. "You know I can't tell you that."

Fighting the urge to curl my hands around his throat and choke the information out of him, I lean forward and rest my forearms on my knees.

"Look. I know how this works. You lunge, I parry. You thrust, I feint. We go round and round, rapiers clashing, until someone gets fatally stuck. Let's just cut to the chase. You need information about what went down on this op and information about her. Anything you need to know about the op, I'll tell you. Anything I've learned about Søren Killgaard, I'll tell you, with the exception of what's not mine to tell. I was entrusted with certain things. I'm not gonna break that trust. And I'll tell you right now that if you ask me *how* she did it, I don't have a clue. But I do know it wasn't an accident. She knew exactly what she was doing."

Downs seems surprised. "So you admit she hacked the NSA's database."

I scoff, "She admitted it right to your face. And technically, I don't know exactly what she did because I wasn't watching, but I do know that you busted through the door screaming bloody murder about an NSA breach, so I think everyone in the room put two and two together without needing a fucking calculator. All that's a sideshow, anyway. You're missing the bigger picture."

He crunches thoughtfully on his antacids. "Okay, I'll bite. What's the bigger picture?"

"*Why* she did it."

Crunch. Crunch. Crunch.

"I'm gonna have to spoon-feed this to you, aren't I?"

"You're saying she wanted to get caught."

"I'm saying the woman does nothing without a good reason." *Crunch. Crunch.* "Hypothetically, why would she want to get caught?"

"So you'd take her wherever you took her. She anticipated that outcome."

He looks dubious. Even his crunching stops. "Uh-huh."

We stare at each other. The ticking of the clock on the wall is painfully loud. My patience—never my strong suit—is already growing thin. "You talk to Chan yet?"

Downs nods. "That we did."

"And?"

"And I think he's almost as in love with Tabitha West as you are."

It's a shot in the dark, but when my jaw tightens, he can see he's hit his target. He crunches the last of the Tums, swallows, and runs his tongue over his teeth.

His tone turns philosophical. "You want to know the problem with love?"

I growl, "No."

He taps his temple. "It messes with your head. Turns a sane man stupid. Take you, for example."

"Let's not."

"You were a spectacular soldier, by any measure. Immaculate service record. Such valiant, almost comically fearless leadership during multiple tours in Afghanistan and Iraq, you earned a Medal of Honor, a Purple Heart, a Silver Star, a Campaign Medal, a—"

"You don't have to recite a fucking laundry list for me, Downs, I've got the hardware in a box on my dresser at home."

"Yet in spite of half a lifetime of discipline, honor, and service to your country, you seem willing to toss it all out the window to protect a skirt. From very *deserved* incarceration, I might add. What she did is a felony. The Computer Fraud and Abuse Act guarantees her twenty years in a federal pen for that little stunt."

I feel the blood rising inside me, hear a marching drum beating out an old, familiar song.

Semper Fi. Semper Fi. Semper Fi.

Always faithful. Not only to corps and country, but also to the people I love.

"A 'skirt'?" I repeat, deadly soft. "A word of advice. Do. Not. *Ever* disrespect my woman within earshot of me again, or they'll be sending you back to Washington in a body bag."

I let that sink in. There's a rustle of movement from the agents by the door, someone getting a better grip on his gun, but I don't break eye contact with Downs.

"That girl you just reduced to an item of clothing is the most beautiful, brave, and brilliant person I've ever had the privilege to meet. Yes, she plays by her own rules, but that's only because there aren't any other rules worthy of her. Not mine, not yours, definitely not any government's. But even with all the power she wields—and believe me, she's extremely powerful—she chooses not to harm anyone or anything. You think breaking a few lines of code in a government website is a prison-worthy offense? If she wanted to, she could break *everything*. She's got a key inside her head to how everything works. Technology, electronics, satellites, weapons, she's got a road map of the entire system. She knows all its vulnerabilities. She could create chaos and disruption on a global scale, but she doesn't. She chooses not to.

"Think about that. If you had the ability to do anything you wanted without ever getting caught, what would you do? Make yourself rich? Change property title records so you owned the Hawaiian Islands? Start a war in the Middle East?"

Seemingly unoffended by my threat on his life, Downs considers my question. "I'd stuff my ex-wife's boyfriend's computer with kiddie porn and make an anonymous phone call to the relevant authorities."

"Exactly my point. Think about the pure *decency* it takes to be able to rule the whole world, and choose not to."

He mulls that over for a while. "But she did get caught."

"You're still not listening. She got caught *because she wanted to*."

"Why would she want to get caught?"

I close my eyes, pinch the bridge of my nose for several seconds, breathe in and out slowly for a count of five. That usually helps when I'm developing a massive headache, but this time, no such luck.

"Don't pop a blood vessel, Mr. Hughes."

I mutter, "Going in circles like a chicken with its fuckin' head cut off makes me want to pop something, I'll tell you that."

"Let's recap. For some mysterious reason known only to her, Tabitha West decided to hack into the NSA's database—"

"Knowing you were on the way, knowing she'd be taken into custody immediately, possibly knowing the exact location where you'd take her." A thought occurs to me. Wheels turn inside my head. Gears start to click, coming together like fingers interlacing. "But maybe that wouldn't even matter. Maybe all she had to do was…"

Set the trap.

My entire body goes cold.

Downs cocks his head and says, "Looks like you just had quite the epiphany, Mr. Hughes. Care to share?"

"The only way you'll catch him is by using me as bait."

"I still have the dagger…you know what has to happen next."

"Let the hunt begin."

I bolt to my feet, knocking the chair over. A sound I'm intimately familiar with instantly follows.

Downs doesn't need to reach for his sidearm because I've got a pair of freshly cocked shotguns and two Glocks pointed at my chest. He looks up at me, his brows raised.

"You know what a margay is?"

Downs nods. "A nocturnal predatory cat native to Central and South America that can mimic the sounds of baby monkeys in distress to lure worried adult monkeys, who the margay then kills and eats. They're a highly intelligent trickster, but small, so they use brains instead of brawn to hunt."

When I blink, surprised, he shrugs. "*Animal Planet*. My ex loved that show. You were saying?"

"I'm saying Tabby just took a page from the margay's book."

A pause follows, but he's quicker than I thought. His face clears with understanding. "She's pretending to be a baby monkey."

"Yep. And I bet wherever you took her, that's where the big monkey is about to go."

He gazes at me for a beat, and then motions for the others to stand down. They lower their weapons—a bit reluctantly it seems—and stand in tense readiness.

"And then what?"

"My best guess? He'll take her back to whatever rock he crawled out from under." My chest tightens at the thought of Tabby alone with Søren, and at the reckless, desperate thing I think she's about to do.

Downs stands. He takes out the bottle of Tums. He shakes a few into his mouth and starts to crunch. "There are miles between those dots you're connecting, Mr. Hughes. And even if you're right, you and I both know he can't just waltz into a secure government facility and whisk away a detainee like he's escorting her to a school dance. Where she went makes Fort Knox look like a wide-open door."

"And yet you don't look like you're not buying it."

Crunch. Crunch. Crunch.

"Had a little convo with the director of the NSA on the way

over—well, you know. Anyway, it seems they've been aware of Killgaard for a while now. More like, they've been aware of the *effects* of Killgaard. Described him as a black hole. Things within his orbit get all"—he makes a wiggly gesture with his fingers—"warped. But the man himself is invisible. He can only be detected by indirect observation, by looking at the distorted things he's left his fingerprints on."

Warily, he adds, "Meaning no disrespect but...like Tabitha West."

Whatever he sees on my face makes him take a small step backward. The agents by the door take a step in.

"Does the NSA know where he is?" My voice is an animal rumble in my throat.

He shakes his head. "Unfortunately, no one knows where he is."

A movement at the door catches my eye. I turn and see two agents walking past. Miranda Lawson is sandwiched between them. She glances over, our eyes meet, and she pales.

It hits me like a lightning bolt.

Heart pounding, I say, "Wanna bet?"

TABBY

*I*n the dark I sit, waiting. Listening. Because the walls are made of concrete, there's nothing to hear except my shallow breaths and the thrumming of my heart.

And Shaggy withdrawing his gun from the holster at his waist.

"If you move, I'll put a bullet in your brain," he says quietly. "Nothing personal."

"I don't know, that seems pretty personal to me."

He doesn't answer or make any other sound. I feel him listening, feel his attention intently focused into the darkness that surrounds us, and on the door.

The electrically operated door, which, with the power out, is more like the lid of a crypt. We're not getting out of here unless someone lets us out.

Shaggy says, "Just stay put. The backup generators will come on in a second."

That's what they all say.

After a while when nothing happens, I start to count. It keeps my mind occupied, keeps me from thinking how Shaggy might actually be able to see in the dark with those cat eyes of his and decide to pull the trigger even if I don't move. Keeps me from thinking about Connor, and what *he's* thinking right now.

Keeps me from focusing on how much I wish he were here with me.

Finally, when I'm nearing six hundred, I hear a noise.

Bang.

It's far away, the sound muffled by the thick walls, the reinforced steel door. It comes again several seconds later, louder and closer than before.

Bang.

"Did you—"

"I heard it," says Shaggy grimly.

"Gunfire?"

"Or explosives. Charges of some kind. Hard to tell."

Another thirty seconds and then—

BANG!

The floor vibrates. My gasp is audible.

Speaking low and rapidly, Shaggy says, "Tip the table over. It's steel, heavy, you'll have to put all your weight behind it to get it over. If you can, drag it left a few feet so it's parallel to the door. Then get down behind it and don't get back up until I tell you to."

I move without thinking. I'm on my feet, the chair kicked out from beneath me, my hands curled around the cold edge of the table, lifting with all my might. When my biceps fail to do the job, I crouch low, set my shoulder under the edge, and shove using the strength of my thighs.

The table topples over with a crash.

I drag it blindly by one leg to the left as instructed, guessing how far I need to pull it to put it parallel to the door. The sound of metal grinding against cement doesn't mask the next earsplitting bang, which produces a tremor in the floor that I feel to the marrow of my bones. I quickly kneel behind the table, listening to Shaggy mutter a curse.

"Drop your weapon," I urge, stress making my voice hoarse.

His laugh is hard and short. "There's a snowball's chance in hell of that happening. Whoever's coming through that door is getting a belly full of lead."

"If you resist, it will only piss him off! Just lay down your weapon and get behind this fucking table—"

BOOM!

Following that deafening blast of sound, several things happen at once.

The door flies open with a scream of rendered metal. A concussion of air, hot and gassy, blasts through the room with such force, it blows the table back, taking me with it. I hit the far wall. The breath leaves my lungs in a sharp gust. There's a crunching sensation in my right shoulder, followed by searing pain. A flash of light, brief but intense, illuminates the room just long enough for me to see Shaggy blown clear off his feet, flung backward until he collides brutally with the wall. His head hits it with a sickening *crack*.

He slides limply to the floor, where he lies unmoving.

Everything takes on the surreal quality of a dream.

Sound is muffled as if I'm underwater. A murky red light permeates the smoky air. The light moves in odd, zigzag lines, cutting this way and that. I roll to my side, cradling my arm, which hangs at an unnatural angle, and try to regain my balance. I get my legs beneath me and shakily rise.

Crowded in the doorway are imposing figures dressed all in black combat gear. Boots, pants, jackets, gloves. Black helmets cover their faces, reflecting a faint green light from within.

Night vision, I think, at the same time I realize what the strange red light is.

The figures in black each carry a rifle with a tactical infrared light mounted on the bore. Five little red dots land in the center of my chest and wriggle there angrily like a nest of wasps.

Sounding very far away, an emotionless masculine voice says, "Target acquired."

The men in black swarm into the room to take me.

CONNOR

I'm pacing. Back and forth across the entryway of Miranda's office, my boots wearing a track in her expensive Turkish rug.

Across the large room in front of a wall of glistening windows, Miranda sits behind her imposing oak desk. Regal. Silent. Watchful. Hands pressed flat against the polished wood.

Her hands are still. Her body is still. She gives no indication of stress.

That's how I know she's guilty. No normal person faced with a roomful of armed men—and one with the attitude of a bear woken early from his winter hibernation—should be that calm.

The quadruplets are behind me, flanking the door as they did in the room where I woke up, standing in the same tense, gun-gripping readiness that seems to be their default.

Downs stands to one side of Miranda's desk, hands in his overcoat pockets, staring out the windows. In contrast to her watchful silence, he's whistling a jaunty tune, rocking back on his heels, enjoying the view.

"My favorite time of day," he muses, looking into the sky, a pale, glittering blue dome beyond the windows. "You can get so much done in the morning, I find. Don't you?"

Miranda says flatly, "I'm a night owl."

Downs glances at her, momentarily disturbed. "Like my ex-wife. Huh."

Then, with a shrug, he returns to his window gazing and whistling.

After a long, uncomfortable silence during which the only sounds are my footsteps thudding against the floor and Downs's merry whistling, Miranda says with a touch of irritation, "I've already spoken with your associates, Agent Downs. I've told them everything I know."

The whistling stops. "*Deputy Director* Downs," he says, looking down his narrow nose at her.

Miranda wears the disgusted expression of someone who's just eaten a bad piece of shellfish at dinner but is too polite to spit it back onto the plate. "My apologies. I've never been a stickler for titles."

More silence, except for my footsteps. Another moment passes before Miranda, exasperated, pleads, "Connor, will you *please* sit down?"

Downs smiles, his pleasant demeanor back in place. "Oh, he's just working off a little steam. On account of his lady friend being taken into custody. I'm sure you understand."

Miranda shifts her weight in her seat and gazes at some fixed point above my left shoulder. "Yes. Well. I'm sure it's very difficult. No one enjoys being taken by surprise like that by someone they think is a friend."

Downs and I share a look. I've told him my theory already, and he allowed me to be in the room while he questioned her on the condition that I not interfere.

He didn't say anything about pacing, however. So back and forth I go.

Honestly, it's the only thing keeping me from tearing this room apart with my bare hands.

"Indulge me if you would, Ms. Lawson. I know you've already been through this, but please tell me what you can about Søren Killgaard."

A muscle beneath Miranda's left eye twitches. "Hardly anything, really. Only what I've learned through this investigation. I'd never heard of the man until a few weeks ago."

Downs smiles his government-issue, "we're all buddies here," totally untrustworthy interrogator smile. "Understood. Just whatever pops into your head. I'm trying to get a more rounded picture. Everyone recalls different things, but when you put them all together, the puzzle begins to take shape, so to speak. Whatever you recall will be helpful."

Miranda's lips tighten, but then it seems she forces herself to relax them into a neutral shape. "Let's see. Well, he's obviously an expert at computer hacking."

Downs chuckles like an affectionate uncle. "You can say that again!"

Miranda offers him a hesitant smile. "And judging by his demands and other communications, I'd say he's quite well spoken. Intelligent, clearly. Educated."

Downs is nodding, saying in a friendly way *yep, uh-huh, that's for sure*, but at the same time, he's slowly moving around to the front of her desk so he can get a better look at her expression as she speaks.

My gaze glued to her face, I turn on my heel and pace left.

"What was your reaction when you received his first demand for money?"

"Panic, quite frankly. I called Connor immediately because I thought it merited a thorough investigation. I saw what happened to Sony when they were hacked." She shudders. "I wanted to avoid that."

"And what did Connor find?"

When she looks to me as if for confirmation of what I might have told him, Downs says, "Unfortunately, he's a bit too upset at the moment to provide anything useful."

When he says the word "upset," he makes a motion toward his head that's supposed to be only for her, a conspiratorial gesture that suggests my mental function is sketchy right now on account of the recent relationship between my skull and the butt of a shotgun. Miranda's mouth makes an O. She nods solemnly in understanding.

"After an initial scan of the network, there appeared to be nothing amiss. Connor then worked in conjunction with my internal IT team to tweak a few things, make the system bullet-proof, et cetera."

"But as it turned out the system wasn't bulletproof."

"That's correct."

"What happened?"

"Information was stolen. Proprietary information pertaining to the workings of the studio, our projects and the like, along with highly sensitive personnel files, electronic communications—"

"Emails, you mean," clarifies Downs.

Miranda nods.

"Anything else?"

"Oh, the list was extensive. I'll have my IT guys catalogue it for you."

"That's all right, I just wondered if there was anything else of particular value that came to mind."

Miranda pauses for slightly longer than seems natural. "Yes, actually. My software was stolen."

Downs lowers his rangy frame into one of the angular modern chairs in front of Miranda's desk, crosses his long legs, removes the bottle of Tums from his pocket, and shakes a few out. As if only half listening, he says, "Oh?"

She drums the fingers of her left hand on the desktop.

"InSight. It's a statistical analysis product I developed myself to measure and predict audience engagement."

Downs tosses back the antacids.

Crunch. Crunch. Crunch.

"Huh. Developed it yourself? Impressive." Over his shoulder, he asks the quadruplets, "Guys, did we know about this InSight thing?"

The one who'd been chewing the toothpick in the other room —at least I'm pretty sure it was him, they all look so freakily alike—says, "It's in the report, Deputy Director."

Downs turns back to Miranda with an apologetic smile. "Sorry, Ms. Lawson. You're not a stickler for titles, I'm not a stickler for reports. I like to leave the paperwork to the bean counters, if you know what I mean. I more of a big-picture guy."

"I do know what you mean. I'm the same way myself. Leave the details to the underlings, I always say, it's the big picture that really matters."

"Exactly! That's exactly what leadership is!" He slaps his palm on the metal arm of his chair. "Well, I can certainly see why you're the big boss around here, I'll tell you what."

When Miranda smiles, pleased by his compliment, I realize Downs is doing his Columbo impression to soften her up, make her think he's a bit of a doofus, get her to let her guard down.

It seems to be working.

Hurry, Downs. Hurry. I turn and pace the other direction.

"All right, Ms. Lawson, I'll get out of your hair in just a moment. Sorry to bother you again, we're almost done. Let's recap. A few weeks ago, this Killgaard individual contacted you via email with a threat of extortion, yes?"

"Yes."

"And after you received that threat, you took the appropriate precautions to prevent any breaches in your network, yes?"

"Yes."

"And then he somehow got in anyway, yes?"

"Yes."

His questions are coming faster. Her answers are easy, automatic. They're getting into a rhythm.

"And once he was in, he demanded more money, yes?"

"Correct."

"And that's when our rapid response team arrived to help, yes?"

"Yes."

"And then Connor and Tabitha West arrived, correct?"

"Yes."

"After which there were several communications between Tabitha and Killgaard, am I right?"

"Yes."

"And the information gathered from those communications led to a team being deployed to Miami, yes?"

"That's right."

"And when did you first meet Søren Killgaard?"

Miranda answers without hesitation, "Two thousand seven."

I stop dead in my tracks. Deputy Director Downs stares at Miranda. The quadruplets tighten their grips on their guns.

It's several long moments before Miranda realizes her mistake. When she does, her face drains of color.

"No. Wait. I-I didn't…I meant—"

"You meant that you first met Søren Killgaard in two thousand seven." Downs speaks evenly, quietly, with a dangerous edge to his voice, the friendly, aw-shucks act vanished. "Mr. Hughes, it appears your gut instinct was correct."

Miranda shoots to her feet. "No! That's not what I meant! I was confused!" Outraged, verging on hysteria, she looks at Downs. Her eyes bulge with fury and desperation. "You were deliberately misleading me! You were trying to put words into my mouth!"

Like a deer that suddenly recognizes it's in the hunter's crosshairs, Miranda skitters back from her desk, panicked, arms flailing, stumbling awkwardly in her high heels, bumping first into her chair and then the wall of windows.

Downs rises. When he snaps his fingers, the quadruplets leap into action.

You've never seen four men in trench coats move so blindingly fast.

~

Stoic, her mascara-streaked cheeks pale, Miranda sits at her desk in handcuffs.

She's waived her right to have an attorney present in exchange for a promise of leniency for her cooperation. She changed her tune of innocence as soon as she had a few shotguns jammed in her face.

The quadruplets didn't take kindly to finding out she'd been hiding knowledge of the man who murdered nine of their own. Law enforcement folks are funny like that.

The quadruplets, Downs, and I stand in a row in front of her desk, bristling and seething as one.

"Let's pick up where we left off," says Downs. His entire demeanor is that of a man barely holding himself back from committing an act of violence. His hand rests ominously on the butt of his sidearm, a fact Miranda doesn't miss. Her face bleaches a paler shade of white.

"You met him in two thousand seven. Where?"

She sniffles, looking down, somehow still elegant and regal despite the handcuffs and raccoon eyes. "In Seattle. I was attending the annual meeting of a professional women's organization called Ellevate. I'd recently founded my own studio and had been invited to speak about young women in business."

"What about them?"

Miranda looks up at Downs, a glint of defiance shining in her eyes. "About how difficult it is for them to be leaders because of all the cocks blocking their path to the top."

With a heavy dose of snark, one of the quadruplets observes, "Feminist."

She snaps, "You try fighting against the patriarchy as a woman in this country and see how far it gets you! If you don't have a dick, the boys club won't let you in unless you're twice as smart and ten times as ruthless. And even then they'll call you a bitch and a cow and a frigid, stuck-up twat, all because you're simply *better than they are*."

"You have a valid point," I say.

That surprises everyone in the room, including Miranda, who blinks at me in surprise.

"But that's a shitty excuse for getting in bed with a terrorist."

Her eyes swim with moisture. She bites her lower lip and then whispers miserably, "You think I don't know that?"

"Back up, I missed something," says Downs, irritated.

"The software," explains Miranda. "InSight. I didn't develop it. Søren did. It was my way to get a real foothold in the industry, to crush my competition, all of whom were men."

Downs looks at me. "You're spooky."

I lift a shoulder. "I know."

"No, I'm serious. You're *scary*. I swear it's like you're the first guy who looked up in the sky and saw half a dozen stars two hundred million light years apart and went, 'Hey, that looks like a really big dipper!'"

"Instincts, I guess."

"Sheesh," says Downs, shaking his head. "Remind me never to try to blow smoke up *your* ass."

Miranda makes a noise of disgust. "Let me know when you two are done jerking each other off and want to get back to the questions."

When one of the quadruplets sets the tip of his shotgun on

her desk, Miranda says scornfully, "Typical male response when faced with an outspoken woman: threats."

After a tense moment, Downs motions with his chin. The shotgun is reluctantly removed.

Downs waves a hand in the air, indicating she should proceed.

Miranda takes a big breath, expels it with force. She closes her eyes briefly. When she opens them again, she's regained her composure.

"Søren came up to me after the speech and introduced himself. He complimented me, empathized with the difficulties I'd described. As a foreigner with an accent, he'd also faced discrimination in this country." She adds wistfully, "Even though he was so impossibly beautiful."

My back teeth are in danger of shattering, I'm grinding them together so hard.

"He said he found it disheartening that at thirty I'd probably already hit the glass ceiling. Although I'd achieved substantial success, my position was insecure. A few flops and my studio would be blacklisted. You have to understand, this business is brutal. The only thing that matters are the numbers on your latest release. Søren implied he'd developed software that would be able to secure my future permanently. He said he'd give it to me at no cost. All he wanted in return was a promise."

I say sharply, "Of what?"

"I didn't know at the time. He said it would be a favor, to be called in whenever he needed it sometime in the future."

Downs asks, "And you didn't find that odd?"

"Of course I found it odd! But he was so incredibly charming. And young, my God he was young. Early twenties or something like that. I had no way of knowing, I never would have *imagined* that such a sweet boy with such an angelic face would turn out to be..." She swallows. "What he apparently is."

"Then what?" I ask.

"Then nothing. Not for years and years. I thought he might never call in the favor. Until…"

When her pale-blue gaze focuses on me, I get a chill all the way down my spine. "Until?"

Her voice is quiet. "Until one day he called me and told me to hire you."

The chill turns to a deep freeze, all the way to my bones. "*What?*"

"He refused to say why. He just said to hire you in whatever capacity I liked, and keep you on retainer. And not to tell you he was behind it. I was happy to accommodate him, it seemed like such a nothing request in return for the software that made my company what it is today. I thought perhaps you were old friends, or someone *he* owed a favor to who needed a job."

Downs looks curiously at me. "And that was the favor?"

Miranda drops her gaze to the desk. "The first favor."

I flatten my palms on her desk, brace my arms, and lean in. "What was the second?"

She moistens her lips, hesitating. "The second favor was to let him pretend to hack my mainframe."

In unison, Downs and I repeat, "Pretend?"

Miranda expels an exasperated sigh. "My God, for two men who pride themselves on being so omniscient, you're seriously dense!"

Downs is losing his patience. "Spit it out, Miranda."

"It was a *game*, all right? He played a game with you! With all of us! A game going back almost a decade! He knew I'd be giving that speech that night, he knew what my weakness was, he knew how desperately I wanted to succeed! So he gave me the tools and set this whole thing in motion!"

Dread makes its way along all my nerve endings, settling into a cold, heavy lump in my stomach. I straighten and cross my arms over my chest. "Explain."

"When he told me he wanted me to pretend we'd been

hacked, of course I said no. For a million different reasons, not the least of which was the high possibility of discovery. I knew the FBI would get involved, knew we'd be under a microscope. It was total madness, and I told him so. I offered him money instead. But Søren replied that if the public and my shareholders discovered that the software I'd used to achieve everything I'd achieved originated from someone of his…history…I'd be ruined anyway. And that's when I realized he wasn't just a talented software architect with a pretty face, because he told me all about the things he'd done."

Her voice wavers. She looks away. "That's when I realized he was a monster."

"Why didn't you go to the police?" snaps Downs.

Miranda morosely picks at the cuff of her sleeve. "Self-preservation, I suppose. My secret would be out. I'd be ruined." Her voice drops to a shaky whisper. "But also because he said no one would get hurt unless I refused. But I did what he asked, and people got hurt anyway."

My gut is telling me in no uncertain terms that something is seriously rotten in Denmark. There are gaps so wide in her story, not even I can connect the dots.

"This is bullshit," I say coldly, staring at her. "What are you leaving out?"

"Nothing!"

"Oh, really? Because from where I'm standing, it looks like you're asking us to believe that Søren somehow knew, years before you and I even met, that my path would eventually cross with Tabby's. That I would approach her to assist me with a job for one of my clients, a woman whose company had been hacked by a supergenius hacker no one had ever heard of before, except Tabby. And that somehow, with his godlike powers of precognition, Søren knew she would agree to take the job, come here with me from New York, and become so desperate to take him down that she'd hack into the NSA's servers, get herself arrested and taken to an undisclosed government location."

Miranda says, "From what I've seen, Søren can predict Tabitha's actions with perfect accuracy. He understands exactly what makes her tick. But the real problem you're having working this out, Connor, is that you think I'm the only person he made a deal with."

Silence takes the room as we all digest that.

"Everyone owes him favors. Politicians. CEOs. Religious leaders. Business leaders. People in positions of power all over the world. He bragged about it to me. Laughed about it. He didn't know in advance who would be in Tabby's sphere of influence when he was ready to make his play. He only had to get enough pawns on the board and bide his time."

The skin on my arms crawls. "Six degrees of separation," I say slowly.

Downs asks, "The movie?"

"No," says Miranda. "The theory that any two individuals can be connected through at most five acquaintances. Søren didn't know in advance what lever he'd have to pull to put Tabby in action, so he acquired himself an army of levers. And when the time was right, he pulled the correct one." She looks at me.

I'm the lever he pulled to get to Tabitha? Horrified, I take a step back.

One of the quadruplets asks, "If he was so desperate to get her back, why wouldn't he just kidnap her like a normal bad guy? Why go to all this trouble?"

Miranda drops her gaze to the silver cuffs around her wrists. "It was important to him that it be of her own free will. He kept saying that 'she has to *want* to come back.' And he knew Tabitha would never come back to him unless he did something to *compel* her to."

It dawns over me like an atomic mushroom cloud, a hot, toxic blast of pure evil.

The chess analogy Ryan and I had talked about had been spot-on. But now I realize it isn't simple chess Søren has been playing.

It's Capture the Queen.

Tabby didn't set the trap for him, as I'd first thought.

He set it for *her*.

Downs says, "Hold on. You're saying—"

I turn and grip Downs's arm. "Wherever you took Tabby, you've gotta get her out of there. *Right. Now.*"

He shakes me off, turns, and walks away a few feet, turns back with a scowl. "Let's recap."

"Five moves ahead."

He looks at me like I'm speaking Cantonese. "What?"

In my mind's eye, I'm at ten thousand feet, looking down at the game board, seeing all the pieces Søren has been moving, all the way back to the beginning.

"That's what Tabby said about Søren. That he'll always be five moves ahead of you, no matter how well you plan. Remember our talk about the margay? Søren *knew* Tabby would pretend to be a baby monkey in distress. He *knew* that she'd anticipate he'd come for her!"

Downs argues, "Why did he wait until now? He could've tried this any time over the last ten years—why now?"

Miranda shakes her head. "I don't know. I'm sorry. I don't know."

"Downs, get her out of there!"

He snaps at Miranda, "Where is he hiding?"

"I don't know! He would never reveal that to me, he's not that stupid!"

I roar, "Get her the fuck *out*!"

Then his cell phone rings. He snatches it out of his pocket, holds it up to his ear, barks, "What?" He listens for a moment. Then he glances over at me, his eyes wide.

I already know what's happened.

CONNOR

*H*ours have passed, and no one is any closer to answers.

The COM center has become government central. Representatives from the CIA, NSA, Homeland Security, the Department of Justice, and the FBI swarm around talking, arguing, theorizing, and generally holding their limp dicks in their hands. There are so many top dogs from so many different agencies, I can't tell who's in charge. I'm not sure they know either.

Since all the security cameras were down at the remote detainment center Tabby was taken to, there's no visual record of what happened inside. And—big fucking surprise—the orbiting satellite was down too, so there are no visuals of what happened *outside*. All they've got so far are seventeen dead guards riddled with bullet holes, one unidentified man in a coma brought on by a traumatic head injury, and a whole bunch of interior steel doors blown apart by small C4 breach charges.

In other words, fuck all.

I've been interviewed—again—by everyone. So has Ryan. So has Miranda, who was finally taken away in tears. The entire studio has been shut down. New specialists from every agency are combing through the network and all the data from the phone call between Tabby and Søren, trying to find anything new.

And I'm losing my fucking mind.

"It's gonna be okay, brother. We're gonna figure it out," says Ryan, watching me with worried eyes as I stalk clockwise around and around Tabby's computer station like a maniac with a severe case of OCD.

"What are we missing?" I ask for the hundredth time, dragging my hands through my hair. "We have to be missing something! She can't just be *gone*!"

Agent Chan, sitting despondently at the next station over, says, "It appears that's exactly the case."

I swing around and glare at him. Ryan mutters, "Great job, Chan. Wind him up a little more, why don't you."

"I'm sorry, but if there were any clue as to her whereabouts, we'd have it by now." More quietly, he adds, "He thought of everything."

"No. I won't allow it," I snarl, making another circle around the desk. "I won't allow him to just *take* her like this. I won't allow him to win. I *will not* allow him to—"

Tabby's computer emits a soft, electronic *ding*.

I abruptly stop and stare down at it. All three monitors are dark, but I know I heard a noise.

Ryan says, "I heard it too. Sounded like an incoming email or something."

Chan suggests, "Toggle the mouse."

I reach down and poke the wireless mouse. The screen in the middle lights up, turning from black to blue. In the center of the screen is a big 3-D picture of the earth, slowly rotating.

"What the fuck?"

Chan rises, comes over to stand beside me. "There's a password box."

The three of us stare at the planet and the box beneath it with the flashing cursor inside like it's Lazarus, risen from the dead.

"That's not an email program," I say. "That's Google Earth."

Chan nods. "Modified to remove all the noise of the home page, but yes. That is indeed Google Earth."

Ding goes the earth, patiently waiting, making its gentle turn.

Ryan says, "Well, the obvious thing is to enter a password, see what happens."

"But which password?" muses Chan, frowning. "From what I know of Miss West, she'd keep the security extremely tight on her personal computer. I'd bet good money you've got only one or two chances to enter the correct password and then the system will self-destruct."

"*Mission Impossible* style," says Ryan. "Cool."

"Not cool!" I feel like a pallet of bricks has been dropped on my stomach. "There's no way to know what password she'd choose!"

Ryan eyeballs me. "Well, brother, if anyone would know, it would be you."

Another cheerful ding sounds. I mutter, "Shit. Chan, didn't you need her password to extract the data from the traceback?"

Chan shakes his head. "No. Her system was up and set to safe mode when we went in. What about Hello Kitty?"

"Yeah," I answer immediately, nodding. But then I shake my head. "No. Too obvious."

Stroking his goatee, Ryan suggests, "Pussy Riot?"

When I send him a sideways glare, he says, "I'm just sayin'."

Chan cups his chin and taps his fingers on his cheek, staring at the screen in concentration. "Do you know her birthday?"

"She'd never use that. Think outside the box. Think like... like a brilliant, eccentric, independent, sarcastic female."

Ryan repeats, "Pussy Riot."

"It's not fucking Pussy Riot, all right!"

"How do you know?"

"I just know! It would be something more esoteric, something only she'd know, something that was kind of a joke..."

When I trail off into stunned silence, Chan asks, "What?"

Goose bumps erupt on my arms. "An inside joke," I whisper. I stare at the screen, remembering.

"It should be something no one else would recognize. Our little code word, don't you think? Something that won't give it away if you accidentally slip and say it in front of anyone else."

Hope rises inside me like a phoenix from the ashes.

I lean over, straighten the keyboard, and slowly, with the utmost care, type in the letters L-O-A-T-H-E.

The password box vanishes. The earth gets bigger and starts to move in double-time, spinning from Africa to North America, and then flies northwest of Canada and zooms down onto Alaska, closer and closer until within several swift seconds, we're staring at a satellite image of...nothing.

"What're we lookin' at?" asks Ryan. "It's all pixelated."

"Zoom out a little," suggests Chan.

I use the roller ball on the mouse to pull back slightly. Now we're looking at a vast forest of pine trees at the edge of a rocky, snow-tipped mountain range. I say, "There's nothing there. It looks completely uninhabited. The nearest town is hundreds of miles away."

Chan points at the screen. "There's a hot springs."

Ryan says, "So all the moose can go skinny-dipping? Wait, is it moose? Mooses? Moosii? What's the plural of the word?"

"Hold on. What's *that*?" I mouse over to the left a bit, zoom in another bit, and when I see what I've found, my heart stops beating and then takes off like a rocket.

Chan leans in, squinting at the screen. "That appears to be..."

"A cat." I pound my fist on the desk so hard, the mouse jumps. "A motherfucking little white cartoon kitty cat with a bow in her hair."

We found her. Somehow she left us a trail of crumbs, and we found her.

"But that's literally the middle of the wilderness," says Chan.

"There's a *tree* right beneath the cat. There aren't any structures. There are no roads. There's nothing."

"Except the hot springs," corrects Ryan.

"The hot springs," I repeat, thinking hard. "Which would produce massive amounts of geothermal heat throughout the surrounding bedrock."

Chan picks up my train of thought right away. "Which means if there are any natural caves in the area, they'd be nice and toasty warm."

We look at each other. Chan breathes, "Holy guacamole. She's underground."

Ryan chimes in, "You think Megamind is operating his evil empire from a *bat cave*? What about electricity? Lights? All his computers?"

"Geothermal energy *produces* electricity. He'd have to convert it with generators, but that's easily done." My mind is working faster and faster, keeping time with the accelerated beat of my heart. "There's no telling how old this satellite image is. It's probably been altered. But even if it hasn't, he'd know to camouflage anything on the ground that could be identified from above. There might be outbuildings, a landing strip, a bunch of things he's disguised. But he can't camouflage this."

I point at the series of numbers on the bottom left of the screen. "Those are her coordinates." I look over and meet Ryan's eyes. He's nodding, grinning, knowing what I'm about to say next.

"It's Hammer time."

He hoots and pumps his fist in the air as I turn my gaze back to the little white cat on the computer screen.

"Hold on, princess. I'm on my way."

~

Within hours, Ryan and I are locked and loaded in the belly of a C-130 en route to Alaska.

We're sharing space with a team of four Marines from the Quick Response Force at Camp Pendleton, the nearest military base to the studio. We took off from there after gearing up, getting an action brief, and fine-tuning logistics.

Turns out the top dogs from all those different agencies worked together like a well-oiled machine once I presented them with a plan.

33

TABBY

J come awake in stages. The first thing I'm aware of is my pounding head. There's a jackhammer inside my skull, breaking it into pieces. My mouth is dry and tastes like ashes. The contents of my stomach are set to a rolling boil.

Where am I?

Fighting the urge to retch, I keep my eyes closed. I swallow several times. My thoughts are foggy. Scattered. I gingerly touch the tender spot on the side of my neck where the needle pierced the skin. Whatever drug was in the syringe his mercs plunged into my jugular when they came for me, it took effect within seconds. Since then, I remember only dreamlike snatches of sensation. Cold wind in my face. The muffled roar of jet engines. The murmur of male voices. The smell of water, faintly sulphurous like rotten eggs.

I slowly lift my lids. Gravity drags them back down. I gather my strength and fight to lift them again, and this time I'm able to keep them open.

I'm lying on my back in an elaborate four-poster bed. Each carved wood post sports a fat white silk tassel around its finial. A white silk duvet is spread beneath me. Above me, sheer white fabric is draped in billowing folds that hang over the sides, long enough to brush the floor.

I'm fully clothed with the exception of my feet, which are bare. My Hello Kitty watch has been removed so I have no idea if I've been out for two hours or two days.

I drop my head against the pillow and force myself to concentrate, force myself to breathe to try to get rid of the fog layer muffling my thoughts.

In a few minutes, my head clears a little, and I manage to sit up. The nausea worsens, a hot churn of pure nastiness deep in my gut. I bite the inside of my mouth, hard, and eventually the bile recedes. When I'm fairly confident I can stay upright without vomiting, I swing my legs over the edge of the bed, swat the hanging fabric away from my face, and survey my surroundings.

The room is roughly oblong in shape, furnished with an eye for austere luxury that stands in stark contrast to the bare stone walls, the natural rock ceiling. It appears I'm in a cave, or a room made to look like one. Underfoot lies thick white carpeting. On either side of the bed are two plain white side tables. A chest of drawers and an armoire, both simple in style but with the subtle sheen and finish of expensive craftsmanship, sit opposite the bed. A full-length mirror leans against the rock wall to my left. To my right is a floor lamp, which provides the only light.

There are no windows and only one door, a solid slab of steel carved through the rock.

I stand, wobble like a newborn foal, and abruptly collapse back to the bed with a weak groan, my hand over my eyes to try to stop the room from spinning.

Soft, ghostly laughter fills the room. It comes from everywhere, all around me, a disembodied, supremely satisfied chuckle that echoes off the walls in waves before dying into silence.

Søren.

He's listening to me. Watching me. Of course. My reaction on waking to find myself this weak and disoriented would be too delicious for him to miss.

My shoulder throbs, but I can move my arm freely, and the odd angle it had has vanished. Dislocation, I surmise, fixed while I was deep in my drug-induced sleep.

I sit on the bed and wait.

To distract myself from any stray thoughts that could put me off the task at hand—thoughts of Connor, for instance, and what he's doing right now—I start a list in my head. All the US presidents in alphabetical order by last name.

I'm up to Taft when the steel door slides quietly open to reveal a corridor beyond.

Holding on to a post for support, I stand. It's risky business. The floor swims; the walls waver. When my head finally clears, I release the post and cross the room, careful as an old woman with brittle bones navigating a steep flight of stairs. At the edge of the corridor, I pause and look inside. It's utterly black, black as midnight at the bottom of the ocean. Light from the room permeates only a few feet in. I see a few feet of floor, glossy as obsidian, and nothing more.

A twinge of panic sends my pulse into double-time.

You've come this far, Tabby. Nine years and not a single whiff of him, and now the bastard is within your sights. You can almost touch him. You can't falter now.

I steel my nerves and step into the corridor. Instantly, the panel closes behind me. I'm engulfed in darkness.

Until I take another step forward.

When I do, blue lights blink on with a subtle electronic *snick* in the floor beneath my foot. I freeze, looking around. I'm in a tunnel about eight feet tall and six feet wide, stretching out perhaps one hundred feet in front of me. The walls and ceiling are the same bare rock as the room I woke up in. The only light is the blue glow beneath my left foot. I carefully take another step forward, and another square of light appears beneath my right foot.

"Pressure-sensitive LED lights," I murmur admiringly. "Clever."

"Thank you." Clear and cultured, Søren's voice emanates through the walls.

Unnerved by the sound of his voice, I freeze. When I'm steady enough to speak, I say, "Let me guess. There are hidden cameras in here too."

"The better to see you with, my dear."

The laughter in his voice fans a spark of anger inside me. I pull myself to my full height, square my shoulders, lift my chin. "You're not the big bad wolf in this fairy tale, Søren. You're the little bitch in the red cape who's about to get eaten for dinner."

Silence. Then, with distaste, "You know how much I dislike cursing."

"Yes. Which is the reason I developed such a dedicated habit of it. I also remember how much you hate being mocked. You didn't like it when I stabbed you either, did you?"

"Such bravado for a woman armed with nothing more than a vicious tongue."

His voice is hard now. I've angered him.

Good. When he's angry, he makes mistakes.

I move carefully down the tunnel. The LEDs flicker on and off under my feet as I walk, leaving a ghostly trail of light in my wake. "No armed guards to escort me? That's quite the dangerous oversight, Søren, considering the last time we saw each other I vowed to kill you. And I will, you know."

"We'll see."

His voice has changed again. There's a smugness to it that makes me uneasy, a secret in his tone. If Søren has a secret, it doesn't bode well for me.

At the end of the corridor, I encounter another steel door.

There are no mechanics visible, no handle or keypad or optical scanner that might make it open.

So I say, "Open sesame."

"Going with sarcasm, are we?"

"In my experience, it can crack almost anything."

Søren chuckles. "Say please."

He draws the word out to two syllables, singsong style, the emphasis on the first syllable. *PLEEEEE-ease.*

Pretending that didn't make all the hair on my arms stand on end, I say, "Oh, excuse me. Where are my manners? *Please*, you motherfucking cocksucking son of a Dutch whore."

Blistering silence. Then, softly, "Every time you curse, Tabitha, it's ten lashings. And if you bring my mother into our conversation again, I'll be forced to employ the branding iron."

My pulse ticks up several notches. "Really. And here I thought you'd never harm me. At least that's what you promised. Do you remember?"

"Like it was yesterday. I had a rather large knife protruding from my chest at the moment. A knife *you*, darling sister—"

"*Half* sister."

"—put there. I promised I'd never harm you, and that I'd always be watching over you, so that if you were ever in peril, I'd be there." His voice warms. "A promise you must admit I've fulfilled quite spectacularly."

I say sourly, "Try not to break your arm patting yourself on the back."

"But you knew I'd come for you, didn't you? *You knew I'd come.*"

His voice echoes around me, filling my ears, filling my body, staining me from skin to marrow. Yes, I knew he'd come. He might be a criminal, a murderer, and a complete psychopath, but he is a man of his word.

"That does raise the question, however."

"Hmm?"

"The Bank of America job? That did me some harm."

His laugh is indulgent. "Don't be ridiculous. That was a minor inconvenience that made you stronger in the end. I did you a favor, Tabitha. I taught you what bumbling incompetents are running the circus."

I snap, "It taught me not to trust anyone. Along with everything else you did."

"Which is the greatest gift I could ever give you. Trust is for children and fools. We are neither."

With a sharp pain in my chest like a knife twisting, I recall Connor's words.

"Trust is better than anything else."

That memory makes me miss him with a feral ache. But he's not here, and I have to stop thinking about him or I won't be able to do what needs to be done. I won't be able to put one foot in front of the other if I think too long about the possibility that I'll never see him again.

Søren says, "What we have is stronger than trust, Tabitha. It can never be broken. We have *blood*. We're *family*—"

"You murdered my family!" I say suddenly, loudly, the words unexpectedly raw in my throat. My head is finally clear, and fury has arrived along with the clarity. But I have to control it, or I'll lose my edge. And when Søren is involved, losing an edge means losing everything.

I drag in a deep breath, let it out, do it again and again, ignoring the trembling in my hands.

"I set you free," he says gently, as if by killing everyone I loved, he'd done me a great kindness.

My hands stop shaking and curl to fists. "We'll have to agree to disagree on that. You know why I'm here."

"You're here to kill me," his disembodied voice replies, matter-of-fact. "Or at least that's why you think you're here. But how will you justify it to yourself? You'll have blood on your hands. Won't my death make you just like me?"

"I'm *nothing* like you."

He sighs. "Your relentless denial bores me. You're *exactly* like me, Tabitha. If you'd only embrace your true nature—"

All at once my patience snaps, and I'm shouting. "Open this fucking door!"

"Now, now," he scolds lightly. "That's another ten lashes."

"I'm not afraid of your threats, Søren! I told you nine years ago that eventually I'd finish what I started, no matter how long you tried to hide! You're a rabid dog who needs to be put down! You could whip me a thousand times and I'd still find a way to kill you!"

That smug, silken laughter again, stoking my rage. "Oh, dear sister. I never said I was talking about whipping *you*."

On silent tracks, the steel door slides open. What I see on the other side makes me gasp in shock.

"No," I whisper, realizing too late what he means.

34

TABBY

*T*he cave the tunnel opens into is vast, the ceiling so high above it's wreathed in shadow. The walls are bare rock, rough-hewn and craggy, a dark gray color veined with pale mineral deposits that glimmer in the dim light. The floor is made of the same rock, polished to a mirror sheen. A long bank of computers sits along the wall to my left. The monitors cast a dim blue glow, which matches the blue glow of the LED strips circumnavigating the room a few feet above the floor. On the opposite side of the room is a sitting area, a modern sofa and three chairs in white leather, a white bearskin rug. Above me to the right is a large, elevated platform with a spiral steel staircase at one end, leading down. The air is warm and still, and smells strongly of sulphur.

Directly in front of me, suspended from a thick woven steel cable attached to a leather collar around her neck, is Juanita.

She's gagged. Her wrists are bound behind her back. She's barefoot, dressed only in denim shorts and a T-shirt with the MMA wrestling logo on the front. The cable from which she's suspended is measured perfectly so that she has to stand on tippy-toe to avoid being strangled by the collar.

When she sees me, she starts to cry uncontrollably. The sound is muffled by the ball gag in her mouth.

I cry out and lunge forward. I'm instantly flanked by four of Søren's guards, pointing high-powered rifles at my chest. They'd been standing just inside the door.

I jerk to a stop. The guards slowly move in front of me, keeping me in their sights.

Twisting on the cable, her bare toes slipping over the polished floor, Juanita softly sobs.

From above comes Søren's voice, floating down like gossamer. "Welcome home, Tabitha."

I look up and see him leaning over the metal railing of the platform, smiling down at me. He's holding a coiled bullwhip in his right hand.

My pulse thundering, I shout, "Let her go!"

His smile grows wider. Light from behind him haloes his golden head. He's dressed in perfectly fitted black trousers and a white button-down silk shirt, the cuffs rolled up his forearms, the collar open at his throat. Like mine, his feet are bare.

He moves away from the railing and begins to descend the spiral staircase, his movements graceful and leisurely, one hand trailing along the staircase rail. He's taller than I remember. More muscular too. His shirt stretches across broad shoulders and the planes of his chest, highlighting a balance of form that would be impressive if only I didn't know what horrors lurked beneath.

And yet for all Søren's polished beauty and grace, it pales in comparison to the sheer, rugged, masculine perfection of one Connor Hughes.

Connor. My heart does a somersault inside my chest.

Don't think about him. Don't think!

When Søren reaches the bottom of the staircase, he pauses for a moment, looking me over. A mad light shines in the depths of his frozen blue eyes. He opens his fingers so the whip unfurls to the floor in a sinister, slow-motion slither.

Rage crackles through me like electricity, as if I've been plugged into a socket and juiced with twenty thousand volts. Every muscle in my body tenses. I growl, "Let her go. Don't make me say it again."

He walks toward me slowly, smiling, rolling his wrist in an expert motion so the whip seems to be a live thing moving before him, gyrating and spinning, the tip slapping lightly against the floor. Beautiful and menacing, he stops about ten feet behind Juanita.

"Or what?" His tone is playful.

Bristling, I answer, "Or I'll make you wish you were dead long before I grant you that wish."

One of the guards takes a step toward me, the bore of his rifle leveled at my heart. "Back down."

I'm staring at Søren when I answer. "I don't know how to back down. I only know how to stand up. So if you want a piece of me, come and get it. But you better be ready to learn your own limits, because I don't have any."

Søren laughs. It's a gorgeous sound, rich and warm, filled with delight. "God, how I've missed you!"

I look at Juanita, trying to convey to her with my eyes that she shouldn't worry, that I'll get her out of this. Trembling all over, she stares back at me, her brown eyes huge, her cheeks wet.

"The feeling is definitely not mutual."

He ignores that. "Even staring down the barrel of a gun, you're fearless! You see, that's exactly why we're so perfect together."

"You disgust me."

"Oh, come now, it must have been tedious living all those years among the peasants. There must be a part of you that's relieved you'll finally have someone of a superior intellect to interact with. Admit it."

I say bluntly, "Sorry to burst your bubble, Satan, but you're not the smartest man I've ever met."

He chuckles. "Now you're simply being ridiculous. Guards." They turn to look at him. When he motions with his head, they retreat, but only to a distance. I've still got four guns trained on me, just from farther away.

"Where were we?" Søren muses.

I take a careful step toward Juanita. Søren allows it, a smile lightly playing around the corners of his sculpted lips.

"Ah, yes. You were demanding I let your little friend go, and I was about to give you a lesson in the quality and craftsmanship of Corinthian leather."

His arm snaps up. I realize what's about to happen a fraction of a second before it does.

"No!" I scream, leaping into motion, but it's too late. Søren's arm comes down with a sharp stroke, the whip cracks, Juanita's entire body jerks, her eyes fly wide open, and her anguish-filled scream pierces the air.

I reach her just as her head drops forward and her body starts to sag. She's going into shock.

If she loses consciousness, she'll asphyxiate.

I grab her, lifting her around the waist so the pressure is off her neck, and pull her against my chest. She's light, hardly a weight at all, her small body motionless in my arms. Her head drops onto my shoulder. From behind the gag, she lets out a soft, animal whimper of pain.

Beneath my fingers on her back, I feel the torn cotton of her T-shirt and the slippery warmth of blood.

"No, no, no, no," I whisper, cradling her against me. I look over her shoulder at Søren. He's watching us, smiling that awful smile. All the light has been extinguished in his eyes. I'm no longer looking at a man. I'm looking at the monster that lives inside him.

The monster hisses, "Time for hard choices, Tabitha," and raises his arm again.

"Promise me you won't hurt her!" I blurt, hating the crack in my voice. "Promise me if I stay here with you, you'll let her go! You'll take her back home, and she'll be safe!"

His lip curls to a faint sneer. "And there it is. Your one fatal flaw. The thing that makes you so utterly predictable. *Sentimentality*. You have my word."

He jerks his head, and one of his guards comes forward. He slings his rifle over his shoulder, unhooks Juanita's collar from the cable that extends so far into the murky gloom overhead I can't see where it starts, takes her from me, and carries her away. I watch her lying limply in his arms, her long dark hair caught up under her neck, her skinny bare legs swaying as he walks. Everything inside me snarls like a pack of wolves.

Søren lowers the whip to his side. We lock eyes. His faultless face hardens. Victory rings in his voice as he commands, "Now, let's begin again. On. Your. *Knees*."

My own voice is flat with hatred. "You better learn to sleep with one eye open, you sick son of a bitch."

"Guard!"

Across the echoing space, the guard carrying Juanita turns back, waiting. Søren gazes at me. One elegant eyebrow slowly lifts.

There's an interval of excruciating decision. I hate him. I hate him with my whole being, with every cell inside my body. And yet I know without doubt what will happen to Juanita if I disobey his command.

And so, with my heart bleeding, I grit my teeth, bend my knee, and slowly sink to the cold stone floor.

CONNOR

*I*t's thirty klicks to the target, which is just under nineteen miles. We're about to do a nineteen-mile hump over rugged mountain terrain wearing a fifty-pound ruck, in full body armor, carrying an M16, in temperatures in the thirties, with a good chance of sleet.

In the dark.

We could've gotten closer if we parachuted in, but then we ran the risk of not only announcing our presence but being shot from the sky like clay birds. There's no telling what Søren's got up his sleeve. I wouldn't put it past the bastard to have his location surrounded with surface-to-air missiles or even an armed regiment of sniper lookouts in the trees.

Which is actually the good scenario.

The bad scenario involves the aforementioned plus antipersonnel land mines.

So we flew into Fairbanks on the C-130, switched over to a Black Hawk to take us into the LZ, and now we've got boots on the ground as the sun sets over the jagged ridge of the North Slope. An icy wind whips the boughs of the yellow cedar and

Sitka spruce into dark, snapping waves. Somewhere in the distance, I hear the lone, plaintive howl of a wolf.

I take a moment to check the compass. I glance at my watch. Then I look at the group of men standing in front of me, Ryan and four steely-eyed Marines named Kasey, Murphy, Reid, and 'Big Swingin' Dick.'

"This should take roughly five hours, boys. We're gonna do it in three."

After five wordless nods, we set off.

TABBY

*F*or long moments, neither one of us moves or speaks. I feel Søren's gaze on me, feel the pleasure he's enjoying at seeing me kneeling at his feet. Submitting.

Outwardly submitting. Inside, I'm a horde of barbarian soldiers with their swords drawn and their teeth bared, foaming at the mouth.

He steps forward. He stops beside me. I hold myself motionless, looking at his bare feet from my peripheral vision, thinking how vulnerable the arch of a foot is. I feel a caress on the top of my head, a stroke of his hand over my hair, and instinctively recoil, jerking away as if his touch burns.

I sense his disapproval in his silence. I know what he wants, and I have to force myself to give it to him—at least long enough to buy some time.

Slowly, swallowing back the hot rush of bile rising in my throat, I return to my submissive pose, head bent, hands on my thighs, balancing my weight on the balls of my feet and my knees. He offers his hand to me like one would for a dog to sniff, or a liege lord for a press of lips on his ring.

Juanita. Juanita. Juanita.

Gritting my teeth, I lean forward and touch my forehead to the back of his hand.

"No kiss?" he asks, lightly mocking.

I don't answer, because the only words in my mouth are those of pure violence.

"All right," he says after a time. "That will do for now. Look at me."

I raise my head and meet his piercing blue stare. In spite of the intelligence there, it's cold. Soulless. So unlike the generous dark warmth of Connor's, those beautiful eyes of his that always looked at me with so much—

No.

I force the thought of Connor from my head, but Søren has already sniffed it out.

His look sharpens. Lightly caressing my cheek with his knuckles, he whispers, "You think you can hide from me? You think I don't know how much you wish you could hate me...but don't?"

I lower my eyes and bite my tongue. Silence is my friend now.

"Come," he says, his voice warm. "I have something to show you."

He turns and walks away. When I don't move, his guards step in. One of them prods me with his rifle. I cut him a look so lethal, he blinks.

I rise unsteadily and follow Søren to the spiral staircase. The guards walk closely behind, our footsteps echoing off the metal. I take in everything around me, memorizing the space, looking for exits. When we reach the top of the staircase, I stop dead.

A few feet ahead of me, Søren says over his shoulder, "Like what I've done with the place?"

The platform we're standing on juts out from the entrance of the mouth of another, smaller cave, with two tunnels at the rear that wind out of sight in different directions. The main space has been retrofitted with steel and glass to form a large, open work area, lit up in a wash of white light. There's a bank of servers behind a wall of glass on one side. Video screens dominate the other wall. In the middle of the room is an enormous, horseshoe-shaped desk forested with buttons, a keyboard in the middle. Behind the desk sit two white captain's chairs.

It has the look of the command room of a starship.

I feel a prod in the small of my back and stumble forward. The guards silently mount the stairs and move to flank me on either side. Søren saunters into the center of the cave and turns a slow half-circle, his arms held out.

"My humble abode. It took a great deal of time and money to complete, as I'm sure you can imagine." He chuckles. "Installing all the equipment was the least of the challenges. You have no idea how difficult the tribal council can be to negotiate with."

"Tribal council?" I repeat, distracted by the wall of video screens. Each one depicts a different view. Dams. Reservoirs. Power plants. Electrical stations. Airports. Docks. Government complexes. Military bases. Manufacturing facilities. Bus depots.

Panic begins to churn in my stomach.

"Yes. These caves are on native Athabascan lands. I had to pay them an ungodly sum to buy the land and their cooperation."

My body turns as cold as my blood. "Alaska."

"Exactly. We're not in Kansas anymore, Toto. Although thanks to the nearby hot springs, it doesn't *feel* like Alaska. I enjoy going barefoot because the rock is so warm underfoot. It's pleasant, don't you agree?"

I don't answer. It's not required, he's just making small talk. Søren leisurely lowers himself to one of the captain's chairs, presses a button on the desk, and all the screens go dark except one. On it is an aerial view of Outlier Studios.

I glance at him. Søren crosses his legs, lowers his lashes, and sends me the most angelic of smiles.

It all comes together with the speed of two fingers snapping.

I say, "Miranda."

"Bingo."

"So you knew all along. Even the press conference was fake?"

He lifts a shoulder, and I close my eyes. *That fucking ice-queen bitch.*

Søren asks, "Just out of curiosity, how did you guess?"

I open my eyes and stare at him, all that glittering perfection hiding such ugliness beneath. "She never asked how I knew you. When we were introduced and I said I'd known you before, I thought it was strange that she never asked when or how. Also, she quoted Machiavelli. The only other person I've ever known to quote him was you."

Søren's smile is cool and composed. "Well, no matter. That loop has been closed."

He turns to the desk and punches a series of keys. The screens blink to life. News anchors giving reports, video from helicopters, headlines shouting "Breaking Story!"

Søren scans all the images, finds what he wants, and presses another button.

All the screens merge to show one enormous image of a fiery crash on a Los Angeles freeway. Three black SUVs are turned on their sides and engulfed in flames. Several more cars are scattered around the SUVs, spun around facing the wrong direction or flipped on their roofs. Traffic is stopped for miles on either side of the highway in both directions.

Søren presses another button and the somber voice of a reporter fills the room.

"Three vehicles carrying police officers and the CEO of Outlier Pictures, Miranda Lawson, have been involved in a severe crash on the I-10. As you can see, the vehicles are engulfed in flames. *No one has gotten out of them.* Emergency crews are on their way—if you would pull out, camera four, there you go—we can see a line of fire trucks and ambulances on the shoulder, inching their way through traffic."

The picture turns to two reporters behind a desk in the news studio, a small inset of the live video stream in an upper corner of the screen. When they continue to discuss the accident, Søren mutes the audio.

Without a hint of regret, he says, "Unfortunately, Miranda outlived her usefulness."

He killed Miranda. He used her to get to me, and then he killed her off like she was nothing more than an annoying insect.

Then I think, *The woman in the Bank of America video. The woman who opened the account in my name... Oh my God, was that Miranda? How far back did their relationship go?*

"Look at all the gears turning!" Søren says, amused. "What's really going to bake your brain later on is how much I know about your new friend Connor Hughes." His voice hardens. "And how he feels about you. Dear sister."

The sound of Connor's name on Søren's lips jerks me out of my shock and sends a blast of pure rage throughout my body. "If you hurt him—"

"No more threats," he interrupts. "Here's the bottom line, Tabitha. I own you now. You're mine. I've waited a long time to get this family back together, and nothing will separate us again. *Including you.* The two of us are going to start our new lives together here, and you're going to forget about your old friends. If you try to escape, I'll kill them all. If you try to hurt me, I'll kill them all. Basically, if you do *anything* that displeases me, I'll kill them all."

He lets that sink in. Then, his tone dropping an octave, he says, "But if you're good, I'll give you the world. That's all I've ever really wanted."

The silence that follows is awful. I stew in it, my mind going the speed of light.

I say, "I have questions."

Søren looks intrigued. "Go on."

"Dismiss the guards first."

When his look sours, I say, "I'll never be comfortable while there are men with guns pointed at my back. You've told me the consequences if I misbehave, and I believe you. If you want us to be a family, you can start by treating me like family. Dismiss the guards."

His expression is unreadable. For a moment, he stares at me, one finger tapping a staccato rhythm on the arm of his chair. Then he makes a dismissive motion with his hand, and his guards leave. I wait until the dull thudding of their boots has faded from the stairs to speak again.

"The place I woke up in."

"Our room."

I force myself not to react to the connotations of those two words and decide to go in a different direction.

"I know how much you like games and manipulation, so I know it amused you to watch me play into your hands. What I don't understand is why now?"

He inclines his head, a kingly nod that indicates he approves of this question. "It took years to find this place. It took more years to prepare it. And during that time, I perfected our little project, the one we dreamed about in college. The thing all the experts said would never happen in our lifetime."

A shiver of dread passes through me. Seeing my expression, he nods again. Then he glances at the wall of glass to my right with the rows of white server towers behind it.

Horror and fascination mix inside me to create an almost irresistible urge to run over to the servers and run my hands along their smooth flanks. I whisper, "*A quantum computer?*"

"One hundred million times faster than the average home PC, thirty-six hundred times faster than the fastest supercomputer in the world, built on a doped diamond crystal that's easily scaled and functional at room temperature."

There's pride in his tone. Though it pains me to admit it, there should be.

A quantum computer is so complex, the algorithms so advanced, the machine can actually think for itself. And not only think.

It can learn.

"Yes," says Søren, watching me reel in amazement. "It's a revolutionary technology that will change the entire world as we know it. I calculate that just its uses in artificial intelligence, robotics, defense, and cryptography are worth well over a trillion dollars."

My voice is faint when I say, "You could win the Nobel prize for this."

"Prizes don't interest me."

I tear my gaze from the servers. Søren is looking at me in anticipation, knowing I'll guess what does interest him. Knowing I'll *know*.

The blood drains from my face so rapidly, I feel dizzy. "You're going to tear the whole world apart. But first you're going to make them pay you for it."

"Not me. *Us*."

"No," I say, my voice turning hard. "I don't want any part of this. Anarchy was never my thing. Hurting people was never my thing."

He rises slowly, with complete grace. His eyes shine eerily in the light. "You wanted to set the world free once. Now we can. You and I, together. It's what I've spent the last decade of my life working toward. It's what we were born for, Tabitha. *It's our destiny*."

Fighting the onset of panic, I back up a step. Søren follows.

"You know me better than that."

"I know that within the last few years you developed an encryption cipher that lets you break into any protected system you want. I've been watching you do it too, dabbling in power.

Flirting with it. You wouldn't do that if some part of you didn't crave it. The only difference between us is your denial."

"You forgot *murder*."

Søren takes another step toward me. I take another step back.

"And yet if I put a loaded gun in your hand right now, you wouldn't hesitate to pull the trigger, would you?"

"That's different. That's justice."

"No, that's revenge. And it would be wrong. You know it. Deep down, you know it. But you're justifying your desire to spill my blood by calling it by a prettier name. You can put lipstick on a pig, Tabitha, but it's still a pig. Murder is murder, no matter how well you try to dress it up."

He takes another step forward. "So if you kill me, in effect you *become* me."

There's a gnawing in my stomach like I've swallowed rats. "Stop trying to mess with my head!"

"I'm not trying, I just am. Because you won't accept the reality of who and what you really are. You put your entire life on pause because of your stubborn refusal to allow all that darkness inside you to come into the light. You knew what I was the second you met me. I never had you fooled like everyone else. And yet you allowed yourself to be drawn in."

"I was seventeen! I had no one! *You were my brother!*"

He makes a soft *tsk* of disapproval. "I was your mirror. And still am. You should've seen the expression on your face when you looked at those servers. Shall I tell you what it looked like?" He prowls closer, growls, "*Lust.*"

"No."

"Greed. Desire," he adds, ignoring my interruption. "You want what I can give you. What no one else can give you but me. Our minds are the same. Our desires are the same. Our needs are *exactly* the same."

He takes another step closer, and now he's within reach. My fingers itch to poke out his eyeballs.

Juanita. Juanita. Juanita, I think, and then, my heart skipping a beat, *But what if she's already dead?*

I have no control over what Søren does, or who he hurts, or how this will end. And in all honestly, I really *don't* know that he'll keep his promise not to hurt anyone if I go along with whatever he wants. After all, the man is a psychopath. They're not exactly known to be reliable.

The only thing I have control over is myself.

So I inhale a slow, grounding breath. I look Søren in the eye and calmly say, "I disagree with everything you just said. But I do have another question."

His brows lift.

"How are you going to call your guards if you can't speak?"

His brows pull together into a frown, which deepens when he sees my grim smile.

In a whip-crack move, I cock my arm back and then punch him in the throat.

37

CONNOR

*W*e're lying on our stomachs at the top of a rocky slope, a line of six silent men scanning the dark terrain below with night vision goggles.

The narrow valley resting between two low hills is much less rugged and densely forested than what we came through. It was a deliberate choice to hump it through the rough stuff, for purposes of both concealment and the probability that the more direct route in through the mouth of the valley would be heavily defended. So far we haven't encountered anything unusual except shitty weather and the discovery that Reid's flatulence could qualify as a lethal weapon.

I've been careful since then to stay upwind.

The rain that made our trek in so unpleasant has tapered off, leaving the sky above us crystal clear. Stars wink and glitter on the black canvas of the heavens. An ethereal, wavering green aurora of light on the horizon is the famous Northern Lights, which none of us take the time to appreciate.

"Two o'clock," whispers Ryan, to my left, his breath a frost of white in the air. I swing around a few degrees and spot what he's already looking at.

"Huey 212," I murmur, eying the bird. "Mounted with twin M240s."

Murphy, lying on my right, whispers, "We've definitely got the right spot."

I agree. A black helicopter mounted with large machine guns hidden under a camouflage canopy is a dead giveaway for a bad-guy lair. Add to that a chain-link fence topped with razor wire enclosing the perimeter of what appears to be only a quiet alpine meadow, security cameras mounted on trees, and a hatch work of infrared sensor beams slicing through the dark. We've got our work cut out for us.

With a toggle on my rifle, I switch my night vision to thermal. "Hello there," I say softly, spotting a warm body in the trees about two hundred meters out. A sentry.

"He's got two buddies," says Kasey at the same time I locate them, another fifty meters south. They're all armed with rifles, spread out in a loose formation around a boulder, which I believe is an ingress point to the caves below. The guards don't appear to be on high alert. One of them is taking a piss. Another is crouched under the low, spreading boughs of a tree, smoking a cigarette. This is good news. They're not expecting company, which means we haven't tripped any silent alarms on our way in.

We lie in silence for another twenty minutes, observing them.

It's the Marine nicknamed Big Swingin' Dick who finally speaks, for the first time since we set out. All he says is one word, spoken in a deep, rumbling voice like the low roll of thunder.

"Dibs."

I whisper, "Happy hunting, soldier."

The quiet spit of his suppressed weapon startles a nearby bird, sending it into shrieking flight. The guards have two bullets in each of their brains in the time it takes me to count to three. They go down, the bird flies away, and then the quiet of the forest is momentarily broken as six men rise to their feet and begin a crouched forward descent through the trees.

38

TABBY

*O*ne of the main principles of Krav Maga is to strike aggressively at the weak spots of an opponent's body in order to quickly neutralize a threat. And one of the most vulnerable spots on the human body is the throat. Even light pressure applied to the trachea causes severe pain. A more aggressive strike can crush the windpipe, resulting in death by suffocation as no air can be drawn upward from the lungs.

The blow I land on Søren's trachea is extremely aggressive.

He stumbles back, clutching his throat, making a hideous gagging sound I find very satisfying.

But because he's not technically neutralized, he's still a threat. And so—because I've been well trained—I'm forced to go after another one of the body's most vulnerable areas.

The feet.

Conveniently, his are bare.

I stride forward, grip him by the elbow, and, as hard as I can, drive my heel down onto the arch of his foot. I feel bone splintering, which is accompanied by the unmistakable *sound* of bone splintering.

Søren drops like a stone.

He curls into the fetal position on the floor, clawing at his throat and gasping for air, his eyes bulging, unable to scream because of the sad state of his trachea.

He doesn't look so elegant anymore.

I lean over him and say, "If your trachea is crushed, you'll suffocate within one or two minutes. If it's badly damaged but not completely crushed, there's a likelihood of severe edema, in which case you've got about seven minutes before your wind-pipe swells shut. Either way, it doesn't look good.

"Now I could just let you die. I planned on that, which you already guessed. However, your point was well taken. The one about if I murdered you, I'd be just like you, I mean. And so what I propose is this. You let me know where you've taken Juanita, and I will give you a pen. With this pen, properly applied, you'll be able conduct an emergency tracheotomy on yourself.

"It'll be messy. It probably won't work. But if you get lucky, you can stab yourself in just the right spot on your neck and use the hollow part of the pen as a breathing tube, allowing you to live long enough for the authorities to arrive. And if you *don't* get lucky, I can rest easy in the knowledge that I gave you a fighting chance, and you died because you were just too lame to save yourself. What d'you say?"

Søren's lips are turning an interesting shade of blue. He flails an arm at me, but I lean back, cross my arms over my chest, and shake my head. "I think you're wasting valuable time here, but hey, it's your life."

His eyes are watering. He nods frantically, pointing at his desk. At the drawer beneath the keyboard.

I open it and find a pad of white paper and two mechanical pencils. "You and your pencils, Søren. Seriously, who uses pencils anymore?"

He rolls to his knees, tries to find his balance, can't. He falls over, collapsing to his side. He jabs his finger in the air repeatedly.

"I'm telling you, there are no pens in this drawer—oh. I found one. Here you go."

I drop the pen and a pad of paper on the floor. He scrambles over to it, wheezing, his entire face starting to turn the same blue as his lips. He scribbles something on the pad, shoves it toward me over the floor, and then frantically unscrews the top of the pen.

"Press F1," I read aloud. *Must bring up a schematic.* It's not like he has time to hand draw me a map of the caves.

I turn quickly to the desk and its sea of buttons, hunting for the F1 key, surprised to find it so easily. I press it, and instantly all the white lights in the cave change to flashing red ones. An alarm blasts. I hear shouts, barked orders, boots pounding up the stairs.

I whirl around and stare at Søren. Like an animal, he savagely bares his teeth at me.

Then he plunges the pen straight into the base of his neck.

Blood spurts through his fingers. His body jerks. He makes an awful gurgling sound, and that's all I can watch. I turn quickly back to the computer because I've only got seconds left before the guards are at the top of the stairs.

I press F1 again to get the alarm to stop, but it doesn't work. There's a different kill key, so I'll just have to do my business with a horn blasting in my ears. Although there are many unmarked buttons on the console, the keyboard is a standard computer keyboard—I start there. I have just enough time to enter a set of instructions and hit the Enter key before I hear an angry shout behind me.

"Stop! Put your hands up!"

Slowly, I raise my hands in the air and turn.

The guards.

Three rush to help Søren. He's sitting upright, although he

looks like he could pass out at any moment. His white shirt is covered in blood, as are his hands. A small silver metal tube protrudes from the base of his throat.

Son of a bitch. He actually did it.

Søren looks at me. He looks at the guard with his rifle trained on me. Then he points sharply at his thigh, a motion I don't understand until the guard readjusts his aim, pulls the trigger, and shoots me in the leg.

39

CONNOR

hen we're approximately ten meters from the fence, a noise breaks the stillness of the night. I hold up a fist, and the team instantly stops.

The repeating electronic bell is faint but unmistakable. We haven't yet reached the fence or the field of infrared beams, but somehow we've triggered an alarm.

Shit. I wonder briefly if there are pressure-sensitive triggers buried in the rocky soil underfoot, but push that aside. It's time to switch gears.

I look at Ryan, make the hand signal for a breach, and point to a spot in the fence. He slides off his ruck, removes a small breach charge, and sets it on the ground adjacent to the chain link. We pull back about twenty meters, each of us with our back to a tree. Then Ryan blows the charge.

In a way, this makes things easier. Or at least more direct.

On my command, we move out in file, moving fast through the mangled chain link. Big Swingin' Dick stays behind as overwatch to lay down suppressive fire if we encounter any hostiles, but we make it to the boulder and the three dead guards without meeting resistance.

When we've established there's no one coming out of the tunnel the boulder concealed, I signal the all clear to Dick. As soon as he's made it to us, I glance at each member of the team.

"Stay frosty. And remember, no quarter asked, no quarter given."

Which basically means that anyone who doesn't surrender gets a bullet in their brain.

Everyone nods.

Holding my M16 at low ready, I lead the way into the tunnel. It's dark and damp, but thanks to the night vision goggles, the details of our surroundings are perfectly visible in gradient shades of green. We move quickly, heading toward a barrier at the end of the tunnel that appears to be a solid steel door or entry gate of some kind, listening to the alarm growing louder. And then we hear another unmistakable noise, this one worse than the alarm.

A single gunshot.

My blood turns to ice. *Tabby!* If she's hurt, I'm gonna go Old Testament-style retribution on that motherfucker. If she's worse than hurt—*No. Don't even go there.*

I clench my jaw and force myself to focus.

The tunnel widens. Silent as ghosts, we move at a steady pace until we reach the steel door. It's about eight feet tall, double that in width. No handle. No lock. No way in.

No problem.

"Blow it," I instruct Ryan. I don't have to ask twice.

After he's set it and we've retreated to a safe distance, we crouch down with our backs turned and wait. Then—*whump!* A flash of light, a blast of heat, a concussion of air blows past, bringing chunks of metal, rock and earth with it. I'm on my feet and charging through the hole in the steel before the smoke even clears.

I run straight into hell.

Red flashing lights and a blasting alarm, hot air and the smell of sulphur, screams of pain echoing off craggy rock walls—it's something right out of Dante's *Inferno*.

Another gunshot. A bullet whizzes by inches from my left ear. I duck and roll, take cover behind a console of computer equipment, and watch as Ryan and Murphy drop to a knee just inside the tunnel, rifles raised. Behind them stand Dick, Kasey, and Reid, flanking the walls. A blistering volley of shots ring out as they all open fire on two guards standing at the railing on the raised platform across the cave. Jerking and flailing their arms, they go down in a hail of bullets.

At the top of my lungs, I holler, "Tabby!"

When I hear her scream my name in answer, I move faster than I've ever moved in my life. It's like I've been shot out of a cannon. I leap to my feet and charge toward the spiral stairs that lead up to the platform from where her scream came. All thoughts of my own safety vanish. I don't heed the bullets whizzing by my body, or the shrieking alarm, or the armed men who leap out at me with rifles raised. I cut them down and keep moving.

I take the stairs three at a time. I don't hesitate at the top, even though there might be a man with a gun waiting there—the woman I love is in peril, screaming my name. Nothing on this earth could stop me or even slow me down.

I fly up the last step, fully prepared to spray death on anyone standing in my way. But I see only two dead guards riddled with holes and Tabby, lying in a pool of her own blood.

I quickly sweep the area. No one else in sight.

Tabby says, "They're gone."

I rip off my helmet and goggles and go to her side. She's white, shaking, curled around herself, gripping her thigh.

It has a big fucking hole in it. And it's leaking. Bad.

"You're okay, princess." I keep my voice completely steady although I'm anything but sure she's going to be okay. In fact, if the bullet nicked an artery—

Nope. Not going there either.

"Søren and two guards," she says through gritted teeth. "They went—" She jerks her head toward an opening in the cave wall, a tunnel that curves out of sight beyond a bank of computer servers. A smear of blood leads to the tunnel. I don't know if it's her blood that he's trailing or if he's injured, but if he isn't, he will be soon.

I shuck off my rucksack, tear it open, dig out the IFAK, remove the tourniquet and the QuikClot pack. I rip a larger hole in Tabby's pants around the bullet hole, quickly tie a tourniquet above the wound—my heart thudding as she groans in pain— and then tear the packet open and carefully press the gauze directly on the wound. The product is coated in a mineral clotting agent that will help stanch the blood flow, but she's already lost a lot.

Then Ryan is at the top of the stairs, gun raised. When he sees only Tabby and me, he lowers his weapon, crosses to us, and takes a knee. "Hey, Red. Funny meeting you here."

Tabby nods, her eyes closed, her lips pressed together so hard, they're white all around the edges. I know she's in excruciating pain. Ryan and I share a look.

"First level's being secured. Doesn't look like there are any more guards than those we've already encountered. Here?"

"Two points of egress, two non-breathing hostiles, and a couple of runners, including the Big Bad." I nod to the tunnel with the smear of blood leading to it.

Ryan checks his watch. "Exfil in twenty."

We share another look.

The Army's Special Operations Aviation Regiment arrives within a thirty-second window. We have to be in the extraction point exactly on time. Which means I don't have long.

Ryan says, "I got her, and I've got your six. Go get some."

"Get some" doesn't mean to a soldier what it means to civilians. When I hesitate, not wanting to leave Tabby's side, he repeats more forcefully, "*Go!*"

I squeeze Tabby's arm and then leap to my feet and follow the trail of blood to the mouth of the tunnel.

~

I know I'm getting close when someone takes a shot at me.

"Where the fuck did you learn to shoot, numbnuts?" I mutter, ducking back around a corner of the tunnel. Not that I'm complaining, but that shot was wide by a mile. After a few seconds when I chance a look around the corner, I can see why.

Two guards are dragging a third man—who must be Killgaard—between them. He's hopping on one bare foot, barely able to stay upright, his arms slung around their shoulders. One of the guards is looking back, moving forward while shooting to the rear.

I take a knee, take aim, and take him out.

When he falls, the other guard spins around, dropping Søren in the process. The guard lifts his rifle and points it at me—

And then he's dead too.

I'm in a loping run before he even hits the ground. When I'm about three meters away from Søren, I hear the noise.

It's a wet, wheezing, sucking noise, like nothing I've ever heard.

He's on his hands and knees, looking at the ground. His breathing is labored. There's something wrong with one of his feet—it's black and blue and looks a bit flat.

Slowly, I move around in front of him. When he lifts his head and looks at me, I realize what the strange noise is. The man has the hollow metal part of a pen sticking out of his bloodied throat.

I snort. Guess he got a close-up look-see at Tabby's temper.

He falls to one side, drags himself to the tunnel wall, props himself up and glares at me. I left my NVGs behind, but thanks to the LED strips spaced every few feet a few inches from the floor, I have enough light to see that the front of his white dress shirt is no longer white, but dark, garish red. He's disheveled, drenched in sweat, and his skin has the waxy pallor of a water-logged corpse.

"So this is the infamous Søren Killgaard," I muse aloud, studying him. "I gotta say, you look like a bag of smashed asshole. And that"—I motion to his neck—"looks like it hurts."

When he just stares at me, his eyes full of fury, I say, "Oh—forgot to introduce myself. I'm Connor Hughes." I add deliberately, "Tabby's man."

His lips slowly peel back over his teeth.

The feeling is mutual, you piece of shit.

"Since it appears you can't talk, I'll keep the conversation short. I'm under orders from the United States government to bring you in alive if I can. The 'if I can' part being the important one."

I let it hang there. We stare at each other. He glances at the rifle one of his guards dropped, only a few feet from his right hand. His gaze jumps back to me. I can see him trying to decide.

Pick it up, I think. *Do me a solid and pick it up.*

A cricket chirps nearby. Another one takes up the song. Somewhere in the tunnel ahead of us, a bullfrog croaks, adding a bass line to the chorus.

Then Killgaard snatches up the rifle and points it at my chest.

But this time he isn't the one who's a few steps ahead of the game.

His head snaps back as the bullet rips through his brain. It leaves a perfect, round hole right between his eyebrows. The rock wall behind him is painted in blood.

Slowly, his blue eyes still open, he slides sideways and slumps over, dead.

Into the silence I growl, "Checkmate, motherfucker."

I lower my rifle and spit on the ground.

Then I turn and jog back the way I came, Killgaard forgotten as I rush back to the one thing in the world that matters more than anything else.

Tabby.

40

CONNOR

*S*he's in surgery for four hours. I've seen war, lost people I love, been through a lot of tough shit in my life, but those four hours are the longest and darkest I've ever spent.

SOAR picked us up right on schedule in the designated LZ. The Black Hawk has a capacity for eighteen fully loaded soldiers, and we were only six, plus one injured woman and one injured girl. Juanita was semiconscious when Murphy and Reid found her, dumped on the floor like trash in a storage room on the first level of the caves. The doctor at the hospital in Fairbanks says she'll have a nasty scar on her back, but she'll eventually be fine.

Physically, she'll be fine. How she reacts mentally to her ordeal remains to be seen. Courtesy of Uncle Sam, her mother and all six siblings are being flown in, which hopefully will help begin the healing process. It's always better to have your team by your side in times of trouble.

We've been debriefed by the CIA, which is exactly as bad as having all your teeth pulled by a medieval dentist. The four Marines who teamed up with us on the op—Murphy, Kasey,

Reid, and Big Swingin' Dick, a man of few words and one hell of a reputation—have gone back to Camp Pendleton, after receiving my thanks and an invitation to join Metrix once they leave the corps, should they be of a mind.

Now it's only Ryan and me, pacing the halls of this cold, depressing, podunk hospital, doing everything I can not to do something I haven't done in over twenty years since Mikey died.

Cry.

"Brother," says Ryan, watching me from his plastic chair in the waiting room. His bulk makes it look like a piece of child's furniture. "It's gonna be okay."

"Yep," I say, and turn around and pace the other direction over the crappy, frayed brown carpet. The chairs are brown too. The walls are a lighter brown. Even the *plants* are brown. It's like this place is one giant turd.

"She's a fighter. You know that."

"Yep."

"She was conscious during the flight to the hospital. That's a good sign."

Conscious, but not speaking. She just gripped my hand and stared up at me, her green eyes huge, her pulse faint.

Her blood leaking all over the goddamned place.

"Yep."

Ryan sighs, realizing that no matter what he says his pep talk won't make me feel peppy.

After another half an hour, a doctor walks into the waiting room. He's a different doctor from the one who attended Juanita. This one, although younger, looks tired and more than a little cranky. Because Ryan and I are the only ones in the waiting room, his glower is directed at us.

"Mr. West?"

"Hughes," I correct without thinking.

The doctor turns his glare to Ryan. "Are you Mr. West?"

Ryan looks startled. "Uh…"

"Who is the husband of Tabitha West?" snaps the doctor.

I step forward, my heart hammering. "Yes. Sorry. That's me."

The doctor sends me a sympathetic stare. "Your wife is out of surgery."

I can tell by the way he's acting that Tabby is anything but dead. But wife—God. That stops me cold. Did she tell him I was her husband? The thought makes me dizzy with hope.

"I can see her?"

"Oh, she's all yours," says the doctor. "Room 204." He turns and walks away.

Ryan says, "Go on, brother," but I'm already running.

I navigate the winding hospital corridors quickly to find the right section of rooms. When I'm halfway down the hall from room two zero four, I hear muffled shouting and slow from a run to a trot.

It's a woman who's shouting, her angry voice echoing down the hall. She's demanding to see someone *right now*, shouting like she's possessed.

I yank open the door of Tabby's room and step inside. Tabby is lying in bed, hooked up to a lot of machines and some hanging bags of clear liquid. A nurse is leaning over her bed, trying to calm her.

"Please, Miss West, you can't get out of bed. The doctor has—"

"I don't care about the fucking doctor!" she roars. "I need to see *Connor*!"

When I say, "I'm here, princess," the shouting stops.

The nurse looks over at me, straightens, and sighs. "Thank the Lord." She leaves, chuckling softly on her way out.

Tabby's eyes eat me up. Without a word, she holds out her arms. It takes me less than a heartbeat to be in them.

She buries her face in my neck and hugs me harder than someone who just woke up from surgery should have the strength to do. I cradle her, kiss her hair, her temple, rock her in my arms as I sit on the edge of the bed, trying to be as gentle as I can while still getting what I need. Namely, contact.

The heartbeat monitor attached to her finger is going crazy, beeping so fast I half expect another nurse to come bursting into the room to see what's wrong.

I release a ragged breath. "Goddamn, sweetheart. Don't ever scare me like that again. I don't think my poor senior ticker could take it."

Tabby keeps her face hidden, her arms tight around my back. She doesn't answer, doesn't take the bait of my weak-ass joke, just burrows in deeper.

"Doctor says Juanita's gonna be fine," I murmur, knowing she'll be worried. "Her family is on their way now. Flying in on Uncle Sam's dime, all seven of 'em. Should be here soon. So, that's good."

Tabby's still silent, holding on to me for dear life. The beeping of the monitor hasn't slowed.

"And me and Ryan are good too, we're okay, none of the boys on the op got hurt. Well, you knew that already."

She still isn't saying anything, and I'm out of people to talk about. She already knows about Søren because I told her in the bird on the way to the hospital.

And speaking of that fucker...

I clear my throat, say softly, "And about Søren."

She stiffens.

I make my voice as gentle as I can. "I know about you being related. And about your parents, what happened. I got filled in on everything while you were in surgery. And I just want to say...I need you to know that I gave him a choice. But he didn't—"

She puts her finger to my lips to stop me.

Maybe she just needs me to shut up and hold her. Maybe she's in pain. *Oh shit—am I hurting her?*

When I try to gently withdraw, Tabby makes a desperate noise and won't let me go.

"Are you hurting, sweetheart?"

She nods.

Now my heartbeat is galloping as fast as hers. "Well, shit, lemme get the doctor! Get you some more pain meds—"

"No!" Her voice is muffled because she's talking into my shirt. "It's not my leg. I mean it is, it hurts like a bitch, but that's not...that's not..."

When she gulps in air and her shoulders start to shake, I realize she's desperately trying to hold back tears. I gently peel her off me and cup her face in my hands. Her eyes are watering. She's biting her lip.

"Talk to me."

She swallows hard, blinking rapidly. Gripping my biceps, she hoarsely says, "I want you to promise you won't call or come visit me. You need to forget about me and go on with your life."

I stare at her, in total shock. "What?"

"I mean it. If you call, I won't come to the phone. If you write, I'll tear it up without reading it. I'll refuse to see you—"

"You're breaking up with me?" I say, astonished and so fucking hurt, it's like my heart's being cut out with a razor blade. "*Now?*"

A lone tear crests her lower lashes and tracks a slow path down her pale cheek. "Of course."

It's only a three letter word but I'm in so much agony, I'm not sure I'll be able to get it out. "Why?"

She looks at me like I'm the stupidest man on earth. "Because I'm not that selfish!"

We stare at each other in silence while the heart monitor goes fucking nuts. Finally, I can't take it anymore. "Tabitha. You just came out of a very long surgery. Your head isn't working right—"

"My head is fine!"

My voice rises. "Then what the fuck are you talking about?"

She's quiet for a moment, and then it all comes out in a blurted rush.

"I know the CIA is here, Connor, I heard the nurses talking! It was nice that they're letting us say good-bye, I don't know what you had to promise them to let them do that, but I know they're going to walk in here any second and put handcuffs on me and take me away and I'll never see you again so if you think I'm the kind of woman who would ask you to spend the next twenty years waiting for me while I rot in a federal prison somewhere then *you don't know me very well at all!*"

She cuts off abruptly, breathing hard, shaking, her face bright red.

And now I understand.

I start to weakly laugh. Relief washes over me in waves.

"This is funny to you?" she asks, outraged.

I pull her toward me and kiss her, very softly, on the lips. "Sweetheart. The CIA isn't taking you anywhere. They want to talk to you as soon as you're up to it, but you're not going to prison."

She blinks a few times, falling still in my arms. She whispers, "What?"

I shake my head, kiss her again. *Her lips are cold. Need to fix that.* "O'Doul. He wrote your letter before he went to Miami. Emailed it to his boss, the Director of the FBI, and sent another copy to the NSA. Said any website cracking you did on the job was at his direct request. He honored your agreement."

"But—but—I went into the NSA's servers *after...*"

"Doesn't matter. He said you were an integral part of the investigation, detailed what you'd done to help, even went so far as to recommend they bring you on as a systems security consultant. Had four agents sign as witnesses so no one could claim it had been faked. Add to that all the intel the CIA got from debriefing everyone involved about what went down... You're clear. Although I think the NSA *really* wants to know how you did it."

Her lower lip trembles. She looks at me with this amazed, disbelieving expression like...well, like she just got sprung from jail.

I grin at her. "You still gonna break up with me? 'Cause I've just gotten used to having you around, busting my balls. Would be a damn shame to let all that hard work you did breakin' me in go to waste."

Tabby drops her face into her hands and leans into my chest, whimpering.

I gather her in my arms. "Deep breaths, princess. They're gonna think you're having a heart attack in here."

She whispers, "I am. I really think I am."

I rub slow circles on her back, inhaling the scent of her hair, her skin. She smells like antiseptic, but beneath that, the warm, sweet scent that's all her.

"Well, before you do, I have a question. It's something I've been dying to ask."

Slowly she pulls away, gazing at me with enormous eyes. The heart monitor skips a few beeps, and then starts back up even more furiously. With a little hitch in her voice she asks, "What is it?"

"How did you signal your location?"

She blinks, looking confused. "My...what?"

"Your location. In Alaska. You know, how we knew where to look for you. Did you gain access to Søren's computer, or—"

"Hello Kitty."

The answer alone is enough to confuse me, but the flat, embarrassed tone of her voice does too. I'm missing something, and I think it might be important. My brows climb. I wait patiently for more of an explanation.

She shakes her head, lets out this wry little laugh, and looks away, her cheeks flaming. "My watch. I installed a GPS chip in it, made some mods to the Google Earth software installed on my machine so they'd talk."

"Wow. I'm impressed."

She shrugs, still avoiding my eyes.

I gently take her chin in my hand. "Tabitha. Why aren't you looking at me?"

"Nothing. It's nothing." She looks down at the thin blue blanket covering her legs and starts to pick at it.

Looks like I'm going on a fishing trip. "Did you think I was gonna ask a different question?"

When she bites her lower lip, it comes to me in a flash that takes my breath away. "Wait. Did you think I was gonna *pop* a question? Like, *the* question?"

When she says, "*No!*" all flustered and embarrassed, I know the real answer is yes.

I take her face in my hands and get so close our noses are touching. Looking into her eyes, I say gruffly, "Do you *want* me to ask the question?"

She sniffs. "I want you to *want* to ask the question."

My heart is doing this gymnastic thing under my sternum, like cartwheels and backflips and all kinds of strenuous athletic shit. I can hardly catch my breath. "And I want you to want to say yes to the question. But…"

She stops breathing and blinks up at me. "But?"

I stroke her cheeks with my thumbs and lean in even closer so my lips brush hers when I speak. "But there's this little forbidden four-letter word I'm wanting to hear you say first."

Beep! Beep! Beep! Beep! Beep! screeches the heart monitor.

Her voice shaking, she says, "Glove?"

I chuckle, shake my head. "You know very well that's five letters. And to make it official you also need the word 'I' before and the word 'you' after. Proceed."

"Um…I slove you?"

"Also five letters. And weird."

"This is all weird."

I'm trying to keep a straight face. "You're telling me. Go on, I'm waiting. I haven't got a lot of time you know. I'm elderly. Could kick the bucket any minute."

She searches my face, stares deep into my eyes, inhales a slow, deep breath. Then she places her hands on both of my cheeks, and very solemnly says, "Connor Hughes, I loathe your sense of humor almost as much as I loathe your face. In fact, I loathe everything about you."

My heart soars. "God, I love it when you talk in code," I say gruffly, and crush my lips to hers.

In a few seconds, a nurse bursts into the room to find out what all the beeping is about.

EPILOGUE

A few months later

"You're smashing me."

"You're complaining?"

"If you didn't weigh three hundred pounds, I wouldn't be."

Lying naked on top of me in his bed on a gloriously sunny Saturday morning, Connor pulls his brows together and sticks out his lower lip, pretending to be hurt. "I am *not* three hundred pounds. Are you saying you think I'm overweight?"

I kiss his chin. "Excuse me, but I'm a delicate flower. You said so yourself, remember?"

He frowns and shakes his head. "No. I can't believe I'd ever describe you as 'delicate.'"

"Well, you did. Although it was right after we'd had sex, so you were probably just being abnormally kind."

He chuckles. "'Abnormally' kind? So now I'm obese *and* cruel?"

I kiss his chin again, adding a nip because I know he loves it when I use my teeth on him. "Oh, definitely," I tease. "You're just a big fat meanie. Everybody knows that."

His grin comes on slow and sultry. His hair falls into his eyes, his face is flushed with afterglow, and the man is so damn gorgeous it almost hurts to look at him.

"There you go talking in code again, woman. You're lucky I like you, or I'd be forced to take countermeasures."

My smile is huge. "*Like* me? Now who's talking in code?"

Very softly, he replies, "Well, I suppose since you're living with me now, I *have* to like you. Even though it's hard because you're such an ugly, unpleasant shrew."

He presses a gentle kiss to my lips and gets the look he always gets when he's feeling especially mushy, all misty-eyed and bashful. It's absolutely fucking adorable.

"Speaking of hard." I roll my hips, pressing my pelvis against his erection. "Are you taking Viagra? Because you're pretty spry for an old man. Three times in an hour, and you're still erect? This thing doesn't quit. It's like the Energizer Bunny."

He adopts a superior tone and looks at me down his nose. "Thing? I'll have you know Zeus isn't a thing. He's a cherished body part and a dedicated servant to your pleasure. In fact, I think you should show him some respect for all the joy he's brought you and give him a kiss."

I start laughing. "*Zeus*? Seriously?"

With total innocence, Connor says, "Of course. King of the gods and ruler of the world. What else would I call him?"

"You're right. Zeus it is. Now get off me, jarhead, I've got stuff to do, and I can't spend the entire day in bed with you." I push at his shoulders, but it's like trying to move a mountain. He doesn't budge.

Inhaling, his eyes closed, he rubs his cheek against mine. He murmurs, "What stuff could be more important than spending the day in bed with me?"

"Oh, only meeting with the head of the NSA to discuss the future of this country's cyber defense programs."

Once I was debriefed by the CIA at the hospital, the NSA came in. And once I was debriefed by *them*, I not only had a migraine but also a job offer.

It's funny how life works. One minute you're steeling yourself for a nice long stint in federal prison, the next you're being asked to consult with Big Brother on secret government spy programs. It's a good thing I have a robust sense of humor.

Connor's eyes blink open. "That's today? It's the weekend."

"It's not like they keep regular office hours, honey."

"Hmm." The mushy look creeps back into Connor's eyes. "I'll let you up on one condition."

I raise my eyebrows, waiting.

In a husky voice, he says, "Call me honey again."

I adore it that he's this big, badass, swaggering military dude who walks around with a gun strapped to his waist most of the time, but me calling him a pet name makes him all gooey.

God, he melts my heart.

I frame his face in my hands and whisper, "You're my honey."

He swallows, exhales a slow breath, says in a husky voice, "And you're my princess."

I nod. "And now that we've established that, please let me up." Just to sweeten it, I bat my lashes and add, "Honey."

Connor kisses me tenderly on the lips and then rolls off me. Standing naked at the side of the bed, he holds out a hand. I take it, allowing him to help me up because my injured leg still isn't one hundred percent solid.

I was in a wheelchair for the first week after surgery, and then on crutches for a few more weeks. I should still be using the crutches but refuse to, even though it hurts to put my weight on my bad leg. I was lucky that the bullet didn't shatter any bones or tear a major artery, but I have a slight limp, which may or may not be permanent. Only time will tell. Aside from the limp and a dull ache in my thigh in the morning and when the weather is cold, the only evidence of what happened is a shiny pink scar on my thigh about the size of a quarter.

I've got a few more invisible scars, but nothing that time won't heal. Under Connor's love and protective care, some of the nastiest have healed already.

Trying not to show worry on his face because he knows it makes me crazy when he worries, Connor steadies me when I wobble.

"You good?"

I bite back a gasp when pain spikes through my leg, and then meet his anxious eyes and smile. "Yep. All good."

I can tell he knows I'm full of shit, but he only nods. We're both proud and stubborn in the exact same way, which makes some things worse, and other things a lot better. Either way, it's good to have someone who gets me, warts and all.

It's even better to have someone who always has my back. To my deep surprise, I *love* being a team of more than one.

I release Connor's big hand and make my way to the bathroom, feeling his gaze on me as I go.

He calls after me, "I'll make some breakfast, yeah?"

"Sounds great. But be sure you make enough. Zeus and I worked up a big appetite!"

His chuckle is drowned out under the sound of cascading water as I turn the knob in the shower and the water comes on.

After my shower, I dry off and head to the walk-in closet. I had no idea when I moved into Connor's enormous loft in the Meatpacking District of Manhattan that a man whose wardrobe consists almost entirely of T-shirts and cargo pants would have so much storage for clothes. His closet is even bigger than the one in my townhouse in Greenwich Village.

"Breakfast is ready, princess!" Connor shouts.

It's faint because his loft is approximately the length of a football field, but I hear it and smile. "Coming!"

I throw on a short silk robe, drag a comb through my wet hair, and then make my way from the bedroom across the vast living area, admiring the view of the glistening Hudson River from the floor-to-ceiling windows. I find him in the kitchen, flipping eggs in a frying pan.

I slide onto one of the leather stools at the big oak island in the center of the kitchen. Now I busy myself admiring another view, this one of a big, muscular male wearing black boxer briefs and nothing else, making me breakfast at his ridiculous gourmet eight-burner stove.

I call it ridiculous because as far as I'm concerned, as long as takeout exists, there's no need for a stove, especially one with *eight* burners. But as I've come to know, Connor Hughes is a man who does nothing by halves.

He turns and looks at me with one eyebrow lifted, a smirk on his handsome face. "I'd ask how you like your eggs, but I already know."

"Oh? And how's that?"

He suggestively looks me up and down, waggles his eyebrows, and then drawls, "Fertilized."

I burst out laughing. "Oh my God, that was awful. You've been hanging around Ryan too much."

He slides the fried eggs onto a plate, adds two slices of wheat toast that have popped up in the toaster, and a few slices of bacon from a plate covered in a paper towel next to the stove, and then presents it to me with a short bow.

I take a bite of the bacon—it's chewy and meaty, perfectly cooked—and moan in happiness.

Connor rounds the island, sweeps my hair off my shoulder, and kisses me on the temple. "Eat up, sweetheart. You're too thin."

I stuff the rest of the bacon in my mouth. Between chews, I

say, "That's probably the most romantic thing a man could ever say to a woman."

Connor leans one elbow on the island and cups my face in his hand. His look changes from teasing to contemplative. He strokes his thumb over my cheek.

Feeling uneasy, I swallow. "Why are you looking at me like that?"

It's a moment before he answers. Streaming through the windows, the sun worships him, glinting mink and gold in his dark hair, bronzing his skin, sculpting his impressive abdominal muscles in highlights and shadow.

"Juanita sent me a text a few minutes ago."

I drop the bacon and sit up ramrod straight. "Is she okay?"

I've seen her several times since returning to New York. The first was at her house a week after we returned from Alaska. Her mother didn't want to let me in, but her siblings convinced her to. Juanita was in far better spirits than I would've been in her shoes. With her pet rat, Elvis, perched on her head, she told me how she'd been on her way back from my house the night she threw the switch, when she'd been nabbed on the street by a group of men in combat gear. A van had pulled up alongside her, they'd swarmed out, and that was all she remembered until she woke up in the caves. I'd hugged her and told her I loved her. She'd laughed and told me to suck a bag of dicks.

Then she showed me the scar on her back—sixty stiches, raw and red—and I broke down and cried.

She rolled her eyes and told me not to be such a pussy.

"She's fine," Connor reassures me in a soothing voice, caressing my cheek. "She's great, actually. She just wanted to find out what time she should come over for our barbeque tomorrow."

My body sags in relief. I wonder if this is what it feels like to have kids, this constant, sick feeling of worry.

"Oh. Thank God. So why do you look so weird?"

"Do I?"

"Very."

He smiles. "So I'm obese, cruel, *and* weird-looking. You poor thing. How do you put up with me?"

"Bacon," I say seriously. "You make excellent bacon. It's your one saving grace."

"Aside from Zeus," he answers in the same serious tone.

I nod. "Exactly. Now explain your face, please."

He tugs on a lock of my hair. "Maybe I was just thinking about how much I like the color red."

I shake my head. "Nice try."

He looks at the ceiling, pretending to think. "Maybe I was contemplating what I should make you for dessert."

"Dessert after breakfast? You know you're a really bad liar, right?"

His eyes meet mine, and his smile fades. His voice drops an octave when he says, "Maybe I was wondering when you were going to put your townhouse on the market."

"Oh. That."

When I look down at my plate of food, Connor puts his knuckle under my chin and forces me to meet his eyes. "Yes. That."

"Um. I can't yet."

His brows shoot up. "Why not? You expecting to move back in?"

"No. I mean, I hope not."

His eyes get wide. I can't tell if the look he's giving me is anger or astonishment.

"You *hope* not?"

Feeling a little defensive, I say, "Well, we haven't exactly talked about the future—"

"I'm in love with you," he says abruptly. "You *are* my future."

That takes my breath away. We've never said 'I love you' to

each other. Even after the day in the hospital, it's always just been 'I loathe you.' Our little inside joke.

I whisper, "So…then…you're just one of those guys who doesn't need the piece of paper?"

Connor looks at me like I'm speaking a foreign language that he doesn't understand. "What. The. Hell. Are you talking about?"

All of a sudden, my face is flaming. I'm embarrassed and uncomfortable and wish we weren't having this conversation. But we are, so I might as well get it over with. I blow out a breath, square my shoulders, and look him in the eye.

"I'm talking about marriage."

Connor's face transforms. He straightens, takes my face in his hands, and breathes, "Yes."

I blink. "That wasn't a question."

"Yes it was. You just asked me to marry you."

Is he fucking with me? "Uh…"

"And I said yes." He flutters his lashes. "Where's my ring?"

He *is* fucking with me! I punch him in the shoulder. "You dick!"

Without missing a beat, he says, "Because I already have yours."

I freeze. I'm pretty sure my heart stops beating, but I can't tell because I've lost all sensation in my body. "You…what?"

Connor gently kisses me. He nuzzles my jaw and then whispers in my ear, "I had this big romantic production planned out—candlelight dinner, horse-drawn carriage ride in Central Park, down on bended knee, the whole thing—but since you beat me to the punch, I'll just give you the ring and we'll call it even."

A little squeaky noise comes out of me.

He chuckles and kisses me again, drawing my tongue into his mouth, gently biting my lower lip. My heartbeat is all over the place. I place my hands on his chest, and they're shaking.

When he pulls away, he's breathing hard. His eyes drift open, and in them all I see is love.

I say breathlessly, "So where is it?"

He brushes my hair off my face. "Where's mine?"

He's teasing, but I'm in no mood for delays, so I improvise. I tear a strip of bacon in half, take his left hand, and wrap the piece of bacon around his ring finger, tucking the ends under so it stays in place. It's a big, crumbly, greasy mess. He stares at it, looks at me, and then looks back at his hand.

I ask, "What do you think?"

"I think I can't wait to tell our kids that you proposed to me with a bacon ring."

"I didn't pro—*kids*?"

He glances up at me with a glint in his eye and a smile playing around the edges of his mouth. "Four."

My mouth falls open. "Four? You want *four* kids?"

He pulls me in against his strong chest, leaving a smear of bacon grease on my arm, and wraps his arms around me. He rests his chin on the top of my head. "You're right. We should have eight. Start our own little army."

I say loudly into his chest, "I am not having eight children!"

He sighs. "Fine. If you *really* want twelve, we'll have twelve. But I think we should definitely consider a nanny at that point."

I fake a growl. "You're extremely lucky that I love you, jarhead, because if I didn't, you'd be missing a few important body parts right about now."

He stills. Slowly he pulls away, looking down at me with shining eyes. He whispers, "Say that again."

I know exactly what he wants to hear, but he isn't giving me my ring, and so I'm not giving him what he wants either. I ask innocently, "You'd be missing a few important body parts?"

He shakes his head. He's so still, I think he might be holding his breath.

"Um…you're extremely lucky?"

He shakes his head again, pulls me closer so our noses are almost touching.

"Honey, you're getting grease all over my silk robe."

"Say it," he demands, and his eyes are so full of need, I melt.

Staring deep into his eyes, I murmur, "I love you. With my whole heart. And I will until the day I die."

He groans and then gives me a kiss I'll remember for the rest of my life, in no small part because he's gripping my head with his left hand and now my ear is full of bacon.

"But I'm still going to keep the townhouse," I say when we finally draw a breath. He does his bristling cat impression, all glaring eyes and hackles raised, hissing through his teeth. "*Why?*"

"Because the loft doesn't have the right wiring for the quantum computer I'm going to build."

He blinks. "Quantum..."

"Computer. Yes. What, you think I *didn't* upload the source code from Søren's system to the cloud before you showed up to rescue me?" I make a *tsk* of disapproval. "Honey. You should know me better than that!"

He's looking at me in total astonishment, which makes me feel pretty damn good. I love being able to surprise him, even though he knows me so well.

He protests, "The CIA said his whole system was corrupted. They examined it for weeks. They couldn't get it to work—"

I bark out a scornful laugh. "You think I'd let the *government* have it? You know what they'd do with that kind of technology! No way, José! They can try to build their own. But if and when they do, they'll have a little white cartoon kitty cat watching their every move."

He looks like he's trying to wrap his head around the idea and not having much luck. "So...that's what you're going to do with it? Watch over the government?"

I lift a shoulder. "That's just a side gig. Its primary function will be saving the world."

After a long, silent interval, Connor begins to laugh. It's quiet at first, a low chuckle, but quickly builds to roar, until finally he's laughing so hard he's gasping.

"I always knew you were a superhero," he says, shaking with laughter and drawing me close.

I wrap my arms around his neck and beam at him. "Can I please have my ring now?"

And the man that I love responds, "Princess, you can have anything you want," and kisses me once more.

ACKNOWLEDGMENTS

Huge thanks to Jim Tierney of Digital Anarchy and Greg Strause of Hydraulx for sharing their knowledge of computer theory, systems architecture and design, and all things automating algorithmic processes that scale.

Thank you to Linda Ingmanson and Letita Hasser for all their help in getting my books to press.

As always, I have to thank Geissinger's Gang for their support and encouragement. Facebook wouldn't be the same without you.

Thanks to Jay for being patient and accommodating when I'm in my writing cave, and for having my back, no matter what. I'm lucky to be on your team.

Finally, thank you to all my loyal readers who have followed me on my publishing journey since my first novel came out many years ago. Without you, this whole writing business is just me amusing myself at a keyboard. I appreciate you more than you know.

ABOUT THE AUTHOR

J.T. Geissinger is a #1 international and Amazon Charts bestselling author of emotionally charged romance and women's fiction. Ranging from funny, feisty romcoms to intense erotic thrillers, her books have sold over ten million copies and been translated into more than twenty languages.

She is the recipient of the Prism Award for Best First Book, the Golden Quill Award for Best Paranormal/Urban Fantasy, and the HOLT Medallion for Best Erotic Romance.

For news and new release notifications, sign up for her reader list at www.jtgeissinger.com

ALSO BY J.T. GEISSINGER

Standalone Novels

Pen Pal

Perfect Strangers

Rules of Engagement

Midnight Valentine

Queens & Monsters Series

Ruthless Creatures

Carnal Urges

Savage Hearts

Brutal Vows

Beautifully Cruel Duet

Beautifully Cruel

Cruel Paradise

Dangerous Beauty Series

Dangerous Beauty

Dangerous Desires

Dangerous Games

Slow Burn Series

Burn For You

Melt For You

Ache For You

Bad Habit Series

Sweet As Sin

Make Me Sin

Sin With Me

Hot As Sin

Night Prowler Series

Shadow's Edge

Edge of Oblivion

Rapture's Edge

Edge of Darkness

Darkness Bound

Into Darkness